THE
DISAPPEARANCE

Bentley Little

A SIGNET BOOK

SIGNET
Published by New American Library, a division of
Penguin Group (USA) Inc., 375 Hudson Street,
New York, New York 10014, USA
Penguin Group (Canada), 90 Eglinton Avenue East, Suite 700, Toronto,
Ontario M4P 2Y3, Canada (a division of Pearson Penguin Canada Inc.)
Penguin Books Ltd., 80 Strand, London WC2R 0RL, England
Penguin Ireland, 25 St. Stephen's Green, Dublin 2,
Ireland (a division of Penguin Books Ltd.)
Penguin Group (Australia), 250 Camberwell Road, Camberwell, Victoria 3124,
Australia (a division of Pearson Australia Group Pty. Ltd.)
Penguin Books India Pvt. Ltd., 11 Community Centre, Panchsheel Park,
New Delhi - 110 017, India
Penguin Group (NZ), 67 Apollo Drive, Rosedale, North Shore 0632,
New Zealand (a division of Pearson New Zealand Ltd.)
Penguin Books (South Africa) (Pty.) Ltd., 24 Sturdee Avenue,
Rosebank, Johannesburg 2196, South Africa

Penguin Books Ltd., Registered Offices:
80 Strand, London WC2R 0RL, England

First published by Signet, an imprint of New American Library,
a division of Penguin Group (USA) Inc.

First Printing, September 2010
10   9   8   7   6   5   4   3   2   1

This book is dedicated to all the wonderful teachers my son has had over the years: Mr. Gary, Ms. Heidi, Ms. Robyn, Mrs. Higgs, Mrs. Mazza, Mr. Mankiewicz, Mrs. Orr, Mrs. Briggs, Ms. Moran, and Ms. Heather. Thank you for everything you do.

Part I

One

The desert stretched out before them, a tan plain dotted by occasional brown brush and bordered at the far edges by small mountains painted purple by the rising sun. Aside from Reyn, who was driving, Gary was the only one in the car still awake, and he shifted slightly in the middle of the backseat, both to relieve some of the pressure that Joan's elbow was putting on his midsection and to move away from Brian's leg, which was pressing uncomfortably close. From the passenger seat in front, Stacy stirred, letting out a muffled sound that was half snore, half snort.

"That's why I love her," Reyn whispered back.

Gary smiled.

They'd been driving since midnight, when Brian had gotten off work at Del Taco, and were now out of California and well into Nevada. If Brian had been awake, he would have insisted they stick to their planned itinerary and stop off in Vegas for a few hours, but luckily for the rest of them he had been out like a light since San Bernardino, and they had decided on the spur of the moment, in the middle of the darkness, in the middle of the desert, to skip Las Vegas and had turned onto a state highway at Baker.

They were on their way to Burning Man, the tribal gathering held each summer in the Black Rock Desert.

Gary knew next to nothing about the festival, only that it had something to do with a big effigy that got set on fire each year like the straw figure in *The Wicker Man*. Stacy had been before, and it was she who'd initially suggested they make this trek. They'd had fun at Coachella together, she'd said. This would be even better.

Indeed, they *had* all gone to Coachella together—all of them except Joan—and while that had been fun and there'd been no problems, it had also been only a two-hour drive from UCLA, with Palm Springs, Indio and a host of sprawling, newly developed desert cities in the immediate surrounding area.

This was totally different.

For one thing, Burning Man was ten hours away, out in the middle of nowhere and lasted a week. For another, it was not a well-planned commercial endeavor but a hippieish "event" where participants were supposed to create a temporary community dedicated to "art, self-expression and self-reliance."

Two days at Coachella had been fine, but Gary wasn't sure the five of them could spend a week together without ending up at one another's throats, and he was glad that their respective work schedules had precluded them from attending all save these climactic three days. Unfortunately, it was also Labor Day weekend, which meant that they were going to be stuck in endless lines of traffic when they tried to return to Southern California.

Joan stirred awake, opening her eyes and smiling at him. She kissed his cheek and wrapped an arm around his midsection. Even here in the car, hair tangled and face groggy, she looked absolutely beautiful, and as always, he was astounded by the fact that she was going out with him. Although he'd seen her around campus before—and noticed her—they had met only last semester in a music appreciation class they had together. He could not remember now how or why they had started talking. He seemed to recall that either she had asked him for a pencil or he had asked her for one, but the memory of that first meeting was vague and hazy. He'd been dating someone else at the time—Meg Wells, a hyperefficient advertising major whose life was so well organized that even the specifics of her leisure activities were accounted for on her PDA—but he'd found himself thinking more and more about Joan, looking for her in the crowd outside the music building before class, going out of his way to walk with her after class, although nothing had happened between them. It wasn't until earlier this summer, after Meg had landed a summer internship at a high-powered advertising agency and abruptly dumped him, that Gary had run into Joan at a party and had gathered up enough courage to ask her out on an official date. It turned out that she was just as interested in him as he was in her—and had been all the past semester—and they moved seamlessly from casual acquaintances to friends to . . . more than friends. *Boyfriend* and *girlfriend*, he would have said, but she didn't like those terms. *Lover* was out, too, as was the perennially unpopular *significant other*.

Whatever they were, they were together, and he was humbled by the fact that he was with someone so clearly out of his league.

There was another snort from the front seat.

Stacy and Reyn, on the other hand, were a perfect match.

Bright white light burst through the passenger windows as the sun surmounted whatever obstacle on the eastern horizon had kept its rays from shining on the highway. There was a chorus of groans and complaints as Stacy and Brian were jolted awake.

"About time," Gary told them.

"Where are we?" Stacy wanted to know.

"Past the nuclear test range," Reyn said.

"Are you serious?" Brian asked.

"Yeah. There was a fence about twenty miles long."

"I don't like that." Brian glanced back out the rear windshield. "Can we go home another way?"

"People drive past here all the time."

"Yeah, and look at the incidence of cancer in this country."

"It's not coming from the Nevada desert," Reyn said patiently.

"I don't want to take chances," Brian said. "You can gamble with your sperm count, but I didn't sign up for that."

They stopped for a late lunch at an Arby's in the small town of Fallon and reached the two-lane road leading into the Black Rock Desert by midafternoon. The traffic was bumper to bumper, and it took them more than an hour to get to a spot where they could drive off the road and onto the playa.

The festival had been going on for five days now, and what Stacy called "Black Rock City" had sprouted from the flat ground like a recycled shantytown in a postapocalyptic world. They could see brightly painted retro shacks and white futuristic domes spread out before them, an assortment of curious flags flying from makeshift towers. People were milling about, gathered in groups, walking alone, working on sculptures, playing instruments, lecturing, listening, dancing. Smoke rose from various bonfires, though the temperature was well over one hundred degrees. A stick-figure effigy atop a high wooden platform—the Burning Man himself—overlooked it all.

"Seems cool," Reyn said unconvincingly.

"Find a place to set up camp," Stacy told him.

They drove around the outskirts of the activity until they found a section of open space between what appeared to be an oversized Lego building (MEREDITH'S

CANDY HOUSE, according to a hand-painted sign) and a black, graffiti-covered block of wood, bigger than their car, whose torn sheet of a flag announced JOE STRUMMER LIVES! Reyn pulled to a stop, and they all got out. It felt good to be able to stretch, and Gary jogged in place for a moment while Joan performed a few quick jumping jacks beside him. The air was heavy and hot, and smelled of smoke and garbage, paint and pot.

Reyn opened the trunk. They'd brought a big ice chest filled with food and drink, as well as three sacks of snacks from Trader Joe's. Gary and Joan had packed a tent for the two of them to share, as had Reyn and Stacy, but Brian had only his sleeping bag. "I'm staying on the ground," he said. "Under the stars. I don't want some advanced polymer coming between me and Mother Nature. That's against everything Burning Man stands for." He grinned. "Unless, of course, I meet a comely young lass who asks me to share her domicile for the evening."

Brian unrolled his sleeping bag on the dirt directly in front of the car, then sat on top of it, listening to his iPod while the two couples each put up their respective tents. Gary and Joan's was the simpler of the two, and they were set up and ready to go before Reyn and Stacy had finished arguing over where to pound in their stakes. Gary walked over to the open trunk and grabbed a bag of spiced pita chips. "Why don't you put everything in the backseat?" Reyn said. "It's cooler."

"What about the ice chest? Should I—?"

"Just put it on the seat. If any of us wants anything, we can open the door and get it." Two bearded, shirtless guys about their age ran by, squirting each other with Super Soakers. "Besides, I don't want anyone else stealing our stuff."

Gary moved the ice chest and snack sacks to the backseat of the car; then he, Joan and Brian ate chips while Reyn and Stacy finished putting up their tent.

"I guess we're done," Reyn said, stepping away from the tent to look at it.

Brian held up the empty pita chip bag. "We are, too."

"So, what's the plan?" Gary asked.

They all looked at Stacy. She was the one who'd been here before, who'd convinced them to come in the first place, and if there was any sort of program, schedule or timetable, she would know.

"Why don't we just . . . explore?" she suggested. She waved her hand toward the motley collection of structures in front of them. "Within Black Rock City there are many villages, and they all have their own artwork, manifestos and music. That's the best thing about being here."

"Aren't we going to be in trouble because we're not building something?" Joan asked.

Gary smiled. "We could dig a latrine."

Stacy sighed. "That's the spirit."

A gray-dreadlocked man in a loincloth danced by, blue zodiac symbols painted on his hairy chest and arms. Behind the Joe Strummer cube, in front of a tie-dyed Bedouin tent, a group of young women in colorful gauzy dresses stood in a circle with their eyes closed, holding hands and chanting.

Brian rubbed his hands in a parody of greed. "Just point me toward the E."

Reyn and Stacy laughed.

Gary looked meaningfully over at Joan. The two of them were the weekend's sober chaperones, the in-place equivalent of designated drivers. Although Gary liked an occasional beer, he was deathly afraid of drugs, and Joan came from a strict religious background and did not even drink. So it was their responsibility to make sure the rest of them did not overindulge or get involved in potentially dangerous activities.

"Oh," Brian said in a tone of exaggerated simplicity. "I almost forgot. I have my own." He reached into the pocket of his jeans and pulled out a wrinkled plastic sandwich bag filled with pills. "Ta-da!"

Gary's heart lurched in his chest. "Where did you get that?" he demanded.

"Don't worry about it, Mr. Clean."

"What if we'd gotten pulled over? What if a cop found that on you? We'd all be in jail right now!"

Brian grinned. "This will all be gone by Sunday. The car will be totally clean on the way back."

Gary was furious. "You stupid asshole!"

"I'll punish him," Reyn promised. "I'll make sure we drive past that test range on the way home."

"Hey, I wasn't joking about that!"

"It's my car," Reyn reminded him.

"Then I'll catch a ride with someone else."

"Let him," Gary said. He reached for Joan's hand and turned away, pulling her with him as the two of them headed through the crowd toward some of the villages and artwork. The festival had an overall theme, as it did each year, but he'd forgotten it and could not tell what it was from the installations around them. Behind a long white wall, onto which were tacked photographs of isolated smiles, he heard the sounds of acoustic guitar and flute. Joan pulled him in that direction, and he allowed himself to be led. "Can you believe that asshole? Carrying drugs?"

"You knew this was going to happen," Joan pointed out. "What did you *think* they were going to do when they got here?"

"I didn't think there'd be drugs in the car with me."

"Just because they're into that doesn't mean that you have to be. As I understand it, that's what Burning Man is all about: letting everyone celebrate in their own way."

"You're very nonjudgmental," he said.

She performed a small curtsy. "It's one of my most attractive qualities."

Smiling, Gary kissed her. "You're good for me," he said.

They walked around the side of the wall and saw a bald woman and a long-haired man seated in folding chairs atop a provisional stage. The woman was playing flute, the man guitar, and they were performing for a group of twenty-odd people sitting cross-legged on the bare dirt. Gary and Joan moved to the back of the crowd and stood there, listening. But the duo did only two more songs before vacating the stage for an angry poet who started shouting his work into a child's Mr. Microphone toy.

Gary and Joan wandered away.

"So, did you tell your parents you were coming here?" Gary asked.

Joan looked shocked. "Of course not!" There was a pause. "You?" she asked.

"Yeah," he said. "Sort of. I mean, my parents aren't the hippest people on the planet, and I don't think they'd ever heard of Burning Man before, so I didn't tell them details about it. But they know I'm here."

"I'm jealous," she said. "I wish I had that sort of relationship with my parents."

"You're jealous of *my* relationship with my parents?" He shook his head. "Your envy is sadly misplaced, young lady."

The sun was getting low, but the air was still hot, and they went through an intricate maze made out of palm fronds before taking refuge beneath a giant umbrella spraying mist on those below it. Finally they made their way back to their own camp. The ice chest was out of the trunk and on the ground, and over it Reyn had fashioned a type of awning to provide shade, raiding the box of black trash bags they'd brought and clamping the ends of three bags between the tops of the car's passenger doors while affixing the other ends to some sticks he'd found and stuck in the ground. Reyn's little hibachi was set up next to the tents, and Stacy was cooking hot dogs over charcoal. She grinned. "Want a wiener?" she asked.

"Already have one," Gary told her.

"I can vouch for that," Joan added.

The others laughed. Stacy used a fork to pick up the hot dogs that were finished grilling. She piled them on a plate, then put on two more for Gary and Joan.

Brian looked apologetic. "Sorry, man. I should've told you I was carrying. I just didn't think about it. Honest."

Gary nodded. "It's all right."

"I guess I assumed you knew."

"It's okay," Gary assured him.

Brian dropped his voice. "Then do you think you can get him not to drive back by that radiated area?" He touched his crotch. "I don't want my guys here contaminated. And I'm sure you don't, either. We have to think about the future, bro. We're not going to be twenty-one forever."

Gary clapped a hand on his back. "I'll see what I can do."

That night there were fireworks. A rave started up in one of the villages and gradually spread outward through Black Rock City, the pulsing music growing louder as additional speakers were improvisationally added. Brian was blissed out and disappeared somewhere in the strobe-accented darkness, while Reyn and Stacy slithered together to slow music that only they could hear. Gary danced with Joan, completely sober. For the first time, he thought he understood Burning Man, and though he wasn't on the same wavelength as most of these people, he still felt part of it all.

The next day, they took Stacy's advice and just wandered around, exploring. In one village, Gary actually finger painted for the first time since grammar school, the distinctive smell of the thick paint bringing on a wave of nostalgia that left him feeling almost giddy. A *Mad Max*–looking Winnebago was tricked out as a lunch wagon, its occupants giving out free veggie burgers, and all five of them ate until they were full before setting off once again across the playa.

That night, the Man was burned, set ablaze to cheers and dancing and revelry. They could have gone over with most of the crowd to where it was actually happening, but they could see the event fine from where they were, and the truth was that all of the heat and walking had pretty much worn them out. Joan drank water, the rest of them beer, and they remained in their camp, enjoying the sight and the sounds and one another's company.

It was shortly after the Man fell that Gary noticed something was wrong.

Very wrong.

He was sitting in place, unmoving, but everything seemed off balance, as though he were on the deck of a seriously yawing ship. He reached for Joan's hand, and it felt *hairy*, like the hand of an ape. As he turned his head to look at her, Gary was suddenly struck with a headache so severe that it felt as though a nail had been jammed through the back of his skull. He cried out in pain and grabbed the sides of his head.

As quickly as it had arrived, the headache was gone.

The lurching, off-balance feeling remained, however, and Gary tried to stand but found that he couldn't; his legs would not listen to his brain. He'd been drugged. He was sure of it, though he did not know how or by whom. An instinct of self-preservation was telling him to get over to the car and crawl into the backseat, to remain somewhere safe until this wore off, but no matter how hard he tried, he could not get his legs to work.

"Joan," he said, but he didn't really say it. No sound came out of his mouth. He wanted to make sure she was okay, wanted to help her if she wasn't, wanted her to help him if she was. For all he knew, she'd been drugged as well. But his muscles remained rigid, frozen, and he sat there, unable to move.

Whatever this was, he didn't think it was ecstasy. Ecstasy was supposed to make you mellow and relaxed, to heighten the sensual component of everything. This was . . .

This was rough.

With a tremendous effort of will, he managed to turn to the side.

Joan was no longer Joan. She was a button-eyed, life-sized rag doll lying unmoving amid the bloody bodies of his slaughtered friends. Two bansheelike shapes emerged from the fog enveloping the outskirts of the scene and picked up the huge doll. Her arms and legs flopped limply as the cloaked and hooded figures lifted her over Brian. His neck had been slit, and both his eyes and his mouth were wide open. Next to Brian, the bodies of Reyn and Stacy were little more than pulped meat.

Gary tried to scream, but only a tiny puff of air was expelled from his mouth. The air became visible, a round, vibrating sphere. It darkened, lengthened, grew wings, then turned and attacked him, a chubby vampiric bat with sharp fangs and cold pinprick eyes. He tried to scream again, and the bat flew into his mouth, forcing its way down his throat, the rubbery winged body disgustingly tactile.

Though he was gagging and choking, he saw through teary eyes that Joan was no longer a rag doll but a little girl, and she was crying and struggling, trying to get away from her mysterious kidnappers. In the background, in the fog, the Burning Man was walking, its limbs, body and head ablaze as it moved in herky-jerky, stop-motion animation away from the carnage that was Black Rock City.

Then all was white.

Then all was black.

Awakening was hard and painful, like being pushed through lava into sunlight after spending weeks in a cold, dark cave. His head felt as though his skull was too small and was pressing in on his brain, and every muscle in his body was throbbing. He was flat on the ground, in the dirt, and he rose to a sitting position. The first thing he noticed was that the sun was high in the western sky. It was noon or just after, although he had no idea what day it was. The next thing he noticed was that Burning Man was winding down. The Joe Strummer cube was gone, as was the temporary structure behind it, and though he could hear the sounds of people moving about, there were a lot fewer of them than there had been before.

Brian was already awake. "What. The. Fuck. Was. That?"

If pressed, Gary would have guessed that Brian was the one who had dosed him. His friend was a good guy and usually respectful of boundaries, but it wasn't too much of a stretch to assume that his judgment might have been impaired under the influence. Obviously, though, Brian had undergone the same sort of trial he had and, as he looked around, Gary saw that his other friends were similarly affected. Reyn was on the ground and moaning, listing slightly from side to side. Stacy was still out like a light.

But where was Joan?

He crawled over to their tent and looked inside. Her sleeping bag was gone, he saw. As was her little knapsack of personal effects. Frowning, he stood, lurching to his feet and holding out his arms to keep from wobbling too much. A great deal of the city had already been broken down, and the rest of it was in the process of being taken apart. The ethos of Burning Man was that the community would be temporary, a piece of performance art, vanishing after its vibrant week in the sun as though it had never existed. Already most of the people were gone, and by tonight the playa would appear as empty and untouched as it had been before their arrival.

Gary's head hurt, and his sense of balance was still shaky, but he staggered over to the car and looked inside. No Joan. He walked around the car, using the door handles, trunk and hood as guides, but there was still no sign of her.

"Joan!" he called. His voice wasn't up to full strength, but it was still strong enough to be heard in and around the immediate area. He coughed, tried again. "Joan!"

The only answer was from Brian. "She's around," he said. "Somewhere."

Gary didn't believe that. Something was not right. He could sense it, and a feeling of panic grew within him as he scanned the desert nearby and saw no sign of her. If she had been drugged as the rest of them had, she should have still been here. If she had not been drugged, she would have gone to get help. But she seemed to have disappeared. He recalled his vision or hallucination or whatever it was, where he'd seen two hooded figures carrying off the rag doll that Joan had become, and he was suddenly certain that there was truth in it. Beneath the delusional trappings, an essential core of reality remained, and he was convinced now that she had been abducted.

Reyn was up and awake, and Stacy was stirring to life.

He didn't like that, either, the fact that they were all coming out of drug-induced stupors at approximately the same time. It suggested a plot, a plan, a premeditated effort to render them unconscious for a specific period of time so that certain actions could be taken during their absence, and he hurried as fast as his acclimatizing legs would carry him to the nearest still-occupied site, where he learned that it was Monday. They had been out for more than a day.

Frantically he searched one disbanding village after another, joined shortly afterward by his recovering friends. No one they encountered had seen Joan or noticed anything unusual, but then, they hadn't been paying much attention, either. That was what happened when something such as this occurred in such a setting: the natural chaos of the crowd made it virtually impossible for individual events to be noticed.

Gary held out a slim, baseless hope that Joan had wandered away, that in some drugged trance of her own she had ended up sleeping it off in someone else's camp. But as the light in the sky shifted from bright white to a more subdued yellow and they found themselves covering the same ground they had trod earlier, that already faint hope dimmed and died. Discouraged, he led the other three back to the car.

He had to face the facts.

Joan was gone.

Two

The playa seemed practically deserted, and the orange of the slowly setting sun was intensified by intersecting clouds of dust kicked up by departing vehicles. The three others faced Gary. It was his girlfriend who had disappeared, and he was the de facto leader on this, the one to make the decisions. Beneath the fear and worry, he could see in his friends' eyes that they were glad they were not the ones to whom this had happened, and while he didn't blame them for that and would have felt the same if he were in their shoes, part of him resented it.

"So, what do we do?" Reyn asked.

"Don't you have to wait forty-eight hours or something before you can report someone missing?" Brian sat on the hood of the car, legs crossed. "I know you're not supposed to get your information from movies, but . . ." He trailed off.

Gary looked back toward the center of what had been Black Rock City. There'd been a minor police presence here all week, and though he didn't know where the cops were from or what their ordinary jurisdiction might be, he figured that they were the ones to whom any crime should be reported. "Let's find the police," he said.

"You mean one of those rent-a-cops?" Brian asked doubtfully.

"I think they're real," Reyn disagreed.

"Whoever they are, I'm pretty sure they're gone," Stacy said. "I didn't see any of them while we were looking around out there."

Shut up! Gary wanted to scream. *Shut up!* Joan was missing and all his friends could do was bicker about the legitimacy of Burning Man's security force. But he knew that wasn't fair. His friends were only trying to help. It was just that every second of delay, each minute they spent not doing something, was time that Joan remained missing. He grimaced as a spasm of pain shot through his lower back and straightened, pressing a hand against his spine. Every muscle in his body was tense. He had a headache, and his neck felt as though it had been used as a punching bag; it hurt no matter which way he turned.

Without further discussion, Gary took out his cell phone, turned it on and dialed 911. But whatever temporary towers had brought this area service for the past week had been dismantled or were gone, and no matter which direction he faced, he got no signal. "Shit!" he yelled—so loudly that Stacy, standing next to him, jumped. He was angry enough to have thrown down the phone, the way characters do in movies, but he wasn't stupid, and instead he tried again, with the same result.

He put the phone back into his pocket. His friends were now trying the same thing themselves, although it quickly became obvious that none of their phones was getting a signal, either.

Gary scanned the dusty and nearly empty plain for any sign of police, but Stacy was right: it appeared as though they'd left. He stood there for several seconds, looking at Brian, Reyn and Stacy, and wondering what to do next.

"Did anyone *see* anything?" Gary asked for the umpteenth time. The other three shook their heads. "Doesn't it seem suspicious that she disappeared while we were all knocked out?"

Stacy nodded vigorously. "I was thinking that, too. Maybe someone saw us all passed out here, some psycho, and he just . . . grabbed Joan, kidnapped her." She shivered. "It could have been any of us."

"Maybe they were planning to get the rest of us, too, only we started waking up!" Brian jumped off the hood of the car, gesturing excitedly. "That means they might not be that far away! They might not have much of a head start!"

"Hold on a minute," Reyn said. "Think about this logically. What would be the point? Anyone who kidnapped someone would be committing a crime, a felony." He glanced at Gary. "No offense, but if someone wanted to rape her, they could've just done it right here; they wouldn't've had to drag her off somewhere. Besides, it would take more than one person to pick Joan up and carry her away, and there aren't bands of white slavers trolling hippie festivals for victims."

"And yet," Brian said, "she's gone."

"You think she just wandered off?" Stacy asked Reyn.

"What I think is that none of us knows anything."

They were all talking too much, and this time Gary did shout. "*Shut up!*" The three immediately closed their mouths, swiveling toward him. Gary took a deep breath. He didn't know about the others, but his own body still felt strangely heavy, and he was pretty sure he was not yet thinking clearly. His friends might have a higher tolerance level for drugs, but he doubted that they were working at peak mental capacity, either. "We need to get to a place where there's a signal so we can call the police. Or else go to the nearest town. But someone has to stay here in case Joan comes back."

"No way," Stacy said, shaking her head. "Not out here in the middle of nowhere. It'll be dark before you get back."

"I'll hang out," Brian offered. "I can always find some way to amuse myself."

"Nothing illegal," Stacy warned him. "We'll be returning with cops."

"No one's staying here," Reyn said. He looked over at Gary. "Sorry, but we can't risk losing anyone else. Joan disappeared while there were still a lot of people around. It would be stupid for us to leave anyone behind now that nearly everyone's gone."

"Then the rest of you go," Gary insisted. "I'll wait."

"No, you won't. You're her boyfriend. You're the one who has to file the report. You know more about her than the rest of us; you can answer their questions."

But Gary wasn't sure he *could* answer their questions. There was so much about Joan that he didn't know. He loved her—he did know that—but they had been going out only a short time, and most of their conversations had naturally revolved around the present and the future rather than the past. There were huge gaps in her history that he couldn't fill, and the type of knowledge he had about Joan wasn't really the sort of hard information that the police would require.

Her parents could answer everything, but he realized that he did not know their names, their phone number or even the city in which they lived. He had the impression that they lived far away, in another state, but Joan had never really told him much about them other than the fact that they were very religious.

Could he get that information through the school? Probably not. There were always privacy issues, and for all the university knew, he was some crazed stalker with whom she had just broken up.

Was he supposed to inform the school that she was missing?

He had no idea.

Gary felt overwhelmed. His first impulse was to call

his dad and ask what he should do, but his parents lived all the way across the country, in Ohio, and he didn't want to alarm them. Besides, they couldn't really help right now. As terrifying as the thought was, as out of his depth as he felt, he was on his own.

"Okay," he said. "Let's go."

On the road that led to the highway, and then on the highway itself, Gary sat unmoving in the passenger seat while Reyn drove, his mind spinning, going over everything that had happened, trying to recall whether anyone at Burning Man had been watching them, or looking at them suspiciously, or had paid extra-close attention to Joan. He was still unable to figure out how or when they had been drugged, and the motives for all of it remained a complete and utter mystery.

He did not notice the name of the town they finally reached, but the second they pulled into the parking lot of the police station, Gary was out of the car and dashing toward the building. It was nearly night now, and the sky in the east was a threatening bluish black. All he could think about was the fact that Joan was out there somewhere and it was getting dark. Running footsteps sounded behind him, and he was only a few feet from the door when a strong hand grabbed his shoulder, fingers digging into his flesh.

"Stop!" Reyn's voice in his ear was low but insistent.

Gary pulled the hand off his shoulder. "What are you doing?"

"Listen to me," Reyn said. "You can't go into that police station."

"What the hell—"

"What if they don't believe you? Huh? I know you're just going to tell them what happened, but your girlfriend's missing, and you probably have more than a trace of some heavy and illegal narcotic in your bloodstream. Automatically, you're going to be suspect number one. They may lock you up now and ask questions later."

Gary looked into his friend's eyes. He hadn't thought of that. None of them had until now.

"Along with us."

"Then what do you think we should do?"

Reyn took a deep breath. "I think we should drive back to Los Angeles."

"We can't leave!" Gary yelled. "Joan's missing! She's out there somewhere!"

"Keep your voice down! What are we supposed to do? Let Barney Fife lock us up? Go back to our camp in case she shows up again? Hole up in a motel room here in Buttfuck, Nevada, wait for the drugs to leach out of our systems and then try to explain to the police why we decided to wait two days to tell them your girlfriend disappeared?"

"You go back," Gary said. "I'll take my chances."

"For all we know, she's sleeping peacefully in her bed in California right now."

Brian and Stacy had walked up. "Reyn's right," Stacy said, putting a sympathetic hand on his shoulder. "She could have gotten a ride back. She could be in her room sleeping it off."

"Maybe she's the one who drugged us," Brian offered. "Maybe she's a—"

"Shut up," Reyn said. "You're just being an asshole."

Gary took out his phone, called Joan's cell. There were five rings, no answer; then her recording came on, asking him to leave a message. The sound of her voice, so familiar and yet now so far away, made him catch his breath. His eyes were suddenly watery. "Call me. Now," Gary said, not trusting himself to say more. He terminated the connection, then punched in the number of her dorm room. It, too, rang and rang, with neither Joan nor her roommate, Kara, answering.

He ended the call, clearing his throat. "So, what do we do?"

"We go home," Reyn said. "Maybe she'll be there by then, maybe not. If not, we say that we thought she'd gotten a ride from someone else, like Stacy said, and we didn't realize she was missing until we returned."

Gary was already shaking his head. "But that's wasting time! What if she *was* kidnapped? What if one *hour* makes all the difference? I can't chance that."

"What good are you going to be to her behind bars?" Reyn demanded. He gestured toward the station, a small building that looked more like a minor post office than the headquarters of a police department. "And do you really think the men on *this* force are the ones best equipped to find her?"

"We get our asses back to California and call some real cops," Brian suggested. "They'll find her."

"But the crime scene's six hundred miles away from Los Angeles!"

"If it *is* a crime scene," Reyn said, "and hopefully it *isn't*, they'll probably come out here themselves with all of their high-tech equipment. If not, they'll call these local yokels, who'll go out and dig through the dirt and report back what they find. Worst-case scenario? You have two police departments on the case."

"No," Gary said, shaking his head.

"I don't like this, either," Reyn told him. "But we don't have much choice."

"I'm going in there."

"You can't!"

Stacy seemed to understand. "Let him go," she told Reyn.

He wasn't waiting for their approval or permission; he was already walking toward the building's entrance. "Wait for me at that Dairy Queen down the street," he said, pointing. "If I'm not there in a half hour, take off without me. I'm not going to mention you guys or bring you into it; it's just me and Joan."

"We'll wait an hour," Stacy said. "Then we'll ... I don't know, call a lawyer."

"A bail bondsman," Brian suggested.

"We'll think of something," she promised. "Go."

He did. From the corner of his eye, he could see Reyn shaking his head and lecturing Stacy as they hurried back to the car. Then Gary was in the station, approaching the uniformed woman at the front desk and asking to talk to someone about reporting a missing person.

He was out of the station in less than twenty minutes. Brian had been right. There was a forty-eight-hour waiting period. Joan might have disappeared, but until she was missing for two days, the cops wouldn't so much as glance out the window to look for her. Gary did tell the sergeant who had volunteered to interview him that he and his friends had been drugged, but the older man didn't seem to care. There was no effort made to draw blood or test him, and the cop's attitude was one of bored disdain. It was as if this sort of thing happened all the time and he was tired of dealing with it.

Gary emerged from the station feeling angry and frustrated. The sergeant had filled out a form and asked some perfunctory questions so that, on the off chance that Joan didn't show up and remained missing after forty-eight hours, they could get a head start on the case. But the policeman made it clear that he had no doubt she would surface within the next twelve hours. "Trust me," he said. "We deal with this every year." *Every time you freaks stage your festival*, he didn't add, though he was obviously thinking it.

Walking out of the building, Gary realized once again how little he actually knew about his girlfriend. Aside from her name and a physical description, he'd been able to give them nothing, and at least three-fourths of their questions had remained unanswered. Most of them were facts that he should know, that he wanted to know, but that he just hadn't gotten around to learning. Things like her parents' names, the names of any siblings, her permanent address, her birthplace. There'd been no hurry because he'd assumed that there'd be time to learn all that. He hadn't known. . . .

He was acting as though she was dead, and he forced himself to push those thoughts from his mind. Right now, she was only missing and, like his friends said, there were alternate possibilities; kidnapping was not the only explanation for her disappearance. And even if it was what had happened, the kidnappers might be hoping for a ransom because maybe her parents were rich, and maybe—

Maybe she'd been raped and murdered and was lying in a ditch.

No. He couldn't think that way.

Gary walked slowly across the small parking lot, empty save for two police cars and an old pickup truck.

The night was dark, and the town had no streetlights. The sky looked as it had when they were camping out at Burning Man: massive and infinite, larger, deeper and darker than it ever was in California or Ohio. Gary walked down the cracked and gravelly sidewalk to the Dairy Queen, whose backlit sign was like a white beacon on the highway. Reyn was right, he decided. They needed to go back to Los Angeles. It felt disloyal to even consider such a thought because he knew she might still be somewhere out in the Nevada desert, but the truth was that he'd done all he could here.

He wished he knew more biographical details. The Los Angeles police were going to ask him the same sorts of questions that these cops had. Maybe more, since he would be filing an official missing persons complaint.

Kara.

Yes.

Her roommate, Kara. Though it hurt him to admit it, she might know more facts about Joan than he did. Gary tried to call the dorm again as he walked, secretly hoping that Joan might answer the phone, although he tried to fool himself into thinking he was *not* thinking that. But once more, it rang without answer, and when the operator's your-party-is-not-answering recording came on, he hung up.

He strode across the Dairy Queen's unpaved parking lot, gravel crunching loudly beneath his sneakers. Reyn, Stacy and Brian were seated at an outside table, eating chili fries and hamburgers by the blue light of a bug zapper.

"What happened?" Reyn asked, hurrying up to meet him.

Gary shook his head. "Brian was right. Forty-eight-hour waiting period. I told them everything and they wrote it down, but . . ." He shrugged.

He'd reached the table. Stacy held out the box of chili fries, offering him some, but the food smelled bad and looked worse, and he shook his head.

"So what do you want to do?" Reyn asked.

"Go back," he said tiredly. "Maybe you're right. Maybe she's there. If not, I'll tell the LA police."

"Have some food," Stacy suggested. "It's a long trip."

"I'll get it." He walked up to the restaurant's window and ordered a hot dog and an extra-large Coke. He probably wouldn't need the caffeine to stay awake, but it couldn't hurt. The food arrived moments later. He ate quickly—they all did—and then they got in the car and took off.

They drove all night, taking turns, arriving back in Westwood by midmorning. School had been in session only for the past week, and things had not yet settled down to normal. UCLA was teeming with students who were going to classes, dropping classes, petitioning to get into classes or just hanging out. The crosswalks of the streets flanking the university were so crowded that in the right-turn lane only one vehicle could get through per green light.

Parking was a bitch, as usual. Someone had stolen Reyn's designated spot by the dorms, but after fifteen minutes of circling around the student lot on the north side of campus, they were lucky enough to spot a red Jeep pulling out. Stacy, who was driving, swerved around a waiting Prius and nabbed the spot. The Prius driver honked at them, yelled something out his open window, but Stacy merely flipped him off as she pulled into the space. "Rich asshole," she said.

They got out of the car. None of them had bathed for four days, and being first drugged and then sleep-deprived had done little to enhance their appearance. Gary glanced down at himself. The dust of the Black Rock Desert still clung to his clothes, and he made an effort to brush off his shirt and pants in order to look slightly more presentable. He looked over at his friends. Brian's long hair was often tangled and disheveled, his clothes typically wrinkled and worn many times before their perfunctory washings, so the difference with him was much less pronounced, but Reyn's short hair was oddly clumped and his clothes were stained, a far cry from his usual fastidiousness. Stacy, too, looked dirty and disheveled.

Sartorial etiquette was the least of their problems, however. Joan was missing, and they needed to find her or report her disappearance. Gary took out his cell phone and tried once again to call first Joan's cell, then her dorm room. There was no answer from either.

It worried him that he could not get ahold of Kara,

but her absence was easily explained. While the fall semester was still young, Gary already knew her schedule almost as well as he knew Joan's, since he and Joan
needed to be aware of the hours Kara would be in and
out of the dorm room. This was Tuesday, which meant
that she was in class until twelve. After that, she usually
ate lunch somewhere on campus or in the village, then
hung around or went to the library until her next class at
one thirty, finally returning to the room around three.

Of course, that only explained why she wasn't there
now.

Why hadn't she answered the phone last night?

He told himself that she was a heavy sleeper or she
hadn't wanted to be disturbed. On the off chance that
she was skipping class and simply not answering her
phone, he decided to check out the dorm to see whether
she was there. She wasn't, and when Teri Lim, who had
the room next door and was one of Joan's and Kara's
friends, saw Gary in the hall, she told him that she hadn't
seen Kara this morning or, now that she thought about
it, yesterday. Teri looked at the four of them oddly, as did
the other students who wound around them and passed
by, but Gary explained that they'd just this moment
come back from the Burning Man festival and hadn't
had time to change. Reluctant to go into too much detail
about what had happened—Teri was an acquaintance at
best—he told her that they'd "lost" Joan and that they'd
been hoping to find her back here.

"I could ask around," Teri offered, "see if anyone has
seen her. Or Kara."

"That'd be great," he said, smiling, though smiling
was the last thing he felt like doing.

"I'll be back."

Joan had given him an extra key for her room. It was
something that was not strictly allowed, so he waited until Teri was gone and the corridor clear before quickly

putting the key in the lock, opening the door and ushering Reyn, Stacy and Brian inside.

He immediately closed the door behind them.

Right away, something seemed wrong. On Kara's desk, her computer was on, Brad Pitt's face smiling out from her screen saver, and the door of her closet as well as the drawers of her dresser were open. Kara's bed was unmade, and her entire half of the room was in disarray, as though she had left in a hurry.

Did Kara have something to do with Joan's disappearance?

Or was Kara a victim, too?

Either way, Gary thought, her absence was a bad sign.

In contrast to Kara's disordered living space, Joan's half of the room was characteristically neat and tidy. While he doubted that there were any clues to be discovered here, he poked around anyway, scanning the items on the top of her dresser and small desk. There were two crumpled yellow Post-its lying on the floor at the foot of Joan's narrow bedstead, and when he picked them up and smoothed them out, he saw that both contained short messages written in pencil. He read the first one. *"Friday 11 p.m. A man called. No name. Said he'd call back."* Gary felt uneasy. What man would call Joan at eleven o'clock at night, trying to determine her whereabouts? And why wouldn't he leave his name? Gary read the second note. *"Saturday, 6 a.m. Man called back. Asked where you were."*

Who could it have been? A friend? A relative? A co-worker? An ex?

Brian had been reading over his shoulder. "You think Kara gave it up? Told some sicko where she was?"

The same thought had occurred to Gary, though he hadn't wanted to acknowledge it, but hearing the idea expressed aloud gave it a concreteness that chilled him to the bone. He could only shake his head no, hoping he was right.

"What is it?" Stacy asked. "Did you find something?"

"A strange guy was calling and looking for Joan," Brian said.

"We need to tell her parents," Reyn said, looking at the notes. "They need to know she's missing. Besides, maybe they can help."

"Maybe she went to visit them," Stacy suggested hopefully. "Maybe she got spooked and ran home."

Gary shook his head. "I don't think so. Joan isn't that close to her parents. And I don't even know where they live or how to get ahold of them."

"We could look through her address book, if she has one." Brian started toward Joan's desk.

Gary saw movement out of the corner of his eye. Teri had opened the door and stepped into the room. He'd assumed that the door locked automatically after closing.

"No one's seen either of them," Teri reported. "And by the way, Joan loves her parents. They're very close. *Brady Bunch* close. She calls them almost every day. They live up near San Luis Obispo in a little town called Cayucos. I went up there with her and Kara for a weekend this summer."

Joan was close to her parents?

And they lived here in California?

Gary felt the first faint stirrings of . . . not distrust, exactly. Uneasiness? That was more accurate. He thought about the few references she'd made to what had seemed a very strict and restrictive upbringing. Had he deliberately misled him, or had he just put the wrong spin on what he'd heard?

"Do you have their number?" he asked.

Teri nodded. "Joan gave it to me in case of an emergency. Hold on a sec." She dashed out the door, and Gary's eyes met Reyn's, although his friend's expression was unreadable. Stacy was admonishing Brian not to look through Joan's desk. Teri returned bearing a torn scrap of paper on which she'd written an address and phone number.

It was just like Joan to give a neighbor her parents' number, Gary thought. Unfailingly prepared, she was always ready for any eventuality. For the first time since he'd awakened in the desert to find her gone, the emotional reality of her absence hit him, and he felt a sharp pang of loss as he took the paper from Teri. What was he doing here? He needed to call the police. Time was wasting.

Still, he dialed the number of Joan's parents.

Teri was backing out of the room. "I have to go. I have a psych class. Tell me what happens."

Gary nodded as he held the phone to his ear. Stacy walked with Teri to the door, the two of them talking in low tones.

He waited. Three rings. Six rings. Twelve rings. A robotic woman's voice came on the line and said, "Your party is not answering. Please hang up and dial again later."

Gary closed his cell phone, shaking his head. He had a bad feeling about this. For about the hundredth time, he tried calling Joan's cell, but now there was no ringing, no busy signal, only a flat, cold silence that sounded like—

Death.

"I'm calling the police," he announced. "It hasn't been forty-eight hours yet, but it's been more than twenty-four. They should be able to do something."

Reyn nodded his approval.

Brian had been examining the contents that were on top of Joan's desk. "What's this?" he asked, picking up a rolled piece of paper slightly larger than a pencil. It looked like a scroll and was stretched between two small sticks.

Gary shook his head. "I don't know. I never saw it before."

"I don't think you should be going through her stuff," Stacy said. "It's not right. She wouldn't want you to."

Ignoring her, Brian had already unrolled the scroll and was reading it aloud:

"O Lord of Heavenly Hosts! Protect me from The Outsiders. Shield me from sin and see me through times of trial and tribulation. Protect me from The Outsiders. Safeguard my friends and family from those who would corrupt us. Protect me from The Outsiders. Let Your light and goodness shine on me and mine. Protect me from The Outsiders. Amen."

Brian looked up, frowning. "The Outsiders? What the hell does that mean?"

Gary didn't know, but his heart was pounding. The prayer was disturbing in a way he couldn't quite put his finger on. He took the scroll from Brian and read the words himself. Joan had told him that her parents were religious and that she'd been brought up rather strictly, but while she refused to drink alcohol, did not take drugs and still exhibited the inhibited demeanor of someone who'd been raised in a repressive environment, she'd given him the impression that she had broken away from all that. He'd assumed that, like himself, she was not religious.

Did she actually say this prayer to herself each night?

The Outsiders.

His uneasiness grew.

Was the prayer to be taken literally? he wondered.

Could there be a group or gang called The Outsiders who were harassing or threatening her? Perhaps that was who was behind this. Maybe she'd been a target all along and had known it. Maybe the prayer had been her way of trying to stave off just this sort of kidnapping.

But she hadn't written the prayer. It was printed on the scroll. She had gotten it from somewhere else.

Her parents?

He needed to call the police. He'd tell them what had happened at Burning Man, give them her parents' address and phone number, tell them about Kara, give them the prayer scroll, explain that he'd already reported Joan's disappearance to police in Nevada. . . .

Brian was opening a desk drawer.

"Stay out of there!" Stacy said sharply.

Gary dialed 911. He was relieved to be able to pass off responsibility to the cops, though he felt guilty that he felt that way.

His call was answered before he heard a single ring: "Nine-one-one. Please describe your emergency."

"My girlfriend's disappeared. We think she's been kidnapped. We were drugged and—"

"Slow down, sir. Start from the beginning."

Gary knew he was babbling, and he was so nervous that his hand was shaking. "My girlfriend's name is Joan Daniels," he said slowly. "I think she's been kidnapped." Following the prompts of the dispatcher, he described what had happened, answering all questions put to him and keeping his voice as reasonable and matter-of-fact as possible. Finally, he gave Joan's dorm, floor and room number.

"We're sending someone over right now," the dispatcher said. "Please stay where you are until the officers arrive."

Three

Although Joan was not Gary's first girlfriend, she was the first one for whom he had fallen so hard. Back in high school, he'd been shy and awkward, and while it was conventional widsom that *all* teens were shy and awkward when it came to the opposite sex, Gary had been so to a much greater degree than other kids. He wasn't quite sure why that was. He'd always had quite a few friends, and his parents were ordinary, well-adjusted people. But for some reason, he had not been able to make that normal transition into the world of teenage romance.

His first real date, which hadn't been until his senior year, had been with Tammy Fieger, whose older brother, Craig, had voluntarily committed himself to a mental institution when she was a freshman. The truth was that Craig had been depressed after their parents' divorce, had had no one to turn to, and had sought help in the only way he knew how. He had stayed in Parkview for less than a month and had been out and back to normal ever since, though he'd transferred to another school, but to the kids at Fairfield High, he was insane, and there was a high probability that his sister shared those genes, which was why no one else had ever asked her out. Even if she wasn't crazy, she had a crazy brother, and that alone was reason enough to avoid her. Who needed that kind of complication?

But Tammy had been nice, he had felt sorry for her, and in the sparsely attended English elective they'd shared, he'd chosen to sit next to her, feeling bad that the other students had bunched together away from her on the opposite side of the room. Her social skills, if possible, were even worse than his own, but that was one of the attractions. There was no pressure on him to be cool or suave, and their mutual awkwardness was actually kind of comfortable. He found it easy to talk to her, and soon they were spending time together outside of class. His friends had liked her, too, and had been very nonjudgmental. Tammy had quickly become an integral part of his life.

So they'd dated, they'd gone to Homecoming and Winter Formal, they'd even had sex; but theirs was no great romance, and well before the end of the year, they'd had a sober discussion about their plans, their hopes, their futures, and had mutually decided to break up. He'd spent the rest of the school year alone and was the only one of his friends who hadn't gone to the prom.

Coming to California had been liberating.

He'd actually had no intention of leaving Ohio and had already been accepted to Ohio State University. But in a weird confluence of circumstances, his Pell grant had come through, he'd received one thousand dollars from an arts foundation that had liked the essay he'd submitted and awarded it first place in their contest, and the company for which his dad worked had offered him a fifteen-thousand-dollar scholarship. He had not actually applied for the scholarship and still suspected his dad's hand (though with a straight face his father consistently denied any involvement), but whatever the reason for the windfall, Gary was grateful. He would have simply taken the money, banked it and gone on to Ohio State as planned, but the scholarship's stipulation was that the funds could be used only for tuition—use it or lose it—

and on a whim, he sent out applications to colleges and universities all over the United States. It was late in the season, and many schools hadn't replied, but by some miracle he'd been accepted to UCLA, where, thanks to his good grades and high SAT scores, he was offered additional financial aid to cover the gap between tuition and the amount of money he had available. It was a once-in-a-lifetime opportunity, and after discussing the situation with his parents, he decided to lock in his acceptance.

The three of them flew out in June, after graduation, to scope the place out.

Gary's conception of Southern California had been formed by movies, music and television, but he was surprised and happy to discover that that conception was pretty close to accurate. They'd left Ohio on a muggy gray day and had landed in Los Angeles out of a bright blue sky. Temperate sea breezes swayed the fronds of palm trees that lined the streets, and while there were dirty industrial buildings beneath the edge of the raised freeway as they headed north toward UCLA, the overall impression was one of a clean, new city where good-looking people lived pleasant, untroubled lives.

Gary liked California immediately, and so did his parents. The guided tour of the campus only served to cement their positive impression of the state, and they'd flown back to Ohio two days later feeling exhilarated. Gary knew he would miss his friends when he moved out west, but the trade-offs were worth it. Besides, he'd be back for holidays. And they could always come out and visit.

At the end of August, he drove out to California by himself. He'd spent nearly half of the essay money on brakes and bearings for his crappy Celica, but it was money well spent because he made it to the coast without incident.

In California, he had fashioned a new persona. What was the use of moving someplace where no one knew you if you couldn't reinvent yourself? So rather than the awkward, slightly nerdy guy he'd been back in Ohio, he became someone different, someone cooler. Although it was impossible for him to change who he really was, he could alter his backstory, jettison some of the baggage he carried, and the Gary Russell who emerged, while fundamentally the same, was more outgoing, more socially self-confident, and that translated into surprising success with the opposite sex.

As a freshman, he'd gone out with several different girls, though toward the end of the second semester, he'd ended up exclusively dating a communications major named Cassie, who introduced him to the campus film society, which hosted weekly screenings of cult movies and foreign films. That was how he'd met Reyn, the club president. Both hard-core David Lynch fans, the two of them had become fast friends, the friendship easily outlasting his brief romance with Cassie.

Reyn was a native Angeleno, and through him Gary became acquainted with entirely new aspects of Southern California. Rather than everything being centered on the school, he was introduced to a much broader swath of life: festivals, flea markets, parks, the beach, and a multitude of fun things to do for free or on the cheap. That summer, instead of going home to spend a couple of months with his parents and his old friends, Gary got a job working with Reyn at Universal Studios, although Reyn, back for his third year, was a tram driver, while Gary was a souvenir stand salesclerk who occasionally doubled for Count Dracula when the man who usually wandered around the park playing the character was out sick or off duty. While he did return to see his parents for a week near the end of August, he felt oddly out of place hanging out with his old friends at their old haunts, and he realized that over the past year Ohio had become not his home but the place he was from. California was now his home.

And life was good. His classes were challenging but fun, he'd scraped enough money together through grants and scholarships to pay tuition for the next year, and he had a work-study job on campus to pay for room and board. Socially, things had settled down, and while he wasn't any more popular than he had been back in Ohio, he was happier. This was where he was meant to be.

That was about the time Reyn started going out with Stacy, then a student at LA City College, whom he'd met at Universal Studios. Stacy was a journalism major who wrote movie reviews for her school paper and occasionally freelanced for an indie film Web site, so the two of them had a lot in common. And that fall, Gary met Brian when the two of them were assigned to be lab partners in a chemistry class. Brian was from the Bay Area, not San Francisco proper but a suburb, and he'd transferred to UCLA to get a name-school diploma after finishing his general ed requirements at a community college. Long-haired and slackerish, he reminded Gary of Tom Weiss, one of his old high school buddies, and while in many ways the two of them were polar opposites, they meshed somehow and started hanging out.

He continued to date various young women he met in various classes but hooked up with Meg at one of the film society's screenings. It was an oddball pairing of the dark satire *How to Get Ahead in Advertising* with the sunny musical *How to Succeed in Business Without Really Trying*, and afterward Meg had participated in one of Reyn's panel discussions. He was never quite sure how their relationship had become as serious as it had, but it progressed quickly from casual to exclusive, and soon afterward Gary found himself living with the unspoken assumption that they were to be permanently a couple. He liked Meg, they never fought, but theirs was not a romantic romance. Though he couldn't put his finger on it, something seemed missing, something wasn't there, and he was secretly grateful when she abruptly dumped him.

Joan was different.

Gary wasn't one of those rubes who'd been brainwashed by books and movies to believe that there was only One True Love for each individual. But the fact remained that what he felt for Joan was deeper and truer than anything he'd felt before. A day into their relationship, he felt closer to her than he had to Meg after a year. Not only was she stunningly attractive, but she was a genuinely nice person. Their relationship was new, and in a lot of ways they were still getting to know each other, but as far as he was concerned, the two of them were amazingly in sync. Their tastes on a lot of things did not coincide, and their interests did not always match, but their attitudes did. Their approaches to life were very similar, and that went a long way toward paving over any minor differences they had.

He loved her.

And she loved him.

All the pieces of his life were falling into place, and while he knew there were bound to be some setbacks and minor inconveniences in the future, he'd seen no storm clouds on the horizon. As far as he was concerned, looking ahead, it was going to be clear sailing from here on in.

How wrong he had been.

Four

When the police arrived at Joan and Kara's dorm room, Gary was standing next to the window looking out at the side of the adjoining building. Brian was sitting in Kara's desk chair, and Reyn and Stacy were seated on Kara's bed. They had opened the door, and though a number of curious students had peeked in as they passed by, none of them had come inside or asked what was going on. It wasn't until the policemen showed up that the four of them had to explain what they were doing there.

There were two officers, and they knocked on the doorframe, identifying themselves as LAPD before entering. One, a heavyset guy in his mid-fifties wearing street clothes, handed out a business card and introduced himself as Detective Williams. The other, younger man, wearing a uniform, did not introduce himself but typed nonstop into a small handheld computer.

"I'm the one who called," Gary said, stepping forward. "I'm Gary Russell."

"What relation are you to the missing woman?" the detective asked.

"Uh . . . boyfriend," Gary said.

The detective turned toward Stacy.

"Friend," she announced.

Reyn and Brian nodded. "Friend," they both said.

"And her name is Joan Daniel?"

"Daniels," Gary corrected. "With an *s*."

"Told you," the younger cop said without looking up.

"That's her stuff there." Gary motioned toward Joan's side of the room. "We looked around a little bit when we first came in, but we've stayed away since. In case there are clues or evidence or anything."

"Tell me what happened."

He explained about their weekend trip to Burning Man, leaving out the story of Brian's smuggled contraband, and described how they had been drugged and then awakened from unconsciousness to find Joan gone. After he told Williams how he'd reported her disappearance to the local Nevada police before returning to check whether she had come back to her dorm room, the detective asked, "How do you think this drug was administered to each of you?"

Gary looked over at Reyn, who gave him a bemused Jim Halpert shrug. There had to have been something they'd all eaten or drunk, something they had in common, but he could not figure out what that might be. Perhaps there'd been a spray of some sort, something airborne, an aerosol mist that they had all breathed. Whatever it was, it had been very localized. The campers to either side of them had been gone when they'd come to, which probably meant that they had not affected.

"I don't know," Gary admitted.

"Excuse me." The other officer looked up at Williams from his handheld device. "There's no Joan Daniels listed on the UCLA student database."

"What?" Gary exclaimed. He leaned over and tried to peer at whatever was on the cop's screen but could see nothing. "That doesn't make any sense."

"Joan *is* a student at UCLA and she *is* missing," Reyn said calmly. "You must have accessed the wrong list."

"It's a listing of all students currently attending this university. And there is no Joan Daniels on it."

"That's ridiculous," Stacy said.

"I've checked it twice. She is not signed up for any classes; she is not registered."

"Then we have a problem," Detective Williams said, turning toward Gary.

"Yes, we do," Gary agreed.

"Yes, we do."

"Because my girlfriend is missing, and it looks like you don't believe she even exists."

The older man's face was set and serious. "I don't know what kind of prank you're pulling here, but it's a crime to file a false report."

"He's not lying!" Stacy said.

The detective looked around. "Maybe all of you are in on this."

"No," Brian said, speaking out for the first time. "She really is his girlfriend and she really did disappear. But . . ." He took a deep breath. "Maybe she isn't who she said she was. Maybe she was conning us and wasn't really a student." He ignored the glares of his friends. "I mean, none of us really knew her for that long—"

"She was in my music appreciation class last semester," Gary said angrily. "You can check with the instructor, Dr. Katz."

"Besides," Reyn pointed out. "We're standing in her room. This is her stuff, her computer, her desk, her bed."

"Her roommate might be missing, too," Gary said. "No one's seen her for two days. Her name's Kara. . . ." He suddenly realized that he didn't know Kara's last name. He glanced around the room. Her things were here. Her name had to be printed *somewhere*.

He felt frustrated, and even as his eyes searched the room, he was still trying to figure out how Joan's name could have disappeared from the school's records. The detective on the computer had to have made a mistake, he decided. It was the only explanation.

"Look through their desks," Gary suggested. "There have to be letters there, forms, papers, things with their names."

"Yeah," Reyn said. "Whether or not you think she was a student, she's still missing. Maybe Kara, too."

"And it's your job to find them!" Stacy glared at the policemen.

"I don't think you realize—" Williams began.

"She could be dead!" It hurt him to say it, and speaking the thought aloud somehow gave it more credence. Gary's mind was racing. He wished he had a photo of Joan, but he didn't. The relationship was too new, and they hadn't taken any pictures together.

Her Facebook page!

"She has a Facebook page," Gary said with relief. "And a MySpace page. You can find out all about her. You can see what she looks like."

Williams looked over at the other policeman, who shook his head. "Dedicated equipment. I can't access that."

"Then use her computer. Or Kara's."

"No. If there has been a crime committed, those may be evidence."

"Fuck!" Gary said, kicking the foot of Kara's bed.

The detective stared at him for a moment, then sighed. "I don't know what's going on here, but I'm willing to give you the benefit of the doubt and assume you're not intentionally misleading us. I don't know who this young woman is, but we will continue to investigate. None of you are allowed back in this room, though. Do you hear me? This dorm is off-limits. I'll need contact information from each of you: names, addresses, phone numbers. I want to see driver's licenses and student ID cards. If everything checks out, if you're right and Ms. Daniels *is* missing, we'll keep you updated. If you're lying, I'll haul all of your asses in and charge you. Do I make myself clear?"

Gary nodded. Already he felt better. At least the cops were going to look into the situation. And once they did, they would find out the truth and start looking for her. And Kara.

But would it be too late?

He tried not to think of that.

Ten minutes later, all four of them had shown ID, submitted to questioning, provided information and been kicked out of Joan and Kara's room. At the last minute, Gary had remembered the phone number for her parents and had shared that with the police, although he kept the original scrap of paper.

They retreated down the hall under the curious eyes of other dorm residents.

"What the hell do we do now?" Reyn asked when they'd exited the building. They stood on the sidewalk as students strode around them, past them.

Brian shrugged. "There's nothing we can do."

Gary's fists clenched.

Brian backed up, palms outstretched. "I'm just saying—"

"Shut up," Reyn told him.

In Gary's mind, he saw Joan alone in a dark, dirty room, naked, bruised and beaten. He saw Kara dead in the desert, collateral damage. "We have to do *something*," he said, but he couldn't think of what. His head seemed heavy, his brain numb and dumb.

Stacy nudged him. "You have to get some sleep," she told him. "You haven't slept for—"

"I slept in the car."

"Yeah, for about ten minutes."

"We *all* need some sleep," Brian said. He yawned, as if to prove his point. "I definitely need to crash."

Reyn put a hand on Gary's shoulder. "It's true. You won't be much help to her if you don't get some sleep."

He was right. They were all right, though Gary didn't

want to admit it. He *was* tired, and likely not thinking clearly, and probably the best thing he could do was catch up on his rest before doing anything. But he imagined Joan bound and gagged, tied to a chair, tortured by unseen assailants.

The Outsiders.

He not only had no idea where she was; he didn't know what was happening to her—and that was the most maddening, frustrating part. Was she being treated well? Was she being gang-raped? Was she dead?

The latter two possibilities seemed the most likely. She had not been allowed to contact him, and there'd been no demand for a ransom. He could think of no reason for her captors to keep her safe and unharmed if they weren't after money.

It was the thought of sexual assault that really upset him, the image that burned in his mind like a white-hot needle, and he was both enraged and deeply disturbed by the idea that hostile strangers—

Outsiders

—were forcibly abusing her while the police sat around and tried to figure out whether or not she even existed.

He wondered if he should take an official leave of absence from school. There was no way he would be able to sit in class, to shuffle from course to course, from mythology to math, while Joan's whereabouts remained unknown. If this dragged on for more than a few days, he wouldn't be able to catch up on all the reading and work in his classes, and the whole semester would be a waste. He'd probably jeopardize his grants and scholarships, too, since to receive the money he was required to maintain a certain grade-point average. Of course, he was also required to keep a full twenty-one-unit schedule each semester to keep the money, so either way he was screwed.

Gary glanced around at his friends. "I am tired," he acknowledged. "But I don't think I can sleep. Is anybody going to their classes today?"

Reyn and Stacy shook their heads.

"I'm on a Monday-Wednesday-Friday schedule," Brian said. "I'm taking a siesta."

"So what's the plan?" Reyn asked.

"I don't know." Gary sighed.

"Sleep on it," Stacy suggested. "We all will. Maybe we'll come up with something."

"Those cops . . ."

"I know," she said. "But they're just doing their job. Once they figure things out—"

"*If* they figure things out."

"Even if they do," Brian said, "they still might not find her."

"Shut up," Reyn told him.

"I'm just saying."

Gary's head hurt. "I'm going back to my place," he told them. It suddenly occurred to him that the phone in his dorm room had an answering machine. He didn't want to get his hopes up, but it was possible that she had called and left a message. "I'll call you guys later," he said, heading toward his own building.

"If we think of something, we'll let you know!" Reyn called after him.

Gary waved, hurrying away, and seconds later he was sprinting toward his dormitory. It was stupid, but in those few moments he had somehow convinced himself that there would be a message waiting for him.

Of course there wasn't—he arrived at his room, drenched in sweat, to find his answering machine sitting there, its message light off, not blinking.

He sat down heavily on the bed and cried. He didn't know where that came from. Worry, stress, tiredness, all of it probably factored in, but he couldn't help himself, and tears rolled down his cheeks, sobs shaking his frame as he faced the fact, *really* faced the fact, that Joan might be dead. He closed his eyes against the emotion and found that he didn't want to open them again.

He lay down, not bothering to take off his clothes or kick off his shoes, and within seconds he fell asleep.

And dreamed.

In the dream, UCLA looked like Burning Man. Instead of the usual brick buildings with their pseudo–Ivy League ambience, the campus was made up of temporary structures fabricated with found objects and recycled materials. He and Joan were seated on a blanket, on some grass, eating a picnic breakfast of dry Apple Jacks. Barefoot students in ragged clothes were running by them, each carrying a log or tree branch. They were running toward the south edge of campus, where a wall was being constructed with the wood, and Gary understood that UCLA was not a university but a fort, and the wall was being built to keep the Outsiders from gaining entry. He told Joan to wait where she was and ran forward to help with the wall, but halfway there, he saw a portion of it collapse and a horde of Outsiders break through. They were cloaked, bansheelike figures whose faces could not be seen within the darkness of their cowls. Turning, he tried to run back to Joan, to protect her, but the Outsiders sprinted past him, and by the time he reached the picnic blanket, she had been whisked away and was gone.

Five

It was after nine thirty when Teri Lim finally left geology. The class actually ended at nine fifteen, but she'd wanted to ask the instructor a few questions about the syllabus. She'd waited until all of the other students who were staying after had asked their own questions because . . . well, because Dr. Prem was cute. The ring on his finger said he was married, though, and his no-nonsense responses forestalled any flirting and made her feel foolish. She asked her questions meekly, nodded at the answers, then walked out of the class and out of the building, sucking in the cool night air, hoping it would reduce the heat on her embarrassed face.

The campus was quiet and nearly empty. UCLA's nightlife was headquartered at Westwood Village, next door, and the university itself seemed to shut down after classes ended. From far away came the faint, raucous sounds of frat parties, mingled with the even more distant sounds of city traffic, the two together creating a soft, indistinct background noise that made the stillness around her seem even deeper, this section of the university feel even more remote and cut off from the rest of the world.

Teri looked behind her, hoping to see other students coming out of Physical Sciences, hoping to see her professor. But everyone else had exited through the main entrance that led to the well-lit parking lot in front of the building, and she remained alone on the dark, winding walkway that was a shortcut to her dorm. To her right, on a bench beneath the dim, hazy light of an old lamppost, a couple was making out, and she let out a sigh of relief, grateful she was not the only one here. Seconds later, however, she was past the bench and walking between two pine trees whose shadowed indentations resembled malevolent beings with pointed heads. The trunks of both trees were more than thick enough for someone to hide behind.

She sped up. Noises from the outside world seemed to have faded away or been swallowed up by the silence, and the only sound she heard was the *tap-tap-tap* of her own shoes on the sidewalk. There were goose bumps on her arms, and not from the temperature. It was hard to see, and she kept her eyes on the ground, not wanting to trip over a rock or branch or crack in the cement. The walkway curved, then straightened, opening out onto a flat expanse of concrete. She looked up.

A man was standing at the bottom of the steps in front of Royce Hall.

Facing her.

Teri quickened her pace. His form was little more than a silhouette, but something about the man seemed off, though for several seconds she couldn't figure out exactly what it was. She finally decided that it was the disquieting way he just stood there, unmoving, in what seemed a strangely formal, almost militaristic stance: arms at his sides, back straight, legs slightly apart.

She was stupid to have taken this shortcut across campus unaccompanied. Especially with Joan and Kara missing. She should have walked with everyone else out to the parking lot and caught a ride back. Or called from one of the campus security phones for an escort. But she was used to being on campus at odd hours in odd places—and by herself—so she hadn't really thought about the danger of walking alone at night.

No. That wasn't precisely true. She'd been nervous from the beginning tonight, ever since leaving the Physical Sciences building, and while she didn't believe in omens or premonitions or nebulous warnings from irrational sources, she thought now that she should have paid closer attention to her gut.

The man took a few precise steps forward, moving from the shadows into the yellowish illumination of one of the walkway lights, and Teri realized what else made her uneasy: she had seen him before. She did not know where, did not know when, but he definitely seemed familiar to her. He was dressed in simple, earthy, homemade-looking clothes that would best be described as peasant garb, and his dark hair was medium-length and parted in the middle, making it appear as though his forehead was topped by a peaked roof.

There was something wrong with him, she saw as he drew closer. He walked in a stilted manner, not as an affectation and not because he was trained to do so, but because he had to: there was something the matter with his legs. It was not just his legs, though. His arms, too, seemed strange, his entire body slightly malformed. She was even more frightened than she had been before, and she clutched her books tightly, her stride growing longer as she attempted to hurry past.

"I need to talk to you," he said.

Teri ran.

The man had some kind of accent, but her panicked mind could not quite place it, and at that moment his speech patterns were the least of her concerns. She kept her eyes on the ground, still afraid of tripping and falling. Her dorm was quite a ways off in another direction, and down another empty path, but she was close to the edge of campus here, and she dashed toward the street, grateful for the presence of life and lights and people.

She didn't scream for help—for all she knew she was in no danger whatsoever and everything was all in her head—but she wanted to get as far away from that man as quickly as possible—

Where had she seen him before?

—and be surrounded by the safety of strangers. Even if he did mean her harm, he would not be able to do anything in the middle of a crowd of people.

And there was a crowd. The sidewalk bordering the school was teeming with students out for coffee or a movie, a trip to a bookstore or a late dinner. Groups of young men and women were walking together, talking, laughing. Teri pushed her way into the midst of them, feeling protected and secure as she passed a couple with their arms around each other, a gaggle of men arguing about politics. She looked over her shoulder, back toward the darkness of the campus, stepped off the curb—

And a car slammed into her, throwing her several feet into the air.

She landed hard on the pavement, on her back. There were screams all around her, but she could not tell who they were coming from because she could not move her eyes to see. She could not move anything at all. She could hear a muffled liquid sound in her head, like the burbling of a fountain, and she knew that was the noise of blood gushing out of her, but she could feel nothing. There was no pain at all in any part of her body. That was a bad sign. Bad.

Even as she thought this, she grew weaker. The act of thinking seemed to take all of her concentration and energy, and keeping her eyes open became a task more difficult than lifting hundred-pound weights. She was slipping away; she knew it, she felt it, and there was nothing she could do about it.

The last thing she saw before her eyes closed for the last time was the man in peasant garb standing over her, looking down, nodding.

Smiling.

Six

Gary awoke feeling anxious, frightened, sad and totally wrung out. Whether what he'd experienced was a legitimate nightmare or had been generated by the residue of whatever drug had been administered to them all back at Burning Man, he had no idea. But the emotions produced by the dream were real, and he could not remember ever having felt worse

The phone rang just as he was sitting up. It was Reyn, and he seemed alert, wide awake, as though he'd been up for a while. He wasted no time with greetings.

"I'm online," Reyn said. "Joan's Facebook page is gone."

"What?"

"MySpace, too." There was a brief pause. "I don't want to sound paranoid, but it seems like someone's trying to erase her, pretend like she doesn't exist. I mean, first her school records, and now this . . ."

Gary's head felt heavy. His brain still wasn't functioning. "Who?"

"I don't know. I thought you might have an idea."

The Outsiders?

Gary glanced at his clock. Six a.m. He'd been asleep for over fifteen hours. Panic welled within him at the thought of all that could have happened during that time. "I'm going to find Joan's parents," he told Reyn.

"I'll try to call them again, but if I can't get through, I'm driving up there. I have their address."

"Don't you think the police have already contacted them?"

"The police don't even think she exists!"

"You're right. At least her parents can clear that up. And maybe they have some idea of what's going on. Where do they live again?"

"Cayucos. I checked: It's about a five-hour drive. I can be back by late afternoon."

"I'll go with you," Reyn offered.

"No," Gary said. "It's the second week of school. There's no reason for you to screw up your classes. I have an excuse. She's my girlfriend. It might not fly with Neilson—"

"Neilson," Reyn moaned.

"—but the rest of my instructors seem cool, and I can probably get away with it. At least this once. I think you'd better stay here, though." Left unsaid was the thought that Reyn should build up some brownie points now because he might need to take some time off later.

Gary doubted that this was going to end quickly.

Or well.

He had to force himself not to imagine what was happening to Joan right now.

"Call me if you learn anything," Reyn told him. "You have my cell. And call me when you get back no matter what happens. I'll see what I can find out here. I think I'll check in with the cops, too. Just in case."

"Thanks," Gary said gratefully.

"You'd better get going."

Cayucos was a picturesque little town on the hilly central coast, halfway between Morro Bay and Hearst Castle. A community so small that Gary was almost past it before he knew it was there, its main street was on a narrow stretch of land between the raised highway and the beach, hidden from view by a line of pine trees bordering the side of the road. It was only an unobtrusive sign near an off-ramp that alerted him to its location, and he pulled into the short left-turn lane, crossed the nonexistent southbound traffic, and headed down a winding, sloping road that led into town.

He passed a couple of oceanfront homes, a gas station, a gift shop. Slowing down at the first cross street, he looked to his right, toward the beach. The road ended less than half a block down, at the foot of a small and refreshingly uncommercialized pier, a narrow wooden platform that ended just past the wave line. Several men were fishing off the side of it. Unlike the piers in Southern California, there was no restaurant at the far end, no shops anywhere along its length. The entire downtown, in fact, was enchantingly quaint and stretched for only a few short blocks. There were a smattering of hotels, a few old buildings from the late 1800s that had been converted into antique stores and bars, a couple of restaurants and that was about it.

Gary continued on, businesses segueing into homes, before finally pulling into the small parking lot of a small library. He had muted the volume of his GPS way back in Los Angeles, tired of hearing the incessant, insistent monotone of its robotic voice giving him directions at every curve and corner, but he turned it back on now and discovered that he had passed the street he needed to take in order to get to Joan's parents' house.

Once more, he picked up his cell phone and attempted to call them. He had tried calling three times this morning already: before leaving the dorm, at a McDonald's in Oxnard, and while on the road, even though he didn't have an earpiece and knew that if a cop saw him on the phone while driving he would get a ticket. There'd been no answer during any of those attempts, and there was none now. He closed his phone.

He was starving, Gary realized. He hadn't eaten breakfast, hadn't had anything at all this morning save a wake-up cup of coffee from the McDonald's drive-through. He should find Joan's parents first, though. That was the most important thing. Afterward, he could grab something to eat.

His stomach gurgled noisily, and there was a pain in his midsection so sharp that it made him wince.

Still, it would only take a few minutes to wolf down some food. Then he could meet her mom and dad and not have to worry about embarrassing himself.

If they were there

Yes. If they were there. He hadn't wanted to think about that, but it was impossible to avoid, and perhaps putting off the meeting a bit longer would help calm his nerves, prepare him. It might also give him a chance to plan out what he was going to say to them if they were there. Because he hadn't really done that yet. He'd been on the road all morning, thinking of nothing else but Joan and Kara and Burning Man, but he hadn't decided how he would tell them that their daughter had disappeared. If he was lucky, the police would have already contacted them, but if not, he would be the one to break the news, and he had no clue how to do that.

He drove back two blocks to the center of town. There were no fast food joints here, but adjacent to the sea wall that separated a public parking lot from the beach was a small white shack, with people eating on plastic tables on the sidewalk out front. Gary turned left onto the short dead-end street, pulled in front of the tiny building and got out of the car. The sign above the door identified the little restaurant as RUDELL'S SMOKEHOUSE.

Inside, there was a refrigerated glass case filled with individually packaged smoked fish and meat. There was even an entire smoked chicken. Taped to the top of the counter was an article from a local newspaper explaining how the Smokehouse and its owner had been featured on a Bobby Flay show on the Food Network. The menu was written in ink on a white dry-erase board, and among the list of items was a smoked albacore taco. Gary had no idea what that was, but it sounded interesting. A woman was chopping vegetables in the area behind the menu board while discussing a bluegrass concert with a man who could not be seen. She looked up at Gary. "My brother'll be right with you," she said.

The unseen man emerged from what looked to be a closet or small storeroom in the back and offered a friendly greeting. Gary asked him what was in the smoked albacore taco. There were a whole bunch of ingredients, including chopped apple and celery, and while the combination seemed weird, Gary was hungry enough to try anything. He ordered two, as well as a Peach Snapple, and took his food out to one of the tables in front. As it turned out, the taco was delicious. He'd never tasted anything like it, and even before he'd finished the first two, he went back inside and ordered another. They were big and filling, but this might have to last him the rest of the day, and it sure as hell beat stopping at some hamburger chain on the side of the highway on his way home.

Looking out at the waves, he felt guilty. How dare he enjoy the view, how dare he enjoy the meal, while Joan was still missing?

Dead.

No, he didn't feel that she was dead, and though he had nothing whatsoever to base it on, the notion was close to a certainty in his mind. Wherever she was, whatever had happened to her, she was still alive. As frazzled as he was, that gave him comfort.

He quickly finished his last taco and his bottle of Snapple and tossed his trash into a nearby container before getting back in the car. Joan's parents' house was located two streets up from the main drag on a road so

narrow and barely paved that it was little more than
a dirt alley. All of the houses on the street were of the
wooden clapboard variety common to seaside communities, and the Daniels home was a white single-story
structure virtually indistinguishable from those to either
side of it.

There was no vehicle parked in the short driveway
or along the narrow road in front of the house, but that
didn't mean anything. Their car could be inside the garage. He pulled in front of the closed garage door and
got out, walking up the flagstone path to the porch. He
rang the doorbell. Waited. No one answered, and he
rang again. He didn't hear any chimes and wasn't sure
the bell was working, so he reached out and knocked.

There was movement as the door gave under his fist,
and he took a step back, surprised. He hadn't noticed
before because, while the door hadn't been latched, it
had been shut almost all the way, but he saw now that it
was not only unlocked, it was open.

This couldn't be good.

"Hello?" Gary called. There was no answer. He hadn't
expected one, and he looked around to see if anyone
else was watching. There were no cars or pedestrians on
the street, no people in their yards, but someone could
very well be looking at him from a window in one of the
houses opposite. He used his foot to push open the door
a little more. "Hello?" he called again.

There was no sound from inside, no sign of movement,
and on impulse, he pushed the door all the way open.
The house was dark, still, and he knew instantly that no
one was home. There was an indefinable but unmistak-
able sense of emptiness that hung in the air of a building
that was uninhabited, and Gary felt that now. Although
he knew he shouldn't, he stepped over the threshold and
inside. His mind was racing through scenarios: they had
been kidnapped and were being held hostage; they had

been kidnapped and killed, their bodies dumped somewhere; they had fled, escaping before their attackers arrived; they had been slaughtered, their bodies left here in the house. Every one of these possibilities ended with him being arrested because the police simply could not believe the coincidence of him reporting both the disappearance of his girlfriend in Nevada and the disappearance/death of her parents in central California.

He'd better make sure he left no fingerprints.

Pushing the door closed with his elbow, so no one from outside could see him, he stepped carefully into the living room. The furniture was oddly mismatched, as though it had all been donated by different families or cobbled together from various local garage sales. There were a few nice pieces, quite obviously recently purchased, but the remainder were worn and used, old and ugly. This was not at all the sort of home that he had imagined Joan growing up in, and its appearance surprised him. From the way she'd spoken, he'd also expected to see a lot of religious articles—pictures of Jesus, pillows embroidered with psalms, framed biblical passages, perhaps—but there was not even a Bible to be seen.

He walked over to a cheap bookcase, situated next to an old television sitting atop a metal stand. There were photos on the shelves, family photos, and he saw Joan dressed in a high school graduation gown, Joan standing by the pier with a friend, Joan in a prom dress, Joan at Hearst Castle, Joan in front of Morro Rock. There appeared to be no pictures of her as a baby, though, or as a young child, and that seemed unusual. Parents usually went crazy with the camera when their kids were infants and toddlers, tapering off after that, but her mom and dad looked to have been just the opposite.

In one photo, she stood between two people who must have been her parents: a man and a woman. The woman was odd-looking, awkwardly built, as though something was wrong with her bones. Her shoulders stuck up too far and looked pointy, while her thin arms hung at strange angles by her sides. Her legs in a dress were bony and too long, and they served to accentuate the peculiarity of her form. *Rickets* was the word that occurred to him, although he was not exactly sure what rickets was and had no idea whether it applied here. The man was an ordinary-looking guy who reminded Gary of one of his father's friends.

In the back of his mind, he wondered if Joan's mother's condition was hereditary, if it was possible that Joan might end up with the same condition. But that concern was minor now. The only thing that mattered was that Joan be found. He picked up a picture of her, intending to take it back with him to show Detective Williams, a recent photo that featured a close-up of her face. He saw the irony in giving a stolen photograph to the police, but it might help him prove that Joan existed and that she was missing. Although his first impulse was to leave a note to let Joan's parents know who had taken the picture and why, he did not think her mom and dad would be returning anytime soon, and he did not want to leave any clues in the house indicating that he had been here.

If Williams asked him where he'd gotten the photo, he would just say that it had been in his room and he'd forgotten that he had it.

Forgotten?

That sounded suspicious, too.

It didn't matter. He would think of something.

Clutching the framed picture, he continued on, moving from the living room to a hallway and the two bedrooms and single bathroom beyond. There were no signs of a struggle in any of the rooms, and all of the furniture and belongings appeared undisturbed. The only thing amiss, the only thing out of place, was in the kitchen: an empty overturned wastepaper basket. Next to it, on the white linoleum floor, was an irregular red spot about the size of a quarter. Gary stared at the spot, noting how it *shone* in the light that entered through the window above the sink, as though it were wet. It might not have been blood, and there might be a perfectly rational explanation for it, but at that moment he could think of nothing else it could possibly be.

And then Gary saw the dog.

He stopped in place, his heart slamming in his chest. The animal was dead, its body lying half in and half out of a little pet entrance built into the bottom of the bigger door that led into the backyard. A shaggy gray poodle, the dog was lying on its side, its open black eyes staring lifelessly into the kitchen, the white rubber of the doggy door sitting atop its distended stomach like a guillotine blade about to slice it in half. There was blood dripping from the dog's mouth, but it looked darker and drier than the spot next to the overturned wastepaper basket.

Gary looked quickly around the kitchen, glancing through the window over the sink to the yard outside. He could think of a whole host of possibilities here, none of them good. He went back over every step he'd taken, trying to make sure he hadn't touched anything, hadn't left behind any fingerprints. He thought of the closets in the bedrooms, the queen-sized bed in the master bedroom, the full-sized bed in what had been Joan's room. Someone could be hiding in the closets right now. Bodies could be shoved under the beds.

He was scared and knew he should get out immediately, but he had driven all morning to get here and couldn't take off without checking first to make sure Joan's parents—*or Joan*—weren't dead or dying somewhere here in the house. He needed a weapon, though, something he could use to protect himself should someone try to attack him. Pulling down his sleeve so the shirt material would cover his hand and prevent him from leaving any fingerprints, he reached out and opened the top drawer. Silverware was stacked in little compartmentalized sections: spoons, forks, butter knives, steak knives. He closed the drawer, opening the one beneath it. As he'd hoped, it was full of larger kitchen utensils, and he withdrew the biggest knife he could find, a carving knife.

He closed the drawer and pulled down his shirt sleeve. He needed the full use of his hands and fingers, just in case. Besides, fingerprints didn't matter here; he wasn't going to put the knife back. It was coming with him. Since he might need the use of both hands, he put the picture frame down on the counter next to the sink, intending to come back for it once all was clear.

Clutching the knife tightly and holding it in front of him, Gary walked out of the kitchen, around the corner of the living room, through the hall and into the master bedroom. As before, all was still. But whereas that had been comforting just a few minutes ago, it now seemed ominous, and he stopped, listening, trying to detect breathing or rustling or any sound whatsoever. Hearing nothing, he stepped forward carefully, prepared for an ambush from any direction.

The closet had one of those sliding mirrored doors from the sixties or seventies, and in it he saw not only a reverse representation of the bedroom, but a reflection of himself holding the knife and advancing. The image was disturbing, and he shifted his eyes to the right, focusing his attention on the reflection of the bed behind him, keeping his eyes on the skirt that covered the open space beneath the box springs, watching for any sort of movement.

Reaching the closet, he grabbed the narrow handle on the far left side of the door and prepared to quickly slide it open, knife at the ready in his right hand. He met his own eyes in the mirror, saw fear there, then pulled the door to the right and cried, "Get out right now!"

There was no one in the closet.

He knew it immediately, but he swept the hanging clothes aside just to make sure.

The closet was empty.

He was glad, but the tension within him still had not dissipated, and he closed the door and turned around, approaching the bed with trepidation. He saw in his mind the oddly shaped woman from the photograph, sliced up and shoved beneath the bed, her bony arms and legs twisted grotesquely around the slaughtered body of her husband. Crouching down, he used the knife to lift up the bed's skirt. At the last second, he thought that he might see Joan under there—but the space was empty. Gary stood on shaky legs, breathing deeply.

He checked the rest of the house. The other rooms were empty as well. He felt relieved, but he was right back where he'd started. *Where were Joan's parents?* He thought of the notes Kara had left back in the dorm room about an unidentified man calling for Joan. He and his friends had told Williams about the notes, had even shown them to him, but the detective hadn't seemed very interested at the time. Gary wondered if the police had bothered to check Joan's and Kara's phone records, to track down the caller.

Or maybe that sort of thing only happened in movies.

An idea occurred to him, and he returned to the living room, where he recalled seeing a telephone on a small end table next to the couch. Beside the phone, as he'd hoped, was an address book. He opened it quickly and flipped through the pages. There seemed to be names and phone numbers but no addresses. Out of curiosity, he looked under *J* for Joan but found nothing. He looked under *D* for Joan Daniels and found only a single word—*Daughter*—along with Joan's cell phone and dorm room numbers.

That was weird.

Gary closed the address book. He'd take it with him and call the listed numbers. Someone might be able to provide him with information. Returning to the kitchen, he picked up the picture frame and headed toward the front door. He wondered if there wasn't something in the garage that he should investigate—

Dead bodies in the car?

—but there was no entrance to the garage from the house, and he didn't dare draw attention to himself by opening the garage door from the outside. Besides, it was probably locked. Once again pulling his sleeve over his hand so as not to leave fingerprints, Gary turned the knob and opened the front door.

Standing in front of the house, next to his car, was a young boy of around seven or eight. The kid had been kicking the car's left rear tire, but he looked up as Gary stepped outside and closed the door behind him. Gary was acutely aware of how suspicious he looked, with his sleeve pulled over his right hand, the knife in his left hand and the address book and picture frame held under each arm. He tried to smile at the boy in an open, friendly manner. "Hi," he said.

"Mom!" The kid took off running. "Mom!"

Shit! Gary hurriedly opened the car door, threw everything on the passenger seat, got in and backed out of the driveway, swinging the car around so it was headed in the opposite direction from the one the boy had taken. This was the last thing he needed. He kept his speed low so as not to draw attention to himself, but he made a beeline for the highway, and once he was out of town, he pressed down on the gas pedal and pushed it up to the limit of sixty-five.

There was a single small rain cloud above him, and a smattering of drops appeared on the windshield. It was already difficult to see through the glass, which was flecked with black spots of unknown origin and yellow blobs of butterfly blood from the trip over, and the droplets of rain made it worse. He turned on the wipers, but they only smeared the glass, turning the highway, cars and surrounding landscape into little more than an impressionist blur. He leaned forward as he drove, squinting through the multicolored streaks. In Morro Bay, a few miles down the coast, he stopped at an Arco station and filled up for the trip back, using a squeegee soaking in a water bucket between the pumps to clean off his windshield. He half expected to hear the sound of sirens as police, alerted by the boy, came speeding after him, but nothing like that happened, and moments later he was back on the road.

Fifteen minutes farther on, just outside San Luis Obispo, a patrol car did pull next to him on the highway. Afraid to glance over, afraid of what he might see, Gary kept his eyes on the road ahead, held his hands at ten and two, and maintained a speed just below the limit. Another police car pulled up on the other side of him, and for a brief, harrowing moment, he was sandwiched between them, certain the two policemen had done this on purpose as part of some tactic to force him to the side of the road.

But then the cop on the left sped away, the one on the right pulled off at the next exit, and he was on his own once again, free and safe. He drove the rest of the way back being extra careful to obey all traffic laws, afraid that if he were pulled over and his plates run, the police might connect him to the break-in at Joan's parents' house. And the dead dog. And maybe the Danielses' disappearance.

Or deaths.

He hit early commuter traffic outside Thousand Oaks, and it took him longer to get back than he'd expected. Gary thought of calling Reyn several times while stuck in a line of cars on the 101 freeway but was afraid a cop would see and cite him. It was after six when he finally reached UCLA and his mercifully empty parking space. He walked slowly into the dorm and up to his floor, intending to call Reyn as soon as he went to the bathroom and got something to drink. Feeling exhausted, he pulled the key ring from his pocket, found his room key and unlocked the door.

The place had been ransacked.

Gary stood in the doorway, too stunned to move. Before him, the contents of his desk, dresser and closet lay strewn about the floor: books, notebooks, papers, pens, pencils, towels, clothes, CDs and DVDs all thrown together in the center of the room. The drawers from his desk and dresser had been pulled out and thrown into the bathroom. Even the bedspread and sheet had been yanked off his now-bare mattress and tossed against a wall.

Gary turned and went quickly to the next room over, banging on his neighbors' door. Two flighty freshmen lived there, Matt and Greg, although only Matt was in. "Someone broke into my room," Gary said breathlessly when the other student opened his door.

"It wasn't me!" Matt said, holding up his hands.

"I didn't think it was you," Gary assured him. "I just wanted to know if you'd heard or seen anything."

"No, man, nothing. And I've been here most of the day, chillin'. I would know if something happened."

"Something did happen."

"I don't know anything about it."

Gary nodded and hurried back next door. He noticed upon second look that, strangely enough, nothing seemed to have been stolen. His laptop and iPod were both still there—on the floor but still there—and if someone had wanted to take something those would have been the natural choices. Instead, it looked as though some crazy person had come in, indiscriminately thrown around the contents of the room and left.

How could Matt not have heard what was going on in here?

For the first time, he wished he had a roommate. Until now, he'd considered himself lucky that he was not forced to share his dorm room with someone else. Sure, his place was a lot smaller than all of the others on his floor, a single-windowed efficiency that appeared to have been constructed to fill the little bit of extra space between the last full-sized room and the stairwell. But it was worth it to have the privacy. If he'd had a roommate, though, maybe this wouldn't have happened. Or maybe the perpetrator would have been spotted.

No, he thought upon reflection. It probably would have happened while his roommate was out as well.

Surveying the damage, he wondered once again who could have done this.

The Outsiders?

He didn't know who the Outsiders were or why he kept going back to them in his mind, but just the thought of Joan's weird little prayer scroll made him uneasy.

Maybe she isn't who she said she was.

Brian's words to the detective came back to him, and while Gary didn't want to give them any credence, he looked at the chaos before him and couldn't help wondering if there wasn't some truth there. If Joan was somehow involved with the type of people who would do something like this . . . He left the thought unfinished.

Should he inform the police?

Of course, he told himself. But instead he phoned Reyn, telling him first about the ransacked room, then about his trip to Joan's parents' house. "So what should I do? Call Williams?"

"I don't know." Reyn spoke cautiously. "I called the police this afternoon. Checked on the status of the case."

"And?" Gary prompted.

"You know, I can't find any trace of Joan online. She's not even on my friends list anymore. She's . . . nowhere." There was a long pause. "The police still aren't sure Joan is real. But Kara is definitely missing. And I have the feeling that we—*you* in particular—are 'persons of interest.'"

"What did they say?"

"It's what they didn't say. I talked to Detective Williams. He asked me a lot of questions, didn't give me many answers, and while he put on this nice-guy, I'm-on-your-side kind of act and was a lot friendlier than he was in Joan's room, it definitely seemed like he was fishing. I got the feeling he was purposely keeping information from me, trying to lead me into a trap."

Gary's heart was pounding. "You think he knows what happened to Joan?"

"No. But Kara? Maybe. Something was sure as hell going on."

Gary glanced around his room. "So do you think I should call him about the break-in here? Or at least let the campus police know?"

"It's your call. But my suggestion would be to *not* tell them, to keep it quiet."

"But they might find fingerprints, fingerprints they could track down. And this would show that *both* Joan and I have been targeted."

"Or they'll find *no* fingerprints. They'll assume you did this yourself to deflect suspicion. And the fact that nothing's been broken or stolen . . ."

"I see your point."

"You're in a no-win situation."

Gary stared at his scattered belongings. "There might be a clue here, though."

"Like I said, it's your call."

Gary took a deep breath. "Maybe I'll ask about the status of the case, feel him out, see how it goes, then decide."

"You know what?" Reyn said. "It's no longer your call. I'm making the decision for you. Don't do it. They're suspicious already, and if you call up *asking* about it . . ." His voice trailed off.

Gary quickly thought it through. "And if they happen to ask where I was all day and find out that I wasn't at my classes, and I can't account for my whereabouts unless I tell them the truth—which is that I went up to visit Joan's parents, who happen to be missing and have a dead dog stuck in their pet door halfway into their kitchen . . ."

Reyn gave a humorless chuckle. "You know how, in movies, characters can't go to the police when a crime occurs because some ludicrous plot twist makes it seem like they're guilty? And so the characters try to solve the crime and end up getting in even deeper shit?"

"That's us."

"That's us," Reyn agreed.

Gary was silent for a moment. "I'm tired," he said finally. "I'm going to clean this place up. I'll talk to you tomorrow. Do you have any classes in the morning?"

"None I can't miss."

"Okay. I'll talk to you then." Gary hung up the phone and looked around, wondering where he should start. He didn't want to do this—there were other things he could be doing, *should* be doing—but he had no choice. Bending down, he picked up his laptop and put it back on his desk. He gathered up an armload of shirts.

Right now, he thought, the police were probably trying to build a case against him for Kara's disappearance.

The other students in his dorm were studying or partying, hanging out or hooking up.

And Joan was still missing.

Seven

It was their first and only trip to the beach.

Reyn and Stacy were supposed to have come with them, but unbeknownst to Joan, Gary had called Reyn and asked him to find some legitimate-sounding way to cancel. He and Joan had been dating for only two weeks, and it was the perfect opportunity for him to spend a day alone with her. Reyn and Stacy had been happy to oblige, going instead to the farmers market and the Grove, leaving Gary free to take Joan to the beach by himself.

The first surprise was that she wore a bathing suit. After hearing about her upbringing, he'd assumed she'd be too uptight to be seen in anything that showed off her figure—he'd had her pegged as an oversized T-shirt girl—but she arrived at his dorm wearing shorts and a Hawaiian shirt, and, once on the sand, stripped down to her suit. It wasn't a string bikini or anything, just a simple peach one-piece, but it showed skin, and Gary was embarrassingly aroused just watching her pull down her shorts.

He spread out the blanket, purposely looking away, and crouched down, sorting through the contents of the ice chest until his arousal was no longer quite so conspicuous. He thought they'd just sit on the blanket, walk along the sand, sunbathe, read, drink, eat, talk, but she actually wanted to go in the water. He'd never swum in the ocean before and was a little wary of the waves, which from this angle looked pretty big and intimidating. But there were kids in the water, and moms, as well as the expected surfers and swimmers, and he and Joan stepped up to the wet sand at the shoreline, holding hands. The water was cold as it swept over their toes and feet, and they both instantly jumped backward, laughing. Gradually, however, one step and one wave at a time, they became used to the icy temperature, and, still holding hands, they ventured farther out into the surf, first ankle high, then knee high.

One wave, larger than the rest, broke closer to shore, almost upon them, and water rolled over their midsections, splashing as high as their chins. As the wave receded, Gary saw that Joan's bathing suit had become see-through. It had been close to flesh-colored already, and now that it was wet, it looked as though it wasn't there at all, the light, thin material revealing dark nipples and a black triangle of pubic hair. Even from this close, she appeared to be completely naked.

Joan did not seem to notice, but he knew that when she did she would be mortified. So he left her in the water, rushed back to their blanket, grabbed a towel and held it out to her as she confusedly walked out onto the sand. It wasn't until she saw where he was looking and glanced down at herself that she saw what had happened. Immediately, she snatched the towel from his hands and wrapped it around herself, face reddening as her eyes scanned the beach to see if anyone else had noticed. No one had, and they walked back to the blanket without speaking.

Gary wondered if she wanted to go after that, but although she remained wrapped up, she made no mention of leaving. In fact, she acted as though it hadn't happened at all, and while he tried to think of something to say that would break the tension, she casually asked him to hand her a can of Diet Dr Pepper. It wasn't until later, after her bathing suit had dried and she'd taken off the towel, after they had strolled along the shore looking for shells, as they were eating their lunch of sandwiches and chips, that she said, "I didn't know that would happen."

It was apropos of nothing—they'd been talking about the sandwiches—but he knew immediately what she was referring to, and he nodded silently, not trusting himself to say anything. Thinking of the way her nipples had looked, and her pubic triangle, he was forced to lean forward and as surreptitiously as possible press down on his crotch with his elbow.

"I guess I should stick to black bathing suits."

Although he didn't know it at the time, he learned later that she'd been not just embarrassed and self-conscious but worried when he had seen her through the translucent material. She'd been afraid that he'd be turned off by her, that her body was not attractive enough, and it was only his rather blatant effort to press down on and hide his erection that let her know he found her physically desirable.

That night, in her room, they made love for the first time, and Gary knew, if he hadn't before, that Joan was the one; that he wanted to spend the rest of his life with her; that he would love her until the day he died.

Eight

Gary was putting away the last of his books when Reyn came over with Brian. Feeling more than a little paranoid, he'd locked his door, and he jumped when the loud knock sounded behind him. "It's us!" Brian called. "Open up!" Gary hurried to oblige, and his friends entered, looking around.

"Not as bad as I thought," Reyn offered.

"Yeah?" Gary whipped out his cell phone. "I took some pictures." He flashed through several shots of the room that showed clearly the extent of the damage.

"Holy shit," Reyn said. "Did they take anything?"

"Not that I can find."

"Maybe it was just a warning."

"Or they didn't find what they were looking for."

"I don't think these people give warnings." Brian was carrying a newspaper, the *Daily Bruin*, which he handed to Gary. Reyn grew silent, as if he knew what was coming. "Check this out," Brian said. "I got it on my way to class this morning." He pointed at the top headline: SOPHOMORE KILLED IN ACCIDENT. Next to it was a photo of a sheet-covered body lying on the ground in front of a car. "That's the chick who gave you Joan's parents' phone number. The neighbor."

Gary glanced at the article. It was indeed Teri Lim who had been killed. Witnesses at the scene reported that she had come running out from the campus path and dashed into the street, where she was struck by a black Jeep that immediately sped away. No one got a look at the Jeep's license plates; one student who saw the accident claimed that the vehicle didn't *have* any plates. Several witnesses told the police that a strange-looking older man in incongruously rustic clothes had arrived just as the accident occurred and that he had hovered over the victim, showing an unusual interest in her condition, before leaving, unseen, immediately prior to the arrival of the authorities.

Teri had died at the scene from internal injuries and the paramedics who arrived were unable to revive her.

Gary looked up from the paper, feeling chilled. This was far too coincidental. He thought about the oddly dressed man who had supposedly watched Teri die and then disappeared into the crowd.

An Outsider?

It seemed likely, and he told his friends what he was thinking.

Reyn nodded. "Makes sense."

"The fuck it does." Brian pushed a long tangle of hair away from the front of his face. "You think Joan's church has some sort of standardized prayer asking for protection from a . . . a gang that's hunting their people down?"

It didn't seem logical when spelled out so bluntly, but Gary said, "Yeah. Maybe."

"It might have nothing to do with that prayer," Reyn conceded. "Or 'Outsiders.' But I'm willing to bet that that weird guy who was lurking around when Teri got killed has something to do with Kara and Joan being missing."

"Then maybe he's after us, too," Brian said.

"I don't think so. We were vulnerable there at Burning Man, but nothing happened to us."

"Nothing?" Brian snorted. "Someone drugged us, man. And maybe they screwed up the dosage. Did you ever think of that? Maybe we weren't supposed to wake up, but they miscalculated and just zonked us out for a while instead of killing us."

"Maybe," Reyn said skeptically.

"But you don't think so?"

"We could've been picked off several times since then. Like Teri. Anyone following us would have had ample opportunity to off us. But no one has."

"That's true," Gary agreed. He looked around his tidied room. "But they are fucking with us." He took a deep breath. "And they have Joan."

"And probably Kara," Reyn added.

Gary nodded.

"You know," Brian said, "my brother's ex-girlfriend's brother is a police dispatcher in Santa Mara."

"Your brother's . . . ex-girlfriend's . . . brother," Gary repeated slowly.

"I know how that sounds," Brian said. "But it wasn't a bad breakup, and Alyssa always liked me. I even met her brother a couple of times, and he seemed cool. I think he'd do us a solid if I asked."

"And what exactly are you going to ask?"

"Here's the thing. When he's at work and it's slow, he runs license plates. He's not supposed to, but he does. He sees a hot babe pass him on the freeway? He writes down her plates, then looks her up. Finds out her name, who she is, where she lives. He does it with cars and trucks he sees in movies, too, or on TV. Sees a cool car chase, writes down the plates. Usually they're owned by rental car companies or movie studios, but one time he ran a plate and it was actually registered to Bruce Willis. Anyway, he can do it backward, too. He can run a name and get address and license information. I figure I'll have him plug in Joan's name and see what comes up.

We might get another address or a next-of-kin or even an alias. At the very least, we'll prove she exists, and we can give that to the cops." He smiled. "Anonymously, of course. I don't want to get Dan in trouble."

"Dan. Your brother's ex's brother."

"Yeah."

"You don't think the cops have already tried that?" Reyn asked. "I mean, if your distant acquaintance the dispatcher can do this, you don't think the detectives assigned to this case could figure out to try the same thing?"

Brian threw up his hands. "What the fuck. I was just trying to help."

"It's a good idea," Gary said cautiously. He glanced at Reyn. "And I'm not sure they *would* try this. My guess is they informed Kara's parents that she's missing, and now the parents are going crazy, pressuring the police for results, and they're trying to find her and probably connect me to it. So I doubt they're doing their best to find out about Joan. Who they don't even believe exists."

"You may have a point," Reyn conceded.

Brian had his phone out. "Calls are being made even as you speak." He quickly used an app to look up the number of the Santa Mara Police Department, and Gary and Reyn listened in as he talked his way through to Dan. After making sure that the call wasn't being recorded or monitored, Brian spun a bullshit story about an amazing one-night stand who'd given him her name but no other information. "I need to know more about her," he said. "I need an address, a phone number, some way to reach her."

There was a short pause; then Brian grinned and gave the thumbs-up sign. "Joan Daniels," he said. "Her name is Joan Daniels."

Seconds later, he was thanking Dan and saying goodbye. Pressing some keys on his phone, he peered for a moment at the tiny screen before looking up. "There are six Joan Danielses registered in Los Angeles County, one in Ventura County and three in Orange County. None of them are the right age, though. The youngest is thirty. You think Joan could be thirty and passing herself off as—"

"No!" Gary and Reyn said together.

For the first time in what seemed a long time, Gary smiled. It felt good but weird, wrong, and the smile vanished as quickly as it had appeared.

"Maybe it's not her real name," Reyn suggested.

He knew Joan. And the idea seemed ludicrous. But it was also the most benign possibility under the circumstances, and Gary found himself clinging to it.

Brian immediately burst his bubble. "My guess is that whoever wiped out her school records wiped out her DMV records, too. I don't know who we're dealing with here, but they seem like some serious dudes. With major firepower behind them."

Gary imagined some sort of shadowy government agency, a black ops organization, and wondered why such a group would be interested in Joan.

Who is she?

The plots of a dozen recent thrillers flashed through his mind.

"Maybe it's a case of mistaken identity," Reyn suggested.

Gary ran a frustrated hand through his hair. "Jesus Christ!" He wanted to lash out, wanted to hit something, wanted to scream. How could this be happening to him? How could it be happening at all?

Reyn looked at his watch, which caused Gary to glance over at his own clock on the dresser and check the time. It was nearly nine.

"We're not going to get anything done tonight," Reyn said. "I suggest we all get some sleep. Tomorrow could be a very long day."

Why? Gary felt like saying. *Do you think we're going to find Joan? And Kara? Is everything going to be solved and put right?* But he simply nodded tiredly and saw his friends out, locking the door behind them and once more looking around his room, seeing it as it had been when he'd arrived back from Cayucos, his belongings strewn about and thrown onto the floor. He shivered, feeling cold, and on impulse he decided to call his parents. It was nearly midnight in Ohio and they were no doubt sound asleep, but he wanted to talk to them. He wasn't going to tell them *everything*, but he needed to let them know what was going on.

In case something happened to him.

He was glad when his dad answered the phone. His father was much easier to talk to than his mother. He'd made the call too late at night to pretend he was just ringing them for a casual chat, so Gary told his dad that his girlfriend had disappeared on a trip with friends to the Burning Man festival. He soft-pedaled the drugging and didn't mention Teri or his ransacked room, but he did tell his dad about Kara being missing as well.

He wasn't sure what he wanted from his father. Advice? Suggestions about what he should do? Deep down, he probably wanted his dad to take over the situation, to fix things, to tell him everything was going to be okay and resolve all problems, the way he had when Gary was a child. But he *wasn't* a child, and his dad was on the other side of the continent. The most he could realistically hope for were some encouraging words. He was momentarily tempted to tell his father everything, particularly when his dad asked sharply, "What are the police doing?"

But instead he said vaguely, "They're working on it."

"Do you want us to come out there?" his dad asked.

Yes! was his honest reaction, but plane tickets were expensive, his father couldn't really afford to miss work, and, in truth, there wasn't a lot that his parents could actually do once they got out here, so he lied and said, "No."

"What's going on? What is it?" In the background, Gary could hear his mother's panicked reaction to his father's side of the conversation, and he quickly told his dad, "Don't make it sound too scary. Keep it light."

"I always do," his dad said calmly, and proceeded to explain what was going on, downplaying the seriousness of what Gary had told him, making it sound as though Joan could simply have had some family emergency that caused her to leave school without informing Gary.

Seconds later, his mom took the phone, and Gary repeated the same thing his dad had just said. Hearing the same story from both of them calmed her down, and after a few pointed questions designed to ferret out any duplicity, she seemed satisfied that nothing was *too* amiss. She started asking him about school and things in general, and for the next eight or nine minutes he chatted with his mother as though everything that had happened since the trip to Burning Man had not occurred.

After she passed the phone back, his dad waited a moment until she was not only off the line but out of earshot and said, "Someone called last night asking for you."

Gary's pulse was racing. "Who?"

"I don't know. But there was something weird about him. He didn't give his name or the name of a company or organization he might've worked for, but after I said you weren't here, he started asking questions about you. Personal questions. Like how old you were and where you were born. I didn't tell him anything. I just hung up on him." There was a significant pause. "Do you think this could be related to your . . . situation?"

Gary could tell from his dad's tone of voice that he thought it was. Gary did, too, but he said, "I've been getting a lot of those calls lately. They're just surveys. I sign up for these contests, and sometimes they're just scams to get you to join a gym or something. I think they sell my name and phone number to other companies."

There was skepticism in his father's "Oh," but his dad didn't push it. They talked for a few moments more, and then Gary said it must be getting late and he should go. His dad agreed but before hanging up told Gary, "Be careful. And if you need anything, *call*." Which told him that his father had seen right through his efforts to minimize the seriousness of the situation.

That made him feel good.

Gary hung up the phone. After arriving back at his room and discovering the chaos within, he had placed the address book he'd taken from Joan's parents' house on his desk, forgetting about it in the ensuing confusion. He'd spotted it again while talking to his dad, and he picked it up now, opening its cover and looking carefully at each entry, turning the pages slowly. There were very few names or numbers listed, and most of those had the same local Cayucos area code. He would call those numbers, just in case, but he doubted the people behind them would be of much help or interest to him.

As he'd discovered back at her parents' house, Joan's dorm and cell numbers were listed next to the single word *Daughter*. That was strange. But stranger still was what lay two pages away, under the letter *F*.

Friend 1, Friend 2, Friend 3, Friend 4 . . .

There were seven altogether. No names. Only the designation *Friend*, along with an identifying digit. Each had an accompanying phone number, and none of the area codes was the same. None was any he recognized, either. He continued looking through the rest of the book, but all of the remaining pages were blank.

Gary turned back to the list of friends, thought for a

moment, then picked up his phone and called the first number on the page.

There was only one ring before someone answered. "Hello?" The voice on the other end of the line was female and sounded more like someone his parents' age than his.

"Hello," he said. "My name is Gary Russell, and I'm, uh, Joan Daniels's boyfriend."

"How did you get this number?" the woman demanded.

"I—"

The line went dead. He tried calling back, but the line was busy, and after ten minutes and at least five times that many tries, he finally decided that the woman had taken her phone off the hook.

But why?

She'd sounded scared, he thought now. The surface belligerence had initially struck him as anger, but, reflecting upon it, there'd been fear there as well. And he was pretty sure it had been the mention of Joan's name that had triggered such a response.

He stared down at the page. He was going further and further afield with these tangents. The likelihood that one of the people listed as *Friend* in her parents' address book had driven out to Burning Man and kidnapped Joan was slim, to say the least.

But there *was* a connection. Like the lines of a spiderweb, all of these threads crisscrossed and wove together, and somewhere in the middle of them was Joan. Although he had no factual basis for such a belief, Gary was convinced that if he followed every lead he came across, he would eventually discover who had taken Joan and why.

He started to dial the number of the next friend on the list—and stopped. What if the next person hung up on him the same way the woman had? He didn't want to frighten off the people who might be able to help him, and he didn't want to set off any alarm bells among the Danielses' circle of acquaintances.

He looked at the list of numbers, looked at the phone, thought for a minute.

And called Reyn.

Nine

They met in the student union, the only ones there save for a gaggle of drunk, giggling sorority types passing through on their way to yet another party, and a handful of dozing, geeky young men with textbooks on their laps who'd obviously planned to pull all-nighters but had fallen asleep in their chairs. Stacy was there, too, with Reyn, and the expression on her face did more to frighten Gary than even his ransacked room. He realized that it had been three days since Joan had disappeared.

She could have been raped hundreds of times since then.

She could be dead.

He tried to focus on the most positive possibility: that she was being treated well, held for a specific purpose and kept safe from harm until that purpose was realized, but as time passed with no word, it was getting harder and harder to buy into such a scenario.

Brian arrived seconds later, wearing Levi's and a pajama top, his long hair even more wild and unruly than usual. It seemed obvious that he'd been asleep before being awakened by Reyn's call.

They all had a rough idea of what had happened, but Gary showed them the address book and spelled out the specifics. Before he was even finished speaking, Brian was taking his BlackBerry from the front pocket of his jeans. "What's that number?" he asked. "I'll check the area code."

Gary told him, and Brian started typing. He looked up from the device. "Lancaster."

"Where's—" Gary started to ask.

Reyn answered. "It's just north of here, maybe an hour or two away. Out in the desert."

"Let's check the area codes of the other numbers," Brian suggested. "See where they are."

One by one, he used his BlackBerry to look up the location of the other six area codes. One was in Maine, two in New York, one in Colorado, one in Illinois and one in Alaska.

"I guess we're not going to be visiting any of *them*," Reyn said.

"Do you think you can find an address for the one in Lancaster?" Gary asked.

Brian grinned. "I'll call our buddy Dan."

"Is he still working?"

"We'll find out."

He was, and though Brian gave another bullshit explanation of why they needed an address to go with the phone number, Dan bought it and provided the information without question.

Stacy shook her head. "Between this guy and those detectives, I'm rapidly losing faith in our law enforcement agencies."

Brian was slowly repeating aloud everything he was being told, while Gary wrote it all down. He'd had a pen in his pocket but no paper, so he used the back page of the Danielses' address book to copy the information. "Joe Smith," he said after he'd finished, and shook his head.

Reyn smiled. "You don't think that's his real name?"

Brian was thanking Dan and saying good-bye. He terminated the call and looked down at the address. "Let's go," he said.

Stacy looked at him. "You don't want to go back and change first? Maybe get out of your pajamas?"

"Nah. I'm good."

She rolled her eyes. "Suit yourself."

"My car," Reyn announced. "I don't trust those death traps the rest of you drive."

Stacy put a light hand on his shoulder. "Maybe you should get some coffee first."

"I'm fine," he told her.

She shot Gary an imploring look, and he nodded. "Let's *all* get some coffee," he said.

There was a pot on a table near the study area, with a stack of white Styrofoam cups next to it, and though ordinarily Gary wouldn't go near that thing—he'd seen those YouTube videos of psychotic assholes spitting and pissing into punch bowls and coffeepots—he didn't want to waste time going to a Starbucks or even a McDonald's. He just wanted to get some quick caffeine and be off.

Ten minutes later, they were heading west on Wilshire toward the 405 freeway. Even at this hour, the 405 was crowded, and it wasn't until they were past Newhall that traffic finally thinned out. They were all wide awake, and though everyone except Brian had had coffee, Gary didn't think it was the caffeine that was keeping them alert. He himself was running on pure adrenaline, as he had been since Monday, and though he'd probably crash at some point, right now he felt as though he could go for another week without sleeping.

They passed Vasquez Rocks, jaggedly black against the purple star-filled sky, and the Universal tour guide in Reyn prompted him to point out the fault-raised cliffs and mention that they had been used in numerous science fiction movies and TV shows over the years, including two separate *Star Trek* films and an episode of the original series. No one was really interested, no one was really paying attention, but the sound of his voice reciting entertainment industry facts was soothing somehow, and it comforted Gary to know that Reyn was along.

There was a loud, sustained honk from behind, and he turned to see a white Dodge pickup riding their tail. Suddenly, it swerved into the right-hand lane and sped past them, going well over the speed limit, twin American flags attached by plastic rods to both the driver's and the front passenger windows fluttering crazily.

"If that guy loves America so much," Stacy said drily, "why doesn't he obey its traffic laws?"

"Yeah, and what's with those flags?" Brian wondered aloud. "We're all Americans here. Is he trying to let us know that he's *more* American than we are?"

Gary couldn't follow the conversation and didn't want to. He was thinking of Joan, wondering what she was doing right at this second. Sleeping, hopefully.

The truck disappeared into the darkness.

According to the clock on the dash, it was one minute after midnight when they passed the green sign announcing LANCASTER CITY LIMITS. Reyn's car didn't have a GPS, but Brian had used his BlackBerry to find the location of "Joe Smith's" address, and he acted as navigator from the backseat, telling Reyn which exit to take and which streets to turn down.

The house for which they were looking was a newer tract home in an unfinished neighborhood that appeared to have been a victim of the recession. Completed dwellings sat next to partially completed frames of houses and flat, empty desert lots. Lights were on in the "Smith" residence, as though the owners were still up at this hour, but the garage door was wide open and there was no vehicle in either the driveway or the garage.

"What do you think?" Reyn asked, pulling up to the curb.

"I think they bailed," Brian said.

Gary unfastened his seat belt. "Let's check it out."

They knocked on the front door, rang the bell, but when no one answered, they walked into the open garage, calling out, "Mr. Smith? Mrs. Smith?" The garage was dark, but illumination from a nearby streetlamp allowed them to see that it was empty.

There was no house next door, and the only one on the opposite side of the street that had been finished was dark and had a Realtor's sign hanging from a post on the front lawn. Yellow light seeped around the edges of a door in the wall that separated the garage from the house, and, knowing there was no one watching, Gary tried the door's handle. It turned, the door swung outward and, after calling out, "Mr. Smith? Mrs. Smith?" again, he walked inside.

His friends followed.

Stacy closed the door behind them as they moved quickly through the house together. Once they'd determined that it was empty, they split up, Gary staying in the living room, Brian going into one bedroom, Reyn into another one and Stacy heading into the kitchen. Breaking into houses was getting to be a habit, and Gary wanted to be in and out as quickly as possible.

The residents had left in a hurry, taking nothing with them. Or very little. Calling out to each other from their respective rooms, Gary and his friends found that nothing seemingly was out of place. All of the furniture was carefully arranged; kitchen cupboards, refrigerator and freezer were well stocked with food; toothbrushes and combs were on the counter in the bathroom. Bedroom dresser drawers were shut and filled with clothes.

Gary found no address book this time, and, after searching through the living room, he walked into the kitchen, passing by the adjacent laundry alcove where

Stacy was opening up the doors of the washer and dryer. Stepping up to the back door, he looked carefully around for any signs of a struggle—

Blood

—but there was nothing obviously amiss. No dead animals. No wet red spots. He opened the door and passed into a covered patio that overlooked what appeared in the darkness to be a lush lawn.

"Holy shit!" Brian shouted from somewhere inside. "I found something!"

It took only seconds to reach the master bedroom where Brian was standing inside an open walk-in closet lit by recessed fluorescent ceiling lights. They all reached the bedroom at once, and before anyone could ask what Brian had found, he pointed to a dark wood cabinet about five feet high that was sitting against the back wall of the closet. The cabinet, Gary saw, was divided into rows of small compartments, and little rolled-up scrolls had been placed in each. Extra scrolls sat atop the case, and Gary picked up the closest of these, unspooling it. Like the one they'd found in Joan's room, it, too, was a prayer of some sort, and it, too, referenced the Outsiders. Only this prayer involved the acquisition of wealth. He read it aloud:

"O Lord our God! Thank You for all You have provided us. You are great and good and generous. Continue to bring to us money and land and earthly possessions. Allow us all of the riches we desire in order that we may use them to praise the glory of You. Protect all that we have and all that we will ever have from the greed of The Outsiders. Amen."

"Sounds familiar," Reyn said, eyebrows raised.

Brian was grinning. "Talk about the pot calling the kettle black. Protect us from those greedy Outsiders.

Oh, and by the way, give us lots of money, land and possessions. In fact, give us everything we ask for. Jesus!"

Gary rolled up the scroll and put it back on top of the cabinet. On impulse, he grabbed another, this from one of the small cubbyholes that made up the body of the wooden case. He unrolled it and read:

> "O Lord our Father! Smite The Outsiders. Suffer them not to live but dispatch of them bodily. Rend their clothing and skin. Spill their blood. Send their vile souls to hell and leave their stinking carcasses to rot. Remove The Outsiders from Your glorious sight forever and ever. Amen."

Reyn shook his head. "Well, that's cheerful."

"Are the Outsiders the good guys or the bad guys here?" Stacy wondered aloud.

Brian grinned. "It's hard to tell the players without a scorecard."

The idea that Joan was involved with the people behind these prayers made Gary uneasy. He knew from what little she'd said that her parents were ultrareligious and very strict, that she'd had a difficult childhood, but the more he learned, the less sense he could make of everything. If she'd broken away from that, why did she have that prayer scroll? And her parents' home didn't look like the house of religious fanatics. In fact, all of the displayed photos of a happy teenage Joan made them seem like loving, devoted parents. None of it added up.

And the prayers themselves freaked him out. He didn't know what about them disturbed him so, but the fact that they were printed on little scrolls, that they each seemed to reference these mysterious Outsiders, that the stilted language sounded so alien, that even the typestyle of the words on those tiny rolled parchments appeared unfamiliar, all conspired to produce within him a feeling of dread.

The others had picked up scrolls and started reading the prayers on them.

It was Stacy who spoke first. "What do we do about this?" she asked, rolling a scroll back up and carefully putting it back where she had found it.

They were all looking at him, and Gary shook his head. He had no idea. They couldn't go to the police with anything they found here, because it would have been obtained illegally. They would be implicating themselves by telling what they knew. He glanced down at the scroll in his hand. What did it mean, anyway? These people and Joan *were* connected, but how deeply and whether or not it had any bearing on her disappearance was anyone's guess.

Although the fact that the Smiths had taken off in the night, leaving their belongings behind, simply because he had called them and mentioned Joan's name, led him to believe that they knew a hell of a lot more than he did about what was going on.

"I have an idea," Brian said. "We'll report the family missing—anonymously, of course—and the police will come and investigate."

Reyn shook his head. "And how will they connect this to Joan, especially when these people left of their own volition, and Joan was drugged and abducted, and the only thing linking the two are some prayer scrolls?"

"That detective has her scroll. He could make the connection."

"But how would the Lancaster police know to contact him?"

"We tell them," Brian said. "Again, anonymously."

Reyn rolled his eyes. "Sure. That's a great idea."

The closet was starting to feel stuffy, although whether that was an actual physical sensation or just a mental projection, Gary didn't know. He put the scroll he was holding back in the cabinet space from which he'd taken it and walked back into the bedroom.

"Are you all right?" Stacy asked.

He nodded, not wanting to speak, though he felt as far from all right as he could possibly be. Brian and Reyn were still sorting through scrolls; Stacy was pulling back the clothes hanging in the closet, trying to see if there was anything behind them. They needed to get out of here soon. As remote as this house might seem, they still could get caught, and he started thinking up excuses, reasons to explain why they were here. If anyone asked, he'd probably say that they'd been invited, that they were simply visiting their friends, the Smiths, who, fortunately for them, were not around to contradict that story.

It occurred to him that their fingerprints were all over this house, but since none of them had their fingerprints on file anywhere—*yet*—that probably wouldn't make any difference.

Thinking of the police made him wonder if Williams had attempted to call or leave a message. He pulled out his phone and quickly checked his in-box. There was a single message, left earlier this evening, and he replayed the voice mail, putting the phone to his ear.

"Gary! I'm—"

He nearly dropped the phone. It was Joan! She was screaming and out of breath, frightened and frantic. The message cut off almost as soon as it had begun, as though someone had caught her just as she'd started talking, yanked the phone from her hand and immediately hung up. He closed his eyes. Horror, worry, relief, anger and fear swirled within him, each vying for supremacy but none gaining a toehold as the competing emotions alternated like the spinning compartments of a roulette wheel.

Gary! I'm—

He imagined her planning for days, carefully working the knots on the ropes that bound her until she was finally free, picking exactly the right moment to make a dash for the one connected phone in the otherwise abandoned building in which she was being held, dialing, calling—

—and then being caught.

Had she been beaten after the phone had been wrenched from her hand?

He glanced down at the small screen of his cell phone, hoping to see the number from which the call had been made, but it was blocked and the only thing displayed was the simple scary word *Unknown*.

Gary played the message again, listening carefully. He was crying, though he didn't realize it at first, didn't notice until he tried to play the message yet again and discovered that his vision was too blurry to see the keys on his phone. He was trying to determine whether there was any identifiable background noise, whether he could hear something behind Joan's aborted plea that would give him any indication of her whereabouts.

His friends gathered around him. He felt a hand on his shoulder, though he wasn't sure whose it was. Without speaking, he held the phone out so they could hear it and played the message again.

"She's alive," Reyn said, and it was the surprise in his voice that cut, that made Gary realize his friend had not believed it until this moment.

"You have to go to the police with this," Stacy said.

Gary, wiping his eyes, nodded in agreement. "I know." Even as they spoke, they were heading toward the garage door through which they'd come in, hurrying faster with each step until they were outside and sprinting toward the car. Brian was a few steps behind the rest of them, and, keyed up, Gary turned and yelled, "Come on!" He was surprised by the anger in his voice.

Then they were in the car and speeding through the darkened streets of the nearly empty neighborhood toward Lancaster's business district and the highway beyond.

No one slept on the way back, but no one spoke, either. They were all lost in their own thoughts, so it came as a jolt of surprise when the car began to slow down and Reyn put on his blinker, glancing quickly in his rearview mirror. "I have to pull over," he announced.

"What's wrong?" Stacy asked worriedly.

"I don't know. It's overheating for some reason. I have to stop before we stall out."

"Shit!" Gary yelled, slamming his hand on the back of the driver's seat.

"Sorry," Reyn told him.

"So much for your great, reliable car," Brian said.

"It's still better than your hunk of junk!"

"Mine made it all the way from the Bay to UCLA. And back again. Four times. And it's still going strong. It may look—"

"What do we do?" Gary demanded.

Reyn was guiding the car onto the shoulder. "Call Triple A, I guess."

They were in the middle of nowhere. Gary wasn't sure exactly where in the desert they'd stopped, but there were no lights, no buildings, no nearby off-ramps. He looked between the two front seats at the temperature gauge on the dashboard. The red needle was pointing directly at the *H*. Through the windshield, he could see steam escaping from the sides of the hood, vaporous mist eerily backlit by the car's headlights.

Reyn switched off the engine and took out his cell phone. They could hear only one side of the conversation, but polite civility gave way to annoyance and finally hostility as it became clear that it would be some time before a tow truck was dispatched. He terminated the call angrily. "An hour. And it's going to cost big bucks. My card only covers a tow of up to five miles. It's at least another fifty to civilization." He shook his head. "Maybe there's a gas station or a garage somewhere between here and there."

"Let it cool off," Brian suggested. "Then we'll check it out. Do you have a flashlight?"

"Yeah," Reyn said. "In the glove compartment. But I don't know anything about cars."

"I do. It could be just a thermostat. We might be able to let it cool down and then take it back slowly. Is there any water in your trunk? Are there any big hills we have to climb?"

"I'm not taking a chance with my engine."

"Maybe a cop'll come by," Stacy said hopefully. "They *have* to assist stranded motorists, don't they?"

"What'll we do with the car?" Reyn asked. "Leave it here?" He shook his head. "I'm waiting for the tow truck."

"Just give me the flashlight and let me take a look," Brian said.

"Fine."

Stacy turned around in her seat toward Gary. "You can call the detective and tell him about the message. You don't have to talk to him in person."

Gary shook his head.

"He kind of does," Reyn said. "He's under suspicion."

Outside, Brian was shouting for Reyn to pop open the hood. Reyn reached down under the dashboard, there was a metallic click, and seconds later Brian was lifting the hood, blocking the view out the windshield.

"I'd better see what he's up to." Reyn opened the driver's door, stepped out and walked to the front of the car.

"That call's a good sign," Stacy told Gary. "I think they'll be able to find her."

Gary nodded. His emotions were still on a roller coaster. Moments before, he, too, had felt optimistic, but right now, stranded by the side of the road, all he could think about was the emptiness of the Smiths' house and how quickly the family must have evacuated it once they'd received his call. That, and how, right after recapturing Joan, her captors had probably moved her to a new, more hidden location.

Once they'd beaten and restrained her.

And every minute that passed allowed them to get farther away.

He checked the message again, looking at the time when it had been left. What had he been doing then? Putting his room back in order, probably.

Why hadn't he had his phone on? He would have answered the call. He could have heard her live. He could have spoken to her. . . .

The hood remained up, but both Brian and Reyn returned to the car. Neither of them was speaking, and it seemed clear that they had had words outside.

Brian shook his head, disgusted. "We're always ending up in the desert, aren't we?" he said, then glanced guiltily over at Gary. "Sorry," he mumbled.

"Let's just be quiet and wait," Reyn said.

"Can you at least leave the radio on?" Brian asked.

"No. It'll run down the battery. I thought you said you knew about cars."

"Forget I even asked."

Moments later, bored, they all got out of the car. They walked around, looked up and down the highway for any sign of a tow truck, sat on the trunk, threw rocks into the desert darkness.

A half hour passed. Forty-five minutes. An hour. "That's it," Reyn said. "I've had enough of this shit." He called AAA again, angrily berating the person on the other end of the line. When he finally got off the phone, he was livid. "She said they contacted Mojave Towing and that the truck should have been here by now but that it's been a busy night and it could be up to another hour."

"*Fuck!*" Gary screamed into the night as loud as he could. He stomped around the dirt and gravel by the side of the road. His muscles hurt, he was so tense. His head was pounding. All he could think about was Joan, and every scenario he'd imagined in the wake of her aborted phone call involved violence, punishment and pain.

"That sounds cathartic," Brian said in response to his outburst. "Let me try it. *Cunt!*"

"You're an asshole," Stacy told him. "*Asshole!*" she screamed.

"*Dick!*" Reyn yelled.

And then they were all shouting obscenities into the darkness, stopping only when a pickup truck sped by. Brian, Reyn and Stacy were laughing, and even Gary had to admit that it felt good to vent. He was still overcome with discouragement and anxiety, but there must have been something to the idea of primal scream therapy because he felt a little less hopeless than he had before.

"Want to start the car and see if we can make it?" Brian asked when they had stopped laughing and calmed down. "If it was just the thermostat or a temperature gauge, we can probably—"

"No," Reyn said firmly.

"Suit yourself."

A while later, the tow truck arrived, slowing as it approached them, yellow lights strobing on the roof of the cab and casting strange shadows on the desert rocks and brush off the side of the road.

According to the white patch sewn into his dark coveralls, the driver's name was John. He asked what had happened, and Reyn handed over his AAA card and gave a detailed explanation of how the engine had at first felt sluggish; then the temperature light had come on, steam had started to engulf the hood and the car had begun to slow.

The driver nodded. He ran the AAA card through a handheld reader. "This here's only good for five free miles," he said. "There ain't nothing within five miles."

"I know," Reyn said. "I'll pay for the rest."

"You have a Visa or MasterCard?"

Gary felt a sudden chill. They were alone here on the highway. In the desert. In the dark. What if this guy wasn't who he said he was? What if he was crazy?

But Reyn seemed to have no qualms. He opened his wallet, took out a credit card and handed it over.

"Where do you want me to tow it?" the man asked.

Gary wondered if there was room for all of them in the truck's cab. Would some of them have to stay here and wait for another ride? He didn't like the idea of them splitting up. He didn't trust this guy.

John.

"Is there any kind of twenty-four-hour garage you can take it to?"

"Our station's the closest, but at night we only do the towing. Everything else is closed. Even the gas pumps. The garage don't open for repairs until eight."

Stacy stepped forward. "Do you think you can take a look at it for us?" she asked, putting on an almost coquettish voice Gary had never heard her use. He glanced over at Reyn, who was looking at Stacy, stone-faced.

"I might be able to check it out when we get there," John allowed. "Let you know the damage."

Reyn shot Stacy a look of irritation, then turned to the tow truck driver. "What do you think it might be?"

"Well . . ." The man walked over to the front of the car. The hood was still open, and he glanced under it for a second, then went and got a halogen light from a box in the back of his truck, hung it off a hole on the hood's interior and peeked inside the engine compartment. He asked Reyn to start the car, checked a few things, then told him to shut off the engine. He slid under the car on his back, wrench and flashlight in hand, then slid back out a moment later. "Can't say for sure," he said, "but it looks to me like it's your water pump."

"All right," Reyn said. "Tow it to your garage."

The driver told Reyn to leave the keys in the ignition, asked everyone to get out of the way, and manuevered his truck until it was directly in front of the car. He got out, unhooked the tow bar, then pulled a lever that let out the winch cable. It took more than a few minutes, but finally the car was lifted onto the flat back of the truck, blocks shoved under its rear wheels.

"You all can get in," he said. "It's time to go."

There was a narrow backseat behind the driver and passenger, and Gary, Reyn and Brian crawled back there while Stacy sat in front with John.

What if he's crazy? Gary thought again.

Then they were on the highway and turning around. Reyn kept glancing through the rear window to make sure the car was not falling off the back of the truck. Two exits and fifteen minutes later, they were pulling off the highway and onto a side road toward the glowing orange ball of a 76 station. MOJAVE TOWING AND CAR REPAIR read the sign over the dark garage behind the pumps.

The tow truck stopped. They got out as Reyn's car was being lowered to the ground.

"I guess you all can wait here until morning," John said. He gestured toward the building. "Office is open. Not much to do, but we have a black-and-white TV in there. Used to be, we could only get one station, but with that converter box, we get quite a few now. Watch what you want. There's a vending machine around the corner if you get thirsty, but drinks cost a buck and it only takes quarters."

"Where are the other cars?" Brian asked.

"What other cars?"

"The Triple A woman told me you were late because it had been a busy night," Reyn explained. "I guess we thought there'd be other cars."

John grinned. "Naw. I just told her that when she called back and bitched at me. Truth is, I fell asleep."

What if he's crazy?

"So you don't have to pick up more vehicles?"

"Not yet. Not unless someone calls."

"Are you the mechanic here?" Reyn asked. "Or just the driver?"

"Mechanic. One of 'em." He'd finished lowering the car and unhooking the tow bar and chains. He unlocked the garage door behind the car, and with a loud, metallic roar, the door rolled up into the ceiling. The keys were still in Reyn's car, and the mechanic got in, pulling it into the first bay. There was a pit in the concrete beneath the car, and after getting out, John grabbed some tools and went below.

"Water pump," he confirmed a few moments later, emerging with grease on his hands. "I had to know. I was curious."

"Can you fix that?" Reyn asked.

"Yeah, but, like I said, we ain't open until eight."

"Well, can you tell me how much it's going to cost?"

"About a hundred parts, a hundred and fifty or so labor."

Gary thought he could hear his friend's sharp intake of breath. He felt guilty, because this probably wouldn't have happened if he hadn't dragged everyone out here on this wild-goose chase to begin with—or, if it had, it would have occurred somewhere in the Los Angeles metropolitan area, probably in the daytime, and wouldn't have cost anywhere near as much.

He wondered if he ought to offer to pay part of it but

didn't know how to even broach that subject until Reyn said, "I'm almost maxed out on my Visa. I only have a hundred or so left."

Gary jumped in. "I'll get the rest." He didn't really have the money, either, but he seldom used his one credit card and had plenty available on his account. He could always just make the minimum payment for several months until he paid this off. Besides, the sooner they got this problem taken care of, the sooner they could get back and go to the police. Whatever it cost, it was worth it.

"We're not supposed to be here," Stacy said in that coquettish voice that seemed so completely at odds with who she was. "If we don't get back by dawn, we'll be in big trouble. You don't seem too busy tonight. Do you think you could do us a little favor and just work on it . . . now? We could pay you a little extra."

The man smiled at her. "I guess I could."

"How long do you think it'll take?" Reyn asked, butting in.

The mechanic shrugged. "An hour, maybe. Two at the most."

"Thank you," Stacy said, smiling.

John went into a small storeroom at the far side of the garage.

"What the hell was that about?" Reyn whispered fiercely.

"Oh, knock it off," Stacy whispered back. "I'm getting us out of here."

They moved away, outside, around the edge of the building, arguing, but when they returned moments later, everything was fine between them.

Brian had already gone into the office to watch TV, and the rest of them joined him, flipping through channels before settling on a years-old *Jerry Springer* show about mothers who'd had sex with their sons' teenage friends. They'd made it halfway through another show about a woman who'd fallen in love with her husband's sister when John walked in and told them the car was ready to go.

In the end, he didn't charge them extra, and between Gary's credit card and Reyn's, they had enough to take care of it.

Then they were off.

There was a surprising amount of traffic on the highway now, all of it heading toward Los Angeles—the same direction in which they were going. The sky was orange in the east, and it grew lighter and lighter as they followed the slow flow of traffic into the city.

The sun was out and it was morning by the time they pulled off the freeway onto Wilshire Boulevard. Reyn was going to head straight to the police station, but Gary asked him to stop by his dorm first so he could get the photo he'd taken from Joan's parents' house. The cops could use it, and he'd decided to say he'd had it in his room and forgotten it was there. If he was asked *how* he could have forgotten, Gary was going to say that his brain had been so rattled by Joan's disappearance that he wasn't thinking clearly. Besides, he saw the photo every day and it was such a commonplace part of his room furnishings that he hadn't even thought about it.

The important thing was that the police would finally have a picture of Joan, proof that she existed, something they could work with to help them find her.

No one trusted Reyn's car, even with the new water pump, and despite his protestations, they switched vehicles and took Gary's Celica to the police station, where they asked the short masculine-looking woman at the front desk if they could talk to Detective Williams. In a flat, intimidating voice, she asked *why* they wanted to see the detective, and Gary said that they might have some information about a case he was working on. She asked

Gary's name, then picked up the handset of the phone directly in front of her and spoke into it, repeating what she'd been told. "Wait here," she said, after hanging up. "Someone will be with you shortly."

Gary was just glad that Williams seemed to be working this early, and he practiced in his head what he was going to say.

A few moments later, the security door to the right of the front desk opened with a buzz, and a uniformed young man about their age emerged to lead them through the station to the detectives' desks. They went down a long corridor, up a flight of stairs and into a large, open room filled with several desks, some manned, most empty. He stopped in front of Williams's partner, the guy with the handheld computer. The nameplate on his desk identified him as Det. Joseph Tucker.

Gary turned to the uniformed guide. "We wanted to talk to Detective Williams."

Tucker smiled harshly. "He's . . . indisposed at the moment. You can talk to me. Wondering how much your bail's going to be set at?"

The young officer was walking away.

"We're done," Brian said, grabbing Gary's arm. "Let's go."

Williams emerged from a restroom at the far end of the room, wiping his hands on a paper towel. "What can I do for you ladies and gentlemen?" he asked, walking up. He threw the wet paper towel at Tucker's head as he was sitting down at an adjacent desk. Tucker ducked, swearing.

Gary handed Williams the photo of Joan, saying that he'd forgotten about it. Then he held out his cell phone, explaining that he'd gotten a call from Joan last evening, though he'd only checked his messages and heard it now. Then he played it.

"Gary! I'm—"

The call was so short, he played it again, just in case the detective hadn't caught it.

"Gary! I'm—"

"I think someone kidnapped her, I think she escaped and I think she made that call," he said. "Then I think she was caught again."

Williams nodded, saying nothing.

Gary couldn't help it. "Now do you believe me?"

"Not necessarily," Tucker offered from the next desk over. "Maybe you recruited a friend of yours to send you that message in an effort to *convince* us that your story was legit."

"Jesus!"

Williams motioned for the other detective to shut up. "I believe you," he said. "But we still can't dig up any proof that a Joan Daniels was ever enrolled in UCLA or lived in that dorm room...."

"Her records have been erased," Brian said. "School, DMV, everything."

Tucker gave him a hard look. "And how do you know that?"

Brian stared back belligerently. "I have my ways."

"Stand down," Williams said tiredly.

"Is there any way you can trace this?" Gary asked.

"Short answer? No."

Gary slammed his hand down on the desk. "She's being held captive! This is an emergency! Can't you subpoena the phone company records?"

"Yes, but that could take—"

"Can't you just *ask* them?" Stacy suggested. "Explain the situation?"

Williams smiled thinly. "The Bush years are over. Privacy policies are back in effect."

Gary was filled with a feeling remarkably close to panic. It was an emotional state that was becoming far too familiar, rendering him simultaneously furious, anxious and powerless, and he wanted to beat some sense into the dull, implacable head of the detective sitting before him. He forced himself to take a deep, calming breath, one of those moves that characters in film did all the time but that seemed so attention-grabbing, obvious and melodramatic in real life. "The only clue we have is this partial phone message, this attempt at contact." He held out his phone. "How can we use it to find her?"

Williams looked at him, glanced over at Tucker, then picked up a pen and a yellow Post-it notepad, handing both to Gary. "Give me your cell phone number, your carrier and the date and time of the message. We'll see what we can do."

He acted as though he was doing Gary a big favor. *This is your job!* Gary wanted to scream at him. *This is what you're supposed to be doing! I shouldn't have to tell you to do it!* But he took the pen and paper, wrote down the information and handed it over.

"Did you ever get ahold of Joan's parents?" he asked. He knew they hadn't, but he wanted to introduce the subject, wanted them to discover that her parents were missing, too.

"No," Williams admitted. "No one's answered at that number."

If the police knew her parents had disappeared as well, they would be much more likely to ramp up Joan's investigation. Gary longed to just come out and tell the detective that they, too, were missing and that there was a dead dog stuck in the pet entrance of their kitchen. But that would involve divulging that he had been to their house, which in the eyes of the cops would probably connect him to their disappearance and would definitely implicate him in the crime of breaking and entering. So he only said, "Don't you think that's suspicious?"

"Possibly," Williams acknowledged.

"Ever think of calling the cops up there?" Brian

asked. "Tell them to check it out? I don't want to over-whelm your little brains, but that just seems like com-mon sense to me."

Gary almost smiled. As always, he was grateful for his friend's fearlessness, but he kept an eye on Williams and Tucker. Cops didn't take too well to open displays of defiance, and he didn't want Brian arrested on some trumped-up charge of resisting arrest.

Williams met Gary's gaze, ignoring Brian. "I believe that your girlfriend disappeared, and we'll do everything we can to find her."

What kind of wishy-washy promise was that?

At least he could take comfort in the knowledge that she was alive.

But he'd *always* thought that she was alive, and the desperation he'd heard in her voice on the phone for those few brief seconds made him even more eager than he had been before to rescue her, to get her back.

Williams must have noticed how lame his promise sounded. "Don't worry," the detective assured him. "We *will* find her."

Gary nodded. "Okay," he said.

But he didn't believe it.

Ten

Gary grabbed the textbooks from his desk. It felt disloyal to be going to class, almost as though he was turning his back on Joan, leaving her to rot in whatever hellhole served as her prison, but he had missed most of this week already, and if he wanted to stay in college and retain his scholarship and grant money, he was going to have to keep up with the coursework. Since this wasn't high school, and there was no one taking attendance, he figured if he could just find out the reading requirements and homework assignments for the next several sessions, he'd be able to get by without actually attending his classes.

In case something else came up.

Which it undoubtedly would.

Besides, there was nothing he or his friends could do right now. They'd reached a dead end in their pathetic amateur investigation, and it was up to the police to carry the ball. This was the perfect time to go back to class. It might even take his mind off everything for a few hours.

Only it didn't. The day seemed to last forever, the hours dragging, even lunch with Reyn passing by in slow motion. Of course, he was running on three hours of sleep, so his perception of time was undoubtedly skewed, but it all seemed so interminable.

Especially when he thought about what Joan was probably going through.

Gary! I'm—

He explained what was going on to Bergman, Garcia, Choy and Bernard, his European history, sociology, classical mythology and statistics professors, and they were all extremely understanding and accommodating. His Shakespeare instructor, Neilson, as expected, was not. Neilson informed him that he did not appreciate truancy, that he kept track of absences, and that if Gary thought he could skate by doing the bare minimum, he had another think coming. Gary nodded politely, took the beating, then immediately walked over to the admissions office and asked for a drop form. There was no way he'd get a fair shake in that class—particularly if he had to miss even more days—and since it was still the beginning of the semester, it was easy to drop the course. He still needed another three units to maintain his scholarship, however, and after talking to a counselor, he discovered that Renaissance literature fulfilled the same requirement. The class was still open, so he picked up an add form and went over to the English department office to get everything squared away. He met with the instructor, Dr. Davies, was given a syllabus, then headed over to the bookstore to buy his texts for the class.

He had a lot of reading to catch up on—in every subject—and he considered going to the library to study. But he felt more comfortable reading in his own room. The artificial silence of libraries put him on edge, made him feel self-conscious about making even the slightest sound or movement, and it seemed easier to study in a more open, natural environment. He grabbed a Monster Energy drink from the refrigerated display case near the cash register—he needed an extra jolt of caffeine to see him through that statistics book—then carried every-

thing across campus to his dorm. He opened the door
to his room—

And three men were waiting for him.

He had time to note that they were wearing odd
clothes, almost Amish-like garb, and that one of them
had a bald and peculiarly shaped head, and then they
were upon him, the one with the weird head grabbing his right arm, another his left, while the third man
punched him in the stomach and closed the door. Gary
couldn't cry out or fight back. He was too busy sucking
in air and trying to breathe. He was jerked erect, and for
several seconds he heard the three men talking in a language that seemed not just foreign but alien. They were
wearing homemade shoes, he noticed as he continued
to raggedly draw in air. Ugly brown things that sort of
resembled moccasins.

Turning his head, he stared at the bald guy, who for
some reason seemed unnervingly familiar.

Michael Berryman. The head mutant from Wes Craven's original *The Hills Have Eyes*.

That was who he looked like.

The man pulled his arm tighter.

The third man withdrew something from a brown burlap sack that was hanging from his shoulder by a rough
rope. A cloth. No, a gag. Gary tried to struggle, but he
was in pain and still out of breath, and he wasn't strong
enough to do more than wiggle in his captors' grasp. The
gag was pulled taut and placed over his mouth, then tied
around the back of his head. He wondered whether the
men were going to execute him or leave him bound here
in the room or take him somewhere. The latter seemed
the least likely. He didn't see how his abductors could
take him down the halls of the dorm, out of the building
and through the campus without attracting suspicion,
although he sure hoped they would try. It was his best
chance.

Gary wrinkled his nose, wanting to spit. The gag tasted strange, he thought. Like dirt or some type of root. And ...

... and ...

... and suddenly he felt calm. Not exactly happy but ... content. The pain he'd been experiencing, the fear and anger that had filled him, all drifted away, replaced by a comfortable tranquillity. He'd been drugged, he knew, but there was nothing he could do about it, and the knowledge lay useless and dormant beneath layers of blissful inertia that were compelling him to relax, to take it easy.

The gag was removed from his mouth. He knew he should scream and fight back, but he didn't want to, he couldn't, and he was led out of his room by the three men, one in front and two behind him. They didn't have to support him on their shoulders or lead him by the hand as though he were drunk; he went along willingly, docile and compliant but perfectly in control of his body. The four of them walked downstairs like old friends and up the concrete path that led out to the street.

Their car, a generic white midsize vehicle with a Hertz sticker on the back window, was parked in a red zone, and a ticket was pressed against the windshield, held down by one of the wiper blades. In a single movement, the guy who'd punched him pulled out the ticket and threw it into the air, where it fluttered down to the ground. For some reason, Gary thought that was hilarious, and he started laughing. He thought he'd never be able to stop, but then he was pushed gently down into the backseat of the car, and he understood intellectually, if not emotionally, the seriousness of his situation.

The car started moving, heading down the street and away from campus.

These had to be Outsiders. And they obviously thought he was part of Joan's religion. Whatever feud these two groups had going, he'd ended up right in the middle of it, and now he was probably going to die.

Only . . .

Only he couldn't get too worked up about it, didn't seem to care. The drug made him not merely lethargic but satisfied, and for the first time in his life he could honestly understand the appeal that narcotics held.

They drove.

The three men seldom spoke, but when they did it was in that strange—*alien*—language, and he could not understand a word of what was said.

He leaned back in the seat, looking at the bald guy with the weird head next to him. He could not seem to stop staring at the man, and this close he saw that not only was the shape of the head irregular, but one eye was bigger than the other and the left side of his mouth was raised up into a sort of permanent smile. The man looked more than a little off, almost retarded, although he definitely didn't act as if he was.

Gary could see details of the clothes of his abductors as well, and he noted with wonder that the shirts had no buttons but were held closed by small pieces of string tied in curiously dainty bows. The pants were leather, but leather that had not been properly tanned and still looked like cow flesh. Lengths of rope acted as belts.

"Where are you taking me?" he asked. He didn't actually care, but he was somewhat curious. No one answered, and he forgot about it.

After a while, he slept.

Apparently, they had driven all night, because when he awoke, it was morning and they were traveling through unfamiliar countryside. He saw chaparral-covered hills and steep sandstone cliffs. They were on a narrow two-lane road whose centerline could barely be seen and whose very asphalt had faded into a gray so pale it was almost white. Gary felt far less sanguine than he had when he'd fallen asleep, and he had the sense that he would feel stronger, angrier, more himself as additional time passed. Not wanting to give any hint that that was the case, he remained unmoving and forced himself to keep a slight smile on his face.

The guy with the weird head said some strange word that sounded like "Micah," and the driver reached next to him on the front seat and handed back a length of cloth.

A gag.

Before Gary could react, the gag was shoved into his mouth, whipped around his head and tied. He tasted dirt, root . . .

. . . and then he didn't care about escaping anymore. He knew he should, but he didn't, and he stared content-edly out at the scenery as his gag was removed. The men to either side were smiling at him, and he smiled back. Through the window, a town passed by: restaurant, gas station, store, trailer court. They bumped over a railroad track, passed by a dry river lined with trees.

What state were they in? Gary wondered. Were they still in California? He didn't know. And it didn't really matter anyway.

Some time later, they pulled onto a narrow dirt road that led through some scrub brush and into a rocky, hilly area. The three men had started talking again, saying words that made no sense, and Gary realized that he was hungry. He couldn't tell if it was closer to breakfast time or lunch, but right now any food sounded good. He was suddenly famished.

The dirt road had narrowed and was now little wider than a biking trail or a footpath. They wound up a small hill, passed between two sentrylike boulders and started down a long, gentle slope that ended at a ranch house and barn. The well-maintained wooden buildings were in a rough bowl-shaped meadow dotted with scrub oak and juniper. Next to the house and barn was a corral, and behind it all was a pasture of dried tan weeds through which a single horse slowly sauntered.

They pulled to a stop in front of the barn, next to a battered, mud-covered pickup truck and a rusted Jeep on blocks. A middle-aged woman was coming out of the house and walking across the dirt toward them. She, too, was wearing drab, primitive clothing, and she wiped her hands on a plain white apron as she approached. She walked with a pronounced limp, as though one leg was considerably shorter than the other.

"Hello!" the woman said, waving, but the driver shouted at her, something short and harsh in that alien language. The woman responded, her words low, hesitant and sounding like an apology. She looked at the ground.

So they *could* speak English, Gary thought.

Interesting.

As the limping woman led them toward the door of the house, which had been left wide open, he glanced around at the surrounding countryside. Apart from this ranch, there was no evidence of human habitation as far as the eye could see, and he realized that it would be the perfect area in which to dump his body. They could dig a hole somewhere on this land, toss him in, cover him up and no one would ever be the wiser. He wasn't worried—if it happened, it happened—but the idea did occur to him, and somewhere beneath the layers of apathy, he realized that that was good, that it was important to maintain an interest, however detached, in what they did to him.

The five of them stepped inside the house. It was simply furnished, just the type of place he would expect a woman who dressed like her to live. There were no rugs or couches or soft furniture of any kind, only crude chairs and tables made from the branches of trees, arranged unartfully in a seemingly haphazard manner on the unpainted plywood floor. There were no electric lights, only kerosene lamps, and like the parking ticket on the windshield, this struck him as hilarious. He started giggling at first, then tried to stop himself, which only made the giggles turn into roaring guffaws.

Then he saw the cabinet in the corner.

And the small spaces within it that were filled with rolled-up scrolls.

He stopped laughing.

The man who'd punched him, the one who appeared to be the leader, shouted some kind of order, and Gary was taken through a doorway into another room and tied to the floor on his back, his legs together and arms spread wide as though he were being crucified. There were shackles on the floor for just this purpose, which made him realize that this was not the first time this had been done, that he was not the first person to whom this had happened. The only piece of furniture in the room was a seat made out of a wooden crate that was pressed against the wall opposite the door.

The shackles didn't hurt, and it was kind of nice to be lying down, even if the wooden floor was hard and dirty. Gary allowed himself to be restrained, then stared up at the dark, cobwebbed ceiling as his captors left the room, closing the door behind them. Moments later, he could hear them in the other room talking, though their voices were little more than indistinct mumbles.

Soon he smelled food cooking, some type of unfamiliar meat, and a while after that the talking ceased. He assumed they were eating a meal, although no one came in to offer him anything. He was starving—he hadn't eaten anything since lunch yesterday—and that hunger, that need for food, cut through the blissful haze engulfing him and gave his comfortable serenity a sharper edge.

Edge was good.

He needed to keep it, hone it.

But such thinking tired him, and even as he tried to remember why he should attempt an escape, he was starting to nod off, to doze, the hard floor beneath his back feeling suddenly much more comfortable, the position of his shackled arms and legs seeming more relaxing than confining.

When he awoke, it was still light outside, but the light had shifted, and the muscles in his back told him that he had been asleep for several hours. He heard nothing from the other room, no talking, but through the window, he heard the woman call to someone, "Keep it down! They're still sleeping in there."

Gary's ears pricked up. The drug had worn off once again, not a lot but some, and that, combined with the now painful hunger in his belly, made him acutely aware of the need to stay alert. He was hoping to hear more words in English, but either someone had said something or she had caught herself, because the next words out of her mouth were in that alien language.

So his abductors were sleeping here. To Gary, that meant that their ultimate destination was still a long way off, and they were planning to travel by night and sleep by day.

Which meant that they weren't planning on killing him.

At least not yet.

He desperately had to take a piss, though he'd consumed no water or other liquid in probably twenty-four hours, and at first he thought he'd just go in his pants, maybe take a dump in there for good measure. That would show those bastards. They'd have to clean him up, find him some new pants, and maybe somewhere in the process, his hands or feet would be free enough for him to fight back. But the thought of it was too gross. Maybe they wouldn't even clean him up and would just make

him sit in it. He couldn't take a chance on that. He'd
puke.

At that moment, there was a change in the limited
light that entered the room, a slight darkening of the
day. Gary moved his head to the right—the only part of
his body he *could* move—and saw the woman peeking
through the window, checking on him. "I have to go to
the bathroom," he told her. "I have to pee."

He figured she would have one of the men escort him
to a bathroom or, more likely, an outhouse, but she nodded, went away and a few moments later limped into the
room through the door. Without speaking, the woman
crouched down next to him, unfastened his belt, unbut-
toned his jeans and took out his penis. Pulling it to the
right, she pointed the tip into a brown ceramic jar. Against
his will, he was aroused by the touch of her fingers, and
his organ stiffened into a partial erection. That made it
harder to urinate but not impossible, and though it took
a while, she held him in place until he was finished and
then walked out of the room holding the jar. She'd said
nothing the entire time, and while he'd felt mortally embarrassed even in his doped-up state, her face retained a
completely neutral expression the entire time. He might
as well have been a cow she was milking.

There were stirrings in the other room, and once
again the smell of food. Onions with the meat, this time.
Potatoes. Tired of waiting for an invitation, Gary yelled,
"I'm hungry!"

There was what sounded like a discussion out there,
and then the guy with the weird head came in. He didn't
tie on a gag this time, but bent down, held open Gary's
mouth and poured in a thick, syrupy liquid from a metal
cup. It had the same earthy taste as the gag, and Gary
wanted to spit it out, but he couldn't move his head,
and it felt like he was going to drown. The only thing he
could do was swallow it.

Then he felt good, and his shackles were removed,
and he was led out through the adjoining room into a
kitchen, where he sat with his three abductors and another man he didn't recognize, while the woman led
them in an alien prayer and then served them plates of
greasy meat and boiled potatoes. The food was horrible,
but he had to eat, and he forced himself to keep the
wretched repast down and not throw up.

The sun began to set as they dined, and by the time
they finished, it was nearly dusk. Gary was led docilely
to his seat in the back of the car as everyone else participated in a conversation he could not understand. He
had no idea why they had kidnapped him, but he hoped
they were taking him to wherever Joan was, although he
didn't know what it would mean for either himself or
Joan if they did.

As before, the man who seemed to be the leader
drove the car, while the same two sat on either side of
him in the backseat. Out of habit, Gary buckled his seat
belt. The rest of them, he noticed, did not. Maybe they'd
get in an accident, everyone else would fly through the
window; then he'd just unbuckle his seat belt, get into
the driver's seat and speed away.

The thought struck him as funny, and he laughed.

He was still laughing when the car struck a deer and
skidded off the side of the road.

They had already traveled up the long slope, past the
boulders, and were in the hills, out of sight of the ranch.
He had no idea where the deer had come from or why
it had leapt in front of the car. All he knew was that
there was a jolting impact, the violent sound of metal
buckling and glass breaking, and then a massive, heavily
antlered deer was on the hood and the car was swerv-
ing sideways off the narrow dirt road. The men to either
side of him were thrown against him, against the doors,
against the seats in front. The driver had somehow man-

aged to keep his hands on the wheel, even as a giant hoof crashed through the windshield to strike the dashboard, but it did him no good. The car still flew down an embankment, smashing into a rock on the way that for a brief second penetrated the rear passenger-side window, split open the bald guy's head and splattered blood all over Gary.

Then the car was rolling over.

And then Gary was out.

Eleven

Reyn was awakened by Colin Clive maniacally shouting, *"It's alive! It's alive!"*—the obnoxious ringtone that Stacy had loaded onto his cell phone as a joke. He'd been meaning to change the sound but had not gotten around to doing so, and he swore this time that he would finally go through with it and switch to an ordinary old-school bell. He looked at the screen for the identity of the caller.

Brian.

"Hey," he said, picking up.

"I can't reach Gary," he said. "You know where he is?"

Reyn yawned. "No. Why?"

"He's been deleted. Facebook, MySpace, everything. Just like Joan. I'd be willing to bet his records aren't in the school's database anymore, either."

Reyn was suddenly wide awake. "What?"

"Yeah. And get this: when I call his cell phone, I get a message that his number is no longer in service."

"Where are you now?"

"I'm going over there to bang on his door."

"Wait," Reyn said. "Have you checked any of *our* Facebook pages?" He saw in his mind a sudden image of Stacy accessing her account . . . and then watching as the photos and text were eaten away and replaced by dead white space.

"No," Brian said. "But hold on a sec." There was a pause. "*I'm* still there." Another pause. "*You're* there." Another pause. "Stacy's there."

Reyn's voice was low and sounded more frightened than he wanted it to sound. "We were all listed as friends on Joan's page."

"Our pictures were on there, too," Brian said.

"I'm calling Stacy," Reyn told him.

"I'm heading over to Gary's. I'll call you when I get there."

Reyn quickly dialed Stacy's number, and she answered on the first ring. It was early in the morning, but she was already wide awake and exercising. He told her about Gary, and before he'd even finished she said, "What about us? Have we been deleted?"

"No. Brian just checked."

"Do you think something's happened to Gary? Do you think it's the same people who got Joan?"

"That would be my guess," Reyn said.

He could hear her audible intake of breath.

"Brian's going over there to check right now."

"We need to call the police."

"We'll wait and see if Brian can find him."

"Do you think—"

"No," he said.

"What if we're all in danger? What if they weren't just after Joan but are after all of us and she was just the first?"

"We have to assume we *are* in danger," he told her.

"I have my art class this morning—"

"Go," he told her. "That's probably the safest place to be right now: in a big crowd with other people. The most important thing is to avoid being alone. Stay out in the open when you're not in class. I'll meet you in the usual place at the usual time. And I want you to stay with me tonight. In my room. It's dangerous to be by yourself."

They talked briefly about their tentative plans for the day, and Stacy promised to leave her cell phone on at all times, even in class. Reyn told her he'd call back as soon as he had any news.

Moments later, Brian called. He sounded out of breath, as though he'd been running. "Gary's not answering his door. I pounded the shit out of it so hard that one of his neighbors came out, and I asked the guy if he'd seen Gary, but he said not for a while, though he didn't know how long." Brian exhaled deeply. "What if he's dead in there?"

Reyn hadn't thought of that. "Find someone to open the door. A manager or whoever."

"Do we tell the cops?" Brian asked.

"Of course!" Reyn was already getting ready to hang up and dial 911.

"What if they think he's just skipped out on them? Won't that make him look more suspicious?"

"They're dumb, but they're not that dumb."

"What about that forty-eight-hour thing? They might not even look for him for another two days."

"I'm calling that detective, I'm telling him what happened, and if he gives me any shit, I'll tell him to shut up, get off his ass and do his job. That's what my taxes are paying him for."

But it didn't work out that way. Williams was not on duty, Tucker was, and with evident glee the detective said that Gary, that *all* of them, had been specifically told to remain nearby where they could easily be reached. The implication was that when—or if—Gary showed up again, he would be in trouble.

"You don't understand," Reyn said, exasperated. "He has not only disappeared, but any computerized evidence that he exists has been deleted. Just like Joan."

"His supposed girlfriend."

"Well, Gary's not a supposed anything. You saw him; you met him; you know he exists."

"Yet he's trying to convince us that he does not. Why do you suppose that is?"

"He's not doing this!" Gary said. Talking to Tucker was like arguing with a crazy person. "It's being done to him!"

"I'm sorry," the detective said politely. "I don't see it that way."

"That's because you're an asshole!" Reyn hung up the phone. It rang again, seconds later, and he answered immediately, hoping it was Brian. Or Gary.

It was Tucker.

"Listen," the detective said threateningly, the anger evident in his voice.

"I don't have to," Reyn told him. "You're still an asshole." He hung up again. Immediately, he called Brian, who had just found a manager whom he'd convinced to unlock Gary's door so they could take a look. Brian kept his phone on as the door was opened, so Reyn could hear the whole thing.

"The place looks normal," Brian said. "Nothing's disturbed, but Gary's not here."

"All right," the manager announced. "Out."

"Gary's not here," Brian repeated, and the words made Reyn's blood run cold.

Like Stacy, Reyn and Brian went to their classes. None of them heard from Gary all day, and each time Reyn called his friend's dorm room, he got the answering machine. Gary's cell phone was still out of service. He did keep calling the police station, and sometime after noon, Detective Williams came on duty. Reyn asked to speak to him and proceeded to describe to the detective what had happened. He left out the little run-in with Tucker, figuring he'd let the asshole explain it himself if he wanted to do so.

Williams definitely seemed concerned, and he asked a lot of questions, making Reyn go over everything twice. Legally, the detective said, Gary would not be considered missing until the day after tomorrow. But he made it clear that, unofficially, he would be looking into Gary's disappearance immediately.

Reyn felt better.

Stacy met him in the student union after her last class. He still had a philosophy seminar he had to attend, so she came with him and sat in, and afterward they met Brian in front of the library. "Did you see anything—or anyone—suspicious?" Reyn asked.

Brian shook his head. "I kept an eye out all day. Either no one's watching me, or, if they are, they're very, very good."

The three of them ate a desultory early dinner at an off-campus burger joint, their cell phones on and sitting in the center of the table. Afterward they split up. Brian had a roommate, Dror, and Reyn encouraged him to tell Dror the situation, since proximity might make him a target as well. Besides, four fists were better than two, should someone try to attack. Reyn and Stacy went to her dorm to get her clothes for the next day, then returned to his, where they tried in vain to study before giving it up and going online to browse through whatever information they could find that even remotely applied.

They found nothing, however, and after a quick call to Brian and one last attempt to contact Gary, they turned in early, exhausted and emotionally wrung out.

Reyn fell asleep instantly.

He awoke in the morning, and Stacy was gone. Next to him on the bed was an empty space and a bloodstain the size of a basketball in the center of the indentation where she had been. "Stacy!" he screamed. There was a low answering noise from the bathroom, what sounded like a moan, and he yanked off the sheet and ran over to the open doorway. Stacy was naked and lying in the shower stall. The water was on, the spray aimed at her midsection, where blood flowed from a gaping knife wound, mixing with the water and swirling down the drain. She tried to say something when she saw him but was in such terrible pain that her eyes closed and the only sound that issued from her lips was a short guttural groan. Reyn rushed forward to help her and was grabbed from behind. He turned to see Joan, holding a bloody knife in one hand and, in the other, a mask that looked like the blank, featureless face of the Burning Man.

Then he *really* awoke, and it was still night, and Stacy was lying beside him, snoring loudly. She was alive; she was safe; she was here. It had all been a dream. He closed his eyes, breathing deeply, and tried to fall asleep.

But he couldn't.

And he remained awake all night, through the long, dead hours that eventually led to morning.

Twelve

Opening his eyes, Gary found himself sitting on the ground, his back against a smooth sandstone boulder. For several seconds, he didn't know where he was or what had happened. Then he remembered the crash, and he looked around for his kidnappers and their car. He saw neither, and he wondered if they had somehow gotten the vehicle working again and taken off without him. That made no sense, though, and he tried to stand up, figuring he could get a better view from a higher vantage point. He was too weak, however, and his attempt to push himself up resulted in an embarrassing slide back down. He waited a few moments, gathered his strength, then tried it again. This time he managed to get to his feet, though he kept one hand on the boulder to steady himself.

The moon was out, although there were no city lights out here and the night was much darker than it usually seemed. He remained in place, allowing his eyes to adjust, and gradually became aware of the fact that there was a slight reddish glow coming from an area off to the left. Moving carefully, putting one foot deliberately in front of the other, he slowly made his way across the dirt in that direction. The reddish glow, he soon saw, came from the taillights of the car, which were still on, though there was no sound of an engine. The car lay downhill from where he stood, in a kind of gulch, its front end mangled, the metal accordioned. He had apparently gotten out of the vehicle after it had crashed, then somehow walked up here, though he remembered none of it.

Now Gary stared down at the wreckage, feeling dizzy and disoriented. He didn't know if the three men were alive in there, but he had no desire to walk over and find out. He hoped they were dead, but he couldn't count on it, and he knew the safest thing to do would be to get out of there as quickly as possible and put some miles between himself and the car while it was still dark. He turned, started to walk off—

—and promptly threw up.

He dropped to his knees, heaving in a way he hadn't done since he was ten years old and had the flu. It was probably a balance thing, an inner ear thing, and he hoped against hope that it would go away quickly so he could try to make his escape, but he remained on his knees even after the stomach spasms had passed, afraid to make any sudden movements.

Slowly, Gary stood. He couldn't see it from here, but he knew that he had to be close to the dirt road that had taken them to the ranch house. He looked down at the wreckage again, closing his eyes after a few seconds to ward off the dizziness, then calculated back to where he figured the road should be. Sure enough, there was a flat area past the rocks that, even with only the minimal illumination of moonlight, he could tell was the trail they'd taken to get from the highway to the ranch.

Gary tried to remember how far it was to pavement, but he'd been blissed out on his way in and things like distance and time had not mattered to him and were now impossible to measure. He was not even positive in which *direction* the highway was, so he reached the dirt road and decided to head left because that felt right. He chose correctly: after ten minutes of walking, the route still wound through rocky hills rather than sloping down to the bowl-shaped meadow that housed the ranch.

With only moonlight to guide him, Gary trudged through the darkened countryside. He had one hellacious headache, and the dizziness had not entirely gone away, but he walked quickly and made good time, and after what felt like an hour or so, he reached the turnoff.

He stopped to rest, feeling tired and discouraged. The road was not as big as he'd expected. He'd assumed they'd been traveling on a major highway, but the route turned out to be a two-lane blacktop that ran straight into darkness in both directions. There were no cars, no lights, no buildings, nothing visible but that unbending track of asphalt cutting through a barren, inhospitable landscape.

Gary's throat felt dry, rough with the afterburn of vomiting, but that couldn't be helped; he had no water with him. And though he wanted to remain here and rest awhile longer, he knew that wasn't a good idea. He needed to keep moving. Even if the men who'd abducted him had been killed, it was more than possible that they were supposed to have been at a certain place by now or that they should have checked in with somebody. For all he knew, the woman and man from that ranch might come speeding out from the dirt road at any second, gunning for him.

He had to get out of here.

Once again, he turned left, for no other reason than that it had worked for him the last time. He kept to the side of the road and, after twenty minutes or so, discovered that what he had taken for the darkness of night was in fact more hills, and that after the road passed through them, it opened onto a flat plain on which he could see, spread out over a wide distance, individual twinkling lights that had to be homes.

He had no wallet, Gary realized. He didn't know what

had happened to it. It had been in his pants when he'd returned to his room after class, but sometime between then and now it had been taken from him.

He patted his front pockets. His keys, too. They'd taken his keys.

So he had no money or ID.

Even if he did run into anyone, he had no way to prove who he was, no way to prove he wasn't an escaped convict or some loony from a mental hospital. And if he lurched out of the darkness to knock on the doors of the cabins or farmhouses whose lights he could see from the road, the people living there would probably shoot him, thinking he was a crazed criminal.

But he wasn't going to walk up to any of those homes. This was *their* country, and for all he knew every single one of those structures housed Outsiders who'd been told of his escape and were on the lookout for him. Logically, of course, that couldn't be true. But it might as well be. Because even if only one out of a hundred houses was theirs, he was dead meat if that was the one he approached.

What was that old bumper sticker joke? Just because you're paranoid, it doesn't mean they're not after you? He *was* being paranoid. And it might be a side effect of whatever they'd used to drug him. But he'd also been abducted from his UCLA dorm by three Amish-looking guys, one of whom looked like a mutant. He had reason to be wary.

He continued on, wondering if one of those lights might be a gas station or a store, wondering if the road curved up ahead and led there. If he could find a pay phone—

Do they even have pay phones anymore?

—he could dial collect and call . . . call . . . call . . . 911? The FBI? Reyn? His parents? He didn't know—maybe all of them.

By the time the sun was starting to rise, his legs were aching, and Gary sat down on a rock to rest. If a car or truck came up the road, he decided, he would try to flag it down and catch a ride. But no vehicles appeared, and after a half hour or so, he decided to keep going. He could tell that the dawning day was going to be a hot one, and he needed to find some water. His parched throat felt more sandpapery than ever, and he kept swallowing saliva constantly, knowing that if he didn't, he would cough and gag and probably throw up again.

In the light of morning, he could see the road ahead, and while he'd made his way through most of the plain and had gone nowhere near any of the scattered shacks and cabins whose lights he'd spotted in the darkness, he saw now that there was something shiny on the road ahead, where it started to slope up the side of a low plateau. Maybe it was a car. Maybe it was light reflecting off the windows of a building. Whatever it was, it was man-made, not natural, and he walked forward with renewed hope, able to ignore the throbbing muscles in his legs, the rumbling in his stomach, the sandpaper in his throat.

A plane flew by, high overhead, the first sign of anything human since he'd left the crash site.

As he drew closer, the shine became brighter until it was a silver glare he could not bear to look at. Then something changed—the angle of the road or the angle of the sun—and though he was still a mile or two away, he could see that the object was indeed a building of some sort, its metal or glass reflecting back the rays of the rising sun.

He was drenched with sweat, but he used the bottom of his shirt to wipe his face and kept going.

The building had once been a gas station, he saw as he approached, but now there was only the skeleton of a Shell sign atop the pole next to the road, and what had been the pump island consisted of bent metal braces affixed to a concrete slab. The office and garage were still being used and were open, however, and though there was no sign on the structure, a crudely painted stencil on the side of a tow truck parked parallel to the road read: TOW-TO-TOW TOWING. It made Gary think of that garage in the desert outside of Lancaster where Reyn's water pump had been replaced—

What if he's crazy?

—and while he felt more than a little nervous, he walked up to the open garage door and called out, "Anybody here?"

There was movement in the darkness, and a beefy, bearded man emerged, scowling. "Yeah? What d'you want?"

Under ordinary circumstances, Gary would have left then and there, just turned away and continued down the road. But he was hungry, thirsty and in pain, and he asked, "Can I use your phone?"

"Ain't got one," the man said, staring flatly at him.

How is that possible? Gary wanted to say. *You have a towing business. How do people contact you when they break down if you don't have a phone?*

Something was wrong here, and all of a sudden Gary wanted nothing more than to get away from this spot as quickly as possible. "Okay!" he said, waving. "Thanks!" He turned back toward the road.

"Wait a minute," the man said, and it was as much order as request. "Is your car out there? Did you break down?"

They were perfectly ordinary questions, totally appropriate under the circumstances, but the big man's tone and demeanor made them seem threatening, as though he was trying to ferret out information. Why did he want to know? Gary wondered. Was the man trying to determine if anyone else was with him or knew he was out here?

What if he's crazy?

He pretended as though he hadn't heard. "Thanks!" he yelled again, turning away, and started walking. He waited for another shouted question or for the sound of running footsteps behind him, but there was nothing. For a brief moment, he thought that he'd misread the situation, that the drugs still in his body had skewed his perceptions and made him read into a perfectly inno-cent exchange a threat that wasn't there. But when he turned and looked back, he saw the bearded man still standing in place, scowling, and he forced himself to give another fake, hearty wave and continue on. His heart was pounding.

Moments later, the rough sound of a powerful engine cut through the still air, and Gary knew that the mechanic had started his tow truck. He kept walking, a little faster now, but he was already thinking about how he could run off the road and strike out across the chaparral if necessary. For there was no way he could outrun a truck. He probably couldn't even outrun the mechanic, not in the shape he was in, and he had just decided to leave the road early when he heard the engine grow loud and felt more than saw the tow truck pull next to him.

"Need a lift?" the man asked, and the belligerence was still in his voice, more obvious now, if anything.

Gary shook his head, kept walking.

"Where's your car?"

Instead of answering, he stepped off the shoulder of the road and into the brush.

"Hey! I'm talking to you!"

Gary increased his speed, striding purposefully be-tween rocks and bushes, heading away from the tow truck at an angle. His heart lurched as he heard the truck's door open and shut. A bird flew up from some-where on his right, startling him.

"Hey!" the driver shouted.

Even as he walked, Gary examined the ground ahead of him for something that could be used as a weapon: a stick, a rock, a broken bottle, anything. It wouldn't have surprised him if the man had a gun, and he kept expecting to hear the whipcrack sound of a shot seconds before he felt a bullet slam through his back, but nothing came. He hazarded a quick glance behind him.

The man was coming.

He didn't have a gun, but he was holding a lug wrench, and he looked angry. He moved with the inflexible decisiveness of the casually violent, and the lug wrench in his hand was held up and outward, like a weapon. "I see you, faggot!" he shouted. "I see you!"

Gary started running. The ground here was sandier than it had been closer to the pavement, and it was hard to move quickly. The countryside was more desertic than he'd realized, and he thought that he was probably out of California. In Nevada, maybe. Or Arizona or New Mexico.

He looked to his left. He hadn't come that far from the garage, and he abruptly changed direction and started heading toward the side of that run-down building. There was no way he'd be able to discover something in the sand that could effectively defend against a lug wrench. He was far more likely to find a tool or weapon he could use in the garage.

He glanced back, praying that the mechanic was still following him, because if the man figured out where he was going, it would be much faster to get back in the truck and then drive back and wait for him to arrive. Gary's only hope was that the mechanic continued to come after him on foot.

He *was* coming after him.

And he was gaining.

Gary pushed himself, trying to ignore the pain in his right leg that had graduated from throbbing to stabbing in the last few seconds. His left leg hurt, too, but it was tolerable. With his right leg, though, he was crying out each time it hit the ground, an involuntary sound that seemed to make him move a little faster. It would have given away his position had he been trying to hide, but the mechanic had been focused on him from the second he left the road and could see exactly where he was at all times.

"Stop right there!" the man ordered. "Don't even think you can get away!"

The garage was close now. He was almost there. But the man behind him was close, too. Gary could hear the grunts of exertion as the mechanic plodded through the sand. The small lead he'd had was gone, and while desperation had kept him competitive, in a moment or two he would be caught, and he expected to feel the blow of the lug wrench against his head before he even made it into the garage to find a weapon of his own. Looking ahead of him on the ground, he saw between himself and the wall of the garage an area awash with black rocks of various sizes. Most of them were embedded in the ground, but a few were loose, and he reached down and grabbed one, turning to heave it at the mechanic.

Under the best of circumstances, Gary had no arm. He expected the rock to go wild, but amazingly it struck the hand holding the lug wrench, and the mechanic cried out, dropping the tool.

Gary wasted no time. He sped ahead, hobbled around the corner of the building, and looked frantically around the open garage for something he could use. His eyes alighted on what appeared to be a sledgehammer hanging from a spot on the wall to his right. He hurried over and grabbed it, turning around just as the bearded man stepped into the garage.

Gary's heart was thumping crazily. He had never been so scared in his life, and the calmness engendered

by the drug he'd been given was long gone. He held up
the sledgehammer with both hands, but it was so heavy
that it was already wobbling in his grip. There was no
way he'd be able to keep this up for any length of time.
If he couldn't bluff his way out of the situation, his only
chance was to land a single clear hit. If he could connect,
he could do damage. Otherwise, he was dead meat.

He wondered if the mechanic had done this before, if
there were bodies buried in the sand nearby.

Judging by the way the man had come after him with
absolutely no provocation, Gary could only assume that
he was *not* the mechanic's first victim.

Gary rested the handle of the sledgehammer on his
shoulder, trying not to wince from the pain caused by
the sudden pressure, hoping his adversary couldn't tell
that he was doing so because he had to, because he did
not have the strength to continue holding the tool aloft.
"Let me go," he said. "Give me the keys to your truck
and let me get out of here."

The big man grinned, hefted his lug wrench. "Faggot,"
he said.

What was all this "faggot" stuff? Gary wondered. It
seemed to be the only epithet the mechanic knew.

Gary pushed it up a notch. "I'll smash your fucking
legs," he said. "Then I'll crush your ugly fucking head."

That seemed to get to the mechanic. His grin disappeared, and his bushy eyebrows beetled into a frown.
He moved a step closer, swinging his weapon. "Try it."

"Give me the keys," Gary demanded. He suddenly
wondered if the man *had* the keys. He could not remember the engine of the tow truck shutting off, and he was
instantly sure that the keys were in the truck, which was
idling several yards down the road.

If he could just get over there . . .

The mechanic rushed him.

It happened so fact that the sequence of events came

to him in a series of images and impressions. The bearded man's face, grimacing and screaming. The lug wrench, swishing back and forth, cutting the air before it. The heaviness of the sledgehammer as he pulled it from his shoulder and swung it in front of him. The drag from the weight of the sledgehammer painfully tensing the muscles in his arms. The screaming face. The swishing lug wrench.

And then the jolt of impact as his sledgehammer hit the mechanic midbody, instantly dropping him.

The screaming stopped, the lug wrench flew across the garage and hit something metal with an earsplitting clang, and the big man went down, blood spewing as he lurched sideways and slammed into a workbench covered with greasy car parts. Gary didn't wait to see how badly the mechanic was hurt. He left the sledgehammer and took off, running for the road as fast as his exhausted, injured legs would carry him. By the time he was out of the garage, he could hear the sound of the tow truck's engine, a low rumble in the stillness of the desert, and he made his way toward it, reaching the vehicle in a matter of minutes.

He'd seen enough movies to know that he should have made sure the mechanic was permanently incapacitated, but fear and panic had made him run, and he turned back, fully expecting to see the man coming after him.

But no one was there and, grateful, Gary climbed into the cab. He prayed that there was enough gas to get him someplace where he could call for help and saw with relief that, according to the gauge, the tank was nearly full. He had never driven a tow truck before, but there was nothing *that* unfamiliar on the dashboard, and he easily got into gear and started down the road.

He passed a rock shop several miles up ahead, and later a feed store, but he did not stop or even slow down until he reached the outskirts of a real town some forty-five minutes later.

Thirteen

Gary called while Reyn was in his Saturday screenwriting class.

Reyn's phone was set on vibrate, and he jumped in his seat, startled, as the silent ringer went off. Quickly, he stood and walked out of class, pulling the phone from his pocket as he strode into the corridor. He'd told both Stacy and Brian not to call unless it was an emergency, and as soon as the classroom door closed behind him, he pressed the TALK button and held the phone to his ear with a trembling hand, assuming the worst. "Hello?"

It was a complete and utter shock to hear Gary's voice. His friend sounded exhausted, and as he listened to the incredible story he had to tell, Reyn understood why. Gary was calling from a sheriff's office in Larraine, New Mexico. He'd driven there in a stolen tow truck after he'd gotten into a car crash, escaped from the men who'd drugged and captured him, walked for hours through the desert and fought off a psychotic mechanic. It was so overwhelming and unbelievable that Reyn made him repeat it again, slowly and with more details. Gary didn't want to, but he did, and when he was finished, Reyn said, "Holy shit."

"The guys who jumped me, the ones who were hiding in my room, they were dressed in these simple, primitive kind of clothes that they'd made themselves, like old-time farmer's clothes. They sort of looked Amish. So if you see anyone like that around campus, get away from them, call the police."

"Do you know who they are?" Reyn asked.

"The Outsiders, I guess. But they didn't talk to me, and when they talked to each other it was in this weird language. Some kind of code, I think. The thing is, they were waiting for me in my room, like I said, but the door hadn't been jimmied. They'd either picked the lock or they had a key or they found some other way in without force. And they did it in the middle of the day in a crowded dorm with tons of people around. So be careful. Be very careful."

"There's news on this end, too," Reyn said.

"About Joan?" Gary asked quickly.

"No. Nothing on that at all. It's about you. You've been deleted."

"What are you talking about?"

"Just like with Joan. Someone's erased your Facebook and MySpace pages. And I have a sneaking suspicion that you're not enrolled in school anymore."

"Are you serious?"

"Never more."

"This is crazy!"

"Yeah."

Gary sounded anxious. "Listen. You've got to go to Admissions and check on this for me. I could lose my grant money. And my scholarships."

"I don't think they'll let me—"

"It's going to be a day or two before I can get back. By that time, I could be totally disqualified. Check online if you can. My student ID number is 1170. Pretend to be me. I'll call you back tonight."

"What if I can't?"

"We'll figure something out."

"Why do you think—" Reyn began.

There was noise in the background, people talking. "I have to go. My time's up. I'll talk to you tonight."

Gary hung up without saying good-bye, and Reyn stood there, cell phone in hand, staring at the closed door of his screenwriting class, not wanting to go back in, thinking how frivolous and trivial it was to sit around discussing the importance of the three-act structure when his friend had been kidnapped and almost killed.

He headed down the corridor toward the outside of the building, speed-dialing Stacy as he walked. She answered on the second ring, just as he was striding through the doorway. "Gary just called me," he told her. "He's in New Mexico."

"Oh my God! Is he all right?"

Walking toward Stacy's dorm, Reyn started to describe what had happened. Almost immediately she said, "Meet me out in front of—"

"I'm already here," he said.

She emerged from the building's front entrance moments later, hurrying in front of a group of young women who were walking out together. She saw him immediately and ran over. "Tell me everything," she ordered.

He knew only the broad outlines, so he couldn't go into much detail, but he repeated what Gary had told him. When he came to Gary's warning about men dressed in primitive farmer's clothes, Stacy's face turned pale. "I think I saw one of those guys."

Reyn's heart was pounding. "When?"

"A few days ago. He was hanging around the bookstore. I remember noticing him because of the weird clothes. He was, like, a middle-aged guy. I thought he was an old hippie or something." She shivered. "But I got a weird vibe off him."

"Was he watching you? Or . . . ?"

"Probably. I mean, I didn't think so at the time, but it makes sense when you think about it now." She threw her arms around Reyn, hugged him tight. "Maybe I'm next."

"We'll make sure you're not."

"Maybe he was one of the guys who got Gary. I saw him the day before Gary was— No! I saw him that same day!"

Reyn had to be blunt. "It doesn't matter. Joan's gone. Kara's gone. Teri Lim's dead. Gary was captured. They're grabbing everyone. They're not leaving any witnesses."

"Witnesses to what?"

"I don't know."

She held him tighter. "What are we going to do?"

"I don't know," he said again.

Brian was with them, holding a steak knife, as they carefully opened the door to Reyn's room. No one jumped out, and Reyn snaked his hand around the doorframe and flipped the light switch. The room was instantly illuminated. They saw right away that no attackers lay in wait, but it wasn't until Reyn had quickly checked the bathroom that they finally relaxed.

Brian dropped the arm with the steak knife and sighed with audible relief.

"We need to get better weapons," Stacy noted wryly, looking at him.

"I did the best I could on such short notice."

Reyn was already at his laptop. "Let's see what we can find out about that town he's in. Larraine . . . Anybody ever heard of it or know how to spell it?" None of them did, so he tried a couple of spellings before he got a match. There wasn't much information available on the town, but he was able to bring up a satellite photo of it, and with the tap of a finger the photo shifted fifty miles east, and he zoomed in on a gas station that must have been the one where Gary had almost been killed.

There were a lot of ranches and cabins scattered

about the surrounding countryside, but he didn't know enough to home in on the one where Gary had been held. A thought occurred to him while he was scanning the image, however, and he got out of the site and started accessing crime logs for Larraine and for the county of De Baca, in which the town was located.

Brian saw what he was doing. "I'll take over here," he said, pushing Reyn aside. "I type faster, anyway. You call that detective. Tell him what's going on."

"Williams?"

"Yeah."

Reyn did, and though the detective didn't have much of a response beyond, "Thank you for sharing that information," Reyn had the sense that Williams was genuinely startled by Gary's story. He asked Reyn to have Gary come into the station once he got back.

Reyn hung up the phone and sat on the edge of his bed next to Stacy, watching Brian type furiously on the computer. He wasn't sure how it had happened, but they'd fallen through the cracks to such an extent that, despite the fact that they were in the very middle of a series of druggings and kidnappings and even deaths, law enforcement was completely peripheral to them. The police were doing very little to help, and although for a brief fraction of a second the four of them appeared to have been suspects in Kara's disappearance, they were not really being persecuted. Whatever was happening was occurring in a netherworld in which they were completely on their own, the sort of universe usually encountered only in movies, and he wondered for the first time in his life if he should buy a gun for protection.

"Found something," Brian said excitedly, looking up from the screen.

Both Reyn and Stacy came over to look.

On the monitor was a month-old crime column from the weekly local newspaper, the *Larraine Roadrunner*.

Brian was pointing to an entry in the center of the screen. On August 6, a woman, Paulette Gaffney, had registered a complaint against her ex-husband, Bill Watt. Watt, she claimed, had been stalking her since their divorce, and he had not only broken into her house but had threatened her with physical violence. She said it was his fault that they were now both "outsiders."

Outsiders.

The word jumped out at them.

Reyn's neck felt as though it had been tickled by the tip of an icicle.

Watt had been picked up but not arrested, and released on his own recognizance.

"That guy has the same last name as the sheriff," Brian said, pointing to a boxed list of local government officials on the left side of the page.

"Could be a coincidence."

"In a town of three thousand? I don't think so."

Reyn didn't, either, and he said aloud, "If the sheriff and his brother are both Outsiders . . ."

Gary's circumstances suddenly seemed much more ominous, and he cursed himself for not getting a phone number from his friend. "Quick," he told Brian. "Can you get me a phone number for the Larraine sheriff's office?"

Brian pulled up another page and began typing rapidly. "It's the De Baca Sheriff's Office in Larraine," he said. "The number's (575) 555-3109."

Reyn picked up the phone on his desk and dialed the number. A woman answered. "Sheriff's office, Maybelle speaking."

He tried to keep his voice calm. "I'd like to speak to Gary Russell. He called me from your office about forty-five minutes ago. I think he's still there."

"I'm sorry," the woman said. "Mr. Russell is with the sheriff. May I take a message?"

"I really need to talk to him *now*."

"I'm sorry. He and the sheriff went out. I don't expect them back for some time. Is there a number at which I can reach you?"

He and the sheriff went out.

A big ball of dread sank to the pit of Reyn's stomach. "No," he said. "That's okay. I'll call back later."

Fourteen

Gary wanted nothing more than to go to bed. He was willing to sleep on a chair, on the floor, in a cell, pretty much anywhere. At this point he didn't care. But he forced himself to remain awake and answer the seemingly never-ending series of questions put to him by Sheriff Watt. He *had* napped for a while on a cot in a back room—the sheriff's office in Larraine was a lot more casual than the police station in Los Angeles—while Watt and a couple of deputies went back out to Tow-to-Tow Towing. They'd found the mechanic just where Gary had left him, on the concrete floor of the garage, and although he was seriously injured, he was still alive.

They also must have found something else in their search of the building because they did not for a second doubt Gary's story, and when he asked if he should have a lawyer present during questioning and whether he'd have to stand trial for attacking the mechanic, the sheriff had shaken his head. "No, it's pretty clear what went on out there. You did what you had to do. I don't think anyone's going to question that."

But they did keep asking questions, and from the tenor of some of them, Gary wondered if they'd found bodies at the garage. Or some other sort of gruesome evidence indicating that the mechanic had done this before.

It was not his run-in with the psycho tow-truck driver

that Gary wanted to talk about, however. It was his abduction.

And Joan's.

He'd told the story several times, stressing the urgency of finding and capturing the group that had drugged and kidnapped Joan and done exactly the same thing to him. The three who had been in the crash with him were probably dead, but if they weren't, they might be able to explain a lot. At the very least, the sheriff and his deputies could put pressure on their accomplices: the woman and man at the ranch.

Watt assigned a deputy to take a formal report, though to Gary's eyes the sheriff seemed much more concerned with the mechanic and the events at the garage than anything that had happened prior to that. He could sort of understand the reasoning—the mechanic's attack on him had occurred within the sheriff's jurisdiction and quite possibly had not been an isolated incident—but the fact remained that there were three bodies in a wrecked car, either dead or injured, and they'd been involved in a crime just as serious. Which made the sheriff's lack of interest seem not just strange but inexplicable.

As the deputy typed into his computer, Gary told the story of his abduction and escape yet again.

"Do you remember anything about the car?" the deputy asked. "Make and model? Color? Did you get a license number?"

Gary shook his head, frustrated. "Like I said, they drugged me. I saw the car when I came to, after the accident, but it was dark and far away and all smashed up, and I couldn't tell what it looked like. Wait," he said. "I do remember something. The plates were white." He squinted, trying to see them in his mind. "I think they were . . . Texas plates."

"Do you recall any letters or numbers? Any at all?"

"No. But if you'll just *go out there*, you can see for yourself." The emphasis seemed lost on the deputy.

"And the men, you say, were dressed strangely."

"Yes. I told you. They looked like pioneers or something. They were wearing, like, *Little House on the Prairie* clothes."

The deputy looked at the sheriff, who had just come back into the room. Gary thought for a brief second that the two of them had heard something like this before, that his description of the men was somehow familiar to them, but he dismissed that idea when the sheriff said, "Let's go out and take a look at this, Herb. See what's what."

Four men took two vehicles. Gary fell asleep in the back of the sheriff's car but was awakened as they approached the garage. Yellow caution tape was strung around the building itself and stretched over the entrance next to the road in order to keep cars from driving in. "Where do we go from here?" Watt asked.

"Keep heading straight," Gary told him.

The car accelerated. "How far?"

"I don't know exactly. I was walking."

They sped over the flat land, and Gary was stunned at how far he'd come. Granted, it had taken him most of the night and part of the morning to get from the crash site to the garage, but he was still amazed that it took them as long as it did to get across the plain in the car. Even the hills beyond the plain went farther back than he expected.

"Are we getting close?" the sheriff asked.

"Not yet," Gary responded.

"Damn. You *did* walk a long way."

The road flattened out on higher ground, the landscape here less desertlike, and Gary was so surprised when the turnoff to the dirt road came up that by the time he shouted, "There it is!" they were past it.

The sheriff stopped, turned around, then pulled his cruiser onto the narrow trail that led into the chaparral. Behind them, the deputy's car did the same.

It had been night when he'd left the crash site, but he was pretty sure he knew where it was, and as they reached the boulder-strewn hills, Gary told the sheriff to slow down. A narrow, winding section of road above a wide and rocky gulch looked familiar, and his careful scrutiny was rewarded when he spotted strewn dirt, scraped rock and crushed bushes. "This is where we went off the road," he said.

The sheriff parked the vehicle, and they all got out. Gary led the way to the edge, passing the boulder against which he'd found himself resting. He looked down the slope. The deer was there but not the car. And definitely not the bodies.

He looked around, confused. How could it have been moved? And so quickly. The car had been totaled. And as far as he could tell, the only towing service within a fifty-mile radius was Tow-to-Tow.

It didn't make any sense.

"The car was right there," he said, pointing. "We were heading back toward the highway and we hit the deer and went off."

"Well, you say you were drugged."

"I was, but my head was clear after the accident. Everything had worn off. It was hours later. And I looked over and saw the car. Right there."

The deputy, Herb, took off his hat and ran a hand through his sweaty hair. "Your head was clear? You told me you were disoriented, that you threw up."

Yes!

"I did. There," Gary said, walking over. He pointed to a dried glop of vomit on the dirt, standing proudly next to it.

The deer was there, and the vomit, but apparently

that was not enough to corroborate his story, particularly when a wrecked car carrying the bodies of three kidnappers had mysteriously disappeared without a trace.

"We-e-l-l-l," the sheriff said, drawing out the word as he looked around at the flattened brush and disturbed ground. "It does look like *something* came through here."

But Gary knew his credibility had taken a big hit, and though he wanted to explain everything all over again to make sure they understood exactly what had happened, he figured it was smart not to push it. They would just go on to the ranch where he'd been held. Maybe the wrecked car had miraculously been moved, but the ranch would still be there.

It was. And it was just as he'd described it. That had to count for something. Still, he could tell already that Watt and his deputies were thinking that his ordeal had made him disoriented and had caused him to imagine things that weren't there and had not happened.

The woman with the limp answered the sheriff's knock with a puzzled expression and a "Yes? May I help you?"

"I'm *back*," Gary said fiercely. "And you're going to pay for what you did!"

Frowning, the woman looked to the sheriff. "What's going on? I don't understand. Who is this man?"

"You know damn well who I am," Gary told her. He turned to the sheriff. "She helped them chain me up in her back room there. She made us all food. Meat and potatoes. They all talked in some kind of code so I wouldn't know what they were saying."

"Ma'am," the sheriff said politely, "according to Mr. Russell here, he was drugged against his will and abducted from his college in California by three men. He alleges that after driving for approximately twelve hours, they arrived here at your property, where he was physically restrained for approximately eight hours, before being once again driven away to an unspecified location. Their vehicle had an accident en route, at which time Mr. Russell claims he escaped."

"I don't know what happened to him," the woman said, "but he was never here before."

"You people kidnapped my girlfriend, too! Joan Daniels! You kidnapped her and you're holding her hostage!"

The woman stood stoically.

He realized he sounded crazy, but there was nothing he could say that would make it seem even slightly more believable, and that only made him shout all the louder. He knew, intellectually, that he should be doing exactly the opposite, talking slowly and rationally, explaining things in a logical manner, but exhaustion and frustration made him even more keyed up. He pointed a finger at her, stared directly into her eyes. "You held the jar when I had to take a piss! You held my cock!"

She did not even flinch. She turned toward the sheriff. "I have never seen this person before in my life."

"She's lying! Search her house. The front room there has no rugs or couches, just a plywood floor and chairs and tables made out of branches. There're no lights, only kerosene lamps. And a prayer cabinet, filled with little scrolls. The next room has chains on the floor, shackles. That's where they kept me!"

"I'm afraid we don't have a warrant to search the premises," the sheriff told him. "And I don't think we have probable cause to obtain a warrant."

"Just walk around the side of the house! Right there! Peek through the window, and you'll see the chains they tied me up with!" He started to move in that direction, but the sheriff grabbed his arm and held him tightly.

"Are you sure Mr. Russell was never here?" Watt asked the woman.

She shook her head. "Never."

"We're sorry to have bothered you, ma'am." He turned to his men. "All right. Let's head back."

Gary wanted to object, wanted to pull out of the sheriff's grip, run to the window of the room where he'd been held and yell, "See?" But he knew that was not possible and that any attempt he made would cause problems for him, not for her, and would further erode his credibility. So he said nothing but allowed himself to be led back to the car. Just before he got in, he turned around to look at the woman in the doorway. Neither the sheriff nor any of his deputies were facing that direction, and Gary expected her to give him a small smile, an acknowledgment that she had won and he had lost, but she did not. She stared at him blankly, impassively, then turned away.

Despite his lack of money and identification, despite the wild-goose chase on which he'd led the sheriff and his deputies, the sheriff's office put him up for the night in a dusty one-story motel with no air-conditioning and an intermittently working ceiling fan—although it was made very clear that this was for one night only.

On top of his worries about Joan and everything else that had happened, he now had to find a way to get out of this town and back to California.

He opened the bag of fast food he'd been given and took out a greasy, soggy hamburger, some cold fries and a watery Coke. Turning on the room's television to alleviate the silence, he watched part of a local newscast from a city in New Mexico whose name he had never heard before. The studio backdrop behind the desk was flat and fake, and the newscasters themselves were unprofessional and sad looking. The newscast depressed him, and he flipped the channels on the TV. Only four stations came in, and he settled on one that was showing an old rerun of *Friends*. He just wanted some noise to distract himself from the dreary silence of his room.

He'd considered staying, finding some way to rent a car and returning to the ranch on his own, but he was in hostile territory and time was wasting. The smartest thing he could do was get back to the real world.

He knew where the ranch was.

He could always come back.

Besides, it was clear to him that it was just a way station, a stopover. Joan was not there, and it was even possible that the woman, the man and whoever else lived at the ranch knew nothing of her whereabouts. The important thing was finding Joan. The aiders and abettors could be dealt with later.

Not for the first time, Gary wondered why he had been taken. He could come up with no plausible scenario, and the only thing that made any sense was that the Outsiders were going to use him as leverage against Joan, were going to threaten to torture or kill him unless she did what they wanted her to do or revealed what they wanted her to reveal.

Would they continue coming after him?

He thought of Kara and Teri Lim. Of course they would.

But then, why had they only taken Joan? Why hadn't they captured or killed the rest of them at Burning Man? Had something changed in the interim?

None of it made any sense.

He called his parents after he finished eating. Gary had never before felt so alone, and more than anything else, he longed to talk to his dad.

He wanted to tell him everything.

He wanted to tell him nothing.

Confiding in his parents *would* make him feel better and would let him know that someone was behind him, but the entire situation was so outrageous that he wasn't sure his parents would believe it. And if they *did* believe it, they would make him get his ass back to Ohio faster than he could say, "Call me Ishmael."

He didn't want that.

So he ended up telling his parents that he'd been the victim of identity theft. Some hacker, he said, had deleted seemingly every trace of him from every computer database in the country. "I'm not even sure my birth certificate is still on file," he said.

"We have to report this," his dad declared. "We have to contact the credit card companies, the DMV, the credit reporting agencies. . . ."

"What I'm worried most about right now is my grant and scholarship money. According to UCLA's computers, I'm not even enrolled in school. And if I'm not enrolled . . ."

"I'll take care of that," his father said. "Don't worry about it."

Gary felt as though a smothering blanket had just been pulled from his face. He wasn't a child anymore, and his dad wasn't the omniscient savior he'd thought when he was a little boy, but it gave him a feeling of security and reassurance to know that his father would call the necessary authorities, individuals and institutions required to get his credit situation and his school funding straightened out. He doubted that Reyn had been able to make any headway on that issue, but he knew his dad would be able to get things done.

At that point, he almost told his father all. But then his mother came on the other line, having picked up enough of the conversation to have some idea of what was happening. "You need to come home. Now." There was authority in her voice but also fear, and he knew that if he said the wrong thing, that fear would tip over into panic.

"I'm okay, Mom."

"Okay? Okay? Your identity's been stolen! They're probably charging automobiles on your credit!"

"My limit's nowhere near that high."

"That's not the point! They could be ruining your credit rating forever or opening up new accounts or ... or God knows what kind of things they can do!"

"We're taking care of that," his dad said calmly.

"I think he should come home. It was a mistake to let him go out there. His girlfriend took off God knows where; his identity's been stolen. For all we know, she did it."

"Mom!"

"I'm just saying. You're two thousand miles away. Something could happen to you, and we'd never know. It's dangerous."

You have no idea, he thought.

"We have perfectly good colleges here in Ohio," she announced.

"I like California, Mom. And UCLA is one of the top schools in the country."

She appealed to his father. "Robert? I need some support here."

"He's fine. What happened is a fluke. We'll make a few calls, get everything straightened out, and things'll be back to normal. The important thing is that you keep up with your schoolwork, keep going to class."

His parents had no idea he was sitting in a dingy motel in a small town in the New Mexican desert, and he quickly wrapped things up and said good-bye, hanging up before he was tempted to tell them all. He promised to call them the following night, but asked them not to try to call him because he had to work tomorrow.

Friends had long since ended, and now a young Bob Saget was hosting a decades-old episode of *America's Funniest Home Videos*. The faded picture and the sight of the 1980s clothes and hairstyles made him feel lonely and disheartened, and he changed the channel to *Extra*, which, although equally dispiriting in content, was at least current.

He sipped the last tepid dregs of his watery Coke and called Reyn. As expected, his friend had not been able to do anything but confirm that Gary was no longer enrolled at UCLA. The attempts he'd made to find out why had all been stymied.

"Don't worry," Gary told him. "I have my dad looking into it. And I'll straighten things out once I get back. I have all my paperwork and everything else, and once I explain what happened, there should be no problem."

"When are you coming back?" Reyn asked.

"That's one of the things I'm calling you about."

There was no bus station in town, but the sheriff had pointed out to him a bench where the Greyhound bus from Clovis to Bernardo stopped each afternoon around one o'clock to pick up any passengers. Gary told this to Reyn, who promised to go online, arrange with Greyhound for a ticket, somehow get him to Albuquerque and then book him on a flight back to Los Angeles.

"I thought your card was maxed out with the water pump."

"Stacy," he said.

"No. I can't—"

"Don't sweat it. You'll pay her back, right? Besides, you need to get your ass back here ASAP."

That was true, but Gary sensed an additional urgency in his friend's voice. "There's something you're not telling me."

"You're right."

He waited, but nothing more was forthcoming. "Well?" he prompted.

"The phones might be bugged. I'd rather tell you in person."

"Then call from your cell. Or go somewhere else—"

"Not here. There."

"The phones here?" Gary said incredulously, looking around at his drab surroundings.

"Yes."

The confidence with which the word was spoken made Gary suddenly feel very vulnerable. He'd thought, after everything he'd gone through, that it would be hard to rattle him, but he suddenly realized how exposed and on edge his emotions really were. Already, his mind was racing, trying to figure out who, what, where, when and why. And how had Reyn found out about it?

They said good-bye, awkwardly, stiltedly, and Reyn took down his number and said he would call in the morning with all of the scheduling details for the return trip.

Gary hung up the phone and moved around the motel room self-consciously, wondering if he was being monitored. Reyn had hinted at no such thing, had only been wary of the phone, but Gary's mind had expanded the paranoia so much that, despite the fact that he was filthy and sweaty and hadn't bathed for two days, he was afraid to take a shower. Someone might be watching. Hell, naked photos of himself could appear on the Internet and haunt him for the rest of his life.

He used the bathroom only because he absolutely had to.

He went to sleep just after six and dreamed that he was back at UCLA. It was a Monday morning, and he was sitting in his European history classs—where Dr. Bergman was standing behind the lectern wearing brown burlap clothes and moccasins. "To become an Outsider," he was saying, "one must—"

Gary jumped up from his seat and ran across campus to Reyn's room.

Where Reyn and Stacy, wearing peasant garb, were rolling up tiny little scrolls. "You're just in time to help us," Stacy said cheerfully.

Gary took off, running through the streets of Los Angeles to the airport, noticing as he drew closer that more and more people on the streets were wearing drab, primitive, homemade clothing. He managed to avoid these people, all of whom seemed desperate to talk to him, dashed into the airport terminal, where he was the only person in sight, and was miraculously allowed to buy a ticket for a dollar and immediately board the plane. Seconds after strapping himself in, they landed in Ohio. His parents were waiting for him in the terminal—and they were wearing simple, hand-sewn clothes. "There's something we need to tell you, son . . ." his father said.

Gary turned to run away, not wanting to hear it.

And the burly, bearded mechanic was standing there with a bloody lug wrench, grinning.

In the morning, he awoke feeling stressed and still tired. His neck was stiff, and with every movement he was conscious of the fact that he could be under surveillance.

Reyn called while he was having a breakfast of tap water to confirm that bus reservations were in place.

"What about the plane?" Gary asked.

"Well . . . that turned out to be a problem. Your wallet was stolen, so you don't have any ID. I could've bought a ticket, but they wouldn't've let you on without at least two forms of ID. Same thing for the train. So you're transferring at Bernardo, transferring again at Albuquerque, but basically, you're on a bus for nineteen hours. I'll be meeting you at the downtown bus station in Los Angeles about this time tomorrow."

"I don't mean to be ungrateful," Gary said. "And thanks for everything you've done. Really. This is above and beyond. You *and* Stacy. But the truth is, I'm starving, and I have no money to buy food. I could pass out from hunger somewhere in Arizona."

Reyn laughed. "Your tickets include meals at the bus

stations in Albuquerque and Flagstaff. I know that first leg of the trip's going to be long, but when you get to Albuquerque, stuff yourself, eat as much as you want. It's all taken care of."

Gary used the pen he had gotten from the sheriff's office to write down the details of the bus transfers, including the numbers and times, on the back of the grease-stained bag that had held his dinner.

He was supposed to check in with the sheriff, and he did so after nine, explaining that he was leaving that afternoon on the bus and heading back to California. The sheriff said that they had his phone number and address on file, and that if anything came up or they needed any additional information, they would contact him. The sheriff, his deputies and his secretary seemed no different than they had yesterday, but Gary wasn't about to trust anyone in this town. He left as quickly as he could.

The morning crept by. He returned to his motel room to watch TV, but he had to be out of the room by eleven, and the bus didn't arrive until twelve forty-five. He would've liked to eat lunch—he'd had no breakfast other than water, and it was four hours to Albuquerque—but he had no money and didn't feel comfortable going back to the sheriff's office and asking if he could borrow some. So he kept moving, walking past the storefronts of Larraine's small downtown, looking suspiciously at the people who drove or walked by. He sat for a while on a bench in a small park, walked through the stacks of books in the library, but he was at the bus stop by twelve thirty. It was early, but he couldn't afford to miss the bus, and when it arrived five minutes ahead of schedule, at twelve forty, he was glad that he'd decided to wait there.

As Reyn had told him, all he had to do was tell the driver his name. He was given a ticket in a passbook envelope, and he walked to the rear section of the bus and found a seat next to no one. The seat was comfortable and soft, the back high and supportive, and he settled into it, feeling grateful. Moments later, the driver announced that they were leaving, the doors closed with a pneumatic hiss, and they were off.

Gary looked out the window as the bus passed a hair salon, a thrift store, a hardware store, a church, as the entire town of Larraine passed by. Then he closed his eyes and smiled.

He'd made it.

Fifteen

Reyn was indeed waiting for him at the bus station, as was Stacy. Brian had a class. Both Reyn and Stacy looked tired, but they were happy to see him. Reyn grinned as Gary stepped off the bus and said, "About time," while Stacy threw her arms around him and gave him a rib-crushing hug.

He hadn't thought he'd be able to do so, but he'd slept on the trip back. A lot. The stress and trauma of the past few days must have caught up with him because although he'd remained awake for the first leg of the journey, he'd slept for six straight hours between Albu-querque and Flagstaff, and then for almost the entire time between Flagstaff and Los Angeles. Although he didn't feel rested, he didn't feel tired, either, and the first thing he asked was whether there'd been any news about Joan. He didn't expect any, but was still filled with a deep and painful sense of disappointment when he was told that Reyn had checked this morning and the police had nothing to report.

"So why were you afraid to talk on the phone?" Gary asked.

"Your buddy, Sheriff Watt."

Reyn explained that Brian had discovered that the sheriff's brother had been stalking his ex-wife, who claimed they were both "outsiders."

Gary thought about how little interest the sheriff had shown in his kidnapping, and the way he had made no effort to confront the woman at the ranch house. It made sense.

"What I want to know is why he didn't do anything." Reyn said. "Why didn't he turn you back in? Why didn't you have some sort of accident?"

"Reyn!" Stacy said.

"They're legitimate questions."

Gary thought about it. "He wasn't the only person I talked to. He wasn't even the first person I talked to. I told my story to the secretary and a deputy before I even got a chance to tell the sheriff. Maybe there were too many people around."

"He could have arranged something," Reyn said. "He got his brother off."

"He still could. He has my name, address, phone number. I had to give him all of my personal information for his report."

"Anyway, that's why I didn't want to say anything on the phone. In case it put you in danger. The sheriff found that motel room for you; maybe he had it bugged."

Gary was trying to figure out what connection a small-town sheriff could have with an entity powerful and sophisticated enough to delete social networking pages and enrollment records at UCLA.

They had left the bus terminal and were walking through the parking lot toward Reyn's car.

"The police," Stacy prodded.

"Oh, yeah," Reyn said. "Williams wants to see you. I filed a missing persons report. Sort of. I mean, it hadn't been forty-eight hours yet, so it couldn't be official. And I had to talk to that asshole Tucker first, who tried to make out like you'd pulled a disappearing act to take the heat off all the crimes you've committed." He smiled. "But Williams took it seriously and promised to look for you. I think he was legit. I told him this morning that you were on your way back, and he wanted you to come in."

Gary thought for a moment. "I'll call him, tell him what happened, let him get in touch with old Sheriff Watt if he wants more details."

"Aren't you going to tell him about the sheriff?" Stacy asked. "I know it's probably out of his jurisdiction, but there must be some mechanism where one law enforcement agency can request the investigation of another."

Gary shook his head. "Williams is all right, but he's barely on board as it is. I'm not sure he even totally believes us about Joan. Getting him to open an investigation of a small-town sheriff in New Mexico because the sheriff's brother's ex-wife mentioned the word 'outsiders' in a police report you looked up on the Internet seems a little far-fetched." He took a deep breath. "Besides, the cops haven't found Joan, they didn't find me, and I'm thinking it's time we went another way."

Reyn frowned. "What's that supposed to mean?"

"I'm not sure yet."

"The police *are* working on it."

"Let them keep working on it," Gary said. "But I'm going to work on it, too."

They reached Reyn's car, and before getting in, Gary stood there for a moment, looking around. There was a wide, crowded street in front of the terminal, and buildings crammed close together in both directions. Above the buildings loomed the Hollywood Hills and, beyond, outlined in the white haze of smog, the San Gabriel Mountains. The air smelled of ethnic food and exhaust fumes, and he realized with a sharpness he had never experienced before that this was where he wanted to live, that even after he graduated from college, he intended to make Los Angeles his home.

With Joan.

Yes, Joan had to be a part of it, too, and as he got into
the car he was filled with a renewed sense of urgency.
The more time passed, the less imperative it would be
for the police to try to find her. Other cases would come
up, and simple human nature dictated that the longer
she remained missing, the less likely it was that they'd
believe she could be found. Even his friends would
probably lose focus. He couldn't allow that to happen.

"What about Kara?" Gary asked as Reyn started the
engine. "Any news?"

"None that they're sharing."

Brian called while they were en route, and Stacy took
the phone from Reyn's pocket to answer. She told him
that, yes, Gary was safely back; then she handed the
phone to Gary so he could describe his ordeal himself.

"Fuck," Brian said when he was finished.

"Yeah."

"It's worse than Reyn said."

"I'm glad to be back," Gary admitted.

"Where are you going now?"

"The dorm. My room."

"I'll meet you there."

Brian was sitting on a bench in front of the building
when they walked up, and the four of them went into the
dorm together. As always, the halls were crowded with
talking, laughing, jostling students, and Gary marveled
at the fact that those three Outsiders had been able to
just walk in, break into his room and kidnap him. Although, amid such chaos, perhaps it shouldn't have been
so surprising.

They reached the third floor.

The door to his room was closed but unlocked, and
Gary slowly pushed it open, taking a quick step back,
just in case. The room was empty. He quickly checked
his belongings, but as far as he could tell, nothing had
been stolen, nothing had been moved. His heart was

pounding as he stared at the spot where the two men had grabbed and held him while the third punched him in the stomach. They had his keys, he thought. And whether those keys were buried along with their dead bodies somewhere near the ranch in New Mexico, or whether copies had been made and distributed to cells of Outsiders all over the United States, Gary knew that he would never again feel safe in this room. He had to find another place to live and sleep. Starting tonight.

"What are you going to do for money?" Brian asked. "I assume your ATM card was in your wallet, along with all of your cash. And I doubt that you can access your bank account without ID—assuming that they haven't cleaned out your account already."

He hadn't thought of that.

"I can loan you a few bucks until your next pay-check," Brian said.

Reyn nodded. "Me, too."

"I'm not sure there's going to be a next paycheck. It's a work-study job. If they've fucked up my school records, they've probably screwed that up for me, too."

"Could you have your parents wire you some money?" Stacy asked. "I'm not exactly sure how that works, but I think it's instantaneous."

"Yeah," Gary said, nodding. "I'll talk to them."

Both of his neighbors, Matt and Greg, suddenly poked their heads inside the room. "Dude!" Greg said. "You're back! People've been lookin' for you."

"Yeah," Matt said. "And one of them was that guy." He pointed to Reyn.

Reyn rolled his eyes. "Thanks," he said. "You can leave now."

"Wait a minute." Gary walked up to Matt. "Did you say *one* of them?"

"Yeah. The other guys were these eco-freaks with, like, hemp clothes and shit."

Gary and Reyn exchanged a glance. "And when," Gary asked, "did these guys come by?"

"This morning. They were, like, skulking around, trying to be all inconspicuous—"

"Which was pretty hard in those clothes," Greg interrupted.

"Yeah. But one of them opened your door, and then he saw us looking at him and pretended he was just passing by, and then he was gone."

Greg nodded in agreement. "We wouldn't've even noticed, but that dude said you were gone"—he pointed to Reyn again—"and so we were kind of watching your place for you. You know, like neighbors do."

"How many of them were there?" Gary asked.

"Two. One of them was a short dude, in his thirties probably. The other one was younger, but there was something wrong with him. He had, like—"

"Ape arms," Matt interjected.

"Ape arms. Exactly. He had, like, these big, long arms that hung way down. Like a monkey's."

"Did they say anything? Did you hear them talk? Did you notice where they went?"

Both Matt and Greg shook their heads. "No. Why? Who were they?"

"No one," Gary said. "Thanks, guys. I appreciate it."

His neighbors looked confused, but they took the hint. "Later," Matt said, and the two of them headed back to their own room.

Gary closed the door behind them, turned around, and his eye was caught by the red blinking light of the answering machine on his desk. He walked over and pressed the PLAY button. His pulse was racing.

It could be Joan.

Gary! I'm—

But it wasn't. The message was from his father, who asked him to call back right away. Gary did, and his dad answered immediately, as though he'd been waiting by the phone.

"Good news," he told Gary. "I explained the situation to both the grant administrators and the people in charge of your scholarship, and they all agreed that these are extraordinary circumstances. So, basically, everything's been put on hold until you're once again officially enrolled. But the money's still yours. So, like I said, talk to your teachers, keep attending your classes, and keep up with the assignments so that once the paperwork's been sorted out, you're already in place."

"Did you call UCLA?"

"That's a slightly bigger hurdle. Your school's got quite a bureaucracy there, and there are some forms you have to fill out, and a couple of things you have to provide, including a copy of a police report and credit statement, before you can be reinstated. That's why I say you need to keep up with your classwork, because this may take a few weeks."

"I have another problem, Dad." Gary felt embarrassed. "I have no money. All my money and identification was in my wallet—"

"You didn't tell me you lost your wallet."

Gary was caught short. "Uh, yeah," he said nervously. "I mean, that's how—"

"You said it was some hacker."

"It was. But he had my wallet. That's how he knew who I was."

His father's voice was stern and disapproving. "How did you lose it?"

"I don't know!"

"You don't know?"

Gary thought fast. "I was at the gym, and someone broke into my locker and took it."

"So you *do* know."

"Yeah."

"I wasn't aware that you belonged to a gym."

"I don't. It's for a PE class."

"I don't remember seeing a PE class on your schedule."

Gary was sweating. He didn't like lying to his father, he wasn't good at it, and his dad could ferret out falsehoods from a mile away. "Look, I was auditing a swimming class so I could swim. It's been hot out here. I left my clothes in a locker, and someone got my wallet. Now he's used that information to steal my identity and ruin my life. Jesus. I think you're getting a little sidetracked here. The point is: I have no money, and I can't draw any out of my account because I have no ID."

His dad was silent for a moment. "Well, you should be able to get money out of your account with your Social Security number and your mother's maiden name. That's usually how it works. They wouldn't let you?"

Now he felt even more embarrassed. "I don't know. I didn't try. I just assumed—"

"Never assume," his dad said.

"Okay."

"I guess that means you didn't call the bank, close your account and open a new one."

"No," he said. "But I will."

"You did call your credit card company, like I told you, and had them close your account, right?"

"Yes," he lied.

"And the DMV?"

"Yeah."

"Well, call your bank and get things straightened out. If there's a problem, let me know. In an emergency, I can contact Western Union and wire you some money." He sighed. "I'm just glad your mother's not here right now. If she heard this, she'd have you on the first plane back."

"I know, Dad."

"I'm not so sure *I* trust you out there on your own."

"I'll be okay."

"Well, sometimes you just have to learn the hard way. Now I want you to call the bank. . . ."

There was another five minutes of lecturing; then Gary thanked his dad again and hung up.

"Wow," Brian said. "What was that about?"

"It's complicated. I need my dad's help, but I don't want to tell him what's really going on, so I have to kind of . . . finesse the truth." He told his friends what his father had said.

"You know," Brian mused, "this could work to your advantage. You could just take the semester off. It's not your fault. It's because of a crime committed against you. You'd probably have no problem. Although it would take an extra semester to graduate."

Gary had been thinking along the same lines. He was already behind in every class, and he had no plans to resume his normal life until Joan was back here safe and sound. Taking the semester off would ensure that his personal problems didn't completely derail his academic career.

But he could think about that later. His dad was right. He needed to get a new bank account, credit card and driver's license. He needed to make sure that no damage was done to his credit and that no exorbitant bills were racked up under his name.

Reyn, Stacy and Brian hovered around Gary's computer while he called his bank, credit card company and the Department of Motor Vehicles. Both his checking and savings accounts were intact, and he was given a new account number with a secret password. His old Visa card was voided, and a report was automatically filed with all of the credit monitoring agencies, alerting them to the fact that he'd been the victim of identity theft. He was told that a new credit card would be sent out to him immediately. The DMV informed him that he would have to come in to one of their offices, get his photo taken and fill out the form for a new driver's license, at which time he would be issued a temporary license and ID card.

Gary hung up the phone. "What are you guys doing?" he asked, walking over to where the other three were clustered around his computer.

Brian looked up from the monitor. "Trying to find out what 'Outsiders' are."

"Any luck?"

"Sure. There's a rock band called the Outsiders, a young adult novel by S. E. Hinton, a line of snowboards . . ."

"Any luck?" he repeated.

Reyn stood straight, shaking his head. "No."

"Whoever they are," Stacy said, "they're flying well below the radar."

"I'm thinking they're based in Texas," Gary said. "I'm pretty sure the car I was in had Texas plates, and we were already in New Mexico and still heading east."

"Does that help us?" Stacy asked.

"It could narrow the search."

It narrowed the search, but it didn't help, and when Gary asked whether someone could give him a ride to the nearest DMV office, Brian shut off the computer.

"I also need a place to stay," Gary said. He gestured around the room. "I'm not staying here. And I can't transfer to another room because once they look me up, they'll find out that I'm not officially enrolled, and then they'll kick me out completely."

"I'd let you crash at my place," Brian said, "but I don't think Dror would be too thrilled."

Gary thought about Brian's roommate. *He* wouldn't be too thrilled staying with Dror, either.

"You can stay with us," Stacy said.

He looked at Reyn. "Us?"

"She's staying in my room. It's too dangerous for her to be on her own."

Gary shook his head. "No, thank you."

"We'll keep it quiet," Reyn promised.

Stacy hit his shoulder. "Bring a sleeping bag. You can sleep on the floor." She shot Reyn a look. "And there's not going to be anything to *keep* quiet."

Gary nodded his thanks. "Okay." He tried to think of what he needed to bring with him besides a sleeping bag. Comb and toothbrush, for sure. A change of clothes.

"It *is* dangerous," Brian noted. "I feel like I'm taking my life in my hands every time I walk out the door. I keep expecting to be jumped and taken prisoner."

"I know," Stacy said. "Me, too."

Reyn looked over at Gary. "You must be *really* paranoid."

"Yeah," he admitted. "Kind of. But I think it's time for us to stop running. We need to take the initiative."

"What does that mean?" Stacy asked. "Hiring body-guards?"

"Yeah," Reyn said. "What *can* we do besides wait for them to strike again?"

Gary faced them. "We can set a trap."

He'd had a lot of time to think about this while he was on the bus.

The men who'd captured him might have looked like rubes, but either they or the people to whom they answered had to have been monitoring his phone calls, his computer use or both. They'd planned the abduction too perfectly. They had to have had access to inside information.

Joan.

Joan could have told them.

No, she wouldn't have, and although he believed that completely, he was still very aware of how little he knew about her. He did know her on the deepest level possible, knew *who* she really was, but the peripherals were obscure, and his knowledge of the details of her life remained frustratingly vague.

Four and a half weeks.

They'd gone out for only four and a half weeks.

It seemed much longer, and the way he felt about her, it was as if they'd been together forever. But he could count their weekends together on one hand, and the actual amount of time they'd spent with each other was in reality very brief.

He recalled his favorite date with her, a trip they'd taken to Disneyland. The amusement park had been crowded, and they'd arrived too late to get on any of the big rides without waiting in a massive line. But she was like a little girl, and though they ended up going on rides like Snow White and Pinocchio, the Enchanted Tiki Room and Casey Jr. Circus Train, she was as delighted as a kid at Christmas. Her enthusiasm was catching, and he was just as excited as she was. They ended up staying at the amusement park until midnight, watching the fireworks and finally going on the major attractions like Space Mountain and Pirates of the Caribbean late in the evening after the families with children had started to go home.

They'd both been bone tired as they took a tram back to the parking structure, and Joan actually fell asleep on the ride over. It was late, and he didn't feel like driving back to UCLA, so he'd found a nearby motel with a red Vacancy sign, and they'd spent the night in Anaheim, with a view of Disneyland through the window of their room.

The next morning, he'd gone to the lobby and brought back a continental breakfast, and they had stayed in bed until it was time to check out.

Gary felt himself tearing up. She seemed at once so

close and yet so far—*weren't those the lyrics of an old song?*—and he was suddenly filled with despair, certain that he would never see her again.

Anger kept him going. He had led everyone outside, and they were now walking slowly together across the campus. He hadn't wanted to remain in his room in case it was bugged, hadn't felt comfortable staying in *any* enclosed space, and even now his eyes were on the lookout for anyone dressed oddly or paying too close attention to their movements.

"They deleted my information, which means they had to access it, which means they know my class schedule. They know your names and faces from the photos on Joan's Facebook and MySpace pages, from mine, too, and they've probably gone to your own pages and looked up even more about you." Gary paused to let this sink in. "But they don't know that we know, and we can use that against them."

"How?" Reyn asked.

Brian was already one step ahead. "We construct a fake schedule for Gary or set up a fake meeting, something that will guarantee he'll be alone at a specific time in a specific place. We talk about it on our phones, e-mail each other about it, and we make it so irresistible to them that they can't not go."

Gary nodded. "Then when they show up, we grab them."

"You're the bait?" Stacy said, shaking her head. "I don't like it."

"You guys'll be there. I won't really be alone."

"She's right. What if there's a whole passel of 'em?" Brian asked.

Stacy raised an eyebrow. " '*Passel?*' "

"It seems like an appropriate word under the circumstances."

"We'll need help," Gary said.

"The police?" Stacy suggested.

Brian snorted. "Yeah. They've been such a great help so far."

"I know it's kind of out-of-the-box thinking," she said sarcastically, "but since law enforcement agents deal with criminals on a daily basis . . ." She held up her hands. "I don't know. It just seems like that *might* be a good choice."

"I told Dror," Brian said, ignoring her, "but I'm not sure he believed all of it. Or any of it. He's a good dude, though. He'll be there if we need it."

"We need it."

"The film society," Reyn suggested. "I can get them. Or at least some of them. Ten to twelve people, probably."

"No offense," Brian said. "But they're not exactly the football team. I doubt they'd be much help."

"The more bodies, the better," Gary told him. "Although we may not even need them at all. According to Greg and Matt, two Outsiders were sent to look for me. That's probably what we'll be dealing with. But there's an intimidation factor with ten or twelve people that you just don't have with four." He nodded slowly, thinking, and as he looked at his friends he allowed himself a small smile. "You know," he said, "this just might work."

Afraid to use e-mail and not wanting to say too much over the phone, Reyn had assembled as many members of the film society as he could corral in so short a time by pretending as though this was the first meeting of the semester. They met where they usually did, in a screening room in the Film Studies department, and Gary was happy to see that of the students who'd shown, nearly all of them seemed able-bodied enough to help. Dror was there, too, Brian's roommate, and Dror was more than able-bodied. A weight lifter, he looked as though he could take on five Outsiders just on his own.

Although Gary didn't exactly get along with him, he was very glad that Dror had come along.

He looked out over the sparse audience. Over the past few hours, he and Reyn had discussed in detail how to broach the subject. Brian was right; this wasn't the football team. The members of the film society were more watchers than doers, and there was no reason to believe that they were willing to participate in any sort of physical activity—particularly one that involved genuine risk. Gary had even suggested that they pretend they were making a movie, a *Blair Witch*–type improvisational film, and *trick* students into going along with their plan.

But the film club was Reyn's baby, he was its president, and though he understood the importance of what they were doing, he was not willing to get society members involved without their consent. So he came up with the idea of honestly explaining the situation and *comparing* it to a similar predicament in a film. Gary, Reyn and Stacy were all fairly well versed in cinematic history, but they still had a difficult time coming up with an appropriate parallel. As Reyn said, they not only had to engage the students on a real, personal level, but they needed to pick a film that would speak to them on a snobbish intellectual basis. They needed something from a director with enough cachet to lure them into action.

They'd finally settled on calling Gary's dilemma "Hitchcockian."

"You're Cary Grant in *North by Northwest*," Reyn enthused. "You're Robert Cummings in *Saboteur*, wanted by the criminals and the police, with nowhere to turn."

"And there's a woman in jeopardy," Stacy said, putting a hand on Gary's arm to soften the words.

"Okay," Gary had agreed.

Now the three of them stood, along with Brian, at the head of this warm, windowless room, turning the real events of his life over the past week and a half into a suspenseful narrative for an audience of movie fans, trivializing the life-and-death stakes of Joan's situation in an effort to convince people who didn't necessarily know or care about her into helping them capture an Outsider.

A couple of them *did* know her, and Gary could see on their faces expressions of shock and horror, along with the determination to do all they could to help. But among the others there were questions. One young woman wearing thick black-framed glasses and a scowl said, "You brought us here under false pretenses. This has nothing whatsoever to do with our mission or with film. I was under the impression we were going to be planning our series for this semester."

"Fuck off," Brian told her.

Reyn raised a hand to calm them both down. "Kate," he said gently. "I know this is a little unorthodox, and you're right—it's not something that directly concerns the film society. But it is an emergency, I'm involved with it, and of course when I needed help, the first people I thought of were all of you." He gestured toward the group before focusing again on her. "Although I completely understand if you don't want to get involved."

She sat down without offering a response, but she did not walk out and leave.

"It sounds like it's going to be dangerous," worried Max Lezama. Gary knew him slightly. He had the physique of a young Don Knotts and some of the same skittish mannerisms.

"I don't think so," Gary said. "Yes, we are going to try and detain one of them for questioning"—he realized that he sounded like a cop—"but that would not be your job. We just need you to stand around and look threatening, maybe block their escape route or kind of *herd* them in the right direction so we can apprehend them."

Max nodded his understanding.

"What if it doesn't work?" another student wondered.

"Why don't you just call the police?" Kate wanted to know. She was still scowling. Gary thought it was probably her natural expression.

"I hate that chick," Brian whispered next to him.

"If it doesn't work ... well, we'll have to come up with something else," Reyn said. "As for why we don't call the police, I think we've already explained that." He raised his hands for silence. "I think you all know what we need. There's no reason to keep debating it. Those who want to help, come up here and talk to Gary. He'll fill you in on the details. The rest of you? I'll see you next week for our first regular meeting." He looked at Kate. "We *will* be planning our fall film series."

Kate picked up her books and left. Max and another student, as overweight as Max was underweight, guiltily sneaked out together, but the eight students who remained were ready and willing to help.

"What do you need us to do?" asked Ed Eisenberg, a tall, athletic guy who'd joined the film society last semester and had an aesthete's taste for Antonioni's ennui and a lowbrow love of American action flicks.

"I don't think the Outsiders will do anything in public," Gary said. "Not after everything that's happened. And I doubt they'll strike unless they're sure it will be successful. So we have to give them the illusion of isolation and make them think I am completely vulnerable. I'm thinking of that memorial path, the one that goes through those pine trees and is nowhere near any buildings." He looked from Reyn to Stacy to Brian. "I'm going to e-mail each of you and tell you how much I need solitude after my ordeal. I'll also call each of you during the afternoon, on cell phones and landlines, and tell you how much I like that path and how I like to walk there at night."

"Do you really think they'll show up?" Stacy asked.

Gary shrugged. "Who knows? I hope so. If they really want to get to me, this would be the perfect opportunity."

"There's one thing I don't get," Brian said. "Sheriff Watt. If he's in on this, why did he let you go? Why didn't he keep you there and hand you over to those Outsiders instead of sending you back here so they can go through that whole kidnapping thing again?"

"I have no idea," Gary said.

"It's a mystery," Reyn conceded.

"Maybe we'll find out when we interrogate those guys." Gary turned to the film society students. "What we need to do now is go out to that path and figure out where everyone's going to hide and what their role is going to be. We need to have at least one person staked out there all day, in case *they* come to check the place out themselves. We don't want them beating us to the punch. Is everybody free right now?"

There were nods all around.

"Then let's do it."

As a group, the twelve of them passed through the center of UCLA, heading toward the hilly north end of campus. Gary kept his eyes peeled as they walked, checking sidewalks and stairways, buildings and open areas for anyone wearing primitive, hand-sewn farming clothes. He saw no one suspicious, though he hadn't expected to, and that was no surprise. What was a surprise was how perfect the memorial path turned out to be for their purposes. He'd remembered it from a walking tour of the campus he'd taken as part of freshman orientation two years ago, but he hadn't been there since, and while his perception of the place was that it was remote-seeming and removed from the main body of the campus with its crowded walkways and buildings, he hadn't expected it to so closely fit their needs. Not only was the narrow, winding path lined with trees, but there were bushes and boulders, a carefully constructed imitation of wild nature that offered plenty of hiding spots and multiple vantage points.

And very few lights along the way.

They walked slowly up the wooded trail, scouting locations along its half-mile length. Gary made it clear that he wanted every segment of the path covered, though he let each individual choose a hiding spot that was most comfortable for him or her. Because there were only twelve of them, and because there were parts of the path so curvy that adjacent segments could not be seen ten feet away from each other, it was decided that the long, straight sections at the beginning and end of the trail need not be covered. The entrance was close to the university's physical plant, which meant that there would probably be other people nearby, and the walkway ended at a parking lot, which would also be pretty public.

It was the middle section they had to worry about, and Gary was very impressed by how quickly everyone found a hiding place. They all turned their cell phones on, making sure to hide the lights, which at night would be very visible, and then they practiced. Several times. Gary walked back and forth along the entire length of the memorial path, clapping his hands at random locations to indicate that an Outsider had accosted him. Each time, someone was there to back him up immediately, and seconds later a horde of people were running up the walkway from both directions to rescue him. It seemed an eminently workable, nearly foolproof plan, and after ten tries, they quit, satisfied.

Gary wanted someone on watch, and Ed took the first shift. He would walk casually back and forth between the parking lot and the physical plant, keeping his eyes open for anyone resembling the description of an

Outsider with which he'd been provided. An hour later, Brian would take over, and someone would keep up the patrol until dark, at which time all of them would take their places.

Thanking everyone profusely, Gary left, taking Reyn and Stacy with him to his dorm room to retrieve a few items.

He thought about Joan. He recalled what it had felt like at Burning Man when he had started to go under, and he tried to remember the last words he'd spoken to her before her abduction. But he couldn't think of what they might have been. In his mind he saw very vividly the temporary structures surrounding their makeshift camp, the Joe Strummer cube and the buildings made of recycled trash. He recalled the hallucination that had not seemed like a hallucination, the rag doll Joan, his slaughtered friends, and the two banshee shapes that had picked up the rag doll and carried it off as, in the foggy background, the Burning Man walked. But he couldn't remember what he'd said to Joan.

He had never felt farther away from her than he did at this moment.

"Do you really think this will work?" Stacy asked.

He looked over at her and hoped he sounded more confident than he felt. "I think so," he said. "I hope so."

Sixteen

Gary walked alone down the tree-lined memorial path, and though he knew Reyn, Brian, Stacy and the others were nearby, watching, waiting, ready to leap out should any of the Outsiders put in an appearance, he still felt nervous.

It was the second night he'd been doing this, and already he was inclined to give it up, to drive nonstop back to the ranch outside Larraine and torture that limping bitch until she told him where Joan was being held or gave him the name of someone who could. He felt helpless, powerless, and everything he did brought home to him the fact that Joan was being held captive. When he slept last night on Reyn's floor in his sleeping bag in front of the television, he saw Joan lying alone on some concrete floor in the darkness of an abandoned building. When he ate breakfast and lunch, he imagined her gnawing on a hard crust of moldy bread. Even when he went to the bathroom, he pictured her squatting over some filthy, smelly bucket.

He thought about his own time in the ranch house, drugged and shackled to the floor, and knew that she was putting up with far worse.

And had been doing so for more than a week.

The very idea made him frustrated, furious, committed to doing anything it took to get her back.

A cold breeze brushed his cheek.

Yet he was still frightened.

There was a bone-crackle rattling off to his left, and his heart lurched in his chest, though he forced himself to keep walking and pretend he hadn't heard. Nothing sprang out at him, and he hazarded a casual glance in that direction, seeing nothing in the darkness until the sound came again and he saw, by the diffused illumination of a far-off streetlight, a sparrow hopping through a small pile of dead leaves.

Maybe it would have been better if he'd assigned someone else to do this. Brian, perhaps. He himself had been through too much recently, and his nerves were fried. He'd never been a nervous person, but he was now, and he could not be entirely sure that when crunch time came he wouldn't panic.

But, no. As scared as he might be, he had to see this through. Joan was *his* girlfriend, this was *his* responsibility, and deep down he not only *needed* to do this; he *wanted* to do it.

Gary kept walking.

He'd finally gone to the police station this morning to talk to Williams. Despite his skepticism, he'd wanted, he'd hoped, that the detective might have turned up something. But the police still hadn't looked in on Joan's parents' house, and no effort had been made to pressure Sheriff Watt about the ranch where Gary had been held. Williams assured him that they had some "good leads" concerning Kara's disappearance, but he didn't believe that, and he'd left the police station feeling more discouraged than he had when he'd walked in.

Gary reached the slow curve in the center of the path where he knew Reyn and Stacy were hidden behind a copse of bushes. For the millionth time, he went over the plan in his mind, looking for loopholes, but once again he couldn't find any. The plan was a good one. Unfortunately, it only encompassed *capturing* the Outsiders. He and his friends had not thought much beyond that point, and though he intended to question the person or persons they caught, he did not know what they would do after that. Turn their captives over to the police? Let them go? Neither of those options seemed right, but Gary refused to think about what that meant.

From the parking lot ahead, he heard the sound of a car starting. He still couldn't see the parking lot, but the volume and clarity of the sound meant that he was close, and he turned around to start his trek back.

And there they were.

There were two of them, and Gary's heart was pounding so hard it actually *hurt*. One of them was holding something in his hand. From this distance, it looked like a length of cloth, and Gary immediately recalled the terrible dirt-root taste of the gag that had been used to drug him.

Ape arms.

The other man had extremely long arms, disturbingly long arms—and Gary knew that these were the two who had come to his room looking for him. He had a sudden flashback to the photo of Joan's mom with her too-long legs and her oddly formed bones.

The men moved toward him.

Why weren't they stopped before they got this far? he wondered. *Why didn't anyone give the signal to alert the others?*

His first terrifying thought was that his sentries had been killed, that Outsiders had murdered one or more of the film society students—

or Reyn or Stacy or Brian

—but as soon as he called out, "Here!" the darkness was filled with the shouts and cries of his cohorts. The noise was intended to confuse and frighten, and it seemed to do its job. The two Outsiders remained unmoving, not advancing, not retreating, but staying in place and looking frantically around as though certain they were about to be attacked but unsure from which direction the attack would come.

Dror arrived first, and not only was he big and fast, but he carried a weapon, a baseball bat that he swung with abandon. Most of the students who came whooping down the path and from behind the trees were carrying makeshift weapons of some sort, nearly all of them bats or knives, and within moments they had surrounded the two Outsiders, who looked lost and frightened.

Gary stepped forward, approaching the two men. They seemed a lot less threatening, a lot less intimidating, encircled by the group of armed students. This was the allure of the gang, of the mob, and it was both dangerous and intoxicating.

The crowd parted before him.

Seconds before, he'd thought that the shabbily dressed men seemed pathetic and sad. But this close, they seemed creepy. He could see that there was something wrong with each of them: Ape Arms' long limbs were genuinely freakish, a physical deformity, and the shorter man's face bore a blank, dull expression that made him appear not quite human. Both of them had odd, identical hairstyles.

Gary was very glad he was not alone.

The shorter one was indeed holding a gag, undoubtedly laced with whatever pacifying drug had been administered to him before, and Gary pointed to the cloth. "Drop it," he ordered.

The man looked at his partner, who said something in that alien language.

The blank-faced man held on to the gag.

Without prompting, Dror stepped forward and quickly yanked the cloth out of the man's hand. The man tried to strike back, but Dror pushed him into his friend and wielded the bat threateningly.

"Be careful," Gary said. "That gag's laced with a drug. It's the same kind they used on me before. Don't touch your face or anyone else," he told Dror. "Make sure you wash your hands before you do."

Grimacing, Dror dropped the cloth on the ground, wiping his hands on his pants.

Gary turned back to the two Outsiders. "Why are you here?" he asked, moving closer. He had no weapon in his hand, but there was a pocketknife in his front pocket, and he took it out, opening it. "And where is Joan Daniels? What have you done with her?"

The short one started to say something, but Ape Arms cut him off, barking an order in that alien language.

"What do you Outsiders want?" Gary demanded.

"Outsider? I'm not an Outsider!" the short one cried. His voice was high-pitched and strange. "*You're* the Outsiders! All of *you*!"

That didn't make any sense, and Gary glanced quizzically at Reyn, who shot him a confused look in return. Under the circumstances, it was not surprising to hear their captives lie. Indeed, it was to be expected. But the vehemence of the response held the ring of truth, and the deep anguish on the man's heretofore dull and inexpressive face made Gary think that his protestation was real. The last thing this man wanted was to be confused with an Outsider.

But if he wasn't an Outsider, who was he?

And what *were* the Outsiders?

The man started crying.

"You won't get anything out of him," Ape Arms said, speaking finally in English and tapping his forehead. "He's simple."

Gary shifted his focus and peered into the long-armed

man's face. The man stared back at him defiantly, and the only thing Gary could think of was the very real possibility that the eyes he was looking into right now had watched Joan as she was being tortured. He was filled with a rage unlike anything he had ever experienced, a fury so white-hot and deep that at that moment he could have murdered this man and felt no qualms.

Gary's voice when it came out was frighteningly flat and low. "I'm going to ask you some questions," he said. "And you are going to answer them. If you do not, I will use this knife to sever your windpipe. After you are dead, I will torture your friend until he talks."

The man sensed the truth behind the words. He tried to look brave, but Gary could tell that he was scared.

Good.

Gary leaned forward. "Now, who are you?" he demanded. "Where do you come from? And what do you want with us?"

Part II

Seventeen

Joan awoke back at the Home.

For several seconds, she thought it was just another nightmare, that she was dreaming it, but there was a tactility to her surroundings that was never present in her dreams, and when she saw that the old photo of Father that had graced each of the bedrooms had been replaced by a newer photo showing him with a thick white beard, she knew she was really here. She sat up slowly, feeling her brain pressing outward against the sides of her skull. Her muscles ached, as though she'd been simultaneously lifting weights and running a marathon.

Where was Gary? she wondered. And Reyn and Stacy? And Brian?

Dead.

No. Father wouldn't allow that.

Then where were they?

Despite the pain in her head, she stood. Aside from the bed, the room had very few furnishings: a hard-backed chair, a small eating table, a freestanding lamp. They were standard issue, and she remembered them from her childhood, but she had lived too long away, was now used to comfort, and her surroundings seemed not just spartan but prisonlike. There was no radio, no television, no computer, no bookshelf. Light came from a fluorescent square in the ceiling. Walking over to the closed curtains, she pulled them open. As she'd expected, as she'd known, there was no window behind the drapes, only a painted scene of green rolling hills, a powder blue sky and a smiling yellow sun.

It seemed like only moments before that she and Gary had been with their friends at Burning Man, sitting around their camp, watching the Man burn and then fall. But how long ago had it really been? Hours? Days?

She had to go to the bathroom, so she tried to open the room's lone door, but it was locked. She began pounding on it. "Let me out!" she called. "Someone let me out!" There was no answer, no response. She called out again, pressed her ear to the door and listened, but heard nothing. She glanced around.

In the far corner of the room was a metal bedpan.

She remembered this, too.

No, she thought. *I can't. I won't.*

But she could. And did.

The girl who brought her food sometime later was one of the Children. Joan did not know her, but her legs and arms were long and bony, and there was a slackness to her features that Joan recognized from some of the others. The girl carried in not a tray but a canvas bag, from which she withdrew a chicken sandwich wrapped in a dirty piece of reused aluminum foil, a carrot, an apple, and a glass bottle filled with apple juice so thick it was nearly opaque. The girl was accompanied by an older man who stood just inside the doorway and was obviously there to thwart any type of escape attempt. Both were dressed in clothing they had made themselves, the type of simple garments Joan recalled from her childhood. Just looking at it made her flesh crawl, and she knew that soon she would be expected to discard her jeans and shirt and sew herself some new clothes.

More than anything, she wanted to escape, wanted to run past the girl and the man and out the door. But she would not get far in the shape she was in. She would be captured and then she would be punished. Joan knew how things worked in the Home. Her best and only hope right now was to garner trust before she attempted to get away or contact anyone. The slight advantage granted to her by not being under constant suspicion could mean the difference between success and failure.

The girl said nothing, not even when Joan thanked her, and Joan wondered if this was one of the Children who couldn't speak. She tried to catch the eye of the man at the door, smiling at him in what she hoped was an open, affable manner, but he remained completely stoic. Seconds after the girl finished placing the food on the small table, the two of them left. Joan heard the click of the door's lock, loud in the stillness.

She was starving. And though she wanted to remain defiant and hated the idea of acquiescing in any way, she needed food, needed sustenance, and she pulled the chair next to the small table and began eating greedily. The food was edible but not very tasty, and the flavor of the apple juice was so odd that she spit back her first swallow and did not take another, in case it was drugged. She considered pounding on the door and letting whoever was out there know that she was finished, but she needed to maintain the illusion of compliance and instead left the remains of her meal on the table.

Now that she'd eaten, it seemed easier to think, though she still had a pounding headache. She wished she could believe that she had been spotted at Burning Man by someone from the Home, but the likelihood of that was nil. No one from the Home would ever attend a festival like Burning Man. No, she had been followed there and then taken, though for how long she'd been under surveillance she could not even guess.

Joan shivered, hugging herself. Had her parents been found, too?

She wondered if they had been captured.

Or if . . .

She started to cry, but quickly stopped herself, wiping away tears before they even spilled from her eyes. There was no time for that now. She needed to keep her wits about her if she ever hoped to get out of here.

Joan glanced up at the framed photo on the wall. Once again, she told herself that Father would not allow anyone to kill Gary and her friends. But this older Father looked different from the man she had known. Not harder—he had always been hard—but crueler, somehow. She could imagine him doing things not merely because they needed to be done but because he wanted to do them. That frightened her.

Could her friends be dead?

No. They might have been drugged, as she had been, temporarily taken out of commission so that she could be abducted without opposition, but they would not have been permanently harmed, and she took solace in the fact that they were out and free and knew something had happened to her. Gary would make sure that she was found, even if he had to go all the way to the FBI to do so. Whether he was back in California or still in Nevada, he would find a way to track her here.

But what if Gary and the others were *not* free?

What if they had been brought here, too, and were in rooms of their own? What if they were right now being brainwashed and beaten into submission just down the hall?

She continued to stare at the photo of Father, at his new white beard, at the flintiness of his eyes.

It was possible.

Joan lost track of time, but for what felt like the next several hours, she went back and forth on this subject. Deprived of any outside stimulation, her mind kept going over the various possibilities, trying to decide what had happened to her friends, her family, Gary. She knew this was a trick of Father's, knew that this was exactly what he wanted her to do, was why she had been left alone like this, but she couldn't help herself, and she was grateful when she heard the sound of the lock turning in the door.

She sat up in bed as the door opened. This time, the girl brought in her bag of food a chunk of cold cooked beef, a slice of freshly baked bread, another carrot and more apple juice. Joan realized that this was dinner. Which meant the last meal was lunch, which meant that she must have awakened in the morning. Along with the food came a book: Father's version of the Bible. Joan felt like throwing it across the room, felt like dumping it in the half-filled bedpan, but she took it from the girl, forced herself to smile gratefully and said, "Thank you."

The girl grinned, pleased, and Joan noticed that her teeth were exceptionally small, like twin rows of little Chiclets. Although she was at least fifteen or sixteen, it looked as though she still had her baby teeth, as though her permanent teeth had never come in.

There was no man accompanying the girl this time, and Joan knew that was a test. Father wanted to see how she would react, what she would do. So she made no effort to get away, made no effort to get information out of the girl, but simply accepted the food and the Bible, and then waved good-bye as the girl backed out into the hall and closed the door behind her.

She was still famished. A side effect of whatever she'd been drugged with, no doubt. As well as the fact that her lunch had not been that filling. She was also thirsty, and while she continued to have doubts about the odd-tasting apple juice, she had no choice but to drink it. She ate first, finishing everything, then waited for several moments, trying to discern any changes in her thoughts or emotions. When there was none, she took a sip. Again she waited.

It took some time, but eventually she finished the juice. She was still thirsty, though, and hungry, and she wondered if that was intentional.

Probably.

Father always had a plan. He left nothing up to chance.

Over the next half hour or so, the ceiling light began to fade in a rough approximation of nightfall, and before it grew completely dark, Joan crawled into bed. She could have turned on the lamp in the corner, but what was the point? She was alone here, and there was nothing to do. She was also tired, although whether that was a side effect of being drugged, a reaction to sensory deprivation or merely the natural workings of her body, she did not know.

She lay there under the thin covers, thinking about her parents, half hoping that they'd eluded capture and were free, and half hoping that they were here somewhere, at the Home. She would not feel so alone if she knew her mom and dad were nearby.

And where was Gary? she wondered. What had happened to him?

Maybe she'd never see him again.

Gary.

She thought of his open smile and his kind face and the tender way he looked at her when he thought she wasn't watching.

Tears came to her eyes as she stared up into the blackness. She said his name aloud, "Gary," and the sound comforted her, made her feel less lonely, though it also filled her with a sadness so profound that her silent tears were converted into sobs, and she could not stop herself from crying, great hiccuping sounds emanating from deep within her gut. She turned over, burying her face in the pillow, trying to muffle the noise.

She cried herself to sleep.

"Gary," she kept repeating. "Gary, Gary, Gary . . ."

Day two.

Or was it? Joan had not been allowed to see outside, had been kept in this room since she'd first awakened here, and although she'd been served lunch, dinner and breakfast, it was possible that the intervals were off, that dinner had come six hours after lunch and breakfast had come one hour after dinner. Breakfast could have been served to her at four in the afternoon and lunch at midnight.

Father was capable of that.

Of more than that.

Boredom made her pick up the Bible after breakfast. She stood next to the curtains, pretending to herself that there was a real window behind it, and opened the book at random, to a page where parents were instructed that disobedient children were to be stoned to death. Immediately, she slammed the covers shut, a chill passing through her, an echo of the fear she had lived with every day until she and her parents had left this place. She'd been gone for five years, had gotten used to life in the outside world, and she'd almost forgotten what it was like living here. That harsh passage brought it all back.

She glanced back at the table, where, next to the toast crumbs and empty apple juice bottle, a prayer scroll lay that had been brought by the boy who had delivered breakfast. Like the girl, he'd been one of the Children, and not only had one of his legs been considerably longer than the other, but his head had been unusually large.

The thought of the Children intensified her chill.

She walked back to the table, dropping the Bible on top of the bread crumbs. Though Father insisted that it was the foundation of everything, the Bible had never held much sway with her. For one thing, there were too many narrative inconsistencies. She could never believe in things like the story of Exodus. After maintaining their religion through two thousand years of slavery, after seeing the Red Sea part, after being provided with manna from heaven, God's chosen people forgot all about Him and started worshipping a golden calf because Moses was late coming down from the mountain? It didn't make any sense. And there were weird anomalies like the story of Adam and Eve, who were kicked out of Eden because God was afraid they would usurp His power. In a strange conversation with what appeared to be another god, He said that humans had already eaten from the tree of knowledge and knew the difference between good and evil, and that they needed to be expelled before they ate from the tree of life and also became immortal.

So she didn't believe the Bible.

But the scrolls still had power for her. They were harsh sometimes, even brutal, but there were no stories in them, only prayers and entreaties, and, in her experience, many of the requests had been answered. That lent them authority. She didn't *want* to believe in the world shown in the scrolls, particularly not the persistent prejudice against Outsiders, but she'd spent her entire life rolling scrolls, writing them, reading them, and old habits were hard to break.

Joan hesitated for a moment, then picked up the prayer scroll from the table. Rolling it open, she automatically read the words aloud:

"O Lord our Father! Praise be to You for rescuing me from the Outsiders. Forgive me for consorting

with evil and show me the light once more. Welcome
me back to the bosom of Your love. Damn the Outsiders for eternity and protect me here in Your Home
forever and ever. Amen."

The second she finished reciting the words, the door
opened and there stood Absalom, smiling. It was as if
he'd been waiting outside the door for her to say the
prayer, as if its recitation allowed him entry. She had not
thought of Absalom since she and her parents had left,
so Joan was surprised at the warm feelings of nostalgia
she experienced upon seeing him again. Like Father, he
was older than she remembered, but the sincerity of his
smile and the kindness of his eyes were as far from Father's stern visage as it was possible to get. A memory
came to her: Absalom tying her shoes for her when she
was five or six, using a thick, rough finger to wipe the tears
from her cheeks and telling her to ignore Luke, the bratty
little boy who'd made fun of her because he could tie his
own shoes and she couldn't.

Absalom stepped into the room. "Welcome back," he
said in the Language, holding his arms open wide for a
hug.

She knew why he was here. It was his job to smooth
things over, to try to make her forget that she had been
drugged and kidnapped and taken to the Home by
force. He was supposed to make her feel missed, wanted
and loved. He was supposed to let her know that all was
forgiven, that she was back and everything was fine. She
wanted no part of that. At the same time, she did like
Absalom and didn't want to hurt his feelings, and she
compromised by smiling and saying, "Hello." She said it
in the Language, surprised and a little bit frightened by
how easily it came back to her.

Behind him, in the hallway, she could see the girl
who'd been bringing her meals. The girl hung back shyly,

though her face lit up when Joan's eyes met hers, as if she was remembering when Joan had thanked her. If Joan recalled correctly, the Children didn't receive many compliments or kind words.

"It is nice to see you," Absalom said in that formal way of speaking that adults always used in the Home. "When Father told me you had come back to us, I was overjoyed."

I didn't "come back" to you! Joan wanted to yell. *I was kidnapped and brought back by force! I never wanted to see this place again!* But she forced herself to answer with a slight acquiescent nod.

"You have been given your old room back!" Absalom told her enthusiastically. "I will take you there. Everything will be as it was."

That was what Joan was afraid of, but she nodded and smiled and followed him out into the hall, the girl moving aside to let her pass. She looked first to the left, then to the right. She didn't recognize this corridor and wondered if it was part of a new addition, though it was also possible that she'd simply forgotten it. Not only had she been gone for several years, but there were doubtlessly things that her brain had blocked out.

"You will be able to eat with us in the dining room again," Absalom continued. "And you may participate in all of the joyous events Father has planned for us."

Joan was filled with a sense of welling panic. She remembered all too well how difficult it had been for her and her parents to escape, and she knew that once she had been reintegrated into the fold, every minute of every hour of every day would be accounted for. She would have no privacy whatsoever. Each move would be watched; each word heard and reported back to Father.

They walked past a series of closed doors. Did any of them lead outside? Even if they did, they would not lead out of the Home, only out of this building—although that might be enough to allow her to get her bearings and, if she could think fast enough on her feet, find an escape route.

She eyed the door on her right, trying to determine whether or not it was locked. If it was and she tried to open it, her attempted breakout would be over before it began. Likewise, if it was open but led to a closet, she would be out of luck as well. She had to be careful. She could afford no mistakes.

Ahead, on the left side of the corridor, a door was open. Joan continued to face forward but glanced surreptitiously to the left, prepared at a second's notice to run through the doorway if it happened to lead outside. There was a tapping sound, a click. In her peripheral vision, she caught movement on the opposite side of the corridor and, surprised, she swiveled her head to the right, where another door was opening to reveal two men standing in a small room filled with skeins of recently spun yarn piled next to what appeared to be a broken loom.

"Absalom!" one of them called.

Absalom paused. "Wait here," he told Joan, shooting a significant look at the girl behind her. He walked into the room to speak to the men, and Joan took a step forward, peering into the open doorway on her left. It looked like an office. Not the type of primitive office she would have expected to find in the Home, but a regular, if bare-bones, office with chairs, a desk and, atop the desk, a computer.

And a phone.

There was no one inside the room.

Joan took a chance. As fast as she could, she ran into the office, slamming the door behind her. She dashed across the floor, grabbed the phone and quickly dialed the number of Gary's cell.

In the hallway, the girl was screaming, though no

words issued from her mouth, only harsh atonal cries. Joan knew she had only seconds to pull this off. There was one ring, two—and then the girl had thrown open the door and was in the room, trying to slam her hand down on the phone and cut off the call. Joan managed to push her away with her left hand while holding the phone to her ear with her right, but the girl fell back and came at her from another angle, still screaming, still calling for help in the only way she could.

Absalom and the other two men entered the room just as the ringing ceased and Gary's voice mail message came on: *"Hello. This is Gary. I'm not able to . . ."*

One of the men lunged for her while the other guarded the door. "Gary! I'm—" Joan shouted, and the phone was ripped from her hand. She was shoved against the desk with such force that the wind was knocked out of her, and then her arms were being pulled back as she was restrained by both men. The girl was still screaming and Absalom was calming her down as the two men dragged Joan back into the corridor.

"Return her!" Absalom said angrily, pushing past them and leading back the way they had come.

She was taken again to the windowless room in which she'd been confined since her arrival and thrown onto the bed, the door closed and locked behind her.

And there she stayed.

Food was delivered while she slept, enough for breakfast, lunch and dinner, so she never saw another person. She knew this solitary confinement was supposed to break her, and she vowed she would not let that happen, but being so alone, with no computer or television or radio, with no book other than the Bible, began to take its toll. She actually found herself looking forward to the day when she could see one of the Teachers or even one of the Children, though that was not something she would ever admit.

She had no conception of time in here, but once, she attempted to sleep after she ate lunch rather than after dinner, and several times she tried to stay awake and not fall asleep at all, in hopes of catching someone bringing food or emptying her bedpan. But she must have been under surveillance somehow because neither ploy worked and, as always, her food arrived and her bedpan was emptied while she was slumbering.

She was given new clothes, Home clothes, which she did not have to make herself, probably because they wouldn't trust her with a needle. She would have welcomed the opportunity to sew—it would have given her a way to pass the time *and* the clothes would have actually fit—but she put on the oversized blouse and pants anyway. Her old clothes were getting dirty, and she no longer felt comfortable wearing them.

The next morning, her jeans and shirt were gone.

Finally, after what felt like a month but was probably only a couple of days, the door was opened again. Joan was daydreaming, thinking about the trip to the beach she had taken with Gary and wondering where Gary was at this moment—whether he was here in the Home or in his dorm room or in a class or at a police station demanding that she be found—when there was an unexpected rattling of the doorknob. She instantly jumped out of bed and faced the door. She'd pictured this moment many times, and in her imaginings she unplugged the floor lamp and used it as a spear or cudgel to attack the person entering her room, but here it was happening, and she was completely unprepared.

The door swung open and in walked Absalom.

Unlike last time, he was not smiling.

And he held in his hand a rope with a muzzle.

"Father wants to see you," he said.

Eighteen

An address.

They had nothing else to show for their long interrogation, for all of their questions and threats, and though they'd gotten exactly what Gary had wanted—the specific location where Joan was being held—the lack of context unnerved him. For Ape Arms gave up the address almost instantly, with a slight, mysterious Gioconda smile, as though he knew of some secret reason why Gary would never reach the place. But after that he would say nothing else, not who he was, not who would be at that location, not why Joan had been taken, not why Kara was missing, not why Gary himself was being targeted. His companion just kept crying.

Gary looked down at the address in his hand.

Joan was in Bitterweed, Texas.

Texas. That was far away, but Gary remembered the Lone Star license plate of the car his abductors had driven, and it was one of the reasons he believed the information to be true. The fact that it was given so freely made him uneasy, though, and while he intended to head out immediately to find Joan, he was worried that he might be walking into a trap.

The two men they'd captured stood before him, unmoving. It was still hard for Gary not to think of them as Outsiders, but if there was any other reliable information they'd obtained during their exhaustive questioning, it was that these two were *not* Outsiders. The very idea seemed to enrage them, and that was the only point on which they would argue or engage, although Gary and his crew were not sophisticated enough interrogators to be able to use that as leverage to pry more information out of them.

But if *they* weren't Outsiders, who was?

That was only one of a hundred questions for which he had no answer. He had the address, though, and once Joan was back safe and sound, *then* he would have the luxury of trying to figure out what was going on.

Reyn sidled up next to him. "What's the plan?" his friend asked, nodding toward the captives.

"We'll have the film society take them out."

Reyn stared at him.

Gary smiled weakly. "Joke." He looked from the tall one to the short one. What *was* to be done with them? If they turned the men in to the police, they risked being arrested themselves. Detaining the men in the way that they had was not immediately obvious as self-defense, and while he might be able to make a case that it was, he would doubtlessly have to do so in court. There wasn't time for that.

On the other hand, if they let the men go, the two of them would probably contact their cohorts immediately and Joan would be taken away and hidden somewhere out of reach.

That was something that could not be risked.

Gary realized all of a sudden that Ape Arms was grinning at him, and he looked away with an involuntary shiver. Something about that smile was extremely disconcerting, and he could tell by the reactions of those around him that they found it unnerving as well.

Who were these people? he wondered again.

Brian had his BlackBerry out and had typed in the

Texas address, using Google Earth to try see where it was and what it looked like. "Check this," he said, and Gary leaned over to see that the area outside the town of Bitterweed, where the address was located, was not available for viewing. Instead of a rural land-scape, they saw a gray screen and the words "Image Not Obtainable."

Brian quickly cross-referenced two other satellite photo sites, but they, too, were blacked out.

"Curiouser and curiouser," Reyn said.

Stacy pulled them away, telling Dror and the others to keep an eye on the captives for a moment, and she led them down the path until they were out of earshot of the others. "I don't know what the plan is now," she said once they'd stopped. "But we need to tell the police what we know."

"She's right," Reyn agreed. "We've done all we can. This is where we hand it off."

Gary was already shaking his head.

"We have to!" Stacy insisted. "Haven't you learned your lesson yet?" She ran a hand through her hair, ex-asperated. "What's your idea? Drive halfway across the country and try to mete out some vigilante justice? Are you going to bring a gun and Rambo her out of what-ever predicament she's in?"

Gary didn't know what he was going to do. All he knew was that he needed to rescue Joan. He looked to Brian for support, but Brian for once was oddly non-committal and lifted his shoulders in a gesture of vague equivocation.

"They killed Teri Lim," Stacy reminded him. "*Killed* her. And kidnapped Joan and Kara."

"And drugged us," Reyn added.

"The point is: this is not something we can handle. We got lucky here tonight. But we're a few college students up against . . . God knows what."

Gary thought for a moment. She was right, he thought, though he hated to admit it. His intentions hardly constituted a plan, and whatever action he took might fail completely. Not to mention the fact that it would take some time for him to actually get to Texas.

Stacy placed a gentle hand on his arm. "We have to turn them over to the police. You know we do."

"We got what we needed out of them," Reyn said. "We tell the cops they were stalking you, file a complaint, let them figure out what to do."

That was a good strategy. He was still worried that *they* might be the ones to get in trouble, that they might be accused of assault or kidnapping or some related offense and would be jailed while the other two were allowed to go free. But they had numbers on their side— twelve to two—and since Teri *was* dead and Kara and Joan *were* missing, it was likely that Williams would believe their story.

Gary gave in. "Okay. We'll take them into the police station—"

"Take them *in*?" Stacy said incredulously. "Has this affected your brain? We call nine-one-one."

Of course.

Gary felt stupid. Grief, fear, stress, lack of sleep, all of it was conspiring to impair his judgment. It probably *was* a good idea to let the police handle things.

Reyn already had his phone out and was calling. After he explained the situation to the 911 operator, Reyn said that this was connected to a case Detective Williams was working on and that the detective would probably like to be informed about it.

They walked back up the path, returning to where the others waited. Both Ape Arms and his buddy had closed their eyes and were standing with their hands clasped in front of them, praying. The two of them were speaking aloud but very softly, and though occasional words could be made out, everyone gave them privacy.

Gary had time to think while they waited for the police to arrive, and he changed his mind about not going after Joan. Maybe his judgment *was* impaired, but he thought the cops were taking too long to show up, and it made him realize that, while they might be highly trained, they had no personal stake in the outcome of this situation. He did. He loved Joan, and he needed to be there when she was rescued from her captors.

The operator had instructed Reyn to stay on the line, and he had. As the police drew closer, he gave them a more specific description of exactly where they were located. Seconds after hearing sirens pull into the parking lot at the end of the memorial path, four uniformed officers came hurrying up the trail. They pushed their way through the circle of students and immediately surrounded the still-praying duo. Moments later, Williams and Tucker strode out of the darkness. Gary hadn't expected them to be working this late and was surprised to see them, but he wasn't surprised by the look of annoyance on Tucker's face, and a sinking feeling in the pit of his stomach told him that they should not have called the police.

Williams immediately put his fears to rest. The detective glanced at the two men, then walked directly up to Gary. "What happened?"

While everyone listened, Gary explained that these two had been stalking him and that because of that he'd been afraid to go out at night alone, so he'd come out this evening with a bunch of friends, and when he and his friends were attacked, they'd fought back.

"And why, exactly, were your friends carrying weapons?" Tucker asked drily.

Gary reminded the detectives about his abduction, how he'd been kidnapped and almost been killed. Williams kept glancing over at the captives. It helped his cause that the two men were dressed oddly and that they had obvious physical problems. They *looked* wrong, and that granted verisimilitude to the story Gary was telling.

"They look like the guys who kidnapped me," Gary said. "Same kind of clothes, everything. I'm willing to bet that they're the ones who wiped all my computerized records. I *know* they're part of the group that has Joan."

"How do you know that?"

"They told us where she's being held. They gave us an address."

"I have no idea what they're talking about," Ape Arms said calmly. He grinned at Gary, and even with the police present, that smile was still creepy enough to send a chill down his spine.

"We have witnesses," Reyn said, gesturing around. "Twelve of them."

"They're liars," Ape Arms said.

"Outsiders!" his friend insisted.

The word put Williams on alert, and Gary thought of Joan's prayer scroll, which the detective must have seen during his examination of Joan and Kara's dorm room. "What did you say?" Williams asked.

"You're all Outsiders!" the short man yelled at the detective.

The men were separated, two uniformed officers guarding each, while Williams interviewed the tall one and Tucker the short one. Gary and the others waited around, trying to listen in, but while the questions could be heard, the answers couldn't, and it soon became clear that the cops were having no more luck obtaining information than they had. Williams returned to where Gary was standing, obviously exasperated. "Do you have any idea what their names are?" he asked.

"Nope. They wouldn't say."

"Still won't." Williams nodded to the uniformed officers. "Bring 'em in. We'll get this sorted out down at the station." He turned to Gary. "You said they told you where Ms. Daniels is being held and provided you with an address."

"We'll need that address," Tucker said.

Brian faced the detective. "Why don't you guys just keep looking for Kara? We'll take care of Gary's *imaginary* girlfriend."

Tucker glared back defiantly.

"We're sorry about that," Williams said, "but we have to go with the facts we have in hand."

"Yeah, and we *told* you—"

"It's all right," Gary interrupted. He was feeling antsy and wanted to speed things along.

"The important thing is that we get everyone back in one piece," Williams offered. "Now, did they give any indication as to Ms. Daniels's condition?"

Gary shook his head.

"Did they say whether anyone else was being held at this location?"

Brian snorted. "They gave us the address. Period. Then they called us Outsiders and prayed."

"I'm going to need you to come back to the station with us."

Gary looked anxiously over at Reyn. They needed to get out of here and get going. Texas was far away and time was passing.

"I know what you're thinking," the detective said. "But the fastest way to do this is for me to call the local police or sheriff and have them check out this address. I'll explain the situation, tell them what we have, and they can go out and look for us. If they find anything, they'll let us know. If they don't, and it turns out we've been given false information, they've prevented us from going on a wild-goose chase."

It made sense, and Gary nodded reluctantly.

"You don't need everyone, do you?" Reyn asked, gesturing toward the students gathered around them.

"Not right now. I need everyone's name and phone number, but Mr. Russell's the only one I need to speak with at the moment." He motioned toward Gary. "You'll have to sign the complaint."

The uniformed policemen had already led Ape Arms and his buddy off to patrol cars, although they had not been handcuffed, and Williams and Tucker took several moments to write down names and numbers, Williams in a small notebook, Tucker on his handheld computer.

"All right," Williams said, nodding toward Gary. "Follow us."

"We'll meet you there," Reyn promised.

"Our car's right over here."

"We'll take my car," Gary said.

Tucker looked suspicious, but Brian shone his flashlight into the detective's eyes and made him turn away. Brian chuckled to himself as the detectives walked back up the path toward the parking lot.

"I guess you all heard that," Gary said to the gathered students. "You guys can go home. You don't have to come with us. But I want to thank you for all of your help tonight. We couldn't've done it without you."

"And things might have turned out very differently if you weren't here," Reyn added.

"Tell us what happens," Dror requested.

Gary nodded. "We will."

"Tomorrow," Reyn promised.

The entire group walked back toward the center of campus, splitting off into different directions once they reached the buildings, and Gary led Reyn, Stacy and

Brian to his parking spot and his car. Fifteen minutes later, they were at the police station and being ushered up the stairs to the detectives' area. Williams was at his desk and on the phone, but there was no sign of Tucker, the other policemen or the two men they'd captured, who were hopefully sitting in some cell right now.

Williams saw them and held up a finger, motioning for them to wait a moment. "Yes," he said into the phone. "I understand." There was a pause. "I'll make sure they do. What's that number?" He fumbled around on his paper-strewn desk for a pen, then grabbed one of the pieces of paper and wrote something down on it. "Thank you," he said. "I'll be in touch."

Williams hung up the phone. "That was Sheriff Stewart, from Bitterweed, Texas. I told him what had happened, told him we have an escaped abductee"—he nodded toward Gary—"as well as three young women—two missing, one a hit-and-run victim—and that we have reason to believe the perpetrators of these crimes are located at the address we were given. I spelled out the details, then described the appearance and behavior of the two men we have in custody, though I couldn't provide any positive ID because they refused to furnish their names, they had no forms of identification, and we have not yet been able to match their fingerprints with any on file.

"Turns out the sheriff and his department know these guys. They've tangled with them before. They're part of a cult based in Bitterweed, known as the Homesteaders, and they've been accused in the past of using terrorist tactics against their enemies, including drugging people and kidnapping them."

"That's them!" Gary said excitedly. "We've got 'em!"

"Not so fast. None of them have ever been convicted, and there's a pending harassment suit against the sheriff that's still making its way through the courts. The sheriff's department would like nothing better than to nail these bastards, but they're more than a little gun-shy, as you can imagine, and they're worried about creating a Waco situation and making these lunatics martyrs to all the wacky fringe groups out there. I laid out everything we have, but they're walking on eggshells, and as far as they're concerned, we can't show probable cause. Right now they're not even willing to take a request to a judge."

"We'll take care of them ourselves," Brian said. "That was our original plan anyway."

Gary nodded in agreement.

"Hold your horses. Sheriff Stewart said he can't authorize any official surveillance, but he's going to station a discreet lookout at the head of the road leading to the compound—"

"Compound?" Stacy said. "They have a compound?"

"Cults always have a compound," Reyn told her.

"—and if any of his men *happen* to see any unusual activity or *happen* to spot anyone resembling Ms. Daniels or Ms. Madison, he'll send deputies in, harassment case or not. I gave him a brief description and am going to e-mail over everything we have. I told him our information's solid, and he knows the importance of finding these young women, so he's going to do everything he can to help us."

"I'm still going over there," Gary said.

Williams nodded. "I thought you might say that. And, frankly, I'm glad. I told Sheriff Stewart that there was every possibility you would not be deterred, and he promised he'd look the other way. No matter what you might try." The detective paused. "I hate to say this—and I'll deny I ever did—but it wouldn't be such a bad thing if you got into trouble somehow and did something that required the sheriff to come to your assistance. *If* you find Ms. Madison or Ms. Daniels, that is."

"What about you?" Stacy asked. "This is your case. Aren't you going to come?"

"No." Williams looked embarrassed.

"Why not?"

"It's complicated."

Gary didn't care why, didn't care whether it was lack of money, a jurisdictional problem or something else entirely. Like Brian, he was glad the detectives weren't coming along. They'd been no help at all up to this point, and the idea of them hogging the glory and claiming success after their mishandling of the investigation into Joan's disappearance set his teeth on edge. Let the local law enforcement guys in Texas get all the credit. It didn't matter to him, as long as Joan was free and safe.

Williams copied something onto a yellow Post-it and handed it to Gary. "Here's the sheriff's direct number. You can keep in contact with him at all times. If you have any problems, if anything happens that you can't handle, the sheriff's men will be there."

"Thanks," Gary said.

"All right. Let's go." Brian was already walking away from the detective's desk toward the stairwell.

It was clear that Williams had more to say and that Stacy wanted to stay and listen, but time was wasting, and Gary started after Brian. "Yeah. I need to get moving."

Reyn and Stacy followed behind them, but Gary didn't turn to look back until they were on the first floor. It gave him a perverse sense of satisfaction to ignore the police, and his only regret was that Tucker hadn't been there as well. The other detective would have gotten much angrier, and it would have been great to just blow him off.

Still, he was in an odd position. Despite Stacy's fears of vigilante justice, Williams and the sheriff in Texas had basically signed off on exactly that, encouraging him to go after Joan on his own, though he had absolutely no idea how. On the one hand, he resented the idea of the police jumping on the bandwagon this late in the game and suddenly getting involved when they'd been completely useless until now. On the other hand, he resented the fact that they were opting out on some technicality and leaving everything to him when he was in way over his head.

Nothing was working out the way it should.

And he was still suspicious of the fact that Ape Arms had provided the address so readily. He and his partner had been sent out here to California to capture Gary again—he was sure of it—and the way they'd practically *invited* him to go after Joan made him sure that his arrival was expected and that a trap had been set for him.

The uniformed officer at the desk buzzed them out, and they stepped through the security gate and through the lobby. Outside, the air felt cool and good.

"We're *renting* a car this time," Brian announced. "I don't trust any of your raggedy-ass jalopies. Mine, either, for that matter."

Gary shook his head. "I can't. I'm still off the grid. My credit card won't work."

"I'll take care of it," Brian told him. "I have a Master-Card that I never use. I think there's a balance of zero on it."

"When the bill comes in, we'll split it," Reyn said. "Three ways. Me, you and Gary."

"Four ways," Stacy stated. Reyn turned toward her. "I'm contributing, too," she said.

"I already said we are."

"*I'm* going to."

"I wasn't trying to disenfranchise you. I just think of us as one entity, one unit. I figured that would be *our* contribution."

"You're a cheap bastard who wants Gary and Brian to pay more." She looked at Gary. "Four ways."

He didn't know how to express his gratitude. Not only for helping to defray expenses but for offering to come along in the first place. He honestly hadn't expected any of them to accompany him. Yes, they were his friends, but they'd already gone far above and beyond. Besides, this wasn't their fight.

Looking from one to another, he actually started to tear up.

Reyn clapped a hand on his back. "We'll get her, don't worry."

"Everybody get a change of clothes, toiletries and whatever," Stacy suggested as they reached the car.

"I'm good," Brian told her.

She ignored him. "We'll meet back at ... where? Gary's?"

"You're forgetting something," Reyn said. "It's nearly midnight. All of the rental car places are closed."

"Then we'll—" Gary began.

Reyn cut him off. "We'll go back to our rooms, catch a few hours of much-needed sleep, then head out bright-eyed and bushy-tailed in the morning."

"No." Gary shook his head in firm disagreement.

"Do you want a repeat of last time? Breaking down in Asswipe, Arizona, while we spend hours waiting for some Homer to find the part that'll fix our alternator? We get some sleep, wait until morning, then rent a car and drive nonstop until we're there."

"We could fly," Brian suggested.

"Yes!" Gary said.

Brian already had his BlackBerry out and was moving his fingers over the screen, tapping the keypad. They waited patiently while he accessed different sites and saved specific information. At the conclusion of it all, he looked up and said, "The earliest flight we could get would be a Southwest leaving LA for Austin tomorrow night at eight. The problem is, we'd have to rent a car for the rest of the trip, which would be a good four hours more. But since we'd be landing in the middle of the night, we'd have the same problem we have right now: we'd have to wait until morning for the car. *And* find a place to sleep."

There was no way Gary was going to wait around all day tomorrow until a night flight—that could very well be delayed—took them to Austin, Texas, where they would have to wait for ten hours for a rental car. His muscles were tense again, and he had to force himself to unclench his fists. "Okay. We'll go in the morning."

"And get some sleep," Reyn said.

Reluctantly, Gary nodded. "And get some sleep."

They were on the road in a new silver Nissan Altima by nine thirty the next morning. Stacy had brought textbooks and schoolwork to keep her occupied on the trip. Reyn and Brian were lugging their laptops, Brian also bringing along his ever-present BlackBerry, while Gary had packed . . . nothing. It was stupid and shortsighted, he knew. They were going to be in the car for a long time, and a book or a game would have helped while away the hours—only he knew that he wouldn't be able to concentrate on anything extraneous. Joan was the only thing on his mind, and nothing could distract him from thinking about where they were going and what they were going to do when they got there.

He hadn't even brought a weapon, and that felt like a mistake to him the second they left. He remembered all too clearly that battle-to-the-death he'd had with the gas station attendant in New Mexico, and that should have taught him a lesson: he ought to be prepared at all times. A sledgehammer was not always going to be nearby when he needed it.

"The sun barfed heat onto the desert," Brian said to no one in particular as they passed one of the Palm Springs exits.

Stacy frowned at him. "What?"

"I'm composing my memoir of this adventure. In my head. I'm memorizing my thoughts and impressions so I can write them down later. This will make an amazing book. True-life trauma makes for instant bestsellers. Especially firsthand accounts of widely publicized events, which, face it, this is bound to be."

"If we play our cards right," Gary said, "no one will ever know about this."

Brian looked at him incredulously. "Are you kidding? This is gold. Four college students setting out on a road trip to rescue their friend who's been abducted by a cult? You couldn't make this stuff up."

Stacy's voice was tight. "A little insensitive, don't you think?"

"No offense, dude," Brian told Gary sincerely. "I'm just thinking out loud. And I know everything's going to turn out okay; otherwise I wouldn't even entertain this thought."

In a weird way, that made Gary feel a little more optimistic.

"It's fine," he told Brian.

Stacy wasn't willing to let it go. "It's wrong," she said flatly.

Brian ignored her. "I read this science fiction story once where, after he croaked, this guy went to a world that was just this wild, overgrown jungle. It turned out that when people and animals died, they just died. They rotted away and became plant food. But when plants died, they went to a kind of veggie heaven, where they grew forever. Somehow wires got crossed, and this dude ended up there with the plants, the only human ever to experience life after death."

"Does that have anything to do with anything?"

"No. I'm just saying."

Gary tuned them out. He was glad they were here, happy they had come along, but their focus was more diffuse than his. He found it impossible to think of anything other than Joan, and talk of any other subject he found not only distracting but annoying.

Disloyal.

Yes. More than anything else, it felt disloyal to him, though that was a fanatic's reaction and he would never admit to it aloud.

Stacy and Brian continued to argue, but Gary said nothing, simply stared out the window, watching the scenery pass by, wishing they were moving faster.

As with the trip to Burning Man, they took turns driving and sleeping. Stacy had gone first, then Reyn. Gary took the wheel after Tucson and didn't give it up until they reached El Paso that night. They had an interim meal at Denny's ("Dekfast," Stacy called it, "half dinner, half breakfast." "Wouldn't that make it *dick*fast?" Brian wondered aloud), and afterward Reyn and Stacy slept in the back while Brian drove and Gary rode in the passenger seat beside him. Outside, the world was dark and flat, the road impossibly straight. They met no others on the highway, and it was easy—*too* easy—to imagine that they were all alone, the last people on the planet. Gary found himself grateful that the rental car had come equipped with satellite radio, that they could listen to music being broadcast from New York. It made him feel tethered to modern life and the world of human beings.

He found himself wondering if the area around Bitterweed looked like this as well. Was Joan chained up in some room, looking out on a barren landscape of endless plains? The thought sickened his heart.

Although he'd not just been anxious to reach Joan

but driven to do so, impelled by a deep primal need to go after her, he had still not thought through the mechanics of rescue. Stacy was right. How *did* he expect to free Joan from her captors? Walk up to the door of whatever this place was and demand that she be released? Try to sneak in through a window and spirit her away, fighting anyone who attempted to bar their escape? What was he going to do?

He had no idea.

Gary continued to stare out the window into the empty darkness, listening as Brian fiddled with the satellite radio, trying to find a song that he liked.

Eventually, lulled by the music and the blackness and the motion of the car, he dozed.

He dreamed about a gigantic farmhouse, identical on the outside to the one in New Mexico where he'd been held but a hundred times bigger. Inside, there was only a single barnlike room where dozens of young women who looked just like Joan were manacled to the floor. At the far end of the room, the psycho from the gas station was trying to start up a chain saw. He intended to cut up the captive women, and Gary knew this because he had a chain saw in his hands as well. They were supposed to work together, moving in from the outside and killing everyone in between. "No!" Gary yelled at the other man. "Stop!" But the gas station attendant didn't understand English, spoke only that weird alien language, and he revved up his chain saw and cut through the midsection of a young woman who not only looked like Joan but screamed like her.

When he awoke, it was still dark. Brian was driving more slowly than he should have been, and Gary tapped him lightly on the shoulder. "What's up?" he whispered. Reyn and Stacy remained dead asleep in the back.

"It's been going on for a while," Brian said. "Wait a sec."

"What?" Gary didn't know what he was talking about.

"There!" Brian pointed through the windshield where, several yards ahead, at the edge of the illumination offered by the headlights, a lone man wearing beige peasant clothes and using a large hooked staff as a walking stick strode purposefully along the side of the road.

"That's the sixth one I've seen in the last ten minutes."

Gary felt chilled.

They passed the man, and though Gary watched carefully through the side window, the man did not turn to look at them as they went by, gave no indication at all that they were there. Glancing in the side mirror, Gary saw the walking man's form, lit red by the taillights, recede eerily into the darkness. He had been dressed like the men who had kidnapped him, like the people at the farmhouse, like the two men they had captured who had given them the address where Joan was being held.

Gary's voice when he spoke was quiet. "What do you think that's about?"

Brian said nothing, only pointed to a green sign coming up on the right.

BITTERWEED 45 MILES.

Nineteen

They had escaped from the Home at night.

Joan had been awakened by her dad, who, with a finger to her lips, bade her get up. Her mom stood behind him, holding a lantern. Joan had not been told this would happen, but it was not entirely unexpected. Like herself, her parents had never seemed happy here, and recently she had noticed them avoiding certain people and spending more time conversing together in low murmurs long after Bedtime, when everyone was supposed to be asleep.

Her mom had been born in the Home, like Joan, but her dad had come here voluntarily, and sometimes, in secret, he told her stories of the world Outside. Father, Absalom and the other Teachers told of the world Outside, too, but theirs were cautionary tales, meant to frighten. Her dad's stories were different. Personal reminiscences. Funny, exciting, but more wistful than anything else. And Joan found herself longing to experience the type of things her dad had. The more she heard and the more she learned, the more stifling life at the Home seemed, and every day it grew harder to follow the rigid rules or feign interest in the mundane tasks required of her.

Though fear of punishment made her outwardly compliant at all times.

Her parents' dissatisfaction, too, seemed to be increasing, but it was when Father had called her in for a personal conference, when she had told her mom and dad what he said, that she really sensed a change in their attitudes. The difference was subtle and probably not noticeable to anyone other than herself, but all of a sudden discontent became disengagement, and though they continued to go through the motions of their daily routines, they no longer seemed a part of that life. Which was why she was not surprised when her dad woke her up in the middle of the night, put a finger to her lips and whispered for her to get dressed; they were leaving.

Joan's heart was pounding as she slipped out of her pajamas and put on the new clothes she had sewn for herself last week. There were things she wanted to bring with her, stuffed animals she'd made, pictures she'd drawn, stories she'd written, but she knew without asking that she would have to leave everything behind, that they would be traveling light.

In the darkness, her parents whispered to her the details of the plan they had concocted. Her dad, it seemed, had been overseeing workers at the Farm for the past week, and while doing so, he had taken the opportunity to stash food, water and other survival needs in backpacks that he'd hidden in the bushes at the edge of one of the fields. Enough for a week. The original plan had been for them to strike out on foot and then try to hitch a ride with someone driving by, preferably someone just passing through on their way to one of the coasts. But as luck would have it, the brakes on one of the farm trucks had gone out yesterday, and Joan's dad had been in charge of getting them fixed. He had done so—and while buying brake pads in town, he'd had an extra key made. He had hidden the key in one of the backpacks and had parked the truck on a trail off the side of the road between the Home and town. He had told Father that the truck needed a new master cylinder, something he could not do, and that he'd left the vehicle at a garage.

Now the three of them needed to get out of the Home, strike out across the fields, pick up the backpacks and walk down to where the truck was hidden. After that, they would be free to go anywhere they wanted.

"We'll go far enough away that no one will ever find us," her mom said. "Not even Father." The words were reassuring, but her tone was not, and Joan could tell that her mom was as scared as she was.

"Do you understand?" her dad asked.

Joan nodded silently. She looked around her room one last time, at everything she would have to leave behind.

Seeing the look on her face, her dad smiled kindly. He told her that he had also taken her favorite stuffed animal, a bunny that her mom had made for her when she was born and that she'd had for all these years, and had hidden it in her backpack with the other stuff. Joan had never loved him more than she did at that moment, and she threw her arms around his neck and held him tight. "I love you, Daddy," she whispered.

"I love you, too," he whispered back.

Holding her mom's thin hand, she waited until her dad had opened the door and checked the hallway to make sure it was clear, then walked with her parents out of the room. They strode purposefully but not hurriedly, not wishing to arouse suspicion. Should someone spot them, it would appear that their family had been summoned by Father or was engaged in performing an assigned duty. Luckily, they encountered no one else, and they walked in silence past the doors of other residences until they neared the end of the third hall.

Still holding her mom's hand, Joan dragged her feet, holding back, trying to slow down. She didn't like where they were going, and though she knew this was the fastest way to get outside, she wanted to turn around and leave the Home through another exit. Ahead, she could see a shadow wavering on the wall, a small, strangely shaped silhouette formed by a candle backlighting an unseen figure standing in the corridor that branched off to the right at the end of the hallway. She was afraid to go around the corner, but her mom squeezed her hand tight, pulling her forward, and Joan held her breath, bracing herself for what she might see.

It was an adult, not a child, but it was one of the Children, and no more than three feet high, with ungainly feet and an oversized head. A man, he grinned dumbly at them, not knowing who they were, not caring what they were doing, and Joan's muscles tensed as she passed by him. She couldn't look at that horrible dumb smile, and she did not relax until they were past the figure and out of the corridor. Glancing at her mom's face, she saw sadness there, sadness and regret. Her mom, she knew, had a soft spot for the Children. She was one herself, though not so bad off as many of the others, and Joan squeezed her fingers tighter around her mom's hand to show that she understood.

Then they had reached the side door, her dad had unlocked it and they were out.

Joan had never been outside at night before, and she breathed deeply. The cool air felt good, strange but good, and she looked up at the sky and saw the bright fullness of the moon. She felt happy and free, and though she'd known all along that they were doing the right thing in leaving, now she was certain of it. She thought of all the stories her dad had told her about growing up Outside, and she was filled with excitement at the knowledge that now that would be her world, too. She was scared, too, of course. The Teachers had drilled a fear of Outsiders into her since she'd been able to speak, and that sort of indoctrination did not give up its hold easily. But she was more eager than scared to leave the Home as she followed her dad around the edge of the building and through a large yard filled with farming equipment and tools. They stayed close to the fence, as far away from the windows of the Home as they could, until they made their way over a dry irrigation ditch and out to the grain field.

"Over there," her dad said, pointing. He was still whispering, though they were several yards from the nearest building and there was no one in sight.

Joan followed his finger to see a line of trees at the far end of the field, a windbreak of tall, skinny poplars filling in the spaces between massive naturally growing cottonwoods. Crouching low, keeping near the high bushes that separated the grains from the vegetable crops, they hurried across the tilled ground, careful not to trip over roots or rocks or furrowed rows. Moments later, they had reached the trees and there, where her dad had left them, were three backpacks. Joan picked hers up, unzipped the top and checked inside. Her fingers closed on the familiar softness of her bunny, and she knew at that moment that everything would be all right.

As they walked between the trees and turned north toward the road, there came a loud scream from the Home behind them. Only it was too loud to have come from inside the Home. It had to have originated outside, in the equipment yard or field through which they had just passed. Joan's heart was pounding. She'd almost screamed herself at the sound, and it was only her mom's hand holding tightly to her own that had anchored her and given her strength and kept her from crying out.

"They're not after us," her dad whispered, sensing her fear. "Someone's being punished."

There was another scream.

Who was being punished? And why? Did this happen all the time? Joan had never heard such a noise before, but her dad was not only not surprised; he seemed to know exactly what was going on.

Joan shivered. She thought of the personal conference she'd had with Father, the way he'd looked at her, the way he'd smiled at her, and more than ever, she was glad that they were leaving. They increased their pace, branches from the underbrush scraping against their legs through the material of their clothes. Then they reached the road, and, with her dad leading the way, the three of them ran over the hard-packed dirt to the pullout where he'd left the truck. By the light of the moon, he opened his backpack, took out the keys to the vehicle and unlocked the passenger door. Joan threw her backpack behind the seat, crawling over the vinyl upholstery to the center. Her mom was right behind her, settling into the passenger seat.

The left door unlocked, opened, and her dad got in. Seconds later, he was starting the truck and pulling onto the road. Moments after that, they reached the paved lane that led to town.

But they did not stop in town. They kept going, gaining speed, heading west.

And they were free.

Joan followed Absalom through a series of hallways to an area of the Home that she remembered only too well. The muzzle was on, covering her mouth, nose and chin with crisscrossing leather straps, and although she could speak, it effectively restrained her head and gave the old man the ability to pull her along like a dog on a leash.

To her right was the Dining Room, and it looked exactly as she remembered: the long wooden tables and uncomfortable benches, the open window leading to the Kitchen, the high beamed ceiling, the walls bare save for the life-sized photo of Father framed at the north end. To her left was the Chapel, and, as was always the case, there were people kneeling on the hard stone floor, both Residents and Penitents, worshipping and praying. Simply looking into the Chapel brought back a flood of sense memories, and her knees could feel the pain of remaining bent on that floor for hours, her arms the strain of holding her clasped hands in perfect position the entire time, her throat, stomach, bowels and bladder the agony of not being able to drink, eat or go to the bathroom.

Absalom yanked on her strap, pulling her forward.

Joan's heart leapt in her chest.

Ahead, the Children were lining the corridor before Father's Room, some standing, some sitting in wheelchairs, a few lying on ambulatory devices that resembled gurneys with steering wheels. She did not want to continue on. Even under the best of circumstances, she was unnerved by the Children, and the thought of passing by them now filled her with dread. Seeing the girl who had brought her food, Joan tried to smile at her, but the child stared back, blank-eyed like the others.

These were not Children like her mom and the others who had been integrated into normal life at the Home. These were the ones who were damaged, the ones who might be entrusted with simple tasks but more often than not were simply housed here, with the vague promise that one day God or Father would reveal their purpose. It had only been five years, but there seemed to be more of them than there used to be, and each succeeding generation appeared worse off than the last, which made perfect sense to someone like her who had learned real science but was probably very confusing to a lot of the Residents, particularly the younger ones.

Joan followed Absalom up the corridor, trying not to look to either side, trying to focus on the old man's back in front of her and the closed double doors of Father's Room beyond. Absalom was walking more slowly here, and she was certain that was on purpose, even though there was no way he could know about her fear of the Children.

Finally, after what seemed like ten minutes but was probably only one, they neared the end of the corridor. Inadvertently, she glanced to her right. At the head of this gathering, closest to the door, was a figure she recognized, wearing a grin she'd never forgotten. It was the little man who'd been standing in the hallway on the night she and her parents had escaped. He looked the same as he had then, with his big feet and oversized head, and he grinned dumbly at her, the same way he had on that night. If the door had not opened at that moment and she had not been yanked inside, she probably would have screamed.

But suddenly she was in Father's Room, and the door was closing behind her.

Joan reached up and began unfastening the muzzle from the back of her head where it was strapped. The room was filled with people, and she was not about to stand in front of them like an animal with this contraption over her face. She expected Absalom to try to stop her, but he obviously knew that there was no way she could escape, nowhere she could go, and he made no effort to keep her from freeing herself. Besides, he had brought her here. His job was done.

Father would take over from this point.

Joan freed herself from the muzzle, letting the leather device drop onto the floor. She remembered with perfect clarity the last time she had been in here, the *only* time she had been in here, and she saw instantly that nothing had changed. At the head of the room was a floor-to-ceiling bookcase filled with religious tomes, and a massive cabinet containing copies of every prayer scroll ever written. Between the two sat the doorway that led to Father's sleeping chamber, and scattered randomly through the center of the long rectangular room, almost like the elements of an obstacle course, were various pieces of antique furniture, not all of which seemed appropriate to the room's purpose. There was a dining table with no accompanying chairs; a Victorian fainting couch; an ornately carved armoire; a rolltop desk; a marble bust of an old man with a long white beard, presumably God; a glass-doored cabinet filled with knives and swords; and an empty baker's rack. Along the walls were wooden benches and, above the benches, painted directly onto the stucco, poorly rendered scenes from the Bible. They were all scenes of violence, Joan noticed now: Cain killing Abel, Abraham preparing to sacrifice his son, Christ being crucified. Father must have painted them himself. He wasn't much of an artist, she thought, and the realization gave her confidence and a strange sense of comfort.

Father wasn't here yet, but the door to his sleeping chamber was open, and everyone was obviously awaiting his arrival.

How old was he now? It was hard to tell. He had fathered her mom and had fathered her mom's mom, and though both her grandmother and her great-grandmother had been young at the time, in their early teens, that probably put him somewhere in his eighties or nineties.

When was he going to die?

Not soon enough, she thought.

She should be grateful for small favors. At least he had not fathered *her*. And he *had* allowed her mom to marry someone else. Although he had wanted Joan to—

She pushed the memory from her mind.

The people in the room, seated on the benches, seated on the floor, standing in the corners, were talking among themselves. Their eyes kept returning to her, though no one would look at her directly. *How many?* she wondered. Twenty or thirty, at least. Not everyone who lived in the Home by a long shot, but enough that the big room seemed crowded. Father had probably called them here specifically to view her perceived humiliation, to drive home the point to both them and her that escape was not possible, that even those who managed to get out would be brought back for punishment sooner or later.

Joan had lost track of Absalom, but she saw him now, standing before the bookcase next to the door to Father's sleeping chamber. He was with one of the other Teachers, a man she recognized but whose name she could not recall. The two men conferred for a moment; then Absalom moved so that each of them was on an opposite side of the door. "Quiet!" they announced in unison, speaking the Language.

The room was silenced.

All eyes were on Father as he emerged from the darkness.

Kara was by his side.

Kara?

Joan stood there, shocked. The last thing in the world she expected to see here was her roommate. The juxtaposition was jarring, her new life intruding into her old life, the Outside world coming into the Home.

And Kara was with Father? How was that even possible? It made no sense on any level whatsoever, and Joan was filled with a profound despair as she saw how her friend was wearing not a look of fear, panic or even coerced cooperation, but an expression of blind contentment.

Converts, Joan knew from experience, were often more hard-core than people who had been born and raised in the Home, and although that had not been true of her father, she had the feeling that it was for Kara. Something in her friend's eyes bespoke not just belief but a willingness—no, a *need*—to impress that belief upon others.

How had this happened? Joan could not seem to wrap her mind around it. Had Kara been a plant all along? Was she the one who had reported Joan's whereabouts to Father? Or had she been recruited *because* she was Joan's roommate?

It was possible that she'd been kidnapped at the same time Joan had been, subjected to brainwashing indoctrination once she'd been brought to the Home, and that was the scenario Joan chose to believe.

Anything else was too depressing and demoralizing to contemplate.

His hand on Kara's shoulder, Father strode between the haphazardly arranged furniture until he was standing directly before her. He was taller than Joan remembered and, as much as she hated to admit it, there was a powerful aura about him, a charisma he exuded that was only intensified by proximity. He smiled at her, but the smile was sharp and dangerous, not warm and welcoming. "It is good to have you back," he said. He spoke in English. For Kara's benefit, no doubt. "I am glad you have returned to us."

Joan wasn't sure how to respond. She wanted to announce loudly that she hadn't *returned*, she'd been *kidnapped*, but while she was angry enough to confront him with the truth, doing so might make her situation worse. She was all alone here, at their mercy, and perhaps it would be smarter right now to lie low.

So she said nothing.

Father smiled, holding his arms wide as though to give her a hug, though neither he nor she made any effort to move closer to the other. "We have always known you would come back to us, and it is a blessing that you are here again. You have experienced the horrors of life Outside, away from the Home, and your inevitable return has brought a new member to our growing family." He put an arm around Kara's shoulder, squeezing.

She couldn't sit still for this. She wouldn't.

"I have seen your joyous future and know why you have come back." He paused. "You are to give me a son."

Joan shook her head.

"Ruth—"

"My name is Joan now."

Father's face hardened. "*Ruth.* I forgive you for leaving the Home. It was not your fault and you are back now, so I—"

"Where are my parents?"

There was stunned silence in the room. She was not supposed to interrupt Father while he was speaking. She knew that, and she'd done it on purpose, to show that she would not be intimidated. But Father's expression was one of rage and hate, and she could tell that he was about to yell at her. Before he could utter a word, she asked the question again: "Where are my parents?" Her eyes met his defiantly.

"You will never see your parents again."

The words were whispered fiercely, not shouted, were meant to serve as a threat, but her heart leapt with joy as she heard them. *Her parents were safe.* If they had been captured, Father would have told her so, would have bragged about it. If anything, he would have used them as leverage, would probably have had them here for her to see. But instead he offered only this vague threat, and inwardly she rejoiced. She didn't have to worry about them being hurt or retaliated against, didn't have to figure out how to help them escape. They were free. She could concentrate on herself and getting out of here as quickly as possible, in any way she could.

Father must have realized that it made him seem weak to be so upset by something *she* said. She was a

nobody. *He* was Chosen. He smiled at her with newly
regained equilibrium. "The Lord our God has instructed
us to be fruitful and multiply, and that is why I have created this haven. So we may follow His wishes and do
exactly that. The Home is not the Home unless it is ever
filled with the voices of new Children." He smiled at
Joan, but there was a hint of a threat in it. "Wouldn't
you like a child of your own?"

"Not with you."

"*Only* with me!" he roared.

She glared at him. "Don't you *dare* touch me," she
spat out. "I wouldn't have a child with you if you were
the last person on earth."

The stunned silence of a few moments previous was
nothing compared to the cessation of sound that suddenly descended upon the room. No one spoke, no one
dared breathe, and for several shocked seconds there
was utter quiet. No one had ever talked back to Father
before, no one had ever addressed him with such disre-
spect, and the fear among the spectators was palpable.
None of them knew what Father would do.

Joan was afraid, too, but she was also angry. Not
just angry. *Furious.* Furious at the way she had been
brought here, furious at the way she'd been raised, furious at the way the people here were treated and, perhaps most of all, furious at what had been done to her
mother. Boldly, she stared back at him, fists clenched,
chin held high.

Father exploded. He lashed out and struck Joan across
the face, not with an open palm but with a fist. The force
slammed her head sideways, and an eruption of pain engulfed her senses. For several seconds she could neither
see nor hear. Then blurred vision returned, along with a
dull roaring that came from inside her head and muffled
all outside sound. She felt wetness on her cheeks, and
for a brief, disorienting moment thought his hand had

been covered with water when he hit her. Then she realized that the wetness was blood.

A punch to the stomach dropped her to the floor, where she curled onto her side, gasping for breath. Through her tears, she peered up at Kara, but her roommate studiously avoided looking at her, concentrating her gaze on the far wall.

"You will have my child," Father snarled, and this time he spoke in the Language so Kara *couldn't* understand. "I will take you again and again and again and *again* until you deliver to me the son that was promised."

Joan searched the faces above her, the faces of the people Father had gathered to watch, looking for support, looking for sympathy, but she saw only uninterested stares and the vacant equanimity of true believers. She would receive no aid or help here.

"Remove her," Father ordered, and strong hands grabbed her arms, yanking her up. It was still hard to breathe, though the wild agony of a few moments before had settled into a pulsing throb in her head. She closed her eyes against the pain and felt herself being dragged away, out of the room, though she could not tell by whom. At first she tried passive resistance, letting them pull her, but the pressure of the fingers digging into her arms became too much, and she was forced to support herself, stumbling on rubbery feet in whatever direction they led.

She was shoved into a room, where she fell forward, collapsing onto the hard wooden floor. Not a word was spoken, and the only sounds she heard were the slamming of the door followed by the click of the lock. She lay there, unmoving, grateful for the respite. After Father's assault and the rough treatment of her escorts, lying unmolested on the floor felt like being in a comfortable bed. She turned her head to the side, closing her eyes. The coolness of the wood felt soothing against her face. Gradually, her tears went away and her breathing returned to normal. The pain subsided, though her left cheek and the area around her left eye felt puffy and swollen.

What was she going to do now? Joan wondered.

What was going to be done *to* her?

She didn't even want to think about that.

She sat up slowly, looking around. Where was she? The Home must have changed a lot in her absence, or she had forgotten or blocked out much of what she'd known about the place, or perhaps the life she had lived here had been so proscribed that huge areas had been off-limits, because this was another room that seemed completely unfamiliar to her. The shape of the room was odd, almost circular, though there were still four recognizable corners, blunted as they might be. The curved, windowless walls, entirely free of adornment or decoration, were made of a different material than she had seen in the rest of the Home: not wood, not concrete, but a tan spongy-looking substance that resembled foam rubber. Illumination came from a series of small slitlike skylights overhead.

In the center of the room were two large rectangular wooden boxes on sawhorses. Made of simple, unstained, unadorned pine, the boxes resembled coffins, and Joan knew instantly that that was exactly what they were. Attendance at funerals had been mandatory when she was a child, but somehow her parents had managed to keep her from that. So she had never actually seen a coffin here before. But she recognized the work, recognized the style, and she thought it was just like Father to lock her up in a room with coffins as part of an effort to intimidate her.

What was she supposed to take from this? That if she did not cooperate she would die?

A new thought occurred to her: maybe there were

dead bodies in the boxes. She would not put that past Father, either, and she walked slowly forward to check.

She reached the coffins.

Peered down.

And saw what had happened to her parents.

Twenty

Bitterweed, Texas, was prettier than its name had led them to expect. Gary had imagined a dusty little town on a flat expanse of dirt, kind of like the one in the movie *The Last Picture Show*. But it was more like a small town on television: quaint buildings nestled between large, leafy trees, a river running under a bridge on the highway at the beginning of the business district. Old-fashioned streetlamps, two to a block, staved off the darkness and cast the entire community in a warm glow, even now in the wee hours of the morning.

As promised, they stopped by the sheriff's office first. Gary wouldn't have expected it to be open at this hour in a town this small, but lights were on as Brian pulled next to the curb in front of the tan brick building. The four of them got out of the car, and Reyn pulled open the glass door. It was unlocked, and a cheap buzzer sounded as they walked inside.

"Is this a police station or a Seven-Eleven?" Brian muttered.

A deputy was sitting behind an old oak desk, playing Tetris on a computer located atop an adjacent cart. He glanced up as they entered and said in a thick Texas accent, "Are you from California?"

Gary looked at his friends. "Yeah," he said.

"The sheriff wants to see you. Hold on, I'll find out if

he's awake." The deputy disappeared through an open doorway into a hallway that led to the rear of the building. "Come on back!" he called seconds later. Glancing silently at one another, Gary and his friends walked around the desk and down the hall to where the deputy stood outside an office, motioning for them to enter.

Sheriff Stewart was as far from the stereotype of a small-town Texas sheriff as it was possible to get. Rather than a corpulent redneck in mirrored shades, he was a slender black man with a soul patch beneath his lower lip. He'd obviously been dozing on the worn couch that sat against one wall of his office, and he yawned as they walked in. "Sorry," he said, and he had no Texas accent at all. "Not much happens here after the bars close, and I was just getting in a little dreamtime before the morning rush." He held out a hand. "I'm Antwon Stewart, sheriff of Camino County. My associate here is Taylor Lee Hubbard, the best deputy on the planet Earth."

The four of them shook hands and introduced themselves. Though there didn't seem to be anyone else in the station, the sheriff indicated to the deputy that he should close the door, and he did so, standing with the rest of them in front of the sheriff.

"I understand that you think one of your friends has been kidnapped by the Homesteaders," Stewart said.

"My girlfriend. Joan Daniels," Gary answered. "And I don't *think* so; I *know* so. We captured two of them who'd been sent after me, and they told us where she was. That's why we're here."

"And you were kidnapped by the cult before and escaped?"

Gary nodded.

"That's rare," the deputy said.

"What happened?" the sheriff asked. "Your detective didn't give me too many details."

Gary explained how he'd been abducted from his

dorm room, drugged, and taken to a farmhouse in New Mexico. He described how, after spending a day there shackled to the floor, he'd escaped following a car crash, and revealed his suspicion that the De Baca sheriff was one of *them*.

Stewart looked over at his deputy before turning back toward Gary. "Would you be willing to testify that the Homesteaders were the ones who did this to you?"

"Hell, yeah!" Brian answered for him.

Gary nodded.

The sheriff smiled. "That would help us out a lot."

"Does that mean that now you can go in there and rescue Joan?" Stacy asked.

Stewart sighed. "It's not that easy. I don't know how much you know about the Homesteaders, but they're a cult. They brainwash people. It's virtually impossible for us to get anyone to testify against them or go on record in any way, shape or form."

"They're scared," the deputy said.

The sheriff nodded. "Even the ones who have escaped, who know things, who've seen things, are afraid. As you found out, these sons of bitches have a long reach. And right now, we're not allowed to even look in their direction, thanks to a court order."

"That they bought," the deputy added.

"They have some pull in these parts," Stewart admitted.

"Well, we're going over there and getting Joan," Gary said. "Even if we have to tear that place down."

"We don't condone what you're doing," the sheriff said. "In fact, we aren't even aware that you're doing it. But if you get into trouble and need help, it's possible that we might be nearby."

"With enough men to storm those gates in sixty seconds flat," the deputy offered.

"Thank you," Stacy told them.

Stewart sat down behind his desk. "Just do us a favor. Wait until morning."

Gary started to object, but the sheriff said, "It's only another hour or so. Besides, it's dark now; you'll be at a disadvantage. And while I have a man out in . . . that general vicinity right now, I won't have my full shift coming on duty until seven."

"We'll wait," Stacy promised.

Gary looked at her.

"Come on. We need every advantage we can get. Besides, we still don't even have a plan."

"What do we do until then?" Brian wondered.

"We have a break room," the deputy said. "There's coffee, some old cookies, I think. You could just wait there."

"Tell us more about this cult," Reyn suggested. "Give us a heads-up on what we should do, what we should be looking for."

Brian raised his hand. "I have a question. On our way here, we saw these cult guys just walking along the highway. For miles. What's that about?"

"Penitents," the sheriff said. "They're members of the cult who have been sent away to live elsewhere. For punishment. After a certain amount of time, they're allowed to return. Homesteaders don't just live here in Bitterweed, in the place they call the Home. This is where they come for training or indoctrination or whatever, and a lot of them do stay, but some of them live in other places, other states." He gestured toward Gary. "As you found out."

Gary nodded. "Like the people at that farmhouse."

"We think they do it on purpose, so we won't know how many of them there actually are—and so that, even if we raid the Home and capture everyone in it, they'll still have people free. We don't even know where these penitents go when they leave Bitterweed. I mean, we've followed some of them, and we do know a few locations, here in Texas, but out there . . . ?" Stewart shook his head.

"Speaking of raids," Reyn said, "what exactly did you go after them on? And what's with this harassment case?"

Stewart sighed. "We first went after them four years ago. A woman came to us, claiming that she'd been raped and held captive against her will."

Gary felt cold.

"At that point, we knew of the Homesteaders—they used to come into town for groceries and gas, supplies and whatnot—but as far as we were concerned, they were just a bunch of religious wackos, neohippie survivalists who kept to themselves and did no harm."

"They've been there forever," Hubbard added. "My dad remembers the Homesteaders being there when he was a kid."

"But they hadn't had much to do with outsiders and no one really gave them much thought. Then this woman escaped, she said, from captivity, and claimed that she'd been imprisoned in the Home for over a year and repeatedly raped by the leader of the cult, who she called 'Father.' We immediately obtained a warrant, but before we could serve it and arrest this 'Father,' our victim had a change of heart—"

"They got to her," Hubbard said angrily.

The sheriff nodded. "They got to her. I don't know how, although I assume it happened in the hospital in Fort Albin, where she was being examined for evidence of rape, but all of a sudden we got a call and it was her, and she was desperate to drop all charges—"

"Scared," Hubbard said.

"She was scared," Stewart agreed. He ran a hand along the back of his neck. "I chose to continue, figuring we had a case even without her cooperation, figuring we could get her cooperation back once we showed her how strong the case was . . ." He trailed off.

"What happened?" Gary prodded.

"She threw herself down a flight of stairs."

"Or was *thrown*," Hubbard said.

"There was no proof. We couldn't prove anything, either way. I arrested this 'Father,' who, no surprise, refused to give us his real name. We checked his prints, but they weren't on file anywhere, and we could find no way to positively ID him. He was not in any system, and we could find no one willing to vouch for his identity. Our guess is that he was born in the Home and has lived there all of his life, but on the complaint we were forced to refer to him as 'John Doe,' as crazy as that sounds.

"I asked the DA to prosecute based on the victim's initial statement, but the case was kicked the second it went before a judge. 'Father' was already free, anyway. He had a high-powered lawyer who got him out of jail after the first night."

"Wow," Stacy said.

"Yeah. Anyway, next time around, it was a boy who claimed he was drugged and kidnapped, a student from College Station whose mother, after the death of her husband, had sold everything she owned and become a member of the cult. The boy had been concerned about her, had started making inquiries, and one day he'd come home to his apartment to find two men waiting for him. They drugged him, abducted him and brought him to the Home."

"That sounds familiar," Reyn said, looking at Gary.

"He was a smart kid. Resourceful. And *big*. Played fullback for the Aggies. He managed to fight his way free, and after he got out of the Home came directly to us, told us everything. So we got a warrant and raided the place, but someone must have tipped them off because we went over those buildings with a fine-toothed comb and found no drugs whatsoever, no indication that anyone had ever been held there against their will."

Gary looked at Reyn. "You're right. Déjà vu all over again."

"We had *dogs*, and even they couldn't sniff anything out. The Homesteaders, of course, were as polite as you please, very helpful, pulling that deferential religious act. We interviewed anyone we could find, but they all toed the party line, claimed they'd never seen the kid before. And we couldn't find that many people. It was like everyone had taken off or was hiding somewhere. We searched the compound anyway, took a lot of pictures, and we did see some weird things: no bathrooms, a kitchen where a cook was butchering a possum, a chapel filled with the strangest-looking worshippers *I've* ever seen, a round room filled with homemade coffins, a triangular room where women were cutting big sheets of paper into little rectangles, huge pictures of our old buddy 'Father' everywhere you looked. But nothing illegal and nothing that was specified in the warrant.

"The kid still stuck to his guns, though, and swore out a complaint, and this time it did go to trial. Again, they had a high-priced lawyer, and the fact that his own mother said he was lying—and, brainwashed or not, she was a damn good witness, very sympathetic—as well as the fact that we had no physical evidence and it was basically a he-said/she-said situation, practically guaranteed that they were going to win. They did, and the kid vowed to file a civil suit, but we never heard from him again.

"Third time a couple came to us, claiming that their daughter had been kidnapped by the Homesteaders. Again, we got a warrant, went in, and there was no sign of her. In fact, the parents themselves disappeared. The phone number they gave us was disconnected, the address false." Stewart breathed deeply. "I'm still hoping that one was a setup. But it's more than possible that someone *made* them disappear.

"After that, the harassment case was brought against us, listing the county, the entire department, and me and my men individually. There've been delays and postponements, so it hasn't gone to trial yet, but it's been winding its way through the system for at least a year. Needless to say, the county attorney has ordered us to stay away from the Home and avoid contact with any of the cult members."

The deputy looked at Gary. "Which is why we're lucky you showed up."

"Exactly. There are four of you who are eyewitnesses *and* victims. We have drugging, kidnapping, breaking and entering, robbery, murder or attemped murder, and it's across state lines and being investigated by Los Angeles police. *And* two of the Homesteaders are in custody. If we can tie all this together, it's a slam dunk."

"I'm not sure about the robbery charge," Gary said. "They broke into my dorm room and trashed it. But they didn't take anything. I don't think I had what they were looking for."

"Oh, you might've. And they might've gotten it. But they won't take anything physical. 'Thou shalt not steal' and all that. They're strict followers of the Bible, even though they're a little loose around the edges. Tell me, have you noticed since then that your credit cards don't work, or—"

"Yes!" Gary said.

The sheriff nodded. "They probably got information off your computer. *That* they don't consider stealing, and it's probably why they were there in the first place. They try to come off as simple, old-fashioned back-to-the-land types, but let me tell you, they use some sophisticated terrorist tactics to go after their enemies. Believe me, I know."

"Why?" Stacy said. "What happened?"

"My credit rating was ruined. So were the credit ratings of my entire staff and half of the county employees. I ended up having to convince my own bank that I was me, and it took two years to prove to them that I owned my own house. Everyone here has a similar story."

"Yep," Hubbard agreed, lips tight.

"Let me tell you about Len Hearn, our then–district attorney. Len had it the worst. He was served with papers for back payment of child support, though he'd never been married and never had a kid. His pickup truck was repossessed and his house was foreclosed on, even though he had never missed a payment on either. Oh, and his bank account was cleaned out, every last dollar he had transferred electronically to a company in Barbados." The sheriff paused. "Len killed himself, blew out his brains with a twenty-two."

"You couldn't get them for *that*?" Stacy asked incredulously.

"No proof," Stewart said. "We called in the FBI, but everything was untraceable. Whoever their computer guy is, he's good."

Outside, there was a lessening of darkness, a hint of pink that showed through the slatted blinds covering the window. Gary glanced at the clock on the wall. Six o'clock. It was Thursday morning. He was anxious to go after Joan.

The sheriff stood and pulled open the top drawer of an old-fashioned file cabinet behind his desk. "One thing that will help you, I think, is getting a look at the Home and its layout." He withdrew a thick manila folder and placed it on top of his desk, flipping it open and turning it to face them.

The first photo, taken from some distance away, showed a sprawling series of single-story buildings framed by a wrought-iron gateway topped with a cross.

The buildings were at the far end of a twin-rutted dirt driveway. "We took these during our first raid. This one's from the road." Stewart slid the photograph off the top of the pile, revealing the next photo below: an aerial view of the property. "This was taken from a helicopter." From this angle, Gary could see not only how large the grounds were but how isolated. The flat buildings of the first photo and a barn surrounded by planted fields were the only structures visible. An irregular red line had been drawn with a pen over a center section of the picture, encompassing the buildings, the fields and a sizable portion of woods.

"The front entrance is here," the sheriff said, pointing with a pencil. "This driveway leads to the road, and the road leads to First Street at the east end of town. The compound's about eight miles from where we are now. I have two men watching the grounds at this moment. Manny Trejo's right here, by this tree." The sheriff moved his pencil. "Ken Faul is staking out the rear of the property from a fire break just outside this part of the picture."

"I thought you weren't supposed to—" Stacy began.

"What the county attorney doesn't know won't hurt him."

"And it might *help* you," Hubbard said.

"If something happened," the sheriff said, "if you got in trouble somehow, if you saw something illegal, if you saw something *suspicious*, Manny and Ken would be in a position to quickly assist you."

Gary nodded. "I understand."

Stewart swiveled the monitor on his desk to face them and with a few clicks of his mouse brought up several rows of thumbnail photos. "More shots are on the computer here. Just click on the ones you want to enlarge."

"Okay."

"I'm going to get some coffee," Stewart said pointedly. "Taylor, why don't you keep me company."

"Sure," the deputy said.

"But—" Gary began.

"We'll be back in fifteen minutes," Stewart told him.

Brian put a hand on Gary's shoulder to keep him from protesting as the sheriff and deputy walked out of the room. "They think we're going to break in," Brian explained, once the door had closed. "They don't want to know about it, but they're giving us time to look over the surveillance photos, to try and find a way inside."

"Oh," Gary said, feeling dumb.

"Huh," Reyn said. "I didn't get that, either."

"You two are so naive," Stacy said. She reached down and picked up the aerial photo. "How *do* we get in?" she wondered. "This place is like a fortress. Even if they don't have guards or people specifically assigned to watch for intruders, they probably have cameras and alarms set up."

"I'm not sure they need any of that," Reyn said, flipping quickly through the rest of the photos. "Look how many people are here. Front, back, sides. Someone's bound to notice us."

"It's harvest time," Gary said. "We might get lucky; they might be in the fields."

"That's a possibility," Reyn conceded.

"How do we get in?" Stacy said again.

Gary had taken the photos from Reyn and was looking through them. The front of the Home did not resemble a home at all, but a generic industrial building. A meatpacking plant, perhaps. Or a warehouse. Both the surrounding farm and the Texas setting would seem to make a Western look more appropriate, but there was no wood, only stucco, no portico, only a flat door in the wall. As Stacy said, it was essentially a fortress, and the disparity between function and appearance was disconcerting.

Inside, the decor was just odd: irregularly shaped

rooms; looms, spinning wheels and other items from a preindustrial era; a restaurant-sized kitchen with a wood-burning stove; primitive, spartan living quarters, and those ever-present framed photos of a white-bearded old man. *Father.* The people were even odder, and like the two they had captured back in California, many of the residents appeared to have some sort of physical deformity or mental handicap.

Like Joan's mother.

He stared at a man with an overlarge head and stumpy extremities, and it suddenly occurred to him that Joan's mother would fit right in with these people. He thought of the prayer scroll they'd found in Joan's room.

The Outsiders.

Realization suddenly dawned on him. *Joan had belonged to the Homesteaders.* She had come from here. And Outsiders were anyone else, anyone who was not part of the cult. Joan and her parents had escaped somehow, and the Homesteaders had tracked her down, brought her back. Her parents . . .

Gary thought of the dead dog in the empty house.

The spot of red blood on the white linoleum floor.

His thoughts must have shown on his face because Stacy said worriedly, "What is it? What's wrong? Did you see something in that picture?" She took it out of his hands to examine it.

He didn't want to say. They were here to help him, and it was wrong to keep information from them, but he rationalized it by telling himself that it was not information, just conjecture. The truth was that he was embarrassed, as stupid and superficial as that might be, and he didn't want them to know that Joan had ever been involved in any way with these lunatics.

Gary looked at the next photo, a picture of the farm. Rows of crops stretched across a long field bordered at the far end by tall, leafy trees. In the photo, one man was riding an antiquated tractor, while a dozen or so others worked with hoes along the rows. If the tractor had been taken out of the picture, the scene could have been one from two hundred years ago.

"They're not as primitive as they make themselves out to be," Brian reminded him, looking over his shoulder. "They erased your electronic footprint. And Joan's. Someone in there is sophisticated enough to hack into the DMV, UCLA, banks, credit agencies. . . . They're not just simple God-worshipping farmers."

"No, they're not," Gary said grimly. "And they're not just here in Texas. They have allies all over, like those people in New Mexico—"

"Like that *sheriff*," Brian emphasized.

"They're not just growing potatoes on that farm, either. Whatever they drugged me with tasted like dirt, like some sort of root. I'll bet they grow that shit right there."

"Duly warned," Reyn said. "We have to be careful."

They spent the next twenty minutes or so looking through the photos on the computer, trying to figure out the best way in. The compound itself was surrounded on all sides by large tracts of open land, so whichever approach they took, they would be easily spotted. Before they even tried to get inside the buildings, they had to reach them, and they went back and forth on how best to do that.

Finally, they heard new voices from the front of the sheriff's office, and Gary glanced up at the window to see that it was fully light outside. They should have gone under cover of darkness, he thought. That would have been the best way to reach the Home undetected. But Stewart had dissuaded them from that, and now it was too late.

The sheriff walked back into the room. "Morning shift's here," he said. "We're ready for action."

"Did you contact your guys who are out there?" Gary asked.

"Quiet night. Nothing unusual. All clear."

"Then we should get going," Reyn said.

They thanked the sheriff, double-checked the phone numbers they had to make sure they were correct, grabbed some fresh doughnuts and coffee from the break room, then went outside. The air was cool and smelled of smoke—someone in town was using a fireplace—but it was obvious that the day was going to be warm. An old man atop a muddy tractor drove slowly down the center of the street.

Gary, Reyn, Stacy and Brian got into the rented Nissan. Reyn drove, with Brian as navigator, and Gary sat in back with Stacy. They pulled around the tractor, still slowly making its way through town, then turned onto a side street just past a feed and grain supply store. The street sloped down a gradual incline past a few blocks of small run-down houses, then turned into a dirt road and began winding through copses of trees and boulder-strewn hillsides, following the lay of the land. They passed a single farm with a walnut tree orchard, and then there was only wilderness.

And then there was the Home.

They could see it from afar, a collection of interconnected buildings on a slight rise of open land. It looked bigger than it had in the photographs and, despite its generic appearance, more intimidating. Along the side of the narrow dirt road, conforming to the boundaries of the property, was a wrought-iron fence eight to ten feet high, in the center of which was the arched gateway topped by a cross that they'd seen in the pictures.

Reyn stopped the car several yards away from the open gateway, parking next to an overgrown bush that hid the vehicle from the buildings. They all opened their doors and got out. "All right," Gary said. "Let's go."

Brian faced him. "And do what exactly?"

"Try to sneak in."

No one moved. Reyn looked at Stacy. Brian looked at Reyn.

"What is it?" Gary asked. "What's going on?"

"You can't come with us," Reyn said.

"What?"

"They know you. They sent people all the way to California to get you. You think they don't know what you look like? They probably have Wanted posters with your mug plastered all over that damn place."

"They know all of us," Gary pointed out. "We were all drugged at the same time at Burning Man, and whoever did that kidnapped Joan and brought her back here. He—or *they*—will recognize us instantly."

"Hence the sheriff's break-in strategy," Brian said drily.

"We'll disguise ourselves as penitents," Gary suggested. "They might not recognize us if we're dressed like them."

"Two problems," Brian pointed out. "We don't have any of their peasant clothes to put on, and we don't know shit about their religion. One short conversation with anyone and we'd be spotted as fakers in three seconds flat."

"I told you we should have come up with a plan before we got here," Stacy said.

Brian held his hand out toward Reyn. "Give me the key."

Reyn tossed him the key, and Brian used it to open the trunk. He rummaged through the backpack he'd brought and pulled out a knife. Some sort of camping knife, it had a green handle with a built-in compass, and a heavily serrated blade that glinted in the early-morning sun.

"What the hell is that?" Stacy demanded.

"These are kidnappers and rapists. Child molestors, maybe. We can't just walk in with good intentions and sunny smiles. We need to be ready."

Thank God, Gary thought. He again wished he'd thought to bring a weapon, and he was glad that at least Brian had come prepared.

"I have one for each of you," he said.

Stacy crossed her arms, shaking her head. "No," she said emphatically.

"I don't think it's a good idea," Reyn concurred.

Gary stepped forward and took the proffered knife. Joan was in that place. If he found out that she'd been raped, he would gut the motherfucker who'd done it, no questions asked. His fingers tightened around the handle. It felt reassuringly solid in his hand. He followed Brian's lead and pushed the knife beneath his belt on his right side, untucking his shirt and pulling it over the weapon to hide it.

"Violence isn't the way," Stacy admonished them.

"We're not going to start anything," Brian countered. "We just need to be able to defend ourselves."

"You're going to end up dead. Or in jail."

"We'll be careful," Gary promised, but again he felt that bloodlust as he thought about what might have been done to Joan.

"I'll go in," Stacy said. "You're Joan's boyfriend, Reyn's your friend, I'm Reyn's girlfriend. I'm the furthest degree of separation from the source. If anyone's going to be able to get by them, it's me."

"They know all of us," Gary explained again.

"We could pull a *Wizard of Oz*," Brian said. "Jump some guards, steal their clothes, sneak inside."

"Or jump a penitent," Reyn suggested. He pointed. Walking down the road, from the opposite direction from which they'd come, was a man like those they'd seen striding down the highway in the dark hours before dawn.

Even this far away, even in broad daylight, there was something creepy about him, Gary thought. The fanaticism and true belief required to make a person walk mile after mile, through some of the most godforsaken terrain known to man, lent the penitent a focus that seemed almost inhuman, and even though his body was clearly tired, almost exhausted, he pushed himself on, continuing zombielike down the road.

And he was smiling.

The smile was the worst.

They watched as he reached the gate, turned in and started up the sloping driveway toward the Home.

"I think the best approach is the simplest," Reyn said finally. "I say we just walk up and demand to see Joan. If they turn us down, we'll think of something else. If they try to capture us, we'll fight back and escape. We'll also have legitimate cause to call in the law." He touched Stacy's arm. "You wait in the car. Pull it up to the head of the drive. Be ready to take off if we run back. If anything happens to us, get the sheriff."

"I like it," Gary said.

Brian nodded, patting his hip where the knife rested below his shirt. "I'm in."

Stacy took a deep breath. "Okay," she said reluctantly. "But be careful. Just . . . be careful."

Brian gave her the car key, and Reyn gave her a kiss. "Keep an eye on us," he told her. "Anything weird happens, call it in. The sheriff has those two men out here." He looked around. "Somewhere. They can be on those guys in seconds."

Stacy held his hand tightly. "I don't like this."

"I don't, either," Reyn admitted. "But it'll all be over soon."

"I think they say that in *The Wizard of Oz*," Brian muttered to Gary.

Stacy returned to the car while the three of them continued onward. They all reached the gate at the same time, and she rolled down the window and blew Reyn a kiss while exhorting him once again: "Be careful!"

If all went right, he'd be kissing Joan soon, Gary thought.

The possibility made his heart race—though with anticipation or fear he could not tell.

They started up the narrow, rutted driveway. The penitent was gone, swallowed up by the Home, and Gary wondered if they were being watched as they trudged up the drive toward the compound. He took out his cell phone and pressed the key to automatically dial the number of the sheriff that he'd input into the device. Nothing had happened—

Yet

—but the sheriff had all but begged them to come up with any excuse to call for help and invite law enforcement to rescue them, and he thought it might be a good idea to have someone on the line, listening in as they tried to talk their way inside—just in case something went wrong.

Gary held the phone to his ear.

Nothing.

The call was blocked.

He asked Reyn and Brian to try their phones, but the result was the same. It made sense. Any organization that had the technical savvy to delete credit histories and bank accounts would have no trouble jamming phone signals.

Thank God they'd left Stacy in the car. Someone needed to be able to go for help.

The three of them looked at one another, putting away their phones.

Kept walking.

Finally, they reached the front entrance of the Home. Gary half expected someone to meet them, to either chase them away or force them inside, but they made it to the door without incident. The building was one story, but it looked bigger close up than it had in the photographs, and just knowing how many interconnected structures lay behind this initial facade made Gary realize how hard it was going to be to find Joan. She could be anywhere in there.

"What do we do now?" he wondered aloud. "Knock?"

Reyn did just that, pounding several times on the door with the side of his fist. The door was so thick, it barely made a sound, and Gary looked down the flat expanse of the building, trying to figure out if there was another way inside.

Then there was a rattle, a click, and the door was opened by an elderly man dressed in the type of peasant clothes that characterized all of the Homesteaders. He greeted them with a too-wide smile, though his eyes were flat. "Welcome to the Home. May I help you?"

"Joan Daniels! Where is she?" Gary hadn't known what he was going to say until he said it, and his words were infused with anger, weighted with all of the emotion that had been roiling within him since Joan had been taken at Burning Man.

The Homesteader's eyes widened. "Outsiders!"

Brian whipped out his knife and pressed it against the man's throat.

"What are you doing?" Reyn yelled.

Gary's heart leapt in his chest, pounding crazily. *They* were the ones who'd be going to jail, he thought. Brian had fucked everything up. He'd committed an honest-to-God crime, and even if they found something now, it wouldn't stick.

But Brian wasn't backing down. "Take us to Joan!" he demanded. "Now! Or I'll slit your goddamn throat!"

Gary expected the two deputies who were keeping the compound under surveillance to run up, guns drawn, but no one arrived. No one came from inside the Home, either, and Brian moved slowly around to the back of the man, still pressing the tip of the knife to his throat. He shifted position, using his left arm to get the man in a headlock and pressing the knife against his back, hostage-style. "You have five seconds to start bringing us to Joan."

"Father will—"

"One!"

"—not allow—"

"Two!"

"Okay!" The blankness in the man's eyes had been replaced by fear. Gary looked over his shoulder toward the road, wondering if Stacy could see what was going on, wondering if she had called for help.

"Let's go," Brian ordered, pushing the man forward.

With a feeling of dread spreading outward from his stomach through his body, Gary followed the two of them into the Home.

Reyn hesitated for a second, then came in as well, closing the door behind him.

Twenty-one

The coffins had been removed, but Joan was still in the same room.

It was the fact that they'd taken the coffins that preyed upon her mind. What had been done with her parents' bodies? Had her mom and dad been given a proper burial? Had they been dumped in a ditch? Cremated? Plowed into one of the fields? Were they rotting in one of the basements? She did not know, and the lack of closure and confirmation was driving her crazy.

Which was probably the point.

The coffins had been removed several hours after she had been deposited in the room. She'd been held against the wall by two big-boned women, while two muscular young men had taken away first the caskets and then the sawhorses. She'd already screamed herself hoarse and cried more tears than she would have thought possible, though she had not been able to look again into those open boxes at her parents. Neither the men nor the women had spoken to her, though she'd demanded to know what they were doing, and after everything had been taken out, the women had pushed her down on the floor and left themselves, locking the door behind them.

That had been a long time ago, and in the interim she had slept on the floor and peed in a bedpan that

had been left for her use. Overhead, the skylight slits
had turned dark, then light, and she estimated that she'd
been in the room for at least twenty-four hours when
the door opened again.

"Eat or die," said the middle-aged man who dropped
a canvas sack of food in front of her, and it was clear
from his voice that he didn't care which one she did. He
was not one of the Children, but she did not know where
he stood in the Home, and she turned away from him,
facing the wall, refusing to give him the satisfaction of
interaction.

He left.

Without taking or emptying the bedpan.

After several minutes, Joan opened the sack, remov-
ing its contents. She sniffed the food that had been
brought: a crusty piece of bread, a stick of celery, a cold
baked potato and, to drink, a canteen of water. All of it
smelled earthy, like fertile soil, and all of it smelled the
same. She refused to eat anything, and in a gesture of defiance she picked up the potato and threw it at the wall.
The bread and celery followed. The water she poured
onto the floor.

The door to the room opened immediately, and two
men strode in. One of them she recognized as Barnabas,
a former friend of her dad's. They'd obviously had her under surveillance and had been watching her as she threw
the food and dumped the water. She expected them to
lecture or chastise her, perhaps even force-feed her, but
instead they merely walked in, Barnabas picked up the
sack and they both turned around and left.

Joan stared after them, frowning, as the door closed,
then locked. There was an odor in the air, as though
someone wearing a heavy floral perfume had just left
the room. The scent had not been there only seconds before, and almost immediately after noticing it, her head
began to feel strange. It was the way she'd felt at Burn-

ing Man, just prior to being knocked out. That memory
had not been part of her consciousness until this very
moment, but she recognized its accuracy the instant it
was recalled, and then . . .

. . . and then . . .

. . . the door opened and her dad walked in, carrying
a tray of mushrooms that looked like little angry people.
He was dead and wearing the same expression he'd had
in the coffin, that terrible wide-eyed, openmouthed look
of surprise, and he approached her on awkward feet, offering her one of the mushrooms. She turned away, and
her mom was standing in the corner, screaming, though
the sound that came out of her mouth was the chirping
of crickets. Her hair was on fire, and the skin of her forehead was starting to melt from the heat and drip onto
her eyelashes like pinkish peach rubber cement.

Joan wanted to run away but her feet were nailed to
the floor.

There was a noise above her, a roaring, like the sound
of a waterfall, and when she looked up, the ceiling was
not the ceiling but a giant version of Father's face. His
mouth was open, and that was where the roaring noise
was coming from. Father was breathing in, sucking all of
the air out of the room, and even though her feet were
nailed to the floor, Joan could feel the power of the suc-
tion. Then her mom and dad and everything around her
were vacuumed up, her feet were yanked painfully from
the floor, and she was sucked into the blackness of Father's open mouth.

Joan awoke in a bed.

She was in a room she recognized but could not instantly place. There were simple square end tables on
either side of the bed, and against the wall opposite her
stood a plain pine dresser. Glancing to her left, she saw
a window.

It came to her then. This had been her bedroom. This was the room in which she'd grown up. There were differences now, such as the style of furniture, but the placement of everything remained the same as it had been throughout her childhood.

She sat up slowly. Her upper arms felt sore, as though they'd been squeezed too hard by careless fingers, and beneath the rough, shapeless cloth of her blouse, her bra was missing. There was an uncomfortable sensation between her legs, and when she pulled out the waistband of her pants and underwear, she saw that someone had stuffed a wadded cloth down there. Joan understood what had happened, and the only reason she had not been raped, she knew, was because she was having her period. Because she was *cursed* and *unclean*.

Thank God for small favors.

No. Not God.

She refused to thank God for anything.

There were voices coming from the living room, and for a disorienting moment, she thought that her parents were out there, discussing the events of the day, that they had never left the Home, that the past five years had been nothing but a dream. It was a moment of euphoria, for despite the fact that they were trapped here under Father's rule, her parents were once again alive and well.

Then she heard the voices more clearly, and the man's voice was not her dad's and the woman's voice was not her mom's. Joan tried to get out of bed, but her head felt as though it had been slammed against a wall. Her brain seemed huge and swollen, and a heavy, crashing pain made her stop moving and cry out. Seconds later, the man and woman who'd been talking in the other room came hurrying in, solicitous looks on both of their faces. He was tall and clean-shaven, with longish hair parted in the middle. She was one of the Children, although the only indication of that was the fact that two of her fingers were fused together. Joan had never seen either of them before.

"Are you okay?" the woman asked, concerned. She was speaking the Language.

"Yes," Joan said in kind, careful not to aggravate her headache by moving too much or too quickly.

"You must have been tired." The woman placed a kiss on Joan's forehead. "I'm glad you're finally up, dear."

Joan frowned. What was going on here?

The man smiled, patting her shoulder. "Hungry?"

They were pretending she was part of their family!

Joan recoiled. She didn't know why they were going through this charade or what they hoped to accomplish, and without moving her head, she shifted her eyes, looking from one to the other. This was Father's doing. Nothing happened in the Home without his approval, and he obviously wanted these two to act like parents to her, though whether they were doing so in order to obtain information or merely as part of some larger brainwashing scheme remained to be seen.

"Would you like some breakfast?" the woman asked.

"Why are you doing this?" Joan demanded, confronting them.

The woman tried to look puzzled, but she wasn't a good enough actress, and Joan caught the sideways glance she shot her husband.

If he really *was* her husband.

"Doing what, dear?"

She responded in English. "Knock it off. I'm not a moron. Whatever I've been drugged with made me hallucinate and put me to sleep, but it didn't make me stupid." Her head was pounding, but she tried to ignore it. "What are you supposed to do? Guard me? Make sure I don't try to escape?"

She'd seen through their deception, and they knew she knew, but they were playing their parts to the hilt.

"Our place is yours," the woman said, switching to English also. "You know that."

Fine. Joan pushed herself off the bed, stood and, despite the thunderous sound of blood thumping in her skull, walked over to the closet and opened its door. Inside were empty hangers dangling from a long wooden bar. She closed the door and headed out into the short hall that led to the bedroom that used to be her parents'.

"Ruth—" the woman began.

"My name's Joan," she said frostily.

The couple looked at each other, confused. Clearly, they hadn't been given much information. They'd probably been chosen for this only because they happened to reside in her family's old living quarters.

Joan walked into the bedroom, noting that the bed was flat against the east wall rather than being centered in the middle of the room the way it had been when her family lived here. These people kept no flowers— her mom always had a vase of cut flowers on the dresser and a potted geranium near the window—and to Joan's eye, the room seemed depressingly devoid of decoration. The only nonfunctional item in sight was a framed photo of Father above the bed.

She walked across the room, moved to open the closet door.

"No!' the man said, breaking character.

Joan immediately twisted the knob and yanked the door open. The closet was dark and, at first glance, appeared to be empty. Then she saw the wooden box on the floor. It was filled with black dirt, and in the dirt grew dozens of white mushrooms of various shapes and sizes.

She frowned. What was this?

"Don't tell Father!" the woman begged. There was fear in her voice.

Whatever was going on, Joan knew she had the upper hand, and she decided to play it. "What is this? What are you doing?" she demanded.

"We only use them for ourselves," the woman said. "We don't share them."

"They help us," the man said.

She understood. These mushrooms were hallucinogenic. They might even be the source of whatever had been used to drug her.

"It's my own soil. I made it myself. And the mushrooms just came up. It's not stealing. I would never steal. They're not part of Father's crop."

"They're just for us," the woman said.

Joan relented. Like herself, like her parents, these were people unhappy with the Home, people who wanted to escape but could not do so physically. Instead, they grew mushrooms in secret and ingested them in order to numb the pain and flee the reality of their lives in the only way they could.

"I won't tell anyone," she said. "But I need you to talk to me. I need you to tell me the truth."

"We can't let you go." The woman started crying. "Father will punish us if we do."

Joan's muscles tightened involuntarily at the idea of punishment. She thought of the screams she'd heard on the night she and her parents had escaped. "What are your names?" she asked kindly.

The man sighed heavily. "I am Mark. My wife is Rebekah."

"My name is Joan. It used to be Ruth, but now it's Joan."

"Joan," Mark said, nodding respectfully. Rebekah was still sobbing.

"How long have you lived in the Home?"

"I came here as a child," he replied. "My parents were Outsiders. Rebekah was born here."

"I don't remember you," Joan said. "Did you know my parents?"

"I worked with your dad on the Farm sometimes," Mark said.

Rebekah wiped her eyes, took a deep breath, banished her tears. "Your mom helped us in the Kitchen every once in a while, but we didn't know them well."

"You knew we escaped, though. You knew we got out."

They both nodded.

"Do *you* want to get out?"

There was a moment of hesitation, as though they still weren't certain they could trust her.

"You're taking drugs," Joan said. "Against Father's laws. You're spending your free time growing mushrooms in your closet and anesthetizing yourselves so you won't have to think about your lives. You're telling me you're happy here? You don't want to escape?"

"Of course we do!" Rebekah said fiercely. "But we can't! No one can!"

"We did," Joan said simply.

"And you're back again."

That was true. Joan thought of her parents in the coffins. *Where were they now?* "I'm not staying here," she said.

The two looked at her, expressionless.

"I was kidnapped and brought here against my will. I'm being *held* here against my will." She swallowed hard. "My parents are dead. *They* were kidnapped. And killed." It felt like a punch to the stomach to say those words. "All we have to do is get out and tell the police, and it'll be all over."

"Father will punish us," Rebekah said again.

Joan backed off. This was too new for them, too much

to handle all at once. But they were unhappy here, they were already doing something forbidden and their sympathies were with her. All she needed to do was nudge them in the proper direction and help them gather the strength to do the right thing.

She also needed to figure out what that right thing was. She needed to come up with an escape plan, the way her dad had. Unfortunately, her knowledge of the Home was not only five years out of date but incomplete. She'd been a teenager when they'd left and had not been exposed to many areas and aspects of life here—which was another reason she needed Mark and Rebekah's help.

"What are you supposed to do with me?" she asked.

They looked at each other. "Treat you like family," Mark said finally. "Father thinks that if we show you that this is still your home, it will make it easier for you to adjust. That's why he put us here in your old place."

Father thought no such thing, Joan knew. He had given her a fake family and put her back in her old bedroom for the same reason that he had paraded Kara in front of her. He wanted to twist the knife.

"How long am I supposed to live with you?" Joan asked.

"We don't know," Rebekah said. She still seemed reluctant to reveal information, as though she suspected Joan was a spy trying to trick them and trap them.

"And now that I'm awake? What happens now?"

Mark answered. "We're supposed to pray with you, read some scrolls together and take you to Chapel."

"Take me to Chapel? Are you supposed to . . . handcuff me or anything?" She remembered the humiliating discomfort of the muzzle Absalom had put on her.

"No." Mark shook his head. "We were told that the herbs administered to you would leave you content and without the desire to escape." He allowed himself a small smile. "We have experienced that effect ourselves."

Thank goodness that aspect of the drug hadn't worked.

Maybe she could use that to her advantage.

"You're to help me cook," Rebekah offered. "Father wants you to help me in the Kitchen."

"So you work in the Kitchen." An idea was beginning to form in her head.

"I enjoy cooking," Rebekah said, a trifle defensively.

Joan smiled. "Me, too."

There was an awkward silence. She didn't want to push, wanted to keep the two of them on her side, so she just stood there, smiling blandly, trying to ignore the heaviness in her head. Rebekah still looked suspicious, worried, no doubt, that Joan would reveal to someone the secret mushrooms growing in the closet.

"Perhaps we should pray together," Mark suggested, closing the closet door.

"Yes," Joan and Rebekah both agreed, and the three of them walked out to the living room, where the prayer cabinet was located.

Mark opened up the dark wooden door of the cabinet, revealing dozens of small compartments filled with scrolls. "You may choose," he offered Joan, and she reached forward, plucking one from the top row. They knelt down together, bowing their heads, as Mark unfurled the paper and read the words:

O Lord of Heavenly Hosts! Protect me from The Outsiders. Shield me from sin and see me through times of trial and tribulation. Protect me from The Outsiders. Safeguard my friends and family from those who would corrupt us. Protect me from The Outsiders. Let Your light and goodness shine on me and mine. Protect me from The Outsiders. Amen.

Joan was silent afterward. She knew that prayer. It was the one her parents had given her when she'd gone off to school, and to her it still had power. She had no fear of Outsiders anymore—she *was* an Outsider now—but it seemed an appropriate entreaty for protection from an enemy, any enemy, and somehow it gave her strength.

Rebekah picked a scroll, and Mark again read the prayer. Then Mark chose a scroll and Rebekah read the prayer. All three scrolls were returned to their respective nooks, and the cabinet door was closed.

"Let us go to Chapel," Mark said.

Rebekah shot a worried look at Joan. "You're not going to try and run away, are you?"

"No," Joan said, and managed to smile. "Not yet."

Chapel was as dreadful as she remembered: the punishing stone floor, the muttering of Residents and Penitents all about her, the ever-increasing pain in her arms as she remained in worship position, her hands clasped in front of her. She hadn't been hungry and hadn't had to go to the bathroom, so she hadn't had to suffer those indignities of the flesh, but the entire experience was just as brutal and grueling as it had been when she lived here.

Mark and Rebekah must have known it, because the first thing Mark said after they'd walked back to their living quarters was: "Would you like to try a piece of mushroom?" His voice was kind, but there was yearning in it, too, and she knew that that was what *he* wanted to do.

She shook her head. "No, thanks." She smiled politely, but deep down she was still shocked that any Resident would do such a thing. She had been brought up strictly—no drugs, no alcohol, no caffeine—and it was a lifestyle to which she still adhered, an approach to living that had stuck, and in her mind the defection of her family was far less blasphemous than the couple's clandestine drug use.

Although her headache was all but gone, only a slow thickness to her thoughts betraying the fact that she'd been sedated, she'd pretended at the Chapel and in the hallways on the way that she was still groggy. She'd lowered her eyes to half-mast and walked in a zombielike fashion. No one had spoken to her or remarked upon her appearance, though several men and one woman had greeted Mark and Rebekah as they passed through the Home.

Not for the first time, Joan thought about Mark's knowing smile and what he'd said when referring to the substance that had knocked her out: *"We have experienced that effect ourselves."* Something about his reaction struck her as significant, and it seemed to her that it might point the way to her escape, though at the moment she could not understand how.

It was midafternoon now, and obviously she *was* still feeling the aftereffects of being drugged because she felt tired. Excusing herself, she went into her old room, used the bedpan and lay down. It was weird being here again, and the superficial changes superimposed over the familiar layout of the living quarters were disorienting. She closed her eyes, intending only to rest for a few moments, but when she opened them again it was dark. For a brief, panicked second she thought she'd been drugged again, but she quickly realized that either Mark or Rebekah had closed the curtains in the bedroom and shut the door.

From the living room, she heard the clinking of knives, and the clanking of pots and pans. The juxtaposition of her groggy, dazed state and what sounded like the everyday noises accompanying food preparation caused something to click in her brain.

She suddenly knew what to do.

Excitedly, Joan pushed herself out of bed and stumbled through the darkness to the door. She pulled it open. The hallway was dark, too, but there was light coming from the living room, and she followed it.

Mark was sitting on the small couch in front of the coffee table, reading a Bible, while Rebekah was unpacking a box of cooking utensils that had obviously just been delivered. "Hey, you're up!" Mark said in an overly familiar manner, and Joan wondered if they had been discussing her while she'd been asleep and decided to go back to Father's script.

"We're making spicy scrambled eggs for breakfast tomorrow," Rebekah said cheerily, and Joan's heart sank.

She moved next to the prayer cabinet, equidistant between the two of them. "You work in the Kitchen," she said to Rebekah. "You help cook meals for the Home. And Father wants me to help you."

There was a slight hesitation. "Yes."

"And you work on the Farm," she said, turning to Mark.

"But I can't get you out." Mark seemed to know where she was heading. He sounded worried.

"But you know *how* to get outside," Joan emphasized.

"Why are you asking this?" He *was* worried.

"You know why."

Rebekah had stopped unpacking the box and stood next to her husband.

"I know how we can escape."

They looked at each other. "We don't want to—" Rebekah began.

"Yes, you do. If you were happy here, you wouldn't be growing—"

"We *are* happy here." Mark quickly cut her off. There was a pleading look in his eyes, and she suddenly understood. He was afraid they were under surveillance. Or he *knew* they were under surveillance.

She shut up. Glancing around, she searched for something with which to write. Finding neither pen nor paper, she held out her flattened left palm, then squeezed together her right thumb and forefinger and pretended to scribble. Neither of them understood her pantomime, and Joan walked around the smallish room until she finally discovered, in the drawer of a bureau, a stubby pencil next to a piece of paper containing a list of names. She tore the paper in half, took it out and placed it on the coffee table in front of them.

"I'm looking forward to helping you in the Kitchen," she said aloud in the Language. "I'm actually a pretty good cook." On the paper she wrote: *We put mushrooms in the food.*

Rebekah was shaking her head violently, but Mark looked thoughtful.

"Scrambled eggs sound good," Joan said. She wrote: *The same kind they used on me. Everyone gets knocked out and we escape.*

"I like eggs, too." Mark took the pencil from her. "They're much better than pancakes." He wrote: *Not everyone eats at the same time.*

"What day is tomorrow?" Joan asked. "I've kind of lost track of time."

Mark sensed where she was going. "Thursday," he replied. He wrote: *Most people will be in the Dining Room for breakfast before Fifth Day services. Only some will be out.*

Rebekah was still shaking her head no.

Joan took the pencil from him. *How many is some?*
I don't know.
Can we get past them?
Maybe, he wrote.

They were out of paper, and Joan turned it over. *Try to find a way*, she wrote. Aloud, she said, "You're going to have to make a lot of eggs. Breakfast is a big meal. I bet a lot of women are working in the Kitchen."

Rebekah took the pencil from her. *Too many*. She underlined the words for emphasis.

We cut the mushrooms ahead of time, Joan wrote after taking the pencil back, *smuggle them in and sneak them into the food when no one's looking. Scrambled eggs are perfect.*

"No!" Rebekah said aloud.

They both looked at her.

"Yes," Mark said softly. He wrote: *We can do it!*

Joan nodded encouragingly. "I'm a pretty good cook," she said again. "I think I'll be a lot of help to you in the Kitchen."

Rebekah picked up the paper, turned it over, read everything on it, then looked from Joan to Mark and back again.

"Okay," she said finally.

Twenty-two

Joan awoke before dawn, feeling anxious.

She had gone with Mark and Rebekah to the Dining Room for supper last night, eating with the Residents for the first time since she'd been brought back, and though she'd been grateful to see no sign of either Father or Kara, the Teachers' table was full, and Absalom and his comrades fixed her with disapproving glances through the entire repast. She'd forgotten how much she disliked these communal meals, with the prayers between each course and the exaggerated politesse, and the fact that everyone around her was overly solicitous and acting sickeningly sweet put her on edge. She was grateful when an end to supper was called and they were all allowed to leave.

Afterward, back at their living quarters, Mark had chosen mushrooms that he assured her, in one of the written notes that had become their only honest means of communication, were of the right type and were strong enough to knock out every man, woman and child in the Home. The three of them had then spent the next several hours chopping the mushrooms so fine that by the finish they were practically powder. From somewhere, Mark had come up with cloth gloves and face masks that each of them wore to minimize contact with the hallucinogen, and he also supplied a small bag into which they scooped the minced mushrooms. Rebekah would carry the bag with her tomorrow and drop its contents into the eggs whenever she got the chance.

"I need some tonight myself," she said. "To relax."

"We will," Mark promised her.

Joan did not know what had gone on behind the closed door of their bedroom after they'd retired, but she had stayed completely sober. This might be her only chance for a long, long time, and she could not afford for anything to go wrong. She needed to stay alert and on top of things at all times.

Now she was on pins and needles.

Either Mark or Rebekah had gone out and brought back muffins, and they were both sitting at the coffee table in silence, eating. A muffin had been brought back for her as well, and it sat there untouched atop a cloth napkin. Had either of them slept last night? Joan wondered; examining their tired faces, she didn't think they had. That worried her, but she couldn't afford to let them see any doubt. They were shaky enough as it was, particularly Rebekah, and at this point Joan needed to show them strength.

Forcing herself to smile, Joan knelt down on the floor next to the coffee table. "Good morning," she said. She picked up her muffin and took a bite. It was rough and dry, tasteless. She grimaced, swallowing hard. "I hope you didn't make this," she joked.

Mark pushed over a piece of paper on which a message had already been written: *We don't want to do this. It is too dangerous.*

Joan was prepared. She'd thought they might get cold feet and had come up with a response. She gestured for the pencil, and Mark handed it to her. *I will take all responsibility*, she wrote. *I will put the mushrooms in the food. If I get caught, I'll say you know nothing. It was all me. They will all believe it. Even Father.* As she pushed the paper toward Mark, she wondered what had happened to the pieces of paper they'd been writing on yesterday. If they had not been completely destroyed and disposed of properly, they could be pretty damning evidence. The three of them had to make sure that no trace of their messages could ever be found.

Mark read her words, nodded to show he understood, then wrote something himself, pushing it across the table: *What if they torture you?*

The words hung there. Even her parents had never spoken so bluntly, though it was a truth known by everyone in the Home, and Joan felt cold reading the question.

Rebekah reached over, grabbed the paper and tore it in half. She tore those pieces in half, then in half again, continuing to rip the paper until the scraps were so small that they could never be put together again and it was impossible to tell that anything had been written on them. Joan understood her fear—she felt some of it herself—and she nodded her approval of Rebekah's action in order to acknowledge that, but she smiled confidently. "When do we start cooking?" she asked.

Joan was not sure she'd ever been in the Kitchen. She had definitely never worked in here, and she was surprised both by the size of the prep area and by the number of women involved. One woman's sole job was to start the fire in the wood-burning stove and keep it lit, and Joan was afraid she would be assigned such a focused and specific duty as well, so she was grateful when Rebekah announced to everyone present that Joan was to be her helper and that she would be teaching Joan the ropes.

Rebekah apparently had high seniority in the kitchen, and no one questioned or even commented upon the assignment. That was good. She was in charge of actually cooking the eggs, of blending together the ingredients prepared by the others, and that gave them a much better opportunity for sneaking the mushrooms into the food than they would have had at a different station.

Food preparation in the Home's kitchen was like a well-oiled machine. It had been done the same way, using the same recipes, for decades, and ordinarily any deviation from protocol would have been instantly noticed. But Joan and Rebekah had worked out a plan ahead of time and had practiced it in the living room: just before the scrambled eggs were done, the older woman would move into position, blocking her from view, and Joan would sprinkle the finely diced mushrooms into the food. The only question was whether heating the mushrooms would diminish their efficacy, and they would have to wait for the meal to be consumed before they learned the answer.

Mark would be in the Dining Room with the others and, like them, he would not eat anything.

If all went well, the Residents would be knocked out quickly and at approximately the same time, allowing the three of them to make their escape. Or try. After they left the Dining Room, she had no idea what would happen. They might be stopped before they got anywhere near the outside. There were doors that could be locked, Residents who could be patrolling the hallways or guarding the exits, and other variables that could not possibly be predicted.

But they had to attempt it.

Joan could see through the serving window opening onto the Dining Room that Residents were arriving. Meals were always served precisely on the hour and Residents were expected to be seated and ready to eat when the food was taken to the tables. So diners did not trickle in. They all came at the same time, and within two minutes the place was filled.

Tamar and Mary, the two women in charge of juicing the fruits, began pouring beverages into cups, while the Children chosen to serve came up to the window with trays and started taking the drinks out to the waiting Residents.

The Children!

Joan had forgotten about them. The ones who were integrated would be eating here with the other Residents, but those with severe mental and physical handicaps ate separately, in a different room at a different time, so they would not be affected by the eggs with the mushrooms. They would still be awake and conscious.

She saw in her mind the small man with the big head and the horrible dumb grin. The thought of running into him in an otherwise empty hallway made her shiver.

It couldn't be helped, though. And even if any of the Children *were* to be wandering around, they would have no clue what was happening. They would not be aware that the three of them were escaping. It would be easy to slip by them.

Rebekah touched her back, getting her attention, and Joan knew that it was time to put her plan into action. Following the older woman's lead, Joan moved directly in front of the stove, picking up the spatula with which she was supposed to scoop the eggs onto plates. Rebekah had disguised the powdery minced mushrooms by placing them into a glass jar identical to those that housed the herbs used for flavoring various dishes, and she handed Joan the open jar, moving into place behind her so as to block from view the fact that she was dumping the entire contents of the container into the eggs.

Rebekah's hand was sweaty when she handed off the jar, and when Joan hazarded a look at her face, the woman seemed pale and frightened. But she shot Joan an encouraging smile, and as soon as Joan was hidden from the rest of the women, she poured in the finely chopped mushrooms, stirred and started plating.

They'd been told that sixty-six people were in the Dining Room for breakfast, and though Joan didn't know how many Residents and Penitents were in the Home altogether, the tables seemed full. The only thing that worried her was the fact that more people ate supper than breakfast, so there were likely to be men and women still out and about. Nevertheless, the majority of the people were here, and of the ones remaining, most were probably in the Chapel. If the plan worked, they should still be able to get out of the Home with little or no problem.

What they would do when they got outside remained to be seen.

Run, she thought, and smiled to herself.

The first tray of plates went out.

Even if the heat of the scrambled eggs had not diluted or negated the effects of the mushrooms, Mark had asssured her that the drug would not kick in for three to five minutes. She ladled quickly, hoping he was right, because if some people started dropping or freaking out before everyone had had a chance to eat, they were screwed.

The food was going out, and she could see through the serving window that the diners were consuming it and liking it. That had been another worry, that the mushrooms would throw off the flavor, but Rebekah had promised that the taste was practically undetectable, and she'd been right. In the center of the room, not eating, was Mark. He was sipping slowly from his cup of juice, looking carefully around, making sure everyone else was eating the way they should be.

Joan finished sending out all sixty-six plates in less than a minute and a half, and though the women working in the kitchen usually started eating only after everyone else had finished with their entire meal, Rebekah had enough clout and had built up enough trust with her fellow cooks that she had convinced them to pause and have some eggs as well before sending out the apple slices and cantaloupe that came after.

Mary swallowed a big forkful, then held up her plate. "Aren't you going to have any?" she asked Joan.

"I'm not hungry," Joan said. She had never felt so tense in her life, and she kept looking from face to face among the women in the kitchen, searching for some sign that the mushrooms were having an effect. If this didn't work—

There was a crash from the dining room, the noise of smashing plates and cups. It was accompanied by voices, but they were muttering, not shouting, and as Joan looked with the other women through the serving window, she saw Mark stand up slowly while all about him diners were falling backward, falling forward, or getting up and staggering about.

Next to her, Tamar let out a short, stifled cry, then stood in place, frozen.

Her pulse racing, Joan's eyes met Rebekah's across a chopping table.

It had worked.

Twenty-three

As they walked deeper into the Home, Gary was reminded of a hive. Not only were the intersecting corridors mazelike, but the few people they saw were all so focused on their own tasks and duties that they seemed to pay no attention to the fact that the three of them were dressed in street clothes, and that Brian not only had his arm around a Homesteader's throat but was pressing a knife against his back.

The lack of interest was definitely strange, but Gary was well aware that this could be misleading, that they could be walking into a very carefully planned trap.

He hoped Stacy had called the sheriff.

"You'd better not be leading us to this 'Father' character," Brian warned. "If I see anyone who even *looks* like 'Father,' you're a dead man. A dead man. Do you hear me?"

The Homesteader nodded and suddenly stopped walking, turning back the way they had come and going down a hallway they had only recently passed on the right.

"Good call," Reyn said.

"I know how these fucks think."

Gary, bringing up the rear of their little party, had taken out his own knife and was carrying it at his side. He had never used a weapon against anyone before, had never even been in a real fight, but Brian's knife was busy, and if they were attacked or threatened by anyone else, someone had to be ready to protect them, to fight back. And he was more than ready to slice his way through a whole army of cultists if it would get him to Joan.

A woman emerged into the hallway from a room that appeared to be filled with piles of white cloth. Her eyes widened as she saw them. "Isaac?"

She tried to approach them, but Brian twisted around so that his knife was visible. "Back off, shut up and Isaac will live."

The man started jabbering in that weird alien language. The woman answered him in the same way.

"Shut up, both of you!" Brian ordered. He nodded at the woman. "You! Get back in that room! Close the door behind you! If you dare to come out of there, I'll slit both of your fucking throats!"

The woman complied, sobbing, obviously frightened and obviously believing he was capable of such action. The man was still trying to talk to her as the door closed, and Brian tightened the grip around his neck, cutting off the words and causing the man to let out strangled, choking noises.

"When I say 'shut up,'" Brian said menacingly into his ear, "I mean shut up." The look he shot Gary over the man's shoulder had none of the hard strength found in those words, but revealed instead a young man terrified, confused and in way over his head.

That makes two of us, Gary thought. He glanced at Reyn. *Three.*

Ahead, the hallway opened out into a large, open chamber that looked like the lobby of a hotel. It had a ceiling that seemed higher than the roof outside, and the walls seemed more obviously wooden. There was something rustic about it, and Gary was reminded of a log cabin. He wondered if this had been the original structure and if everything around it had been added on later.

Straight across the room was a different hallway. To their right, yet another corridor headed off in a separate direction. Gary was beginning to get worried. They were being drawn deeper and deeper into this compound, and it was starting to feel to him like a trap. Their buddy Isaac or his girlfriend back there could shout out a warning, and he, Brian and Reyn could be instantly surrounded by hordes of militant Homesteaders. They'd taken so many twists and turns through this jerry-rigged building that there was no way he would be able to find his way out again without a guide, and he wasn't sure how effective threatening to kill Isaac was going to be. He had the feeling that the man would be willing to sacrifice himself for the common good and that his compatriots would be only too happy to let him do it.

Wasn't that how cults worked?

Gary pushed past Reyn and got in front of Brian and his hostage. "Enough of this bullshit. Where's Joan?"

Before the man could respond, they heard the sound of smashing dishes. The noise came from nearby, and Gary saw Isaac turn his head to the right. From down the adjacent corridor came another crash, and though their smartest move would be to stay as far away from people as possible, they all moved immediately to the head of that hallway. Something was definitely wrong, and maybe they could turn that to their advantage.

"Where's Joan?" Gary asked again. He wasn't about to let this bastard off the hook. "Is she down there?"

"I do not know where *Ruth* is," the man said defiantly.

What the hell did that mean?

Brian tightened his grip again, making Isaac cough, but he shot Gary a look of concern, and Gary understood why. The man was bolder than he had been, he felt safer here, and that might mean they were in trouble.

"Look," Reyn said, pointing.

Down the corridor, two men stumbled slowly out of an open doorway, then leaned against the wall opposite the door, staring upward.

"They're tripping," Brian said, recognizing the behavior. He grinned. "I could get into this cult. Just joking," he added quickly, glancing over at Gary.

Gary had no idea how his friend could joke around at a time like this. Even if they managed to find Joan and get safely out of the Home—which seemed increasingly unlikely—they would probably end up going to jail, thanks to Brian's irresponsible actions. Gary thought about Father's high-powered attorneys. He and his friends would be charged with everything the Homesteaders *should* have been charged with: kidnapping, assault, attempted murder. . . .

If they ever did get out of here, he was going to kick Brian's ass.

There were other noises coming from the open doorway through which the two wasted men had stumbled, including voices. One of them, a man's, said something that sounded like "Joan."

Gary dashed down the corridor without thinking, leaving Reyn, Brian and their hostage behind. He didn't know if they were following him and at that moment didn't care. The only thing he cared about was finding Joan.

The two men were still leaning against the wall, staring upward, frozen. Directly across from them was the entrance to what looked like some sort of mess hall or banquet room, with a doorway wide enough to fit four people abreast. Inside was chaos. Four rows of long tables stretched nearly the length of the huge room, and most of the people at the tables were lying face forward in their food, though some of them had apparently fallen backward and lay in ungainly positions on the floor. Here and there, other men and women were stumbling against each other or walking in circles. Four or five stood like statues, unmoving.

"Gary!"

He froze. Joan! He had no idea where her voice was coming from, but she'd seen him and was calling to him, and he swiveled around crazily, trying to figure out where she was.

And then he saw her.

How long had it been since she'd been taken from him at Burning Man? A week? Two? He had no idea; his brain could not focus. It felt like years. But she was here now, and she looked wonderful, and she was hurrying toward him from the far end of the room, dodging everyone in her way.

"Gary!"

She was wearing the same sort of drab peasant outfit as everyone else, and it didn't look as though her hair had seen a brush for days, but she was Joan, and like a beautiful painting in an ugly frame, she shone in these surroundings, looking even better than he remembered. He was filled with a complex emotion, at once joyful and sad, angry and relieved, a new emotion that combined all of these feelings into a coherent whole and revolved entirely around her.

He shoved the knife between his belt and his jeans, on his right side, reaching for her as she ran into his open arms. There were a few seconds when it felt strange, when the size and shape of her seemed unfamiliar; then the points where their bodies touched conformed to each other, melded together, and it was as though they had never been apart. Gary kissed her, but it wasn't a long, lingering movie kiss because she pulled back almost instantly and said, "We have to get out of here!"

"What's going on?" he asked, looking around.

"I'll explain later. We have to go." She glanced over her shoulder, and a man and woman were there. "Mark, Rebekah, come on!"

His hand had dropped immediately to the knife when he saw the couple, but apparently Joan knew them and they wanted to escape as well. Holding Joan's hand tightly, not willing to let her go for a second, Gary moved back into the corridor, where Reyn and Brian stood, confused.

"What are you doing?" Joan said, shocked.

She was looking at Brian, whose arm was wrapped around their hostage's neck while he pressed a knife against the man's back. "He's our insurance policy," Brian said.

"Gary?" He could hear the fear and confusion in her voice.

"We'll talk about it later."

They were moving back the way they had come. "Does anyone know a quick way out of here?" Reyn asked. He moved next to the couple behind Joan. "Can you lead the way?"

The man—Mark?—nodded. "Follow me."

"The sheriff should be here any second," Gary said hopefully. "We left Stacy in the car and she was supposed to call for help."

But he wasn't sure that was what had happened. They'd been in here for a while now, and at the very least, the two men Stewart had ordered to watch the Home should have been kicking ass and taking names.

Maybe they'd been captured.

Maybe Stacy had.

No doubt Reyn had had the same thought, but neither of them dared say it aloud. They followed Mark back into the huge rustic room—what Gary thought of as the lobby, as though they were in some resort hotel—

and turned left into the nearest hallway. Isaac began to chatter away in that weird language, obviously directing his speech to Mark, but Brian did something that made him cry out and shut up.

They entered a storeroom of some sort and passed through it, exiting through a doorway on the opposite side into another room filled with low cots and cribs. The room was empty, but there was something eerie about it, and Gary was happy that they passed through quickly and entered another corridor.

"Where are we going?" Joan asked.

"The Farm. It's closest," Mark said.

The corridor curved—

And there was Father.

Gary knew who he was immediately. There'd been no mug shots of Father in the sheriff's file because lawyers had gotten them removed when the case was dismissed, but his framed visage had been displayed on the walls of every photographed room. He'd appeared grim and forbidding in the pictures, but he looked far more frightening in person, and the dark eyes of the tall, stern man who stood in the center of the hallway, white beard hanging down to the center of his chest, blazed with an anger so strong that Gary completely understood why his followers were afraid of him.

Behind Father in the corridor, standing, sitting, crawling, rolling wheelchairs and pushing carts, were men, women and children, fifteen or twenty of them, all horribly malformed. Gary saw a woman with only one arm, no legs and a few strands of iron gray hair combed over the top of her otherwise bald head, being pushed in a modified stroller by a broad-shouldered man no taller than a child. A skinny, pasty-looking teenager who did not seem to be able to close his mouth was drooling into a thick rag tied around his neck. A figure of indeterminate gender lay atop a table equipped with wheels, laughing toothlessly.

"What the *fuck*?" Brian said.

"The Children!" Joan exclaimed, and there was fear in her voice.

"Yes, Ruth, the Children," Father said. He had a strong, deep voice, the type suited for oratory, and his piercing, angry eyes took all of them in. What Gary saw there frightened him, and for the first time he thought they might not make it out of there alive. He used his right hand to withdraw the knife from his belt, still holding protectively on to Joan with his left.

If he thought there would be talk, discussion, negotiation, he was wrong. With a rigid finger, Father pointed at them and shouted an order in that strange language.

Rebekah screamed.

Joan clutched his hand even tighter.

The Children swarmed. As Father stood untouched and unmoving amid the sea of running, rolling, crawling humanity, Gary, holding tight to Joan's hand, turned to run. He had a knife in his hand, as did Brian, but neither of them were killers, and though they might have wielded the weapons for protection, their reflexes were too slow, impeded by conscience and morality, and by the time they'd made the determination that to attack was their only choice, it was too late. Gary's wrist was grabbed, the weapon jerked from his hand. All of the words coming at him were in that alien language, and hands were clawing at him, claws were handling him. He saw faces so distorted they looked more animal than human, more monster than animal, feeling soft, squishy flesh and hard, reptilian skin. Trying to fight back, he went down under a horde of hideous assailants. "Joan!" he cried as they were wrenched apart.

Punched in the gut so hard he couldn't breathe, Gary

knew he was going to die, and at that precise second someone shouted out, "Stop right there!"

The voice was not only normal but familiar. Sheriff Stewart.

The assault continued, but it grew weaker, and shouts in English overrode the alien screams as law enforcement officers broke up the melee. Gary kicked one of his attackers and managed to pull free from a long-legged man who was tugging on his right arm. He stood, looking frantically about for Joan. Batons raised, Stewart and four deputies he didn't recognize were yanking people up, shoving them against the wall and shouting for compliance. Joan and Reyn were free and standing just behind the sheriff. Brian was still fighting with a man who had hold of his neck.

Face hurting, eyes watering, Gary lurched to the right, staggered around the edge of the fray and embraced Joan. "Are you okay?" he managed to get out.

She nodded, but her body was tense, and the expression on her face was anxious and agitated. He was about to tell her that everything was all right, the cavalry had arrived, they were safe, when he saw where she was looking. He suddenly understood her worry, and he glanced around, searching in every direction. His eyes moved over the combatants, up and down the corridor, did the same thing again, but the result did not change.

Father was gone.

Twenty-four

Joan stood with Gary and their friends next to the sheriff's car as two deputies brought out a line of stumbling, mushroom-impaired Residents tied together with plastic restraints. They were placed in front of the Home, in the shade of the wall, next to the fifty or so others who had already been taken out.

All of the law enforcement officers in Bitterweed, on duty and off, had been called in, as had the six extra posse members who usually helped out in the event of an emergency, but they were still overwhelmed by the sheer number of people they had to round up. Other agents from other jurisdictions had been summoned to handle the overflow, but it would be a while before any of them got here, and until then local law enforcement had to subdue and restrain the entire population of the Home by themselves. Not all of the Residents and Penitents would be charged and arrested, of course, but all of them had to be interviewed, once they were sober, and after that the determination of what to do with them would be made.

There were deputies stationed all around the Home, at every entrance, in case someone should try to get away, and Joan still had hopes that Father would be captured, but as one hour passed by, and then another, such an outcome seemed increasingly unlikely. The sheriff had told them they didn't have to wait around, they could go back to town, but she wanted to stay. She wanted to see what they found, who they found, what happened.

Finally, the last group was brought around the corner of the building from the area of the Farm, all shackled together. There were Teachers in this group, and she saw the look on Absalom's face as he was led out with the others. There was nothing kind about it now. He had no warm smile for her, only a hateful glare that told her what she already knew: this was not over.

She remained stoic as his eyes bored into hers. But inside, she was like jelly. She had left the Home, had lived in the real world, was an official Outsider. She was not the girl she had been. But somehow being here again, seeing these people, brought it all back: the fear, the anxiety, the paranoia.

She turned away, trying to make it seem casual and natural, not wanting him to know that she was afraid. Her heart was pounding crazily, and she needed a drink of water; her mouth was completely dry. The sheriff walked up to them. He looked tired but pleased, and he actually smiled as he said, "Thank you." He pointed to Stacy. "Especially you, for calling it in. The tape of that call is going to get us out of a whole heap of legal trouble."

"I just hope you put them away for a long time."

"With your help, with the help of all of you, I think we'll be able to do that." The sheriff moved in front of Joan. "Ms. Daniels." He nodded politely. "How are you feeling?"

"Nervous," she said.

"Understandable, understandable." There was a short pause. "When we're done here, after we go back to the office, if you're up to it, I'd like to get a statement from you. Not to add on too much pressure, but you're the reason for all this. You're the linchpin of our case, and we really need your cooperation in nailing these guys."

"I'll give you a statement; I'll testify in court—I'll give you whatever you need."

He looked relieved. "You don't know how glad I am to hear you say that."

"Is that all of them?" Gary asked, motioning toward the numb, passive Residents lined up against the wall. Separated from the others were the Children. Several of the more severely disabled, the ones in wheelchairs or lying on gurneys, had already been taken away in ambulances.

"That's all we were able to find. So far. I have a group of men searching the barn and looking through the fields. We're going to go back in and do another search of the compound in a few minutes." His jaw tightened. "We haven't been able to locate their illustrious leader, the one who calls himself 'Father.'"

Joan had been afraid of that.

The sheriff faced her. "Do you have any idea where he might be? Are there any . . . secret hiding places or . . . I don't know, escape tunnels?"

"I have no idea," she admitted, but she motioned toward Mark, who stood with Rebekah off to her right in an ill-defined no-man's-land between the sheriff's car and the restrained Residents. "Mark might be able to help you, though. He and his wife are the ones who planned everything with me. He lived here a lot longer than I did, and he's been here the entire time. He'll know what to look for."

She convinced the sheriff that Mark could be trusted, and, after talking to him, Stewart allowed Mark to lead him and a team of four men into the Home so they could systematically search each room, closet and corridor for Residents or Penitents who might be hiding.

Kara was in one of the groups that had been brought out, although she had not eaten breakfast and was considerably less groggy than the men and women to whom she was shackled. With Deputy Hubbard's permission, and under the watchful eye of another officer, Joan was allowed to go over to speak to her roommate—although the conversation was more than a little one-sided. Kara not only refused to respond to her questions; she wouldn't even look at Joan. She kept her eyes on the ground, and after several minutes of this, Joan gave up and walked back to where Gary was standing by the car. She still wanted to know why her roommate was here, what had happened, how she had ended up with Father, but those questions weren't going to be answered today.

One of the Children with mental problems began howling and a couple of others responded in kind. Using a loud, authoritarian voice, a Teacher ordered them to stop, and they did.

Time passed. Ten minutes. Twenty. A half hour.

Gary tried to speak to her a couple of times, tried to ask her questions, but Joan waved him off. She wasn't in the mood to talk right now; at the moment she was content to just stand here and wait.

The day was warm, and they were in the direct sunlight. The metal of the car was hot against her back. But she didn't care. She was grateful to be outside, and even standing here doing nothing, she felt freer than she ever had inside the Home.

Mark emerged, leading the sheriff and his men out of the building through the same door they'd gone in, but no one else was with them. Their search had uncovered nothing. A moment later, the sheriff told them what they'd already guessed.

Father was nowhere to be found.

He had escaped.

Joan sucked in a deep breath, turning around, away from the Home and the Residents and Penitents lined up against it. She saw her reflection in the window of the car, a ghostlike image superimposed over the solid reality of the backseat. She hardly recognized herself, and she realized that she had not seen her own reflection in many days.

"Are you all right?" Gary asked softly, putting a hand on her back.

Joan nodded, but in her mind she saw the look on Absalom's face when they'd led him out, and she shivered.

This was not over.

PART III

Twenty-five

Sitting in the sheriff's office, Gary could not stop shaking. He'd been fine when it all was happening. Adrenaline had taken over. Even afterward, waiting outside, watching the Home being raided and everyone rounded up, he had been able to maintain his cool. But he'd started shaking the moment they'd returned to town. His emotions had caught up with the knowledge in his brain, and he realized not only the scope of what they'd come up against but how close they had come to death. Even thinking about that army of deformed people—

The Children

—made his blood run cold.

He had no idea where the Children were right now or, indeed, where most of the men and women from the Home were being held. A handful of them were in cells here in the building, and he assumed those were the ringleaders, the ones in charge, though the sheriff, understandably, had not had time to explain exactly what was going on.

He only hoped they would not be arrested themselves. In an effort to head off trouble and get everything out in the open, Reyn had volunteered the information that Brian and Gary had been carrying knives. For self-defense, he'd emphasized. In all of the chaos, that fact might never have come out, so Gary wasn't sure that offering it up was such a wise strategy. Brian was pissed. Nothing had been said about his taking Isaac hostage, but it was bound to come out eventually, and he was already blaming Reyn for that.

Gary was sitting next to Joan on the couch in Sheriff Stewart's office. His arm was around her, had been ever since they'd arrived, but the two of them had not had time to talk. Well, they'd had the time but not enough privacy. He felt awkward saying what he wanted to say in front of the others, and he was waiting until they were alone.

A deputy Gary did not know brought them soft drinks and potato chips from the vending machines—it was after lunch and they were starving—and they set upon the food greedily. The Fritos bag Gary picked up crackled noisily as his hands shook, and he noticed when Brian popped open his can of Dr Pepper and spilled it all over his pants that his friend's hands were shaking even worse than his. They were all nervous wrecks, and only Stacy, who had not come into the Home, retained any measure of composure.

"How did you find me?" Joan asked Gary. She opened up a package of Doritos. "How did you ever figure out that I was here in Texas?"

It was a long story, but he wasn't sure she wanted to hear it right now and he wasn't sure he wanted to tell it. "They sent someone after me. Two people, actually. They were caught and gave us the address of the Home. I think they thought we'd be captured if we came here. I don't think they were doing us a favor."

"You almost *were* captured," Stacy said.

He nodded. "That's true."

Joan was eating her Doritos. She no longer seemed to be paying attention to him.

"I went to your parents' house," he told her. "In Cayucos."

"They're dead," she said simply.

"What?"

"My parents are dead."

He had no idea how to respond to that. The only thing he could think of to say was, "How do you know?"

"I don't want to talk about it."

"Did you tell the sheriff?"

"I don't want to talk about it."

Gary shared a glance with Stacy, hoping she could indicate to him how he should react, what he should do, what he should say, but she shrugged her shoulders helplessly, raising her eyebrows in an expression of cluelessness.

"I got their address from Teri," Gary continued lamely. He suddenly realized she did not know that Teri Lim was dead. He shut up. There was a minefield in every explanation, and he doubted that she could take much more bad news.

Her parents were dead?

Had the Homesteaders killed them? That would be his first guess, and he thought about the dead dog and the blood on the linoleum floor of their kitchen. If Joan hadn't told the sheriff yet, Gary would. Drugging and kidnapping were bad enough, but murder would put those bastards away for life.

Where was Kara? he wondered. Had she been placed in a cell? She might be able to shed some light on this.

From outside came the sound of a helicopter. No. Helicopters. Plural. At first he thought they were from other law enforcement agencies, but seconds later, Stewart came into the room, frowning. "The press has arrived. I'll try to keep them away from you—"

"No need of that," Brian said. "I'll talk to them."

The sheriff fixed him with a hard glare. "I was thinking of Ms. Daniels."

"Oh."

"Could we have a minute?" Reyn asked the sheriff.

"Take all the time you need. I'm going out there to try to deal with this. If you need anything, ask Taylor. I'll be back as soon as I can."

"What the hell are you thinking?" Reyn turned on Brian as soon as Stewart was out of the room and the door closed behind him.

"I'm thinking of getting some national exposure."

"Do you know what would happen if you spoke to a reporter? *Every* reporter would try to talk to you. Then they would start looking into your background. They'd find Isaac, who would reveal that you held him at knife-point. Then they would ask *why* you held him at knife-point and whether this was part of a pattern, and they would comb through your past and find every little thing you ever did wrong and broadcast it to the entire world. Do you want that to happen?"

"No," Brian admitted.

"Okay, then. Just keep your mouth shut."

Stacy put a finger to her lips, motioning for them to stay quiet. Phones were ringing all over the building. From the front of the sheriff's office, they could hear Stewart shouting above the *thwap-thwap-thwap* of the helicopters. "I want no one in here! Is that understood? No one gets past these doors! Taylor? You and Billy drag out that podium we have in the conference room and set up some sort of press area in the parking lot out back! We'll direct them there! I don't know how long it's going to take them to land and find their way over here, but we don't have much time!"

The helicopters were getting louder, and there seemed to be more of them.

"Who's at the compound?" Stewart shouted. "They'll be going there first! Stall them! I don't want anyone saying anything—'No comment' the shit out of them—but keep them there as long as possible!"

The tactic must have worked because while the sheriff's office seemed to be in complete chaos for the next fifteen minutes or so, as far as Gary could tell, no reporters made it into the building.

After that, things calmed down, though the sound of the helicopters never completely went away. Stewart returned, and one by one, they were taken to another room and interviewed, their statements recorded, dictated to a stenographer and signed. Joan went first, Gary next. The questions were easy, and he answered them honestly, describing everything that had happened since the trip to Burning Man, leaving out only those incidents that would cast himself or his friends in a bad light. Between Joan's eyewitness account of her captivity, what had been found in the Home and what he and his friends had to say, the Homesteaders were going to be in deep shit.

Joan had been crying after her interview, and she was still crying when he returned, sitting on the couch with Stacy, the two of them holding on to each other's hands for support. Gary took over for Stacy as she went over to Reyn, and Brian left to do his interview. He held Joan close and told her over and over again that everything was going to be all right, the worst of it was done.

He hoped it was true.

After a while, she stopped crying, but they continued to sit on the couch, arms still around each other. If they weren't where they were and what had happened hadn't happened, he thought, it would have been nice.

A deputy walked past the door, leading a too-tall woman with too-short arms.

One of the Children.

The tactile memory of slimy skin and rough claws made him shiver. From what Gary understood, the Children were the product of incest, the offspring of Father and his daughters. Or granddaughters. Or great-granddaughters. The idea sickened him, and he thought about the photo of Joan's mother, wondering if she was one of Father's progeny. The possibility that Joan could be related to that man made his blood run cold.

Had Father tried to . . . ?

Gary pushed the thought from his mind, refusing to consider it.

It was evening by the time they were through. There was no motel in town or the department would have paid to put them up for the night. There wasn't even a bed-and-breakfast, but the sheriff had invited them to sleep at his house, and his wife had set up couches and cots in the living room. The bed was made up in the guest room for Joan. Just as Antwon Stewart defied the stereotype of a Texas sheriff, his wife, My, left any preconceptions about a sheriff's wife in the dust. A petite woman with a thick Vietnamese accent, she wore silk pajamas with no shoes and served them homemade spring rolls and pho for dinner. She was friendly and chatty and kept up a lively conversation throughout the meal, but Gary could understand only about a fifth of the things she said, so he ended up nodding a lot and pretending to agree with whatever she told them.

The sheriff had dropped them off but had not remained for dinner, and although he advised his wife not to turn on any television news so as not to disturb Joan, Mrs. Stewart asked after they'd finished eating whether any of them would mind if she put on CNN.

"It's fine," Joan said, managing a small smile. "I think we're all curious."

Mrs. Stewart turned on the TV, and after showing the results of a tropical storm that had hit South Carolina, a shot appeared of the Home, taken from a helicopter earlier that afternoon. The anchor gave an update on "the situation in Bitterweed," revealing that authorities were questioning cult members, trying to discover the whereabouts of the sect's mysterious leader, known only as "Father," who had authorized the drugging and kidnapping of at least one UCLA student and who might be behind numerous other crimes over the past two decades. A picture of Father, taken from one of the framed photos found throughout the Home, was shown on-screen.

"At least people know who to look for," Stacy said hopefully.

Gary said nothing. He was watching an aerial view of the Home, thinking that much more shocking revelations would be revealed to the world over the next few days as the law and the press learned more about the Homesteaders.

Hopefully, they would be long gone and back in California by then.

Stacy already had her cell phone out. "I have to call my parents," she said. "They're bound to see this on one of the stations, and I have to let them know I'm here before they find out about it on the news."

Reyn and Brian took their cells out as well, calling their parents, and Gary knew that he should do the same. Even if the sheriff was able to keep his promise and shield them from the media, their names were bound to get out eventually. Especially Joan's. His mom and dad were already worried about Joan, and if they heard that she'd been kidnapped by a cult in Texas—or, worse, that she'd once been part of that cult—they'd hop a plane to California and physically *drag* him back to Ohio. He needed to get ahead of this and put his own spin on it before they learned about it from some third party.

But he made no effort to move his arm from around Joan's shoulder. She had no parents to call, and right now it was more important for him to be there for her than to try to head off an uncomfortable confrontation with his mom and dad.

Well, his mom.

His dad would be okay. He could reason with his dad.

His mom would freak.

Stacy, Reyn and Brian had retreated to opposite corners of the room and were talking in hushed, hurried tones. He'd call his own parents later, when Joan was going to the bathroom or taking a shower or something. He pulled her closer to him, squeezing her shoulder reassuringly. She leaned her head against his arm. "I love you," she said softly. It was the first time she'd said it since they had been reunited.

"I love you, too," he said.

Gary fell asleep that night on a narrow couch, staring upward at an unfamiliar ceiling. He dreamed that he was one of the Beatles and they had just finished playing a concert in a massive stadium. Afterward, they ran backstage and Father was in their dressing room. He was having sex with the groupies who had been meant for the band.

And one of them was Gary's mom.

The trip back to California was uneventful. Joan was still not volunteering information about her ordeal, and Gary did not want to pressure her. She would talk when she was ready.

The backseat of the car was crowded and uncomfortable, with three people shoved into such a small space, but no one complained. They stopped a lot to stretch their feet and switch driving duties. It seemed much harder to stay awake on the trip home than it had on the way there, and the desert scenery seemed infinitely more boring. The only times they were all awake at once were the beginning of the trip, the end of the journey, and whenever they stopped for a meal or a bathroom break.

It was night when they reached Southern California. "Should we check in with the police?" Stacy wondered as they pulled into Westwood Village. "Tell them what happened?"

"Fuck 'em," Brian declared.

"I'm sure Sheriff Stewart has called Detective Williams and told him everything by now," Reyn said.

"Even if he hasn't, so what? Kara's free. Her parents are probably coming out to pick her up. And if they want to keep looking for Joan—or, more accurately, *start* looking for Joan—let 'em."

That reminded Gary that neither he nor Joan was officially enrolled in school anymore, and as that was something else of which she was not aware, he explained to her what had happened to all of their computerized records. Before showing up to class again, they were both going to have to go to Admissions and try to get everything straightened out.

"My Facebook page is gone, too?" she said incredulously.

"Everything."

"I didn't know they were so tech savvy," she admitted.

Reyn was driving, and he found a parking spot near his dorm. "After we unpack," he told them, "I need to take the car back. I don't want to pay for an extra day."

"I think we have to," Stacy said. "We were supposed to turn it in in the morning. I think we're already being charged an extra day. We might as well get some use out of it."

"I'm taking it back anyway. We don't have a parking sticker for it, and if we leave it here they'll tow it."

"I'll follow you in my car and pick you up," Brian offered, getting out.

"Deal."

"Thanks," Gary said gratefully. "I—"

"Don't worry about it," Reyn told him.

They took their personal belongings out of the trunk. Tossed casually near the wheel well were Brian's knives. Gary had been surprised when Sheriff Stewart had not confiscated them, and even more surprised when the man had said, "Get these out of here. I don't want to see them again." It had been a thank-you for helping the sheriff's department to get the Homesteaders, and it was also a way of keeping things simple, not muddying the waters. No one else had seen the knives, and if any of the cult members claimed to have, Stewart would just say they were crazy. The best thing for everyone would be for the knives to just disappear, but with Father still on the loose, Gary knew Brian would not get rid of them.

Neither Gary nor Joan had any belongings to take out of the trunk, but they waited patiently while the others unpacked. They had not talked about it, but Gary could not imagine that she would want to sleep in the same room she had shared with Kara. At least not the first night. Not after everything that had happened.

He was right.

He caught Joan looking in the direction of her dorm building, and when she saw him watching her, she shivered. "I'm not staying in that room," she said. "I can't."

Gary put an around around her. "You don't have to. We'll just go in and get your clothes, toothbrush, whatever else you need. You can stay with me."

"I'm not sleeping in your room, either," she told him.

He frowned. "Where, then? The car? I mean, we're kind of running out of options."

"I'll switch with you," Brian offered. "Dror and I can move into your place and you can live in ours."

"No one would want to live in your place," Stacy said. She smiled at Joan. "You can move in with me."

"Wait a minute!" Reyn objected. "*You're* supposed to be staying with *me*."

"I was," Stacy said. "But I'm going back to my own place. There'll be two of us there now."

"I don't like it."

"We'll be fine. It's on the top floor, far away from the elevators and the stairs, and surrounded by very responsible people. Not to mention the fact that we're just going to walk inside, lock the door and stay in until morning."

"They were waiting for me in my room," Gary pointed out.

"You will all come with us to check the place out," Stacy said. "Once you leave, *then* we'll lock the door and stay in until morning."

"I still don't like it. Make sure you stay away from the window, too."

Stacy gave a single nod of acquiescence. "In case anyone climbs the building, we will keep the window shut."

"What about Gary?" Joan asked. "I don't want him to—"

"He can stay in my room," Reyn said. "As long as he doesn't mind camping out on the floor. I'm not sharing my bed with him."

Gary smiled politely. It didn't matter what they did, he thought to himself. The Homesteaders had hacked into the school, the DMV, and every credit agency he'd even looked at. Finding the residences of his friends would be a piece of cake.

But he said nothing. Not yet. Tomorrow he'd talk to everyone about it, but tonight they all needed a good sleep. Besides, paired up, they should be all right. For one night at least.

How many cult members were there? he wondered. The Home had been pretty well cleaned out, though Father and maybe a few others had escaped. But how many were spread across the country, hiding in farmhouses like the one in New Mexico, living in little pockets amid the unsuspecting families of small-town America? Father could be amassing an army right now, an army whose sole pupose was the destruction of Joan and her friends.

Now he was just being paranoid.

Wasn't he?

"Cell phones on at all times," Reyn advised. "We need to keep in contact with each other."

Gary nodded in agreement.

Stacy patted Joan's shoulder. "Come on, roomie. Let's go get your stuff. Then I'll show you around your spacious new digs."

Twenty-six

The weekend passed quickly and, thank God, uneventfully.

On Monday, Joan spent the morning in the registrar's office, along with Gary, filling out forms and explaining to a succession of clerks and administrators the broad outlines of what had happened. Neither of them was officially reinstated yet, but the machinery was in motion and they'd been assured that everything would be fine. Eventually.

It was much easier dealing with her instructors. She didn't give them any details, but even the ones who didn't care whether she showed up or not were perfectly willing to allow her to remain in their classes, do the work and take the tests—even if she wasn't officially enrolled. She met with each of them before class began to find out what she'd missed, and while there was a lot of reading to catch up on, there hadn't been any tests and weren't any coming up in the next few weeks. It would be pretty easy to get back up to speed.

It was simple talking to her teachers; her fellow students were a different situation altogether.

She started sensing something wrong in physical anthropology, her first class of the afternoon. She arrived early to speak with the instructor and was in her usual seat before any of the other students arrived, but Janie

Kendricks and Rob Magnussen, who usually sat to either side of her, purposely chose desks on the opposite side of the room, and by the time the entire class had assembled, there was a visible boundary of empty desks around her. That seemed strange, but the room was large, the class small, there were a lot of empty seats and the configuration could have been just a coincidence.

It was in her psych class that she truly knew there was a problem. As before, she spoke to the professor prior to the start of the class, but there were a couple of students from the previous session who'd remained behind to talk to the teacher, and by the time she finished writing down her reading assignments and the address of a Web site on which one of the instructor's monographs was posted, the rest of her class had started to arrive. Moving away from the lectern toward her seat, she nearly ran into Leigh Lathen. She and Leigh had known each other since their freshman year and had always been friendly, but now the other woman scowled at her and fixed her with a glare so hostile that Joan was taken aback.

It had to have something to do with the Home. Though she'd given no interviews and done everything she could to stay out of the spotlight, Joan's name and face were all over the newspapers and TV—especially those damn cable channels. She didn't even want to *think* about what was happening in cyberspace.

Maybe Leigh was religious and somehow offended by her connection with a sect that mainstream America considered a cult. Maybe she had a friend or relative who was a Resident or Penitent and had been arrested. Maybe . . .

She gave up. The truth was, she had no idea what the problem could be. It bothered her, though, that Leigh seemed to be upset, and, determined to set things right, she tapped the other student on the shoulder.

Leigh whirled around. "Leave me alone!"

"I'm sorry. I—"

"Why would you do something like that?"

Joan looked at her, confused. "What?"

"You know."

"I have no idea what you're talking about."

Leigh turned away.

"Whatever you *think* I did, I *didn't*," Joan insisted.

"Right."

Other students were looking at her, Joan noticed, and the expressions on their faces mirrored Leigh's: a mixture of anger, antagonism, disappointment and disapproval. Curt Souter was staring at her as though she'd shot his dog. Marie Pearcy looked like a woman whose husband had been seduced by Joan and stolen away.

What was going on here?

"Marie . . ." she began.

"Don't you even talk to me." The other student focused her gaze on the professor at the front of the class, her mouth set in a hard, straight line.

The lecture began before Joan could find out what the problem was. She paid attention, took careful notes, but was aware at all times of the unfriendly glances directed at her by her classmates. It was a weird sensation, made all the more difficult because she didn't know why it was happening or what was behind it. The lights dimmed as the instructor began a PowerPoint presentation, and that made her think about the Homesteaders' new facility with computers. Her MySpace and Facebook pages were gone, she was not officially enrolled in this class due to the hacking of Father or one of his minions, and it was not much of a leap to assume that her classmates had been sent malicious e-mails bearing her name. She could clear this up quickly if she could just talk to the other students, but after class ended they shunned her, refused to speak with her and exited the classroom quickly.

Frustrated and discouraged, Joan packed up her books and looked toward the front of the class where the professor was preparing for his next lecture. Her teachers would probably be next, sent falsified messages threatening them or propositioning them or telling them she wanted to drop their classes. Father was playing with her, piling on the problems one layer at a time in an effort to break her, and she knew that she had to be strong in order to survive the onslaught. So did Gary and Stacy and Reyn and Brian.

What would happen after the psychological noose was tightened? How far would Father go in order to get back at her?

She knew the answer to that. He had spent five years tracking her and her parents. He had killed her mom and dad and kidnapped her in the middle of a counterculture festival filled with thousands of people. He would stop at nothing.

Father's sense of revenge was Old Testament.

He would not stop until she was dead.

Outside, the campus was bathed in autumn light, orangish and indirect, and though her watch said it was shortly after two o'clock, the light made it look like four. She looked around for Gary. He was supposed to meet her here, but there was no sign of him. Her pulse quickened slightly. It was probably nothing, but she knew what Father was capable of, and she was the one who had insisted that the four of them be alone as little as possible.

The walkways were crowded, but Gary was tall and usually easy to spot. Today, she knew, he was wearing a red shirt. Glancing both to her left and to her right, she saw no one who looked even remotely like him.

But . . .

But she saw a *very* tall man with a very bald head standing alone on the grass next to a marble sculpture.

He seemed to be the only person who was not moving, and though he was kind of far away and it was impossible to tell for sure, it looked like he was watching her.

Joan's breath caught in her throat.

She turned away. Not quickly, not obviously, but casually, subtly. She focused her attention on a building, on the sky, scanned the walkways for Gary once again, then pretended to randomly glance over at the sculpture.

The bald guy was still there, still unmoving, still staring in her direction.

She turned away again, her mind racing, trying to come up with a plan. He couldn't do anything in public, she reasoned, not now, in broad daylight, in front of all these witnesses. This was the perfect place to confront him, and though the sharp pain in her stomach made her wonder if this was what an ulcer felt like, Joan forced herself to be brave. Instead of fleeing, as she wanted to do with every fiber of her being, she took a deep breath, crossed the crowded walkway and started across the lawn toward the man.

He made no move to get away, and she saw as she approached that he was not looking at her but still staring in the same direction where she had been. He seemed as much of a statue as the sculpture next to him, and for a brief second she thought that he might be some art student's amazingly lifelike project. Then she saw the white cane leaning against the marble and realized that he was blind.

She relaxed a little. But some of the Children were blind or deaf, too, and she kept glancing around to make sure this wasn't a trap and she wasn't about to be jumped by Homesteaders hidden in the bushes. She approached slowly. "Hello?" she said softly in the Language.

There was no response.

"What is your name?" she queried.

He turned his head in her general direction, a quizzical look on his face. "I'm sorry. Are you talking to me? I'm afraid I only speak English."

The sigh of relief that escaped her made her realize that she'd been holding her breath. "I'm sorry," she said in the Language, keeping up the pretense of being a foreign student. She turned, walking much more briskly back the way she had come. Gary was now heading up the walkway in the middle of a crowd of students, looking away from her toward the building, expecting to see her waiting by the steps as they'd arranged, and she tapped him on the shoulder. He started at her touch, nervous even here, and she realized how on edge all of them were.

"I didn't mean to startle you," she said.

He bent down, kissing her. "No problem. It's just . . . you know."

"Yeah." She tried to smile. "I need to ask you something: Did you notice anything strange in any of your classes today? Was anyone acting weird toward you?"

He frowned. "How do you mean?"

She explained that no one would sit by her in anthropology and that the students in her psychology class had been hostile and shunned her.

He tried to make a joke of it. "What are you, in junior high?" But she could tell from his eyes that he was worried.

"I think they're attacking us with computers. They have a lot of information about us, and Father will use everything at his disposal. There's no telling what they might do."

"We have credit freezes, everyone's been alerted, all the companies—"

"I don't just mean online. There's no telling what they might do *physically*."

He nodded. "I bought you a present. Come with me to my car."

That was a non sequitur if she'd ever heard one. "What?"

"I bought you something." Sensing her confusion, he added, "It's for protection."

He'd parked in the north lot instead of leaving his car in his usual spot by the dorm and walking—an effort to vary his routine, which was something they'd all discussed and were trying to do. The parking lot was closer than the dorm, but it still was quite a trek, and though at first he refused to tell her what he'd bought, wanting it to be a surprise, his silence in the face of her constant questioning began to seem silly, especially as they had another five minutes to go. "I got you a baseball bat," he finally admitted. "Big Five was having a sale and my sociology class was canceled, so I sped over there and bought it."

When they reached the car, Gary opened the trunk and pulled out her bat, a dull red length of aluminum. "Here it is," he said, hefting it. "You can fight off anyone with this. It won't work against guns, but unless I miss my bet, Father and his people are less mechanically inclined."

"They don't use guns," Joan agreed. She paused. "At least, I don't think they do. I didn't think they used computers, either."

Gary rested the bat on his shoulder. "You can swing at any part of a person and it'll work," he said. "Legs, arms, midsection. Anything'll put them out of commission. Don't aim for the head unless you have to, though. That'll kill them."

There was an awkward pause, and Gary placed the bat back in the trunk. "So where do you think he is? Any ideas?"

She shook her head.

"There seem to be cult members—"

"Homesteaders," she said.

"What?"

"We—*they* like to be called 'Homesteaders.' "

He eyed her strangely. "We?"

"You know what I mean. What were you trying to say?"

"Just that there are *Homesteaders* all over. In Texas, New Mexico, maybe even here in California. I was just wondering if you know where any of them might be located. Or even how many of them there are."

"I was brought up in the Home. I don't know anything else. I do know some of the others who've gotten away...."

"The people in your parents' address book."

"They might have some ideas. But I'm sure they're in hiding by now. News travels fast on that network, and even if you didn't scare them off with your clumsy investigation"—she smiled at him—"they've seen the news and they've scattered to the wind."

"So what do you think happens next?"

Her smile faded.

"Joan?"

"I think he's going to come after us," she said.

The phone rang in the middle of the night. Not her cell phone or Stacy's, but the landline, the one that belonged to the room. By the time Joan groggily lifted her head from the pillow, her brain still echoing with the dream of an endless hallway filled with horribly malformed Children, Stacy had already walked over to her desk and picked up the telephone. "Hello?" she said. Her eyes grew wide and frightened. She put her hand over the mouthpiece. "It's a man," she whispered fearfully. "I think it's one of *them*. He's speaking some language I never heard before."

Fully awake now, Joan jumped up from the air mattress on which she'd been sleeping and grabbed the phone from Stacy's hand. She was prepared to hear Father's voice, but it was someone else, though the words the man was saying could not have been more terrible. "Your flesh shall be rent for your crimes," he stated in the Language, and it sounded as though he were reading the words from a scroll. "The Lord has sanctioned your punishment, and when you are dead you shall dwell for eternity in the fiery pit of Hell—"

Joan hung up the phone.

"Who was it?" Stacy asked, her voice quavering. "Was it . . . ?"

"It wasn't Father, but it was one of them."

"They know my number!" Stacy was on the verge of crying. "They know where we are!" She grabbed her cell phone from the nightstand, casting frightened glances at the telephone on the desk, as though she thought the object was possessed by a demon.

"Who are you calling?" Joan asked.

"Reyn!" Pressing a speed-dial number, Stacy quickly brought the phone to her ear. "We just got a phone call!" she said without preamble. Reyn must have answered. "Joan says it's them!" There was a short pause, and Stacy turned toward Joan. "They got one, too!"

She tried to remain calm as Stacy and Reyn described details to each other over the phone, but inside Joan was just as frightened as they were. This might be just a scare tactic, part of the psychological assault, but she was by no means sure of that, and it could very well be that someone was on the way right now to carry out the threatened punishment. She crouched down next to her air mattress and reached under Stacy's bed for the baseball bat.

"I'm calling the police!" Stacy shouted into the phone. "I don't give a shit what Gary and Brian think!"

She hung up and called 911.

Reyn arrived before the police, as did Gary. Brian

elected not to join them. His phone had not rung, and he was setting up his computer to record any calls. He planned to wait by the phone in case one came in.

A single uniformed officer showed up to take the report. Gary and Reyn seemed offended that the case had been given such a low priority. They'd expected to see one of the detectives they'd dealt with before—even though it was after one o'clock in the morning—and they kept emphasizing that Joan was the student who'd been kidnapped by the cult in Texas. The policeman, Officer Garcez, assured them that the detectives would be given his report in the morning, but he seemed tired and put-out that he had to be here at all, and Joan wondered how seriously he was taking this.

Stacy was still upset, and she explained the sequence of events several times to make sure the officer understood what had happened. Joan filled in her part of the story, providing a translation of the message up to the point where she'd hung up the phone.

Reyn was the one who'd answered the call that came to his room, but he'd put it on speakerphone and Gary had confirmed that the language being spoken sounded like the same one his kidnappers had used.

Officer Garcez was taking things a little more seriously now, and he called in to a supervisor, giving a report over his two-way radio before he'd even finished writing everything down. Joan was still holding on to her bat, though she was leaning on it at the moment, treating it more like a cane.

They all heard the supervisor's reply, although Garcez acted as though they hadn't. "We're going to look into the cult connection," he told them. "We have your phone numbers and we know where to reach you. If we need additional information, we'll be in touch, and if you see, hear or experience anything else unusual, call and let us know." He finished writing on his pad, then closed it, obviously preparing to leave.

"That's it?" Stacy said incredulously. "You're not going to station someone outside our door or have someone watch the building?"

The officer allowed himself a small smile. "It was a phone call," he said. "Do you know how many times a night people report obscene phone calls?"

"They weren't obscene phone calls," she reminded him. "They were threats. From people the police are looking for. Fugitives. And they're part of a pattern."

"We'll check into it," he said in a voice that was probably meant to be reassuring but that just sounded patronizing. "Lock your doors, don't let anyone in you don't recognize, and if you receive any other calls, let us know."

"Can't you put some kind of device on the phone?" Reyn asked. "To trace incoming calls?"

"No," the officer said simply. He was already making his way toward the door, and it was clear that he didn't want to be here.

Joan put a comforting arm around Stacy's shoulder, still holding on to the bat with her other hand. She was glad Gary had given her the weapon because she felt much more secure with it in her possession, and in her mind she saw Father coming over, forcing his way into the room, and herself using the bat to bash in his head, swinging it like a baseball player until his head was nothing more than a bloody pulp and he was dead.

She could do it, Joan thought, and the realization scared her.

"So what do we do now?" Stacy wondered aloud as soon as the cop had left and the door closed behind him.

"I'll stay here with you," Reyn offered. "You and Joan take my room," he told Gary.

Stacy was already shaking her head. "No way. I'm not staying here."

"Then we'll switch—"

"I'm not staying here, either," Joan said.

"Then we'll *all* sleep in my room," Reyn told them, "although God knows where everyone will fit." He looked toward Stacy and Joan. "And don't forget: They know where I live, too. I got a phone call also."

"There's safety in numbers," Stacy said, and Joan had to agree.

Reyn nodded. "All right, then. Get what you need and let's go. It's late, I'm tired and I have an early class in the morning."

Joan gathered her toothbrush and hairbrush from the bathroom, putting them back into her suitcase along with her clothes. She picked up her suitcase in one hand, her baseball bat in the other.

Father was just trying to scare them, she told herself again. Soften them up before making an actual assault. They still had some time.

But she didn't relax until they'd walked to Reyn's dorm and were in his room, with the door closed and locked behind them.

Twenty-seven

This time, Gary was awakened by sirens.

Reyn was already up and peering out the window, his face illuminated by pulsing flashes of red light. "What's going on?" Gary asked, sitting up. Beneath the oscillation of the sirens, he heard the faint, constant cry of a far-off alarm.

"I think it's your dorm," Reyn said, and his voice was so calm and matter-of-fact that for a moment the meaning of his words didn't register.

Joan and Stacy, on the bed, were still sleeping, and Gary looked over at Reyn's alarm clock. Three fifteen. They'd been asleep for less than an hour. He'd thought the commotion of the phone calls and the cops would be enough turmoil for one night.

He suddenly realized what Reyn had said. "My dorm?" Gary crawled out of his sleeping bag and looked with his friend out the window. Sure enough, a fire truck with extended ladder was parked two buildings over, where smoke could be seen billowing upward through several open windows, illuminated from within by yellow-orange flames.

Gary stumbled, reaching for his shirt. He bumped into the bed, and Stacy, instantly awake, said in a panicked voice, "What is it?"

Reyn answered. "It looks like there's a fire in Gary's dorm."

Stacy immediately flipped on the light. Gary found his socks and shoes and started putting them on. Within seconds, everyone was getting dressed and ready to go out. Moments later, the four of them were hurrying through the empty hall and down the stairs. Ignoring the walkway, they made a beeline across the lawn toward the fire engines with their flashing red lights. There were several trucks in front of the building now, but the sirens were off, Gary noticed. And the alarm was silent. The scene before them seemed anomalous without those sounds, deprived of the noise that gave it context, and the sound track of quiet murmuring that accompanied the garish visual made it all feel very surreal.

All of the residents of the dorm were outside, on the sidewalk, on the grass, in the parking lot, many in their bare feet or only partially dressed. Thick black-gray smoke was pouring from the front-facing windows, streaming upward into the sky, and heat from the fire had blown out the glass. Shards glittered on the ground in front of the building, crunching under the boots of the firemen walking in and out. Occasional flames were still visible from one of the upper windows, though the fire seemed for the most part to have been extinguished.

Looking up at the dormitory, Gary didn't have to be told.

The fire had started in his room.

He glanced around and saw his neighbors, Matt and Greg, standing next to a light pole, both of them wearing nothing but pajama bottoms and holding on to laptops as though someone might try to snatch the devices from their hands. "Hey," he said, walking up to them. "What happened?"

"Dude!" Greg said. "Where've you been? We were

pounding the shit out of your door trying to get you out of there! We thought you burned up!"

"I was out."

"I can see that," Matt said, taking in Joan and Stacy and their disheveled appearance. He nodded admiringly.

"What happened?" Gary asked again.

"Who the hell knows?" Greg said. "I was asleep, and then the alarm went off and I smelled smoke, and I yelled at Matt to get up, and we grabbed our laptops, and we tried to save your sorry ass, and then people were screaming and the smoke got too thick and we bailed."

"And here we are," Matt added.

Joan pulled him aside. "It's them," she said.

"I know."

From off to his left, he overheard one fireman talking to another. "It was an accelerant with a really low flash point, that's for sure. But I'll be damned if I can figure out what it was. I never smelled anything like that before in my life. And did you see that burn pattern?" He shook his head. "We need a *real* investigator on this one."

"So what do we do?" Joan asked.

Gary didn't know, but from his point of view right now, their options were narrowing. He didn't see Father giving up and going away, and every outcome he could imagine involved a confrontation. He thought of his battle with the psycho at the gas station and wondered if another such event was unavoidable.

"Hey," Greg was addressing Reyn. "Do you know if the school has, like, fire insurance on all this? I lost some valuable stuff in there."

"Do you think they'll stop?" Gary asked Joan.

She shook her head. "Never. We crossed Father and we won. That's not something he'll ever forgive or forget."

"But the others . . . don't you think they're grateful to

be free? And in the eyes of true believers, doesn't this make him seem fallible? Won't he lose followers?"

"Never," she said again.

"So they'll keep coming after us."

"They believe in an eye for an eye," she said.

Gary met her gaze. "What do you believe?"

Joan turned away, uncomfortable. "I'm not one of them. That's why we left."

Stacy was already calling someone on her cell phone.

"Who are—" Reyn began.

"The police. They need to know about this."

She was right, and Gary found that he was glad she was calling. The cops may have been useless when it came to investigating Joan's disappearance, but the Bitterweed sheriff's department had saved his ass back in Texas, and he trusted law enforcement for protection. Wasn't that their motto? "To serve and protect?" Or "To protect and serve?" The word *protect* was in there somewhere, and right now he and his friends *needed* protection. Especially Joan.

Besides, Tucker might be an asshole, but Williams seemed like a good guy. And Gary knew that it would be a huge feather in the detectives' caps if they were the ones who caught Father. Police and sheriffs' departments all over the country were looking for the man, and the one that nabbed him would get not only bragging rights among their peers but a whole heap of good publicity.

"When are we going to be able to go back in?" Matt was asking a fireman.

"Not for a while."

"What if looters steal all my stuff?"

"*No one* can get in," the fireman said. "Not even looters."

"Thanks for nothing!" Stacy flipped off her phone, scowling. "They said the fire department handles its own investigations," she reported. "If the police need to be called in, the fire department will decide."

"Did you remind them about the Homesteaders?" Gary asked. "I mean, the cops were only here an hour ago and now this happens. It seems like things are building. Who knows what could happen by morning."

"They don't care." Stacy shook her head disgustedly.

Matt tapped Gary on the shoulder. "Did you lose a lot of stuff?"

He hadn't even thought about it. "Yeah, I guess," he said. The truth was, he didn't really care. He had more important things on his mind.

Greg breathed deeply. "This might sound weird, but don't you think this fire smells good? I mean, all fires smell good. But this one *really* smells good."

"It does have a distinctive odor," Reyn told Gary. "I was just thinking that myself. And it smells *familiar*, though I can't quite place it."

Gary, Joan and Stacy sniffed the air. It was more woodsy than would be expected from a dormitory filled with books, clothes and electronic equipment, Gary thought. And maybe it did smell kind of fragrant, like aromatic pipe tobacco. But it was not anything he recognized.

Joan was looking around, scanning the faces of the ever-growing crowd, and Gary asked what she was doing. "Looking for them," she answered, and he mentally kicked himself. He should've done the same thing when they'd first arrived on the scene. If there *had* been any Homesteaders around after the fire had started, watching from the shadows and waiting to see what happened, they were long gone now.

Firefighters were emerging from the open front doors of the building, dragging dripping, deflated hoses with them. The blaze appeared to be out. No more flames were visible, and even the smoke coming out of the windows had died down to occasional wisps.

Gary glanced over at Reyn's dormitory, its rectangular bulk dark against the night sky, the refracted red from the fire engine lights reflected in blank windows. Was it next? What about Joan's room or Stacy's? Or Brian's?

"I don't think we should go back to your place," he told Reyn. "If they know where I live, they probably know where you live."

His friend nodded. "Agreed."

Stacy had her phone out again.

"Who are you calling?" Reyn asked.

"Brian." She looked down at the small screen. "Wait a minute. He left a text." Her fingers typed on the tiny keyboard. "He says, 'Don't call. Busy.' What the hell does that mean?"

"His recording," Gary said. "He's waiting for the Homesteaders to call him so he can record it."

"That guy knows his computers," Reyn admitted. "He might even be able to trace them."

"I'm calling anyway." Stacy started pressing numbers.

"Call his cell," Gary advised.

"That's the only number I have."

He must have picked up right away, because she started telling him about the fire. "*Gary's*," she said after a short pause. She listened for a moment. "No, I'm saying you should get out, too. You could be next." She put her hand over the phone. "He says he's not going anywhere. He's ready for them if they come."

"He probably is," Gary said.

"What?" Stacy said into the phone. She listened again, facing Gary. "He says if they can't even be bothered to call, to hell with them." She looked surprised, then took the phone away from her ear. "He hung up on me!"

Gary and Reyn both chuckled.

"You think that's funny?"

"A little," Reyn said.

"I'm sure he'll be fine," Gary offered.

Stacy faced him. "Yeah? Well, what about us?"

She was deeply frightened, he realized, and while he appreciated Brian leavening the tension and his friend's bravery gave him hope, she clearly didn't see it that way. Brian's attitude had made her feel that even *they* weren't taking the threat as seriously as they should. She was even more worried than she had been before.

"I think the most important thing right now," Reyn said, "is that we continue to vary our routines. For all we know, they have people watching us, have had people watching us ever since we got back. We can't make it easy for them. Yes, we go to classes at specific times, and we sleep in the same rooms, but we can make everything else a variable. Take different paths to class, eat at differ-ent tables or restaurants, make sure we're not providing them with a blueprint to get at us."

"I say we take it *to* them," Gary said.

"We don't know where they are," Stacy pointed out. "Or who they are."

Reyn nodded. "We're going to have to play defense."

"Set another trap?" Gary wondered aloud.

"I don't know how we'd do that," Reyn admitted. He looked over at Joan. "Any ideas?"

She shook her head. "I'm out of my depth here. And, to be honest, you guys probably know as much as I do at this point."

"I'm not going back to *any* of our rooms," Stacy an-nounced. She obviously didn't want anyone else over-hearing their conversation because she backed onto the grass, away from the crowd, motioning for them to fol-low. "I think we should rent a hotel room," she said, her voice lowered.

Reyn shook his head. "There're only a few hours left until morning. By the time we find someplace, it'll almost be time to get up again. Besides, we'd have to use a credit card. And right now, I think we'd better assume that they have the ability to track our cards and know where we go."

"He's right," Gary agreed.

Joan nodded.

They spent the rest of the night in the student union, taking turns sleeping on chairs that they'd pulled into a wagon-train circle, with one person awake and on watch at all times. Joan had brought her bat, and it was passed to each person standing guard, first Reyn, then Gary. It was Joan's turn to play sentry after that, but the clock on the wall said it was five thirty and Gary knew he would never be able to fall asleep for just an hour, which was when Reyn needed to get up for class, so he stayed awake and let the others get some extra shut-eye.

Brian called him on his cell phone at six, and Gary moved away from his friends to the middle of the room to take the call. Brian said he'd taken a pill he'd been saving for just such an occasion and stayed awake all night.

Gary was in no mood to lecture.

"No one called," Brian said, disappointed. "I was ready to record that sucker and turn it in to the cops, but either they lost my number or I'm not important enough to bother with. Probably they were too *busy* to call," he quipped. "You know, with the fire and all."

Gary smiled. It helped to have someone not take things so seriously.

"So what's the plan?"

"Everyone's trying to figure that out," Gary told him. "Right now, I guess we keep our eyes open and just try to get through the day."

"That's not much of a plan," Brian pointed out.

"Yeah, well . . ."

"Need another knife?"

"Joan has the baseball bat I bought her."

"What about you? What if they come after you?"

"I think I'm pretty safe here on campus."

Brian snorted. "Are you kidding? If you'd been in your room last night, you'd be dead. They *kidnapped* you on campus. You need a knife."

"Maybe," Gary conceded.

"Meet me in front of the bookstore at seven forty-five. They don't open 'til eight."

"I can't carry a weapon to class! Give it to me later."

"Name the where and when."

"I'll call you."

Reyn had awakened, and Joan was stirring, so Gary said good-bye and returned to the circle of chairs. He tried to smile. "Up and at 'em," he said. "It's a new dawn."

Before their first class, Gary took Joan to Subway for breakfast, something neither of them had done before. Stacy studied in her car, with the windows rolled up and the doors locked. Reyn parked his own car in the west lot, rather than leaving it near his dorm. They were all making an effort to vary their routines and throw potential tails off their trails, but Gary couldn't help thinking it was futile. These were people who had nullified his driver's license and erased his school records. Did he honestly think they wouldn't find him if he ate breakfast at a new location?

No.

The only thing that gave him any comfort at all was the fact that every police department in the western United States was on the lookout for Father, and his picture—the same one that had overlooked every room in the Home—had been on TV constantly ever since the raid. Even casual viewers would know that he was a dangerous and wanted man if they happened to run across him. Of course, if Father shaved his beard and changed his hairstyle, no one would ever know who he was. But

that would be a victory in itself and not something that
he thought would happen.

He still held out hope that Father would be located
and caught. From a logical, rational perspective, it was
not only possible but probable.

And yet . . .

And yet his gut told him exactly the opposite. It was
nothing more than a feeling he had, a vague, floating, un-
substantiated notion that Father could not be stopped,
that he would find them wherever they went, whatever
they did. But Gary believed it utterly, and it frightened
him to the core.

His cell phone rang in the middle of classical mythology, and Gary jumped in his seat, startled. The students
around him turned to look, and Dr. Choy, at the head
of the room, frowned. Cell phones weren't allowed in
class, but ever since Joan had been kidnapped at Burning Man, his had been on all day every day.

Gary's first thought was that it was Joan and that
she was being attacked. His second thought, immediately upon the heels of the first, was that it was Reyn,
calling to tell him that Joan *had* been attacked and was
missing.

Or dead.

He hurried out of the classroom to answer the call,
pressing the TALK button even before he reached the
door. "Hello?" His voice sounded as frightened as he
felt.

"Gary?"

It was his dad. The classroom door closed behind
him, and he was alone in the corridor save for a couple
dressed in black who were making out next to one of the
windows. "Dad?" he said.

"Why didn't you tell us?" His father's voice was
accusatory.

Gary feigned ignorance. "Tell you what?"

"Your girlfriend, this *Joan*, was kidnapped by a cult, a cult that she used to be *part* of, and now that cult leader is loose and on the rampage."

He should have known they'd figure it out.

Actually, he was surprised it hadn't happened sooner. He'd been expecting a call immediately after returning from Texas, but somehow his parents had missed that initial round of news stories. Thank God for small favors. Although he should have taken the initiative and called them first.

"Your mother and I saw *Dateline* last night, and they had a whole thing about it."

He could hear his mom in the background, shouting, "*Let me talk to him! I want to talk to him!*"

His dad's voice lowered. "As I'm sure you can guess, your mother is very upset."

"Listen, Dad—"

"The police rescued her and now she's back in school, but this madman is still after her. They explained all about it."

It sounded as though the part he and his friends had played in the events had been left out, and for that Gary was grateful. Sheriff Stewart was definitely a class act.

His mom grabbed the phone. "What are you doing with a girl like that?"

"A girl like what?" he said angrily. How dare his parents pass judgment on Joan. They'd never even met her.

"She was in a cult! We didn't raise you that way. Maybe we didn't go to church that often, but—"

"Mom," he said, trying to keep his tone even, "you know nothing about Joan. And you know they make things up for TV. How else would they get ratings?"

"It was on *Dateline*!"

Once again, he realized how far he'd come since his Ohio days. He was a real Californian now, and whether that meant he was more cynical or more sophisticated than he had been, the fact was that he no longer saw things the way his parents did. They were nice people and he loved them, but their world was much simpler and much more black and white than the one in which he now lived.

"They made it look worse than it was," he said.

His dad took the phone back, got on the line again. "I know how you feel, Gary. She's your first real girlfriend, and you think you're in love with her—"

"I *am* in love with her!" he blurted out. He cringed even as he said the words, embarrassed to be talking to his dad that way, but he stood his ground.

"Maybe you are," his dad conceded. "Maybe you are. But hear me out. You're too young to be tied down right now. And something like this can only make it more difficult. There is national media attention focused on this girl. And she was kidnapped and held captive at some cult compound in Texas. She's going through things you can't possibly understand."

Right then, he almost told his dad everything.

Almost.

But he didn't. This was one of those pivotal moments, an end-of-childhood moment, and though he wanted more than anything to have his dad speed out here to California and rescue him, he knew it would be wrong to involve his parents. He couldn't endanger them like that, and he realized that this was the first time *he* was making an important decision that affected all three of them; *he* was deciding what should be done for the good of the whole family. "Most of that stuff is made up," he lied. "You know how the media sensationalizes everything."

His dad sounded skeptical. "It seemed pretty well documented. And they were talking to law enforcement officers who were involved in the case, who were *there*."

"Dad, I can handle it. And she needs me right now." His voice almost broke on that last sentence. He was saying it for strategic reasons, for dramatic effect, but it was true, and though he hadn't known Joan that long, he realized yet again how much he loved her. No matter how long he lived, he would never feel this way about anyone else, and going through something like this together could only make their relationship stronger. That was something he didn't know how to describe.

But, miraculously, his dad seemed to understand. "Okay, Gary."

"What?" He could hear his mom screaming in the background. The sound was suddenly muffled as his dad put his hand over the mouthpiece and said something to her that he didn't want Gary to listen in on. "I've got to go," his dad said a few seconds later, coming back on the line.

"Over my dead body!" his mom screamed.

"I'll call you later."

"Okay," Gary said. There was a short beat. "Thanks, Dad."

"No problem. Love you."

"Love you, too."

He returned to class, shooting the instructor an apologetic smile, hoping the expression on his face conveyed the importance and seriousness of the call. A half hour later, after the session ended, he found Reyn waiting for him outside the classroom. Reyn had had a free period, and he'd called a friend of his, who had a friend who was out of town. If they took over house-sitting duties, the friend said, they could stay at this guy's place for the next week. It was a two-bedroom duplex in Van Nuys, just off the 405 freeway, ten minutes from campus if there was no traffic. All they had to do was feed the fish and water the ficus.

"We can all stay there," Reyn said. "Even Brian, if he doesn't mind sleeping on the couch."

"That sounds great." Gary felt surprisingly relieved, as

though getting away from UCLA would offer them some sort of protection. "I'll call Joan and Brian, tell them."

"I already called Stacy. It's fine with her, although she has a late class today until six. My last class is at three, but I'll stay with her."

"Should we—"

"I'm going to meet Ernesto for lunch so he can give me the key to the place. Wait for me at three on that bench outside the library, and I'll give it to you. You and Joan can go over there first, and we'll meet you there after Stacy's class." He grinned. "If you two wanted to provide a hot dinner to show your appreciation, I wouldn't be opposed."

"Consider it done."

The crowd around them was thinning out. "I'd better get going," Reyn said. "See you later."

"Later."

Reyn met his friend at an El Pollo Loco in Encino to pick up the key and stopped by an Ace Hardware on the way back to make four extra copies. "There's no garage," he explained when he met Gary and Joan outside the library, "so you have to park on the street—*if* you can find a spot. The stove and oven are broken. They're both gas, but the gas has been shut off so the place won't blow up."

"We'll make do," Joan told him.

Brian was with them. They'd already asked him to stay in the duplex, but he'd declined. "I like to be where the action is," he said. "Besides, Dror's got my back." He had agreed to drive over with them, however, just to see where the place was, and he took out a pen, writing down Reyn's directions on his hand.

"I have some paper," Joan offered.

"That's all right. This is easier."

Reyn gave each of them keys, Brian included, then looked up at the clock in the tower. "I've gotta get going. Stacy's out in ten minutes and it's all the way across campus. See you between six thirty and seven."

"Dinner will be waiting," Joan promised.

Reyn was already starting to hurry away.

"Did you try these keys yet?" Gary called after him.

"No! Let me know if they work!"

And he was lost in the crowd.

The three of them stood there for a few moments more, pretending to talk but in reality scoping out the surrounding area, looking to see if they were being watched. There was no sign of oddly dressed Homesteaders, and none of them noticed anyone loitering suspiciously nearby or taking any interest in their presence.

"I'll follow a couple of car lengths behind you," Brian said as they started making their way toward the east parking lot. "See if you're being followed."

"Are we paranoid or what?" Gary tried to joke.

"No," Joan said soberly. "We're realistic."

And that, he realized, was the truth.

Brian stayed for only a few minutes, to make sure they got into the duplex and to check it out. There was a medium-sized living room, a small, narrow kitchen, a single bathroom with a shower-tub, and two bedrooms, both with full-sized beds. It was connected to a bigger unit in the front, but while it was modest, it felt homey, and Gary liked it immediately. He was reminded of Sheriff Stewart's house in Bitterweed, for some reason, and that connection cemented his positive impression of the place.

"Even if I wanted to stay, there's no room," Brian noted.

"The couch," Gary said. "The floor."

"That's all right. I'll stick with my bed."

Joan carried her suitcase into one of the bedrooms,

and Brian motioned for Gary to follow him outside. He'd managed to find a parking spot in front of the duplex, and he headed over to his vehicle. "Brought you a knife," he said. He opened the trunk and withdrew a long blade encased in a leather sheath.

Gary was hesitant. It was much bigger than the one he'd carried into the Home and looked almost like a small sword. "I don't know. We have the bat. . . ."

"If Father and his hemp-shirted goons come crashing through that door in the middle of the night to kill you and rape Joan, you're going to thank your lucky stars you're sleeping next to this."

He was right, and Gary picked up the weapon, hefting it in his hand, surprised by how heavy it was and at the same time reassured. "Thanks," he said.

"No problemo."

Joan appeared in the doorway behind them. She saw the sheathed knife but said nothing about it. More than anything else, that brought home to him how seriously she took their predicament.

"Gotta go," Brian said, slamming the trunk. "Call me tonight. If I don't hear from you by eight, I'm calling *you*. And if you don't answer your phone, I'm coming *over*."

"Right back at you."

Joan had walked up behind him, and together they watched Brian drive away, standing on the sidewalk and waving until his car had turned the corner at the end of the block. "So what's for dinner?" Gary asked.

"Let's go in and see," she said.

The apartment had a working microwave and a refrigerator, but the refrigerator was empty and the only food that could be found in the cupboards were packages of Top Ramen and Cup O'Noodles.

Joan grimaced. "I don't think so."

"Any ideas?"

"I can actually cook in a microwave, you know. Real food."

"Like what?"

"How does pasta sound?"

"Pasta Roni?"

She hit his shoulder. "No. Real pasta. Sort of. I get, like, Ragú or something, chop up some extra vegetables and herbs, heat it up, cook the noodles and voila! A nice home-cooked meal."

"Sounds good," he admitted.

She took his hand. "Let's go to the store and do a little grocery shopping."

He smiled. "We're getting awfully domestic, aren't we?"

"Is that a complaint?"

"No. I think it's great."

She squeezed his hand. "Me, too. Come on."

They drove down the street to the nearest supermarket, an Albertson's. He grabbed a cart from the front of the store and followed her up each aisle as she compared prices and picked out items. "Do you want something for dessert?" she asked.

He shook his head. "I'm not much of a dessert fan."

"I eat when I'm under stress. I'm making brownies."

"In a microwave?"

"It can be done, believe it or not. Watch and learn." She threw a box of brownie mix into the cart.

He liked this. It was fun. And for a few moments he almost forgot that Father was out there, angry and after them. Then they were in the produce department, where suddenly he smelled dirt, roots. He whirled around— and Joan was holding out a bag of loose mushrooms she'd chosen. "I usually mix these into the sauce," she said, frowning at his reaction. "Gives it a richer flavor. Are you all right?"

"Fine. I'm fine." But the smell was still in his nostrils

and he was remembering the rag his kidnappers kept putting over his face. He felt nervous, jittery, and he found that he didn't like being out in public like this. He felt exposed, and he made Joan hurry up so they could get out of there and get back to the duplex.

Reyn and Stacy arrived ten minutes before the dinner was done. Joan and Gary had already set the table and were watching the news, waiting for the microwave's timer to beep, when their friends came in. "I was joking," Reyn said when he saw the table. He breathed deeply. "But it smells good!"

The food *was* good, and they all overate and then retreated to different chairs or couches to complete the reading assignments for their various classes. Reyn turned on a radio and tuned it to a jazz station, keeping the volume low. "I can't study in silence," he said apologetically. "I need some noise."

The evening was nice, but the aura of foreboding that hung over Gary refused to go away, and when they quit studying and went into their respective bedrooms, he had a hard time falling asleep, despite the fact that he'd been up almost all the previous night. When he finally dozed off, he dreamed, a horrible nightmare in which, like zombies from *Night of the Living Dead*, Homesteaders surrounded the duplex and started breaking windows, knocking down doors. He tried to grab his knife, but too many hands were on him, clawing, scratching, hitting, pulling. Homesteaders were everywhere, and as he looked frantically around, he saw that Joan had already been killed, that her bloody body was being torn apart. Through a gap between the lurching forms of his attackers, he saw the open doorway, and behind it the short hall, where an army of peasant-clothed Homesteaders was filing into Reyn and Stacy's room. Over the grunts and screams and sickening wet crunches, he could hear

Father's deep, booming laughter, loud, raucous and happily amused.

In the morning, he awoke with the dawn, and for the first few confusing seconds thought that his dream had been reality. But Joan was dozing next to him, he could hear Reyn and Stacy murmuring in the other bedroom, and with grateful relief he realized that everyone was still alive.

So far.

Twenty-eight

Brian hated communications law. It wasn't the subject matter; although, for the most part, the course was pretty dry going. No, he hated the length of the class. And its time slot. It was a course required for his major, so he had to take it, but it was only offered in one big chunk, on Wednesdays from four to seven, and that made the class unbearable. By that hour, he'd been at school for most of the day and his brain was tired. It also encompassed his dinnertime, so he was hungry. Students were allowed a fifteen-minute break at five forty-five, halfway through, and a lot of them got snacks from the vending machines on the first floor or coffee from one of the service clubs that'd set up a concessions table outside the building, but others just bailed, leaving and not coming back, and today Brian thought he might try that himself.

It had been a few days since they'd returned from Texas, but he still hadn't adjusted to normal life. In a weird way, he'd *liked* the roller-coaster ride of the past two weeks. On some adrenaline-junkie level, he'd even liked that terrifying foray into the Home, although he could hardly believe now that he had held a guy at knifepoint and forced him to take them to Joan. It seemed as though that had been another person, and thinking about it from a distance, he realized how lucky he was that he was not behind bars.

But that was why he was finding it difficult to get back into the rhythm of things here. After so much danger and excitement, it was hard to go back to being a regular guy doing regular things in a regular way—although Father was still loose and probably after them, if the events of the past two days were any indication. So he wasn't exactly Joe Average. But compared to the adventure they'd had in Texas, life at UCLA was still a lot more sedate than being on the road.

And sitting through a class like comm law was sheer torture.

The session was not even halfway over and he'd already dozed off twice, though he doubted the instructor had noticed. A pompous windbag who loved the sound of his own voice and seemed to believe that a point worth making once was worth making thrice, Dr. Meyer seldom paid much attention to inconsequential minutiae such as the reactions of his students.

Brian had been taking notes on the lecture in the way that was expected, but in the margins of the notebook he'd been jotting down ideas. He still thought the best plan was to take the fight to Father, to get Dror and those film geeks together again, bring along the pigs if necessary and hunt the bastard down. But since none of them had any idea where to take the fight *to*, the next best thing would be to prepare themselves for the showdown that was inevitably going to come. Reyn's little namby-pamby plan of hiding and hoping no one would notice them was idiotic. The only reason they'd been able to get into the Home had been because *he'd* thought to bring knives, and Brian knew that their best chance now was to arm themselves the same way.

That was what he'd been jotting down: simple alarms they could set up around their rooms, places they could hide easy-to-use, easily accessible weapons, people they could enlist to help them. They'd beaten the cult the last time, and Father would do everything he could to ensure that didn't happen again. So they needed to be ready.

Brian smiled to himself. Too bad his dad wasn't still around. The old man would be shocked that his hippie son not only knew his way around weapons but was willing to use them. *Had* used them.

Some of his dad's asshole-ness must have gotten passed down through his genes.

Brian's brain had drifted away, lost the thread of the lecture, but his attention was once again focused on the front of the room when Dr. Meyer suddenly stopped speaking. The instructor was folding up his laptop, and the students around him were standing and stretching or gathering their belongings, and Brian understood that it was break time.

Just as well. He'd brought a Big Gulp to class with him, hoping the caffeine in the Coke would keep him awake, but he'd finished the drink early on and now desperately had to take a leak. He looked around for Tina, a chick he was interested in whom he usually managed to chat up during the break. She was already out the door, on her way to get coffee from the table in front of the building, no doubt, and he figured he could quickly go to the bathroom and worm his way next to her in line before she actually got her decaf.

He shoved his books under his chair, checking his phone to make sure he had no messages waiting as he followed the crowd through the door. He didn't like using the restrooms next to the elevators—too crowded— so he usually walked down the hall to the bathroom opposite the Communications department office. The office closed at five, and there were no other classes at that end of the building at this hour, which meant that he was able to get in and out quickly.

He passed through the throng of students who were waiting for the elevator, lining up for the restrooms or

making their way down the stairs. Once he turned the
corner, the corridor was empty, save for a female instructor weighted down with book bags who was just entering
the little-used back stairwell at the far end of the building. The sound of voices behind him grew muffled, faint,
indistinct, before being swallowed up in the silence, and
by the time he approached the closed door of the Communications department office, the only noise he could
hear was that caused by his feet on the hard floor, which,
despite the fact that he was wearing sneakers, sounded
like the clicking of boots.

Tina was probably downstairs by now, lining up.

He reached the restroom, went in, quickly relieved
himself and washed his hands. The dispensers were out
of paper towels, so he wiped his wet hands on his pants.
He came out of the bathroom—

And saw an old man in peasant clothes, holding a
whip.

Brian stopped. The guy was coming toward him from
the rear of the building, where the door to the stairwell
was still closing slowly. He'd been holding the whip in
front of him, using both hands, but when he saw Brian,
his left hand dropped the tip of the lash and his right
hand flicked the leather handle, causing the whip to
crack.

How the fuck had they found him? Brian wondered.

He started walking away from the man, toward the
front of the building, toward the elevators and his classroom and other people. Behind him, the whipcracks
grew louder, more frequent, more insistent. The old guy
was gaining on him, and unless he wanted to start running away like a little girl, he was going to have to deal
with the man.

Brian stopped, turned.

The old man was closer but not as close as expected,
and Brian examined his face, trying to figure out if he

looked familiar, if he'd been at the Home. Brian didn't recognize him, but both the plain homemade clothes and the poorly shorn hair clearly marked him as one of the Homesteaders.

The man stared hard at Brian and cracked his whip with extra vigor.

These were religious freaks, weren't they? They were supposed to take the Bible literally and follow everything to the letter, right? He decided on a confrontational approach. "Thou shalt not kill. Ever heard of that rule? It's one of the big ten. Maybe you guys should try following it."

The man kept coming, cracking his whip. He said nothing, and the expression on his face was blank.

"Fuck you," Brian said disgustedly. He was more scared than he dared let on, but he turned calmly to walk away, not wanting to give the son of a bitch the satisfaction of seeing him run—

And two more Homesteaders were coming toward him from the front of the building.

Carrying knives.

The blades were remarkably similar to the ones he'd brought to Texas, and it occurred to Brian that they might be the very same ones. These guys were out for revenge, and they could've easily broken into his room and found them in his closet. They probably could have found his schedule somewhere in the room, too, although their resident computer whiz could just as easily have looked it up online.

Neither of these two was wearing an expression, either. Their faces were just as blank as the old man's, and as they approached, knives extended, they reminded him of zombies.

No.

Soldiers.

Following orders.

Suddenly he was much more afraid. People acting on their own, even out of strong emotion, could be reasoned with, talked to, convinced to alter their course of action. But people following orders, doing the bidding of others, had no ideas or convictions they could be argued out of. They were merely performing a task.

Brian thought quickly. One or more of the doors in this corridor might be unlocked, but if he tried to open them and failed, he would have wasted valuable time. The bathroom was open, but he didn't think the door could be locked from the inside and he didn't want to trap himself within a confined area—particularly not with people carrying knives.

He decided the best course of action would be to try to get by the guy with the whip. The old man might get in one or two lashes, but that wouldn't be fatal, and if he ran fast and hard enough, he could knock the old fuck off his feet and speed past him, escaping down the back stairs.

Assuming there weren't other Homesteaders waiting for him in the stairwell.

The men with knives quickened their pace, and Brian screamed at the top of his lungs, an incoherent cry intended to startle his attackers and throw them off their game. Simultaneously, he rushed the old man, keeping his head down as he charged so as not to be whipped in the face. The whip was more powerful than he'd anticipated, however, and either the Homesteader was more adept with it than expected or he was extraordinarily lucky, because even as Brian ran, the lash sunk into the flesh of his neck and instantly wrapped around it three times, cutting off his flow of air. Brian floundered, fell and desperately tried to claw the whip from his neck. His mouth and nose were frantically trying to suck in oxygen, but the passage to his lungs was blocked, and the braided leather acted as a barrier between his head and his body. He knew that he was dying, and he kicked his feet, jerked his body around, trying everything he could to breathe again.

Then a knife stabbed him in the lower back, and he could no longer move his feet. With one hard, jolting yank, the whip was pulled away, and another knife sliced into the back of his neck. He tried to use his hands to push himself up off the floor, but his arms were weak and his muscles wouldn't obey his brain.

The three men spoke together, calmly, unhurriedly, in the strange language of the Home.

This can't be happening, Brian thought. Not on a modern college campus, not in a building with hundreds of students in its classrooms.

But it was happening.

The last sight he saw was his own blood spreading slowly across the shiny white floor toward the wall.

Twenty-nine

Reyn looked up. "He's still not answering."

"Brian always answers his phone." Gary was worried. This was the fourth time they'd tried to contact their friend in the past hour, and each time they'd been put directly into voice mail. Outside the coffeehouse, the light was fading. The sun was almost down, and most of the campus was now in shadow. The security lights lining the walkways were already on. Both Joan and Stacy were in lab classes—different lab classes in different buildings—and he and Reyn were waiting here, next to the window, where they could see the entrances to each building.

Reyn said aloud what they were both thinking. "Do you think something happened to him?"

"I hope not," Gary said, but that was a lame response and he knew it. He finished his coffee and stood. "We need to find him."

"But Stacy and Joan . . ."

"They'll be in class for another twenty minutes. We'll be back in plenty of time."

Reyn nodded, but Gary could see that he was worried. If something *had* happened to Brian, they might be putting themselves in harm's way. And the fact that Joan and Stacy were in class didn't necessarily mean that they were safe.

Still, it was a risk Gary was willing to take. Right now, Brian's silence concerned him more than anything else.

The two of them left the coffeehouse. Outside, it wasn't quite as dark as Gary had thought. Looking through the windows from inside the lighted building had made the exterior world look like night, though in reality it was still dusk. "I know he has a class right now," Gary said, "but I can't remember what it is." Brian had flirted with several different majors, and it was hard to keep track of what he was studying.

"Isn't it that long class? The one he was dreading on the trip back?"

"Yeah. But what was it?"

"Wasn't it some type of law class?"

"Communications law!" Gary suddenly remembered. He frowned. "But what building's it in? And what room?"

"Somewhere near the Communications department, I assume." Without mentioning it, both Reyn and Gary had automatically reoriented themselves and started off in that direction. Reyn had his phone out, and while it wasn't as sophisticated as Brian's BlackBerry, he was typing on the small keypad and trying to access the school's current course catalog. "Fourth floor," Reyn announced. "Room 411." He shut the phone, shoved it into his shirt pocket, and they both strode more quickly toward the Communications building.

There were very few students out at this hour. Some were in classes, but most were studying or had gone home or were eating dinner. The two of them pretty much had the walkway to themselves. Gary was focused on their goal, had his eye on the square, blocky structure ahead, with its asymmetrically lit windows that gave the front of the building the appearance of a primitive computer terminal. So he was surprised when Reyn nudged him with an elbow and pointed. "Look," Reyn said quietly.

Between the bushes, moving away from them, was a dark-haired man wearing familiar-looking peasant clothes.

Gary didn't wait. He took off running, leaping over a low hedge border and dashing over the short expanse of grass. He hit the bushes hard, branches scraping his arms, leaves slapping against his face, but he refused to slow down. He was not athletic, had never played football, but he brought the man down with a flying tackle just as the Homesteader emerged into an open area near an intersecting sidewalk.

He fell onto his quarry, who tried to scramble out from underneath him and get away. Gary twisted the man's neck until the Homesteader turned onto his back, then sat on the man's chest, his knees pinning down the cult member's arms. The guy beneath him looked perfectly normal. His bones weren't strangely shaped; his head wasn't oddly formed; he didn't appear to be slow or impaired in any way. *A convert*, Gary thought. And that was good. In movies and on TV, fanatics and true believers inevitably held out against any questioning, steadfastly refusing to divulge information even while being tortured. But in real life, most people weren't that strong. And anyone weak-willed enough to voluntarily join a cult would not have the fortitude to withstand a hard interrogation.

"Call Joan," Gary told Reyn, who was just catching up. "Make sure she's all right." His fear was that Homesteaders had been sent out to distract the rest of them while Joan was attacked and captured—or killed.

Reyn whipped out his phone and punched in her number.

Gary turned his attention to the man beneath him. "You were following us, weren't you?"

The man smiled, his teeth eerily white in the ever-increasing darkness.

"Why?"

There was no answer.

"Where's Father?" Gary demanded.

The smile grew wider.

Gary punched the Homesteader in the face. His fist didn't connect directly with the man's nose, the way he'd intended. Instead, it sort of hit the side of the nose and the cheek. But it had the desired result, and Gary felt the hardness of bone beneath his knuckles, the warm wetness of blood.

"Where's Father?" he asked again.

The man was crying. He seemed surprised by the pain, as if he never thought such a thing could happen to him.

Gary held up his fist again. "Tell me where Father is! Tell me why you're here and what's going on! Now!"

"God doesn't want—"

"God wants me to beat the shit out of you," Gary said. "That's why I'm here and you're there. Now talk!"

The man recovered his composure and, through his tears, smiled again, blood covering his gums and seeping between the cracks of his teeth, distorting the look of his mouth and giving him an almost inhuman appearance. "Father is coming."

Father is coming.

The words sent a chill stabbing straight to Gary's heart. "Where is he?"

There was only the bloody smile.

A student walking by on the sidewalk to their left had noticed the commotion and was looking at them suspiciously.

"Get the police!" Gary yelled at him. "Now! This guy's a rapist! I caught him!"

The student ran off, taking out his cell phone as he did so. Thankfully, the guy was rattled and not thinking clearly or he would have noticed Reyn standing there and talking on *his* phone.

Or he would have realized that he didn't have to *go* anywhere to make the call.

Or he might have stood there and used his phone to take a picture.

Things could have gone so much more wrong, but miraculously they hadn't, and Gary quickly tried to think of a way to incapacitate the Homesteader. He wanted the man to remain in this spot but didn't want to be around himself when campus security or the police arrived. He and Reyn needed to get out of there fast. Looking around, he saw a recently planted sapling in the center of the grass. The small tree was being supported by guide wires secured to the trunk and attached to stakes in the ground. If he could—

The man bucked beneath him, the force and suddenness of the movement throwing him off, and before Gary could right himself and reestablish his hold over the Homesteader, the man had scrambled away, jumped to his feet and dashed into the bushes. Every instinct he had was telling him to take off in pursuit, but Gary knew that he had no hope of catching up to the man now, and at the moment his chief concern was for Joan. If *he* was being shadowed, it was a certainty that someone, or several someones—

Father

—had been sent after her.

Reyn was talking to Joan on the phone right now, and when he told Gary that she was in the library, working on research with a group of students from her lab class, a flash of panic shot through him. She wasn't in the lab? She'd walked all the way to the library without telling him? At this point, any variable at all was cause for worry, and he took the phone from Reyn. "Stay where you are!" he ordered. "Father is coming! That's what the Homesteader said. I caught one and—"

"I know. Reyn told me." There were others with her, so she was trying to sound calm, but he could hear the worry in her voice.

"He just escaped!"

"I know."

"Don't—" Gary had to stop and gulp air. He was hyperventilating and couldn't finish his sentence without pausing to catch his breath. "Don't go anywhere!" he said, and took another breath. "We'll meet you there! Where are you, exactly?"

She was still trying to keep her voice calm in front of her classmates. "We're in study room A on the sixth floor of the library, against the back wall."

"I know where it is. We'll be there as soon as we can."

"I'll stay right here." There was a pause. "You be careful, too."

"Always."

They said good-bye, and he handed the phone back to Reyn. "We have to get over there."

"I'm calling Stacy first." He paused before pressing her speed-dial number. "Do I tell her to stay where she is or go to Joan?"

Gary thought quickly. "We should probably stay together. There's safety in numbers."

"It'd be harder to get all of us if we were spread out," Reyn said.

"Not if there's a group of them and *they're* all spread out. We can defend ourselves better if we're together."

Reyn nodded, pressed the number. "Stacy!" he said as soon as she answered. "We just ran into a Homesteader. He said Father's here and on his way. I need you to leave class and get over to the library as quick as you can. Joan's there. We're heading over, too. We ..." He trailed off, then shook his head as he changed his mind. "No. Stay where you are." He looked over at Gary. "You get Joan," he said. "I'll get Stacy. We'll meet . . . ?"

"In the library. Study room A. Sixth floor."

"In the library. Study room A. Sixth floor," he repeated.

There was no time to waste. Gary waved to Reyn and took off running. Reyn started running after him, several steps behind, and before their paths diverged, he heard his friend say to Stacy, "That's who we were looking for. He's not answering his phone. We thought something might've happened to him."

Then Reyn turned toward Stacy's building, and Gary ran toward the library.

It was dark now, and the entire campus seemed little more than an amalgam of hiding places. He glanced suspiciously at every person he passed by, hyperaware that any one of them could be a fanatic cult member ready to attack. Ahead, in the gloom, the hulking mass of the library resembled nothing so much as the exterior of a haunted castle.

An icy shudder passed through him.

Father is coming, he thought.

Father is coming.

Thirty

Joan put down her cell phone.

Tessa and Vy were arguing over something in the course textbook. Craig was on his laptop, looking up something entirely unrelated to the class.

She glanced slowly around. The study room was completely enclosed. There was only one door, and a wall of windows looked out into the library, so if anyone tried to approach through the stacks, she'd be able to see them immediately. This was probably one of the most secure places she could be on campus, but she felt vulnerable, at once trapped and exposed, and though she'd promised Gary she'd remain where she was, Joan wanted nothing more than to get out of this room and out of the library. First instincts weren't always right, though, and she knew that it would be much smarter for her to—

The lights in the library began flashing, accompanied by the clanging of an alarm.

"Fire!" Tessa cried, snatching up her books.

All of the students in her study group hurriedly gathered their materials, preparing to make a run for the stairwells. They were on the sixth floor, and if there was a fire, they wanted to get outside as quickly as possible. Joan had the same gut reaction, but even as she grabbed her books and notebooks, she was thinking of the fire last night, in Gary's dorm. The ringing alarm sounded exactly the same and the parallels were impossible to ignore. The fire in the library—if there really *was* a fire in the library and someone had not simply set off the alarm—must have been set by the same person.

Father is coming.

Tessa and Vy were already out of the room and running, and Craig was holding the door open for her. "Come on!" he yelled.

She followed him—and saw a Homesteader walking up the aisle between a long row of bookshelves.

The lights flashed off again, on, and the Homesteader was closer, much closer, moving fast, though he was still not running.

Panicked, she dashed to her left. Another Homesteader was coming up *this* aisle, heading toward her as though he'd known all along that this was exactly where she would be.

She ran in the direction of the north stairwell, acting on instinct rather than intellect, aware on some level that she was going into the most remote section of the library and that most of the other students on the floor had probably run to the south stairwell, which was adjacent to the elevators. The rhythmic flashing of the lights, accompanied by the constant ringing of the alarm bells, lent the space ahead a surreal aspect that only intensified her fear.

And then the alarm stopped, the sudden cessation of noise creating a silence so heavy it pressed against her ears.

Joan froze. She heard no voices, no footsteps. She'd lost Craig and had no idea where Tessa and Vy were. Downstairs by now, probably. Along with everyone else.

Was she the only one left on the sixth floor?

No. The Homesteaders were here.

She ran toward the stairwell door as quickly as she

could, her heart pounding crazily. It was the terror she'd felt back at the Home multiplied by ten. Here in the outside world, Father might not have the absolute power that he'd had in his own fiefdom, but the Home was gone and he was angry, and there was no telling what he might do.

She reached the door and pushed it open. The stairwell smelled familiar, as though someone wearing a heavy floral perfume had just left the area. Immediately, her head began to feel strange. She recognized the feeling and tried to turn around and go back the way she'd come, but hands reached around from behind her and grabbed her arms, pressing them to her sides. Looking down, she saw that the hands were clawed, that the skin was blue, the long nails black, and then a bag was put over her head, a bag that was wet and smelled of old licorice.

And then she was out.

Joan awoke to see Father staring down at her.

It was night, and his features were illuminated by the soft, flickering glow of candlelight. His eyes were hard, his mouth set within the overgrown beard, and he was holding a Bible, though the way he was clutching it in his hands made it look as though he wanted to rip the book in half rather than read it. Joan was in a prone position, lying on something hard, and when she tried to lift herself up on her elbows, she found that she couldn't. She was being held down, though she couldn't tell if hands or straps were keeping her in place, and she realized at that moment that she could not feel anything below her neck. Her body was totally without sensation. Maybe *nothing* was holding her down, and with a feeling of rising panic she wondered if she was permanently paralyzed.

She tried not to let the fear show on her face, though

she had no idea whether or not she was successful. "Where am I?" she demanded.

When Father didn't answer, she said, "Gary's coming for me."

"He's dead," Father stated flatly. "All of your friends are dead. *Ruth*."

Joan couldn't keep the reaction off her face this time. The effect his words had on her was physical. It was as if he had punched her in the stomach. She could tell from the smug satisfaction in his voice that what he said was true, and she was filled with a sudden deep despair. At that moment, she wished she was dead herself. Her parents were gone . . . Gary . . . her friends, and all that was left to her was the one thing on earth she wanted most to avoid: Father. She wished he would kill her, but she knew that was not going to happen. Eventually, she would die, but he wanted to make her suffer first, wanted to make her pay.

"I am building a new Home," he said in the Language, "and you have been called upon to assist me."

"Never," she said in English, though she was not brave enough to look at him.

He shoved his face in front of hers. The candlelight created pools of shadow on his features, giving his eyes an almost skull-like appearance. "You will bear me sons," he intoned. "In pain shall you bring forth children."

Her vision blurred. She closed her eyelids tightly as the tears overflowed and ran down the sides of her head, not wanting to see Father's expression of triumph.

He continued talking to her, but somehow she was able to block out his voice. Closing her eyes helped, but there was also a type of white noise in her head, a dull humming that was probably a residue of whatever had been used to drug her, and she found when she concentrated on that sound, it caused Father's voice to fade into the background. His voice grew louder and he might have been yelling at her, but she lost herself in the hum and, eventually, she drifted off to sleep.

When Joan awoke again, she was alone. It was still night, but the environment around her was darker. Candles had either burned out or been taken away. She glanced around surreptitiously, trying to figure out where she was. She assumed Father and his people had taken her off campus. But were they even in California? How long had she been out before waking up? How much time had passed? Hours? Days? Weeks?

She was gratified to find that not only could she move her head, but she could wiggle her fingers. And there was feeling again in the lower half of her body. She was definitely strapped—she could feel the ropes holding down her arms, legs and midsection—but at least she was able to see her surroundings.

She was lying on a bed in a small room of primitive construction, in what appeared to be part of an old shack or cabin. The lone candle illuminating the room was behind her head somewhere, so she couldn't see it, but its flickering orangish glow threw into relief the whorled wood of the walls and allowed her to view the framed photo of Father that was hanging where a window should be. There had to be a door into the room—indeed, she could feel cold seeping in from outside—but, like the candle, it was behind her and she couldn't see it. Other than the bed on which she lay, there didn't seem to be any furniture.

Joan listened for any sounds from the world outside or from other rooms in the cabin. Her ears were still slightly plugged up, and at first she heard nothing. Then, from the stillness, came a low, muffled muttering.

Voices in prayer.

How many of them were there? And what were they praying for? The death of the Outsiders? Continued evasion of the police? All of Father's prayers were selfish and self-serving, asking for favors or begging for revenge, and she had no doubt that he was leading his current group of followers in a plea to save his butt.

The idea that the great and powerful Father was engaged in such a pathetic and prosaically craven pursuit gave her hope and strength, and she immediately began testing her bonds, attempting to discover if any of them were loose and whether she had any hope of escape. Gary and her friends might be dead, but that was even more of an incentive. Their deaths needed to be avenged, and she would not rest until Father had paid for his crimes.

She was crying, thinking about Gary, and for some reason the image that stuck in her mind was one of him eating a sandwich at the beach, staring out to sea while she watched him, unnoticed. But she made no noise, and even as her tears overflowed, trickling down the sides of her head into her ears, she was moving her hands and feet back and forth, trying to create some wiggle room. Her legs felt cold. In fact, the entire lower half of her body felt cold, and she realized with horror that her pants were off.

Had anything been done to her? She couldn't tell. But even if nothing had happened yet, it would—

You will bear me sons

—and she struggled even harder to free herself.

The prayer had stopped, and now Father was talking. She could not hear the words, only the rhythm, but he was in full fire-and-brimstone form, and she could imagine what he was saying. How many people were with him? she wondered. Almost everyone from the Home had been captured, but she had no idea how many people in the rest of the country were followers of Father or how quickly he could gather them. Although maybe he didn't want them all with him. Spread out, they could provide a fugitive network, allowing him to evade police indefinitely as he moved from one house and one state to another.

Joan gave up trying to break free of her restraints. There was no progress, for all her effort, and already she could feel pain in her wrists and ankles where her skin was becoming chafed and rubbed raw. She needed to save her strength in case an opportunity arose.

Who was she kidding? There weren't going to be any opportunties. Gary was dead, Reyn and Stacy were dead, Brian was dead, and she was tied down to a bed in some filthy shack, where she would spend the rest of her life—however short or long that might be—being raped by Father.

In pain shall you bring forth children.

She started to sob again, and this time she couldn't help uttering small desperate cries of hopeless despair.

Behind her, she heard Father's heavy footsteps.

And even heavier breathing.

Thirty-one

By the time Gary reached the library, it had been evacuated and scores of students stood before the building in the growing darkness, clutching books and backpacks, watching as policemen and firemen came and went through the open doors. Every so often, another student or two would be ushered out. Gary scanned the crowd, looking for Joan, and when he didn't see her, he moved to the front of the assemblage, hoping to find her being escorted to safety, but very quickly the trickle of people being led from the building dropped to zero, and he realized with a sick feeling in his gut that she was missing.

He was filled with rage and frustration, much of it directed at himself—*he should have gotten here faster, he shouldn't have let the Homesteader go*—and he wanted to run into the library and find Joan, wanted to speed across campus and chase down the bastards who had nabbed her, but he had no idea where she was, and he stood there impotently, unable to act.

At the edge of the crowd, Gary saw a shadowy shape, a short figure with an oddly large head, and as the squat form wove in and out between the evacuated students, an unwelcome shiver passed through him. It wasn't the man he and Reyn had caught on their way to the Communications building, but he had no doubt that it was a Homesteader, one of the Children. From the corner of his eye, he thought he saw additional movement to the side of the library, and when Stacy tapped him on the shoulder and Reyn said, "Hey," Gary jumped.

"Where's Joan?" Stacy asked immediately.

He shook his head, unable to say the words, and realized that he was on the verge of tears. They had rescued Joan once before. What were the odds that the same thing could happen twice? Would Father, who was on the run, kidnap her to convert her back to his religion or press her into servitude? No. He probably wanted to punish her. She was probably already dead.

Stacy's phone was out, and once again she was calling the police. This time, she got Williams on the line. "We think she's been kidnapped again," Stacy told the detective, explaining what had happened.

Listening to her describe the situation, Gary came back from the brink. Father probably *did* want to punish Joan, but he wouldn't do it by killing her. He would keep her, hold her, torture her.

Gary thought of the case Sheriff Stewart had told them about, the woman who'd been imprisoned in the Home for over a year and repeatedly raped by Father. He tried not to, but he couldn't help imagining Joan being assaulted by the old man, and the pictures in his head made him want to strangle the son of a bitch with his own beard.

Sirens sounded from streets on different sides of the campus.

"What?" Stacy said into the phone, shocked.

Gary held his breath.

She looked over at them. "Someone's been murdered in the Communications building!" she announced.

Brian.

Gary met Reyn's eyes, seeing on his friend's face a mirror image of his own feelings.

Stacy said a quick good-bye and got off the phone. "He's coming over himself this time."

"To the murder site first," Reyn said.

Gary nodded. "Which doesn't help Joan."

There was a commotion near the library entrance, and the three of them pressed forward, along with the rest of the crowd. The cause of the disturbance had been discovered. A piece of cloth had been set on fire and placed near a smoke detector in order to make the alarm go off. A firefighter carried out the smoldering black fabric using a pair of long metal tongs, and another fireman rushed up carrying a metal container. The burned cloth was dropped inside.

Reyn sniffed the air, and an expression of excited recognition passed over his features. "I remember that smell now! I know where I've smelled it before!"

Gary breathed deeply. The smoke did indeed have the same woodsy odor as the fire that had destroyed his dorm.

"It's Abrego's Pitch!"

"What the hell's that?"

"It's sap that was used by Indian tribes as a kind of fire starter. The Spanish even used it in their lamps when they couldn't get oil. It's from a native tree that was nearly logged to extinction. We learned about it in my California habitats class last semester." He looked at Gary. "As far as I know, the only place this tree grows is on a preserve in the Mojave Desert. It's protected, but there's, like, an on-site research facility run by the school. We went there for a lab class, and that's where I smelled that smell, as part of a demonstration."

"I'll bet that's where they're going," Gary said excitedly. "I'll bet that's where they're taking her. How far away is this preserve? And how big is it?"

"Big," Reyn admitted, and the note of discouragement in his voice made Gary's heart sink. "It's part of the Angeles National Forest, on the desert side of the San Gabriel Mountains, and it probably takes up fifty square miles. There are canyons, trails. . . ."

"So we'd never be able to find them," Gary said dejectedly.

Reyn paused, thinking. "The thing is," he said, "on another part of the preserve, in a canyon where we hiked and took notes on local plants, we passed an old abandoned ranch—a house, a barn, some stables—and I remember a big white cross painted on the rock wall above it."

Stacy was shaking her head. "Sounds kind of hinky, don't you think? They escape from their compound in Texas, are on the run from the law, and instead of hol- ing up with one of their own in Texas or New Mexico or Arizona, they decide to camp out in a California wildlife preserve—one with a public nature center, no less—so they can raid the local trees for pitch to start fires at UCLA. It doesn't add up."

She was right, Gary thought. And yet . . .

And yet how much of what had happened to them made any kind of logical sense? From Joan's mysteri- ous disappearance at Burning Man, to her roommate Kara's conversion, to his own abduction, to the Home with its deformed incestuous offspring, everything that had occurred had followed an absurdly irrational ratio- nale. Were they now going to start applying the test of ordinary reason to a situation that until this very second had been its polar opposite?

"I think she's there," Gary said.

Reyn nodded. "I agree."

"Do you know how to get to this preserve?"

Reyn's phone was out and he was already accessing a GPS app. "I will in a minute."

Stacy sighed, shaking her head.

Around them, some of the students had started to wander off. A fireman was announcing that the library would not reopen until it had been thoroughly searched, and the rest of the crowd started to break up. The excitement was over, it was getting late, and they began heading toward other classes or the student union or the dorms.

There was movement in the darkness to the left of the library building, and though it was too dim for him to be sure, Gary thought he saw two figures in peasant clothes hurrying behind the bulky, blocky structure. His pulse quickened, a primal fear response. A split second later, another man appeared, this one standing purposely in a square of light thrown onto the grass by one of the library's windows. He faced their direction, and though he was too far away for his face to be seen, Gary had the distinct impression that he was smiling.

The man was oddly shaped, with a squat body held aloft by incredibly long legs. He was obviously one of the Children, and just the sight of him sent Gary into a rage. Fists clenched, he started forward.

"No," Stacy said, grabbing his arm.

He turned to her.

She was looking in the same direction, an expression of alarm frozen on her face. "Don't follow them. They're trying to get us alone. Stay with the crowd."

He peered into the darkness at the long-legged man still standing in the square of light and felt a tingle of fear. She was right. The man was attempting to lure them into the shadows, away from everyone else, and doubtless there were others waiting nearby to ... to ...

To what?

Kill them.

Yes. The Home was gone, Father was ruined, and he was out for blood.

Stacy had already manuevered her way between the

departing students and was flagging down one of the campus policemen standing in front of the library doors. She spoke quickly, but whatever she said to the officer must have had the ring of truth because the man immediately returned with her and asked with some urgency, "Where is he?"

Gary pointed into the darkness at the side of the library, but the Homesteader was gone. In the few brief seconds he had turned away, the deformed man had disappeared. "I don't know," Gary said. "He was right there."

"We'll find him," the policeman said grimly.

The three of them followed the officer around the side of the building. He had his flashlight out—a long metal cylinder that obviously doubled as a weapon when needed—and was shining the beam in a swiveling arc in front of them. But there were very few bushes or hiding places, and the area seemed to be completely deserted. They reached the spot where light from one of the library windows fell upon the ground, and Gary looked back at where they'd been standing. He knew all of a sudden that they would find nothing. All of the Homesteaders were gone.

He was right. They circumnavigated the entire building, but aside from a handful of students strolling past on a nearby sidewalk on the opposite side of the library, they saw no one. Certainly no malformed men in beige peasant clothes skulking around the shadows.

"There's no one," the policeman said. "Or, if there was, they're gone."

"We didn't imagine it," Stacy said.

"I believe you."

"Well, thanks for checking it out," Gary said. "But we've got to go." With every second that passed, Joan was farther away, and he was anxious to be out of here and on the road. As tenuous as Reyn's connection might

be, he fully believed that Father and his followers were
taking her to that nature preserve, to that ranch with a
cross painted on the canyon cliff above. The notion rang
true to him, and his mind had already begun concocting
a scenario where that painted white cross was a secret
symbol indicating that the ranch below was a stop on an
underground railroad for religious fanatics, a safe haven
for abortion clinic bombers, child-molesting polygamists
and weapons-hoarding sect leaders.

Stacy held out her hand. "Thank you, Officer Sanders."

"I'll keep my eye out for these people," he promised
her. "And I'll tell everyone else to watch for them, too.
They probably *are* the ones who set off the alarm."

"We'll take my car," Gary said, leading them away
from the library toward the north parking lot. A few
students were still hanging around, watching the firemen and policemen, and a young woman with a camera, probably from the school newspaper, was crouching
down on the cement, trying to find the right angle for a
picture, but by now most of the crowd was gone.

They hurried. The walkways leading between the
buildings to the parking lots were not very crowded, but
that would change in a few minutes when classes got
out, and they didn't want to get caught in the rush. Gary
cast a quick glance toward the Communications building. None of them had made an effort to call Brian again
since all of this had started, and though he knew why, he
didn't want to think about it.

Reyn still had the directions he'd accessed displayed
on his phone, and as they strode quickly toward the
parking lot, he was describing the route they needed to
take. The sidewalk wound between two grass-covered
mounds, and far off to the left Gary saw the tree-lined
memorial path where they'd set a trap for the Homesteaders who had come to abduct him. Although the
area before them was clear and open, for some irrational

reason he kept expecting the tables to have been turned, kept waiting to be jumped by a gang of Father's followers, but they made it to the parking lot without incident. "I'm over there," Gary said, pointing.

They hurried down the main aisle, past several rows of vehicles.

"Oh my God," Stacy said as they approached.

Gary's car had been vandalized. All of the windows were smashed and the tires were flat. He ran forward and looked inside. The seats had been slashed.

They knew his car.

What else did they know?

His parents' address.

The thought chilled him. The important facts of his life were all listed online, he realized, and the Homesteaders' hacking had gained access to that. They knew almost everything about him.

Now they were acting on it.

He wanted to call his parents immediately, but there was no time. Joan was his first priority right now, just as she was Father's, and he needed to find her and get her away from those lunatics.

"They're here somewhere," Stacy whispered, looking around the parking lot. "I can feel it."

Gary could, too, and he looked about, seeing pools of darkness in the gaps between the evenly spaced lights. The parked cars and trucks offered far too many hiding places for his liking.

"We need weapons," Reyn said all of a sudden.

He was right. Gary mentally kicked himself. How stupid could they be? If Brian were here, *he* would have brought weapons. He recalled the comforting heft of Brian's swordlike knife in his hand. If only he had something like that right now . . .

But it was back in the duplex, along with Joan's baseball bat.

Reyn had taken the ring of keys from his pocket and was holding it in his fist, individual keys protruding from between each knuckle. Gary thought of an idea. He hurried around to the trunk and opened it, rummaging through the wheel well until he found a tire iron. He saw in his mind the crazed, grimacing face of the bearded gas station attendant, and though the recollection of that encounter made his stomach knot up, he knew that the heavy tool would be an effective weapon. Closing the trunk, he swung the length of tempered steel back and forth, hearing it cut through the air with an audible *swish*.

"Gary?" Reyn said.

Gary could tell from Reyn's tone of voice that he'd seen something, and he quickly turned. Reyn was staring down the row at a figure standing several car lengths away.

It was a man with a whip. He had emerged from between a beat-up Honda Civic and an old Chevy and was flicking his wrist, the whip in his hand cracking loudly several times in quick succession. The man was wearing the handmade clothes of a Homesteader, and his gray hair was cut crudely in a style Gary had never seen before. Behind him, from between the same cars, came another Homesteader, this one wielding a large knife.

"Back up slowly," Gary said, and the three of them did just that, not wanting to turn their backs on the men.

The old guy advanced, cracking his whip again, and Gary swung the tire iron in front of him, his heart pounding.

"You! Put that down! Now!"

At the sound of the voice, Gary turned to see a campus policeman getting out of one of the electric vehicles used to patrol the parking lots. He came from behind Stacy, walking quickly, pointing a nightstick at the Homesteader with his right hand while his left hand unhooked a walkie-talkie from his belt. "Martinez," he said.

He'd obviously been notified about the Homesteaders, probably by Officer Sanders. "North lot. We have two of them, one with a whip, one with a knife, threatening three students."

The Homesteaders ran.

"Wait there!" the policeman ordered Gary, Reyn and Stacy, and took off after them, shouting into his walkie-talkie. Seconds later, the Homesteaders and the policeman were nowhere to be seen.

"Do we wait?" Stacy asked, confused.

"No," Gary said.

"We'll take my car." Reyn told them. "I parked in the east lot. Let's go."

Stacy called the police station again as they ran, trying to get ahold of Williams. He was not in his office, was already on campus, but by the time they reached Reyn's car, the dispatcher had put her through to the detective, who was with a forensics team on the fifth floor of the Communications building. Gary listened in on her side of the conversation, his eyes meeting Reyn's over the roof of the Focus, neither of them liking what they heard.

Stacy swung the phone away from her mouth, an expression of shock on her face. "It's Brian," she said, her voice little more than a whisper. "He's been stabbed. He's . . . dead."

Gary had suspected that already, had *known* that already, but it was another thing to have it confirmed, and hearing the manner of his friend's murder took the breath out of him. He had to inhale deeply just to keep his respiratory system functioning. Involuntarily, his gaze shifted toward the center of campus, toward the Communications building, though it could not be seen from this angle. He tried to remember the last thing he'd said to Brian or that Brian had said to him but couldn't.

Stacy continued to talk on the phone as they got into

the car, explaining to Williams what had happened and where they were going. It was clear from her side of the conversation that the detective was trying to talk her out of it, but whether that was because he didn't believe Father and his followers were actually out in the desert or because he thought it was dangerous for them to go there alone was considerably less clear. Even Stacy wasn't sure, she admitted, after terminating the call, but she hoped the fact that she'd hung up on Williams before he could finish would cause him to at least send some other cops after them.

"We *can't* do this alone," she told them.

Gary and Reyn said nothing.

The official name of their destination was the Mojave-Abrego California State Preserve, and there were several ways to reach it, although even the quickest route took two and a half hours, which meant that they wouldn't arrive until after midnight. Gary told himself that that meant it was a two-and-a-half-hour drive for the Homesteaders as well, but rather than reassure him, the thought tormented him. That was a long trip. Did it really seem plausible that they would transport Joan so far? Wouldn't it make more sense for them to take her to a hiding place closer by?

Or kill her?

He refused to let his mind go there, but the worry nibbled around the edges of his consciousness.

As the freeway passed through the sleepy suburban communities of the San Fernando Valley, Gary grew ever more anxious. Reyn had recognized the smell of the smoke, but was that really enough to go on? Was that lead concrete enough that they should spend the next several hours in the car after Joan had been abducted yet again and Brian had been murdered? What if they were wasting their time on a wild-goose chase?

"I know it's where they took her," Reyn said, and

though he was probably just trying to convince himself, his words had the effect of calming Gary. Despite the seemingly illogical logistics, he thought the same thing. Father's people *had* taken Joan out to the preserve.

They had traveled this road before, and as the city faded into desert and they passed by the jagged, angular rocks where Reyn had told them episodes of *Star Trek* were filmed, Gary was overwhelmed by memories. He remembered Brian and Reyn arguing behind the raised hood of this car while waiting for AAA after the water pump broke, remembered all of them getting out their frustrations by yelling obscenities into the desert night. "*Fuck!... Cunt!... Asshole!... Dick!...*" The sadness he felt threatened to sap whatever energy he had left, and once again he thought that Joan was probably dead.

Her fate wasn't a certainty, though, and the image of her face installed a renewed vigor in his determination to confront Father. Even if she *was* dead, Gary was going to make sure that that bastard paid for it and that he could never harm anyone else ever again. Gary still had his tire iron, and Reyn had one in the trunk that he could use, along with a hammer and an assortment of screwdrivers. Stacy had also found a wicked-looking corkscrew in the glove compartment. Not the greatest weapons in the world, but at least they were armed.

Somewhere in the middle of the desert, they turned off on another road, a two-lane highway that ran along the foothills of a mountain range that could be sensed more than seen in the darkness. Theirs was the only vehicle traveling in either direction, and while the lights of a few far-flung buildings were visible when they first exited the freeway, those quickly disappeared and they drove through a landscape that was black and featureless, able to see only the small section of blacktop illuminated by the Focus's headlights.

They had stopped speaking quite a ways back and drove for the next hour in silence.

There were no green road signs telling them how far away the preserve was located, and only the eerie glowing screen of Reyn's phone on the seat next to him told them that they were on the right track. Indeed, even when they reached the turnoff to the preserve, it was only a dark wooden sign planted parallel to the road that indicated they were there, and if Reyn had not remembered it and been looking for it, they probably would have driven right past without noticing.

This road was dirt. And narrow. The desert had given way to foothills, and the single-lane trail wound through what appeared in the gloom to be a lot of scrawny trees and dry brush. They passed a turnoff that led to a low, dark building where a single lightbulb illuminated a bare side wall and slab of concrete.

"Nature center," Reyn said.

He followed the curving dirt road away from the building, and several miles later it began winding through a forest of stunted pine trees. They went up a small hill before dipping into a rocky canyon carved into the mountains beyond. The car slowed as they approached the towering black cliffs.

"Almost there," Reyn said grimly, and added, "I think."

He was right.

Rounding a curve, Reyn suddenly had to slam on the brakes. If they'd been going even five miles an hour faster, they would have had an accident

Jesus Christ, Gary thought as he took his hands from the dashboard and peered through the windshield. *How many of them are there?*

The road ahead was blocked by cars, Jeeps and pickups with license plates from various states, more than a dozen of them, parked and double-parked in no particular order, the vehicles protruding into the road at assorted angles, making further progress impossible.

Reyn quickly shut off the headlights.

They waited for a moment, expecting Homesteaders to come at them, expecting to be attacked, expecting at the very least to see someone running away to warn Father that they were here. But the vehicles were all empty; no one had noticed their arrival. The three of them looked at each other, their faces barely lit by the dim illumination of the dashboard lights. It was impossible to read what his friends were thinking, so Gary just blurted out, "I'm going to get Joan." He opened his door.

"You don't even know where she is," Reyn said.

"Up this road, I assume. That's where that ranch is, isn't it?"

"I'm coming with you."

Gary shook his head, motioned toward the parked cars. "There are a lot of people here. If one person can't sneak her out—"

"Maybe two or three people can," Stacy interrupted.

"No. Listen," Gary said. "I'm going to find her, see what I can do. If it's not possible, I'll come back and the three of us'll figure something out. But right now, I want you to get this car turned around and ready to go in case I do bring her back *and* do as much damage as you can to those other cars so they can't come after us."

"We don't know whose cars they are," Stacy objected. "They might not be the Homesteaders'."

"They are," Gary and Reyn said at the same time. They both smiled. The first time all night.

All three of them got out of the car, Gary taking his tire iron with him.

"All right," Reyn said, agreeing to Gary's plan. "But you come back for us if there's *any* problem."

Gary nodded.

"If there's any *question* about there being a problem," Stacy added. "If there's a minor *inconvenience*."

"Deal."

Gary hefted the tire iron in his hand and was about to start off when Reyn said, "Wait," and walked back to the trunk. He opened it, drawing out a long screwdriver. "Slip it in your belt," he said, handing the tool to Gary. "Just in case."

Gary nodded and also accepted a long metal flashlight. "Thanks." He pointed it at the ground and turned it on, testing it to see if it worked. It did. Reyn pulled out a lug wrench for himself and closed the trunk.

"I'll be—" *back*, Gary started to say, and thought he saw a man-sized shadow detach itself from the darkness before them and slip behind a pickup truck. The hair on the back of his neck prickled and gooseflesh instantly overtook his arms. Before he could say anything or even switch on his flashlight, the shadowy figure emerged from somewhere off to their right, running crazily toward them.

"Outsiders!" it yelled in a man's voice.

They all jumped back, startled and frightened, and Gary managed to switch on the flashlight, aiming it upward. He had time to register that it was indeed a man, that he was dressed in Homesteader garb, that he did not appear to be deformed, and then he was upon them. Stacy was the one closest to him, and with one wild leap he jumped on her. She screamed, tried to fight him off, but he grabbed her head in both hands and twisted.

She fell to the ground, limp, the Homesteader on top of her. The man raised his arms in triumph. Stacy's eyes were open wide, as though she'd seen something surprising, and her mouth was open. The expression on her face, the last expression she would ever have, was one of shock and horror.

Reyn swung his lug wrench without pause, without

thinking, an instinctive reaction accompanied by a terrible wail of pain and loss and rage and hate. The steel
tool slammed into the back of the Homesteader's head.
With the force of such an impact, Gary would have expected the contents of the man's skull to splatter outward. Instead, brain and blood overflowed like the yolk
from a cracked egg, and the Homesteader fell onto his
side, dead. His legs were still lying atop Stacy's back, and
Reyn, continuing to make that terrible sound, kicked
them off her. He bent down, touched his fingers to her
throat, pressed his ear against her cheek, but as much
as he might hope and wish that she remained alive, she
was dead, and he put his arms over her and hugged her
awkwardly, sobbing.

The same thing might have happened to Joan, the
same thing could be happening this very second, and
without saying anything to Reyn, trusting that his friend
would do what needed to be done despite his grief, Gary
took off, keeping to the side of the dirt trail but following it forward. He held the flashlight in one hand, the
tire iron in the other, prepared to encounter another
Homesteader at any second and ready to attack first if
he did.

He met no one on the way, and with the beam of his
flashlight trained on the ground directly in front of him
so as to illuminate pitfalls, he did not see the ranch house
until he was almost upon it.

It was the sound of voices that alerted him, a chorus of chanting louder than his footfalls on the dirt that
caused him to stop and look up. The canyon had broad-
ened, and off to his right, past scattered trees, against a
cliff so tall and dark that he could not see where in the
night sky it ended, sat the ranch Reyn had told them
about. There were three or four buildings, although they
were little more than vague black smudges in the gloom.
The middle one, however, had lights in its windows, dim,

flickering lights generated by candle or lantern rather than electricity, and he assumed it was from here that the voices originated.

Still shining his flashlight on the ground so he would not trip over holes or rocks or roots, still holding tightly to his tire iron in case he should meet anyone on the way, Gary walked slowly forward toward the ranch, eventually finding a footpath that led between trees and over a dry creek bed to the buildings. As he drew closer, he could see the white cross that Reyn had described, gray in the darkness and taller than a man, painted on the rock wall directly above the ranch house.

No guards or sentries had been posted outside, as he'd feared, and Gary shut off his flashlight and hid for a moment behind the thin trunk of a polelike pine, trying to determine the safest approach. Through the curtainless window straight across from him, he could see a large space—what had probably been a living room once upon a time—and a group of silhouetted figures standing there holding hands. There were at least ten people in this prayer circle, he estimated, plus who knew how many in the building's other rooms. Somewhere inside was Joan, he was sure, but at the moment he could think of no way to find her, let alone rescue her.

He was about to try sneaking around to the back of the house when, from down the trail behind him, from the way he had come, an explosion ripped through the night. He started, nearly dropping the flashlight, and turned, looking toward the source of the sound. He saw fire through the trees, bright, thin flames a half mile back that caused orange light to dance up the face of the opposite cliffside.

Reyn, he thought.

And smiled.

Thirty-two

Joan vomited.

It was her best and only defense.

The door had closed behind Father—she could hear it, if not see it—and there was suddenly more light in the room. He had brought his own candle or lantern. She expected him to come around and confront her, but he did not, and in the silence of the room she heard the rustling of clothes, the sound of pants falling to the floor. She knew what he was doing, and her stomach knotted up with dread. Moments later, he presented himself. He was naked and aroused, and she was sickened by the sight of his body. He was old and decrepit, and his sagging chest and scarred, wrinkled skin revolted her.

How old was he? She'd tried to calculate his age while at the Home and determined that he had to be at least in his late eighties or early nineties, although when she'd told this to Mark and Rebekah, they'd both said with complete confidence that he was over two hundred years old. She'd considered that idea ridiculous at the time, more brainwashing propaganda, but the thought chilled her now. She would believe anything at this point, and her eyes focused on a scar near his right shoulder that looked like it might have come from an arrow.

He moved in front of her.

"You will bear me sons, Ruth. God has willed it."

That was when she vomited.

The idea came to her spontaneously. In a quicksilver thought process focused solely on self-preservation, she recalled how germophobic Father had always seemed to her with his endless cleansing rituals and his insistence that others carry out his wishes, and simultaneously she remembered how as a child she'd been so squeamish that she could make herself throw up just by thinking of gross and disgusting things. Her brain put the two together, and as he approached her, she thought of excrement floating in milk.

And puked.

She turned her head to the side so she wouldn't choke on her own vomit, but the spew only went so far and some of it flowed back into the indentation where she lay on the mattress. She felt a disgusting warm wetness against her cheek, smelled a horrible putrid stench and promptly threw up again.

Father stepped back, horrified, his erection gone, and though she could tell from the expression on his face that he wanted more than anything else to hit her and beat her and hurt her, to *punish* her, he could not. He was too repulsed, too afraid of contamination, and he gave her a wide berth as he walked back around the head of the bed and began putting his clothes back on. Joan could hear him gagging, trying not to throw up, which explained why he wasn't lecturing her and railing against her, and several seconds later, he was out of the room, taking his light with him and slamming the door.

She flipped her head away from the part of the mattress on which she'd thrown up, and while that lessened the smell somewhat, or at least the immediacy of it, she could still feel the cooling puke on her shoulder and side, and the sour taste still filled her mouth. It was all she could do not to vomit again, though she doubted there was much left in her stomach to regurgitate.

She was safe for the moment, but she knew that
Father would probably send someone else in here to
clean her up, and then she would get it even worse. The
self-preservation instinct never thought ahead or con-
templated consequences, and she realized now that her
actions could very well have hurt her in the long run.

Now that she considered it, though . . .

If they untied her in order to change the bedsheet and
wipe her off, she might be able to get in a few licks, might
be able to bite or kick or hit or even get away. She quickly
thought about her options. She might have a chance here,
and she needed to prepare herself to take it.

Unless Father *didn't* send someone to clean her up,
and punished her by making her suffer and lie in the
puddle of her own drying vomit.

Or decided to kill her.

To hell with the consequences. She was glad she'd
done what she had, and even if she ended up being
beaten, raped or killed, she took great satisfaction in
knowing that she had pierced Father's implacable, ar-
rogant armor. Just remembering the look of horror on
his face, the sound of him gagging as he quickly put on
his clothes, gave her a feeling of victory.

From somewhere outside came an eerie cry, an ago-
nizing wail that was faint but clear. She still had no idea
where in the world she was, but the primitive walls within
her sight line suggested country rather than city, and lying here in this dim room, hearing that wail, she imagined some sort of monster prowling through the woods.
She shivered, frightened on an instinctive gut level. The
cry came again. In fact it never went away, only ebbed
and flowed in its intensity, and now it sounded human,
the cry of a man in serious physical or emotional pain.

There was a commotion in the other room, and at first
she thought it had to do with her and what she had done,
but when no one came in, and she heard Father yelling

and was able to make out the words "you" and "again," she allowed herself a glimmer of hope. He was angry. At his own people. And that was good. It meant things were not going according to his plan.

She wondered if the Homesteaders had been discovered, if they were going to have to leave this place—wherever it was. Maybe they would forget about her in their haste and leave her behind and she would be rescued.

Maybe they would just kill her because it would be too much trouble to take her along.

She tried in vain to make out what Father was saying. He was still yelling, and she could also hear the movement of feet, many feet.

What was going on in there?

She listened.

Waited.

Thirty-three

Gary faced away from the far-off fire and focused his attention once again on the ranch house in front of him. He had no idea what had happened and could only assume that Reyn must have figured out a way to blow up one or more of the Homesteaders' vehicles. He'd probably dropped a match down one of the gas tanks or something, and while the sound of the explosion and the sight of the flames had immediately filled him with a sense of gratification, he wished his friend had found a quieter way to decommission the cars.

Seconds after the blast, a line of men and women came running out of the ranch house. It was too dark to see any of them clearly, but he discerned no limps, no malformed appendages, nothing to indicate that any of them were Father's Children. They carried neither lanterns nor flashlights and moved without speaking through the darkness, not taking the road but jogging single file down a parallel path he had not noticed before.

He counted twenty of them, maybe twenty-one or twenty-two. It was hard to tell. Were these *all* of the Homesteaders who were left? Gary wondered. Were these all of the penitents and all of the followers from throughout the entire country? He hoped so but doubted it. Not that it really mattered. Because while there might still be pockets of believers scattered among various other states, Father was here. That was the important thing.

Cut off the head and the body will die.

Gary didn't know where he'd heard that before, but it was true, and he knew that if Father were captured—*or killed*—his followers would dissipate; the Homesteaders would be through. Gary looked toward the path down which the men and women had gone, wishing there was a way for him to warn Reyn that they were coming, but even if his cell phone worked in this canyon, he didn't want to draw attention to himself by speaking aloud or inadvertently give away Reyn's position by setting off the ringtone of his friend's phone. Besides, at the rate the Homesteaders were moving, they would reach Reyn before Gary could take out his phone, turn it on and make the call.

He needed to concentrate on finding Joan and getting her out of here before they came back.

The room behind the window he'd been watching now appeared to be empty, but Gary didn't dare trust that that was the case. Carefully, he crept forward, crouching low, until he reached the building. He paused, waiting to see if he'd been spotted, but no one came out, and though he listened, he heard no sound. His right hand was starting to hurt, and he loosened his grip on the tire iron, which he'd been clutching as tightly as he could.

Moving slowly, he sidled along the wall until he reached the window, then allowed himself a sneak peek around the edge of the frame. He saw a sparsely furnished room lit by two lanterns at opposite ends. There were no people, which meant no Joan, and he quickly pulled himself back, not wanting to be discovered should someone enter. His heart was pumping loudly enough to muffle his hearing, and he wondered if Joan was in the house at all.

Maybe she was dead.

No. She couldn't be. But he crept along the side of
the wall more quickly, with renewed purpose, and when
he reached another window on the side of the building
and found it dark, he shone his flashlight through the
glass without hesitation. Weakened by the dusty glass,
his beam shone upon a bed, a table, a chair. Through another doorway across what had to be a hall, he could see
dim flickering, as from a candle, and he hurried around
the next corner in an effort to reach that room.

Only . . .

The rear of the house had no windows. His flashlight
beam played upon a solid wood wall facing the cliff behind the ranch. A feeling of panic welled within him, and
he forced himself to calm down as he retreated back the
way he'd come. He reached the front of the house, making sure to stay in the shadows—

And there was a gunshot down the road.

A gunshot?

One of the Homesteaders must have gotten Reyn.

It was like a punch to the gut, and his first instinct was
to run and check on his friend in case there was something he could do.

Another gunshot.

Two shots? Reyn had to be dead. But Gary could
not allow himself to stop and dwell on it. He had to find
Joan—although how he could hope to get her out of
here now he had no idea.

He clutched his weapon tightly. As far as he could tell,
he was all alone. No one seemed to have been left behind when the Homesteaders had run out to investigate
the explosion. Even if someone was in the house, Gary
had his tire iron and could easily subdue—

Kill

—the person. It was time for him to take action, and
without further thought he ran to the door through
which the Homesteaders had exited. It had closed but

was knobless and unlocked. He put his flashlight down on the ground, then yanked the door open, rushing inside, both hands on the tire iron, ready to swing.

As he'd seen from the window, there was no one in the front room. From a hook next to the door hung a lantern, and another lantern was suspended from a bigger hook near the door on the opposite side of the room. Between the two, in the center of the floor, was a round table on which sat a large black Bible. The table's chairs had all been pushed against the wall, and on top of the seats were piled boxes filled with prayer scrolls.

The room smelled woodsy, piney, the same distinctive odor that had characterized the fires at his dorm and at the library. If Reyn had not recognized the scent, Gary would not be here right now, and he was grateful to his friend for remembering where he had encountered the pitch before.

Unless, of course, Joan wasn't here.

In which case Reyn and Stacy had died for nothing.

Anger nearly overwhelmed him at the thought, and he ran through the room, tire iron over his shoulder, ready to take out anyone in his way. He almost tripped over a metal bucket near the opposite door. It was filled with a thick black liquid, and he had time to register that it was probably the pitch before he was in a short hall. He spotted the dark room he'd seen through the window, as well as what appeared to be a kitchen, but there was another room at the back of the house, with a faint light glowing around the edges of the doorway, and he hurried over and ran in.

And there was Joan.

She was lying on a bed in the middle of the windowless chamber, facing away from the door, and she looked awful. She was half-naked, and her cheeks, neck and shoulders were covered with what looked like drying vomit. Her face was red and swollen. But she was alive, and the instant he moved in front of her, she burst into tears. Tears began falling from his eyes, too, but this was no time to dawdle, he had to get her out, and he immediately he began working on her restraints—thick rope that had been tied into slipknots over and over again until the slack was down to nothing.

"We're getting out of here," he said. And because he didn't know what more to say, he said it again: "We're getting out of here."

"How—" She tried to talk through her tears but the words were little more than hiccupped sobs. "How did you find me?" She sniffled hard and heavily. "Where *are* we?"

"It's a long story, but we're on a ranch in a nature preserve in the middle of the desert. And we've got to get out of here fast. The Homesteaders are gone, but they could be back any minute." He wished he had a knife or longer fingernails. He was still on the first knot and not getting very far.

"Are we in California? What day is this?"

She'd been drugged. He should have known, should have guessed, and as he finally started to unravel the knot keeping down her left hand, he hoped that she would be able to walk. There was no way he'd be able to carry her.

His mind was racing, covering twenty topics a second. He was trying to release her from her bonds and at the same time figure out how to get out of this canyon without being seen. They probably wouldn't be able to use Reyn's car, he figured, so he was trying to estimate how far it was to the preserve's nature center and how long they would have to remain hidden until someone showed up to open the place in the morning. And shouldn't he tell Joan that he loved her? That was how it worked in movies during rescue scenes. The protagonists usually kissed, too, although that was not going to happen. She had thrown up, and it still smelled, and he was trying to hold his breath as much as possible so he wouldn't gag. And—

There was noise from outside the house.

A voice.

"Ruth!"

Father.

Gary froze for a second, then began furiously pulling at the knot. A fiber from the rope stabbed his index finger, but he ignored it and kept working.

"Ruth!"

The voice was louder.

He could sense Joan's panic, but somehow that calmed him. One of them had to keep a level head, and he focused on the task at hand as his fingers finally loosened a loop of rope, pulling the end free. At least both of them were smart enough to keep quiet. He finished untying her arms, then untied her right leg while she took care of the left. Quickly, Gary helped her sit up, then stand. Picking up a corner of the bedsheet, she bent down, wiping the vomit from her chin, mouth, neck and shoulders. Gary pulled off his T-shirt and put it on her. It was long but not quite long enough, and she tugged down the bottom hem.

He didn't kiss her, but he hugged her. "I love you," he said.

"I love you, too."

"Ruth!"

Father was in the house.

Gary picked up his tire iron. They needed to get out of here. Now. They could no doubt find a hiding place within one of the rooms, but they would be found very easily if they did so, and when the Homesteaders returned, escape would become virtually impossible. If they were ever to make it out, this was the time. He peeked around the corner. The hallway was empty, and he turned back toward Joan, motioning silently for her to follow. Still holding down the bottom of the T-shirt, she moved next to him—

—and screamed.

Gary swiveled around.

Father.

He was standing in the center of the hallway, and Gary had never seen eyes so cold in any human being. He had no idea how Father had gotten here so quickly. It was as though he'd just *appeared*, and a jolt of fear passed through Gary as he looked upon that fierce, hard visage. Every instinct he had was telling him to run back into the room and slam the door, but when Joan screamed again, it broke the spell, and anger filled the space within him. This was the man who had kidnapped Joan, who was responsible for the murders of Reyn and Stacy and Brian and Teri Lim and Joan's parents and who knew how many others. He was an evil motherfucker whose twisted preachings had caused the ruination of dozens, perhaps hundreds, of lives over several generations.

"The Lord shall smite you!" Father shouted in a deep, booming voice.

Gary rushed him.

He hadn't known he was going to do it until he did, but he raised his tire iron and charged, intending to beat the bastard's brains out.

Father stumbled back, and at that moment Gary knew for sure that he was just a man. He saw alarm on the bearded face, but evidence of Father's humanity, rather than engendering sympathy, served to stoke Gary's fury. He dashed down the hall, ready to bring down the tire iron on the son of a bitch's head.

Father retreated into the front room and from somewhere produced a weapon of his own: a long shepherd's staff. It must have been leaning against a wall, and Gary cursed himself for not having noticed it earlier. Nevertheless, that overgrown cane was no match for his metal rod, and he moved into the room, Joan right behind him.

With his beard and his staff, Father looked like Moses, but he was quicker and more agile than he appeared, and before Gary knew what had hit him, the long length of wood had lashed out and struck his arm—*hard*—causing him to cry out in pain and drop the tire iron. Father smiled cruelly.

Scrambling, Gary grabbed the tool and backed away, instinctively crouching low. The staff swung around again, barely missing his head. He was close enough to Father to do some damage, and he hit the old man's shin with the metal bar. There was definitely a connection—he felt the solidity of the impact through his hand—but Father's reaction was not what he expected.

Because there was no reaction.

The man's legs did not buckle; he was not knocked off his feet; he did not even cry out. Instead, he stood his ground, and his staff came crashing down on Gary's back. Gary fell to the floor, pain whipping through his body from the point of contact like lightning, a jagged bolt that hit muscle and organ and bone on the way. He rolled to the right, wincing in agony as the end of the staff hit the floor inches from his face.

Looking up, he saw Father's hard eyes and thin, heartless smile. He cringed, waiting for the blow that would kill him.

With a wild, animalistic cry, Joan launched herself at Father. She leapt on him, knocking him over, clawing at his face with her raked nails as he went down. "I hate you!" she screamed. "I hate you, I hate you, I hate you! You're a liar and a murderer and you're wrong! You're wrong! You're wrong! About everything!"

It was a strange thing to yell, especially under the circumstances, but Gary understood. And he knew how hard it was for her to say those words. She'd been brought up in Father's religion, and no matter how far she'd strayed, no matter what he'd done, there'd always been a part of her that still believed.

Father threw her off, but Gary lurched to his knees and instantly took her place, landing hard on Father's chest, pinning down the old man's arms.

And then he was pounding Father with his fists, hitting him hard, and it felt good. His knuckles connected with Father's nose and cheek and jaw, and with each blow there was a satisfying crunch. Blood splattered and soaked into his beard, and though the old man did not make a sound, and even stopped struggling after the first few seconds, Gary kept whaling on him.

It was Joan who said tiredly, finally, "Stop."

He paused, watching her get shakily to her feet, his mind still filled with thoughts of the evil this man had done, every fiber of his being focused on punishment and revenge. Gary was shaking, adrenaline pumping through his bloodstream, but slowly he stood, looking down all the while. Father did not move. He did not even appear to be breathing.

Was he dead?

Gary wasn't sure, but part of him hoped so. He didn't relish the idea of being a murderer, of killing a man, but the truth was that he would feel much better if Father was no longer alive.

He stepped away from Father's body toward Joan, who had backed up and was standing near the hallway door. His knuckles hurt, and his fists were covered with blood. He wanted to find a bathroom and wash up, but they had to get out of here before the other Homesteaders returned. If the others came back and found Father dead, they would kill both him and Joan on sight.

"Look out!"

In the split second before Joan's warning cry, he

heard the tap of wood on wood, and his mind instantly put the two together. He reacted instinctively, dropping to the floor and rolling to the side just as Father's staff slammed onto the floorboards where he'd been only seconds prior. Gary jumped to his feet. Bloody and very much alive, the old man stood there like some unstoppable monster, grinning, the few teeth that remained in his mouth dripping red.

Before Gary's rattled brain could even contemplate a reaction, Joan had picked up the bucket next to the door, taking several quick steps into the center of the room and throwing the contents of the bucket right into Father's face. The thick black liquid splashed onto him and around him, causing him to cry out and drop his staff, pitch running viscously down his head and off his flailing arms.

Thinking fast, Joan grabbed the hanging lantern and dashed it onto the spreading puddle.

Glass shattered, and the floor exploded with a *whoosh*, a breath-sucking vacuum that pulled the air around them into the center of the room, creating a fireball that shot up to the ceiling. Within seconds, everything was in flames, and Father was caught in the middle of it all. His beard was burning, as were his clothes, and he screamed in agony as he staggered around, bumping into a wall, then bouncing back and hitting the table.

He looked like the Burning Man, Gary thought, and recalled the hallucination he'd experienced after being drugged at the desert festival. In his vision, the Burning Man had lurched jerkily, like a Ray Harryhausen figure, and that was the way Father looked now as he headed blindly toward the line of flaming chairs, arms outstretched.

They had to get out quickly, before the fire spread, and Gary pulled Joan by the hand toward the part of the house he had not yet explored. The last room was indeed a kitchen, and next to a dilapidated wood-burning stove was a door that led outside. He pushed Joan ahead of him, and the two of them emerged into the open air, gasping for breath. Without pausing, they hurried around the corner to the front of the building, where smoke was pouring from the window and the doorway, the billowing black backlit by flames. Gary smelled the unique woodsy odor of the fire starter. *Abrego's Pitch,* he suddenly remembered.

With a final anguished cry, a sound more monster than man, Father stumbled outside, through the open front door, and fell to the ground. Joan gasped, grabbing Gary's hand, squeezing it tight, but Gary stood there impassively, watching the old man's death throes, taking a grim satisfaction in the way the burning figure jerked weakly beneath the flames before collapsing in a charred heap.

Joan was crying, turning her face to his shoulder. He felt her warm tears on his skin. On the other side of her, his eyes registered movement, but he couldn't make out what it was. Seconds later, he saw Reyn running from the darkness into the light of the flames.

Reyn!

For a second he was confused. *Isn't Reyn dead?*

His friend stopped next to him, shouting to be heard over the crackling fire that had almost completely engulfed the house. "Sheriffs are here! A whole group of them!" Reyn was breathing heavily. He didn't have the lug wrench, Gary noticed. "Williams must have called! They shot one of the Homesteaders who tried to attack! They're arresting the others!"

"I heard an explosion," Gary said numbly.

"Me." Reyn held up a book of matches he took from his shirt pocket. "I made a wick, put it in one of their gas tanks. Just before the sheriffs arrived."

Was it over? Was that it? Gary didn't know, but he

was still filled with a strong sense of urgency. Reyn, he saw, was politely looking away from Joan, who was no longer holding onto the hem of the T-shirt. She noticed at the same time he did and, embarrassed, pulled the shirt down on both sides until everything was covered.

Gary looked over at Reyn. "Are there a *lot* of cops?"

"Sheriffs. And there were three cars' worth. There might have been more coming. I don't know."

"Can they handle all those Homesteaders?"

"I think so. They're armed, they've already shot one of them, and these guys don't seem like they're willing to be martyrs." He glanced anxiously around. "What about—"

"Father?" Gary nodded at the burning form in front of them. "You're looking at him."

Reyn's eyes widened. "What happened?"

Gary shook his head. "It's a long story." And he stood there, staring silently, watching as the blackened, smoking form lost the last vestiges of its human shape and became a smoldering lump of nothing.

This is for Joan, he thought. *This is for Stacy. This is for Brian.*

This is for everyone.

Thirty-four

Joan pulled away from Gary's bare shoulder and wiped her eyes. She could not look at Father's burning body, so she faced the opposite direction, where the darkness of the canyon was suddenly rent by flashing blue and red lights as a sheriff's car arrived.

The vehicle pulled to a stop several yards away, on a flat section of ground. A deputy not much older than herself emerged from the passenger door, with a heavy-set middle-aged man walking around the car from the driver's side. Both had their weapons drawn, but before they could say anything, Reyn shouted, "She's the one who was kidnapped! We're the ones who came after her!"

The deputies approached, still not putting away their guns. "Is anyone else here?"

Gary gestured toward Father's blackened form. "Just him."

Joan could not look.

"He's the one who was in charge of everything, the leader of the cult. They called him 'Father.'"

The deputies were taking no chances. Their weapons were still out as they walked up. The young one could not seem to take his eyes from the fire. "What happened?" he asked, motioning toward the billowing smoke.

Gary told him. From the beginning. It was an abridged

version, but it started at Burning Man and hit the highlights. The two deputies listened without commenting, although it seemed pretty clear that they were familiar with at least part of the story, maybe from Williams, maybe from the news. When Gary came to his description of finding her tied up, Joan tuned out, not wanting to hear it. In her mind, she saw Father's wrinkled, naked body, and her muscles tensed as she recalled the disgust and terror she had felt.

Gary finished talking. The older deputy was calling someone on his walkie-talkie, though there seemed to be no real urgency in the request he made for someone to come and put out the fire. Joan herself didn't care if the entire canyon burned down.

The young deputy looked at Joan, his eyes quickly taking in the T-shirt before glancing respectfully away. "Do you need shoes?" he asked. "Or a blanket? There's an extra pair of boots in the car. They might not fit perfectly, but you could put them on."

"Thank you," she said sincerely.

He hurried back to the vehicle, returning a moment later with a pair of clunky hiking boots and a gray flannel blanket. She unfolded the blanket, twisted it into a type of sarong and tied it around her. She leaned on Gary while she put on the boots one at a time. They were too big for her feet and she wasn't wearing socks, but it was better than going barefoot.

"We have a *lot* of questions," the young deputy said.

Gary nodded tiredly as Joan finished tying the shoes.

"I'm going to have to ask you to come with us to the office. It's back in Palmdale, about forty miles away."

Joan stood and all three of them nodded their acquiescence. The older deputy had walked over to Father's corpse and was bending down, examining it. Joan hazarded a quick look and saw that the flames engulfing the body appeared to be completely out.

Another sheriff's vehicle pulled up, this one an SUV.

"Do you need a ride?" the young deputy asked. "We'll probably be out here for a while, but we can take you back."

"No, we have a car," Gary replied.

"My car," Reyn said.

He was crying, Joan noticed, and she suddenly wondered where Stacy was, where Brian was. In all the commotion, she had not thought to question why they weren't there. She started to ask, but then her eyes met Gary's, and at that moment she knew. She was filled with a sudden aching sense of loss, and she looked again at Reyn, wanting to say something, wanting to comfort him, but the expression on his face was one of such complete and utter devastation that she knew anything she said would be useless and ineffectual, would probably make things worse, so she remained silent.

"Wait by your car, then," the deputy said. "Someone will be heading back shortly to transport the detainees. You can follow them." He spoke into his walkie-talkie, informing the law enforcement agents who were rounding up the Homesteaders that the three of them were coming.

She felt exhausted as they started walking across the flat ground to the dirt road, the trees, rocks and walls of the canyon pulsing blue and red in time to the car lights.

Father was dead.

She was glad, but she felt no happiness. Her parents were dead, too. So were Stacy and Brian. The Home, the site of her childhood, was gone, and though she had long ago left behind Father's teachings, seeing a curled scrap of burned paper tumble past—one of the prayer scrolls—brought home to her what was lost and filled her with a sadness she'd not expected and could not explain.

Gary was here, though, and that was all that mattered. She loved him, and he loved her, and they had survived. She glanced over at him, seeing in his shadowed, soot-covered face the older man he would become. She knew that no matter what else happened in her life, no one else could ever be there for her to the extent that he had, no one else would do anything as heroic or self-less. But she also knew that they were young, that things changed, that despite the way they felt at the moment, they might not stay together forever. Ten years from now, they might be married—or they might be strangers, living on opposite sides of the country, involved with other people, with the events of this semester having receded into memory, recalled with decreasing frequency as the years passed by.

That was tomorrow, though, and today was today, and she took his hand, held it tightly and together they followed Reyn, walking up the dirt road, into the darkness, into the future.

ABOUT THE AUTHOR

Born in Arizona shortly after his mother attended the world premiere of *Psycho*, **Bentley Little** is the Bram Stoker Award–winning author of numerous previous novels and *The Collection*, a book of short stories. He has worked as a technical writer, reporter/photographer, library assistant, salesclerk, phone book deliveryman, video arcade attendant, newspaper deliveryman, furniture mover and rodeo gatekeeper. The son of a Russian artist and an American educator, he and his Chinese wife were married by the justice of the peace in Tombstone, Arizona.